Bus Station

Michael W Hare

ISBN 978-1-964097-54-1 (softcover)
ISBN 978-1-964097-55-8 (ebook)

Printed in the United States of America.

INK START MEDIA
265 Eastchester Dr Ste 133 #102
High Point NC 27262

PROLOGUE

It was a warm day. The sun was shining bright and it was a hundred with no rain in sight. Quite a lot of people were on the streets of Atlanta, but not many were entering a bus station on the corner. Being July, you would think that there would be a lot of people trying to get out of the heat. The building looks like any other red-brick building. A woman came to the glass door and entered. You could tell she looked good for her age with long brown hair, which was her natural color. She was tall and had a decent shape. She looked around the building taking in everything and wondering why she was there. She thought the room was quite plain, having white walls and white-tiled floors with no design. The only contrast of color was the blue plastic seats. Still looking around, she saw the glass doors leading to the bus platform and on the other side of the room were grilled windows for ticket sales.

The man behind the counter watched as the woman approached. She looked nice in her red dress and black heels that clink with an echo.

"My name is Jennifer Conner, and for some reason, there is a ticket for me."

The man looked up into her green eyes and said, "Hold on a minute," as he looked on this computer. Before he looked down, he noticed the gold chain with a cross on it. "Are you with the rest of that church group over there?"

Jennifer looked across the room noticing quite a few members of her church. They were singing while others prayed. "Yes, I am. It is the reason I am here."

While he checked on the computer, she noticed that he looked like a farmer. He had on blue overhauls with a red-checkered shirt. He had to be in his sixties; his hair was pure white and had washed-out blue eyes. When he looked up at her, she saw the wrinkles around his eyes.

"Madam, we do have a reservation for you, but you're on a different bus than those people." He printed out her ticket and said, "You will be leaving through door number 6 over there," as he pointed it out.

Jennifer took the ticket and looked over to some of her friends and wondered why she was not with them. She walked over to the seats close to her door and sat down to wait.

CHAPTER 1

Jennifer sat and looked at the people across the room but did not see her husband. She started to go over her life trying to find out why she was here. She grew up in Gering, Nebraska, with her parents and no siblings. Her mother's name was Debbie, and she looked just like her mother with brown hair and green eyes. Her father Henry was six-feet tall, muscular, and working in a sugar factory carrying fifty-pound bags of sugar each day. He had brown hair too but had blue eyes, and he was hardly home; but when he was, he was usually drunk. He was quite abusive with his wife, but she never left him because of her.

Jennifer was an A student all through school and became a favorite of her high school principal. Mr. Wright came up to her one day and asked if she would like to make extra money.

"I need a part-time person to work in the office. Would you be interested?"

Jennifer jumped at the chance and said she would love to do so since it would not interfere with her classes, and she did not have too many friends. The girls thought she acted too good for them since she never wanted to hang out. When she got the job in the office, they began to hate her and always found ways to pick on her. They got together and planned a way to get her in trouble. Since working in the office, her grades went down a little but still hold a B average.

The girls waited till the teacher in science left her room when one of the girls went in and got the grade book. She erased Jennifer's B, made it an A, and hurried out. Later in class, the girls told the teacher that they saw Jennifer messing with the books. The teacher looked and noticed the grade changed and went straight to the principal.

Jennifer was working in the office when he opened his door and told her to come into his office.

Mr. Bright said, "I have three girls who say that you changed the grades in this book that I am holding."

"Sir, I never saw that book before," she said, starting to cry.

"Well, I am sorry, but I must take the words of other girls when so many said they saw you. You will no longer work in this office and will have to leave school. We will schedule an appointment with your parents to see when you can return to school."

Jennifer was quite upset knowing that she was not guilty but was more afraid of her father.

She picked up her things and left the school yard, dreading going home knowing the principal had already called her parents. When she got home, her father was waiting for her and was quite angry.

"What have you done?" he yelled.

"I have not done what they said, Dad. I was set up by those girls."

"You expect me to believe that all those girls are against you? And now I will have to take a day off of work because of you."

Jennifer yelled back at him, "You should believe me," and turned and walked out of the room.

It made her father that much more angry, and he ran and grabbed her. He turned her around and slapped her face knocking her to the floor. "Do not you ever walk away when I am talking to you."

Jennifer got up crying as her face stung. "You are always mean and never listen, and I am not Mom. You can just batter me around."

He smacked her again, and she ran to her room and locked the door. He yelled through the door, "You will get more of the same when you come out."

Jennifer lay down on her bed and started crying hysterically. She thought to herself that as soon as it is dark, she would leave and never come back. She knew they could not stop her; she just turned eighteen.

Jennifer packed her book bag and one suitcase with clothes, sliding them under her bed till everyone was asleep. She opened her upstairs window, which was just above the porch and walked out on the roof tying a sheet to her bags and lowered them to the ground. She knew with her savings that she would be all right for a while. She wanted to get as far away as possible. There were two bus stations in Gering, one was too far being downtown. The relay station was about a mile away. It took her a half-hour to make it; the station was about to close for the night. The ticket agent was about thirty, and he told her there was not a bus till eight o'clock in the morning, and it will head to Atlanta, Georgia.

"How far are you going, Miss?"

She thought for a minute and said that was where she was going. Jennifer bought her ticket for a hundred and twenty dollars.

Reggie closed the office and sat on the bench with her. He was a blue-eyed blonde that she though was quite cute. He asked if this was her first trip, trying to make conversation.

"Yes. I am going to visit an aunt," she lied.

"Well, I hope you have a good trip, and it is good that you have a heavy coat. It will be quite cold by morning. Well, I got to get home. Have a safe trip," he said. He got up from the bench and left.

Jennifer felt quite alone sitting there till morning. When the sun rose in the morning, it was still cold, and she felt frozen to the bench. Soon she saw the bus and was happy to get out of the cold. She knew her parents would be up and would soon be looking for her.

The bus stopped in front of her, and the driver opened the bus door and climbed down.

"Are you waiting for this bus, madam?"

"I am. Here is my ticket," she said, handing it over.

"Oh! I see you are going to Atlanta."

She said yes, handing him her suitcase. He put it under the bus and said, "Climb aboard. We will be leaving shortly." He told her his name was Bill and he will be with her till Chicago. She liked the fact that he looked good for his age with brown curly hair and brown eyes. She got on the bus with her book bag and looked for a seat. Jennifer saw an empty seat next to a girl that was about her age.

"Is this seat taken?" she asked.

"No. You are welcome to it," she said.

Jennifer put her book bag on the overhead shelf and sat down. Once the bus left the station, Jennifer felt relieved. She was also quite nervous and a little excited not knowing her future.

After a while, the girl next to her said, "My name is June, and where are you going?"

Jennifer turned to her, telling June her name. "I am going to Atlanta to get a job and hopefully stay."

"I am going there too. I have a boyfriend waiting. I have talked to him for a year over the internet and decided it was time to meet him. I am also hoping to live with him if he will let me," June said.

Jennifer said, "I am running away. My parents would not listen that it was not my fault at school. When my father hit me, that was all I could take."

June felt sorry for her and said, "Come and live with us for a while."

Jennifer said, "I appreciate your offer, but I am sure you two need time alone for now. I hope we stay in touch with each other."

June smiled and said, "Just give me your number."

She gave June her cell phone number, and they were both tired and soon fell asleep until they reached Chicago.

They found out that they had to change buses because this bus was going on to New York. They collected their luggage and walked into the station. They found out it would be another hour before their bus would get there. June suggested that they had dinner at the Burger King in the station. Jennifer was quite hungry and had not eaten since last night. She ordered a Whopper with cheese meal and so did June. They finished their meal and looked around the station till it was time to line up for their destination. The new driver stood at the door and checked their tickets, and they took their luggage to the man who was loading the luggage under the bus. They both climbed on the bus and found seats about midway down the aisle. June took the window seat and Jennifer put her book bag up on the shelf and sat next to her. Soon the driver entered the bus and made the announcement.

"The next stop will be in Lexington, Kentucky. It should be about seven hours, so I'll dim the lights for you folks so you can get some sleep. My name is Frank, and if you have any questions, feel free to come up front." As he pulled out of the station, he said, "Have a good night. See you in Lexington."

After several hours, the driver announced on the intercom, "We are pulling into Lexington, Kentucky. There will be a half-hour stop here for those going on to Atlanta. Those getting off here, I hope you had a pleasant journey, and there will be someone to help you to collect your luggage from the bus."

Jennifer and June woke up and saw it was still in the middle of the night. June said, "Why don't we get a drink and snacks out of the vending machine? I do not think I can sleep anymore. How about you?"

Jennifer said that was a clever idea. They left the bus together and entered the station. They got a Coke and some chips after getting their change. June decided on some donut sticks and said, "There is enough for both of us." They took their snacks back to the bus just in time. The new driver was checking the new passengers on the bus and putting their luggage underneath.

The driver got his seat and soon pulled out of the station. He began his announcements. "My name is James. I will be with you until Atlanta. We should be getting there a little after eight this morning, so I will dim the lights so you folks can sleep."

Jennifer and June sat and ate their snacks, looking out the window as the lights went by.

"I hope Jeff is waiting for me when we get there," June said.

Jennifer said, "You should call him and tell him."

June picked up her cell phone and called. After a few rings, a male voice answered. "Jeff, this is June. We should be there at eight."

"Do not worry," he said, "I have my alarm set for seven. See you there."

June said, "I cannot wait to see you."

"I know. I am anxious too," Jeff said.

"Well, I will let you get back to sleep. See you soon," June said as she hung up. June felt better and returned to sleep, and in a little while, Jennifer closed her eyes.

Jennifer woke up with the sun shining in her eyes not knowing where she was.

June came awake saying, "What time is it?"

Jennifer looked at her watch and said, "A little after seven."

June said, "We must be in Georgia," looking out the window.

Then an announcement came from the driver saying, "We will be in Atlanta in the next half hour, so you need to get everything ready to depart."

Jennifer got up and collected her book bag and set it on her lap. They were watching as they made it through the suburbs of the city.

Soon the announcement came. "Welcome to Atlanta, Georgia. This is your final destination. Make sure to take all your belongings with you as you depart the bus. We are pulling in the station now. The temperature is ninety-five. Hope you had a good trip."

CHAPTER 2

ATLANTA

When the bus pulled into the station, Jennifer grabbed her book bag and made her way slowly off the bus. The heat hit her right away. She removed the coat she was wearing. June broke out in a sweat exclaiming how hot she was. They went over to the man who was taking the luggage off the bus. They showed the man which was their suitcases; after he handed them theirs, they made their way inside.

Just as they entered, June saw Jeff and left Jennifer with the suitcases while she went over to him. June gave him a kiss before walking back to her hand in hand with a young man. Jennifer noticed that he was quite handsome with his curly blond hair and beard. He smiled at her with his large brown eyes. She could tell he was a big man and quite tall and muscular.

June said, "This is Jeff, and this is my new friend Jennifer."

Jeff's look made her feel naked, which sent a chill down her body. She knew right away she was not going to like him. Jennifer smiled as said she was glad to meet him, not wanting to cause her friend any problems.

June said, "If it is all right with Jeff, you can stay with us till you find a place."

Jennifer knew that he gave her the creeps and said that she would be fine at a motel. "You two have a lot to catch up on and do not need me hanging around."

Jeff said, "I understand, and I know one that is not too expensive. It is just over in College Park. We can drop you off at the Economy Lodge over on Virginia Avenue."

Jeff picked up the suitcases and Jennifer followed them out to the parking lot. Jeff walked over to a black Chevy van and opened the back door to put in their suitcases. June climbed up into the front seat, and Jennifer headed to the side door after handing Jeff her suitcase. Jeff closed the back door and then the side door before heading around to the driver seat. Jennifer looked around at the red interior design of the seats. The seat was cloth and not leather. Jeff started the van and pulled out of the parking lot after paying the man at the ticket booth. Jeff blasted the radio on the drive to the motel, and Jennifer wasn't too happy with his type of music. She wasn't into rap and was glad when they made it to the motel.

Jeff hopped out of the van and collected her suitcase from the back. June got out when Jennifer did and gave her a big hug.

"Here. Put my number in your phone. If you need anything, call. You better stay connected. I will worry," June said.

Jennifer laughed and said, "I am sure I will be calling every day."

June said, "I will be waiting to tell you how things are going with me too."

Jeff had already got back in the van saying, "We should go."

June hugged Jennifer one more time before climbing back into the van. Jennifer stood there and waved goodbye as they left the driveway of the motel.

Jennifer made her way into the lobby of the motel and up to the desk.

The lady looked up and said, "Welcome to Economy Lodge. I am Jean. How can I help you?"

Jennifer said, "I was wondering if you had rooms to rent by the week."

"Yes, we do. They are two hundred a week and include breakfast."

Jennifer pulled out her wallet from her purse and put two hundred on the counter. Jean took it and said, "Let me print you a receipt." She got the receipt and made up two key cards saying, "You will be in room 225 on the second floor. There are vending machines up there including an ice machine. Just out of this door to the right are washing machines and dryers. The housekeepers are always here at eight, so if you need your room cleaned, let them know. If not, you can still get fresh towels and other supplies. Just let them know."

Jean said, "I hope you have a pleasant stay, and you will have to walk around the building. The room is at the back of the motel, and you have a choice of an elevator or stairs."

Jennifer said thanks and left the lobby, heading around the building. Having luggage, she took the elevator to the second floor and walked down the corridor to her room.

After sliding the card in the slot, she opened the door and walked in. First putting down her suitcase, she then looked around. On her left was a small room with a vanity mirror on the wall over a large counter with a sink, which led to another room with a toilet and a tub with a shower. Walking back out, she went into the main room which had a queen-size bed. The walls were a light blue and the comforter on the bed and the curtains were green. There was a large dresser and a flat screen TV above it. In the corner was a table and chairs next to the sliding glass doors, which lead out to a small balcony that was just above the swimming pool. She was thinking she could sit out here in the evenings. The room had central air and the thermostat was over the nightstand, which was white like the dresser.

Jennifer put her suitcase on the bed and went over to the closet next to the dresser. She emptied her suitcase between the dresser and the closet. She left out a red T-shirt and matching shorts, which she took to the bathroom with her book bag. Opening the book bag, she placed her toothbrush and hairbrush on the vanity. Taking out her soap from the bag, she turned on the shower. Getting undressed, leaving her clothes on the vanity, she went and took a shower. Drying off, she walked out of the bathroom with her clean clothes and got dressed.

Jennifer sat in front of the mirror and blow-dried her hair and thought she needed to eat something. There was a list of advertisements for restaurants in the neighborhood including some that deliver. She decided to take a trip around the area, so she decided that Waffle House would do since it was on Virginia Avenue. Jennifer put on her tennis shoes, which would be comfortable for walking. She picked up her key card and put it in her shoulder bag and headed to the door. She decided to take the stairs down to the parking lot and then walked back around the building to the road. When she made it to the road, she looked up and down the avenue noticing what stores were there. She turned left seeing that the restaurant was a few blocks down. It was quite warm, and she was beginning to sweat. There was not much wind from the cars going by. She walked down the street to the traffic light so she could get to the restaurant, which was across the street.

Jennifer felt the blast of the air conditioner as she entered. The place was quite busy, and every table was occupied. A server noticed her standing at the door and said there was a booth in the back following me. Jennifer followed her and was led to a seat.

When she was seated, the server said, "Welcome to Waffle House. My name is Molly. Can I get you a cup of coffee to start?" Jennifer looked up seeing that the lady was quite young, still in her teens. She had red hair and green eyes and was quite skinny. Jennifer said that would be fine as she looked at the menu. Molly soon returned with the pot of coffee and said, "Are you ready to order?"

Jennifer said, "I will have the breakfast platter." Molly asked how she wanted her eggs. Jennifer said she would like them over easy.

She was on her second cup of coffee when Molly returned with her food. Jennifer began to eat after putting strawberry jam on her toast. The eggs and the hash browns were good, and she finished by sopping up the yellow with her toast. Jennifer had another cup of coffee, and Molly dropped the bill on the table. When she was finished drinking, she picked up her purse, taking a five out and leaving it on the table. She got up and walked to the cashier with her bill. The cashier took her money and asked, "Was everything alright?"

Jennifer said that it was and collected her change. Jennifer left and crossed back at the light and headed to the motel.

Jennifer walked into the lobby to find a newspaper for job listings. A paper machine sat just inside the door with the *Atlanta Journal.* The machine took quarters, so she went up to the desk for a change. This time there was a man on duty saying, "May I help you?"

"Yes," she said, "I need some change for the machine."

He was an older man in his fifties named George. He took her money, gave her change, and asked, "Anything else I can help you with?"

"No. That is all I need for now."

"Well, I hope you have a good day and hope to see you for breakfast tomorrow."

Jennifer thanked him and went to get the paper out of the machine. She left the lobby and headed back to her room.

Entering her room, she walked over to the table and sat down. She removed her shoes before opening the paper. Looking through the classifieds, she couldn't find any secretary jobs listed. She felt a little disappointed and thought tomorrow there would be some. She sat there while reading the rest of the paper. Jennifer decided to take a little nap and did not wake up till night with the phone ringing. She picked it up, said hello, and realized it was June on the line.

June said, "I called to see how you are doing and tell you about my day."

"Well, it was fine, but I did not find any job prospects."

June said, "I am sorry, but it is only the first day, and you'll have to have patience."

Jennifer said, "You are right, so how was yours?"

June said, "I had a wonderful day after we left you. He took me to Six Flags, and we rode all the rides. Had lunch in the park, and after we left, he took me to dinner. It was a fancy place with waiters and a show."

"Wow! I'm sure it was exciting," Jennifer said.

"It was, but I will talk to you tomorrow. I am so tired," June said goodbye and hung up.

Jennifer was feeling hungry and checked out the ads on the dresser and decided to call Papa John's. The person answered the phone giving the name and asking for her order.

She said, "I would like a large pepperoni pizza with a medium Coke. I would also like it delivered to room 225 in the Economy Lodge in Virginia."

He said, "That will be fifteen dollars, and it will be there in about thirty minutes."

She said that would be fine and gave him her phone number. While she waited for the pizza, she began thinking about the anger she felt toward her parents and a little frightened that she would not get a job.

I am never going home. I must make it.

To calm down, she turned on the TV and watch a comedy of *Abbott & Costello*.

Soon there was a knock at the door. Someone called, "Pizza delivery."

Jennifer got up from the couch, got the money, and opened the door. A young man stood there in a Papa John's uniform handing her the pizza. Jennifer handed over the fifteen dollars and said thanks. He smiled saying, "Enjoy," and left. She took the pizza and the drink over to the table and sat down to eat after unpausing the show. She sat and watched while she ate. She was full after only two slices and sip her drink as she finished the movie.

I'll keep the rest for tomorrow night, which will save me some money.

Jennifer got up and took a shower putting on her black negligee. She slipped her dirty clothes in the laundry bag and walked back into the bedroom. Yawning, she got in the bed and was soon asleep.

In the morning, the sun shone in her eyes, and she looked at the clock; it was almost nine. She knew she had to get up and that breakfast ended at ten. She hurried and got out a blue pair of shorts and a matching tee and put them on. Slipping on her tennis shoes, she headed downstairs after locking her door. She told the housekeeper her room did not need cleaning today. Walking down the stairs, she hoped that there were some jobs in the paper today. She was a little nervous and was hoping her money did not run out before she found a job.

When she entered the lobby, she found Jean was working and was happy to see her. Getting change for the paper machine, she got a paper. She put the paper on one of the dining room tables. She made a cup of coffee from the breakfast bar. She had time to read the paper first before getting her breakfast. Opening the paper to the classified, she sipped her coffee as she read. Taking a pen from her purse, she circled three secretary jobs, which made her heart leap for joy. She was hungry now, so she made her way over to the breakfast bar. She poured the batter in the waffle maker, and while that cooked, she refilled her coffee. When it was done, Jennifer ate her waffles and finished her coffee. Picking up her trash and throwing it away, she went back over to Jean at the counter.

Jean looked up, saying, "How was your breakfast?"

Jennifer said, "It was good, and I was wondering, do you have a map of Atlanta? I have not ever been here before."

"I am sure there is one in those brochures in that rack," Jean said, pointing across the room. Jennifer went over to the rack and saw all the places she could visit and finally found a map of Atlanta. Going back to the breakfast bar, she refilled her coffee, said thanks to Jean, and headed back to her room.

She had to set her coffee down in the corridor to get the key card out of her purse to let her in. She slid the card in, and the door clicked open. She put her foot in the door, so it wouldn't close as she picked up her coffee and entered. Taking all her stuff over to the table, she sat down and read that all three jobs had their application online. She pulled out her map of Atlanta to find the nearest library in College Park and found it on Main Street, which was a thirty-minute walk.

Jennifer finished her coffee before gathering up everything she would need to take with her. Putting the key card back in her purse and brushing her hair, she was ready to go. First, she went down the corridor to the vending machine and got money out of her purse for a bottle of water. She knew it was quite hot, and she would dry out quickly on her walk. The day was already in the seventies and climbing. She walked back to the elevator and let it take her to the first floor. She made it around the building to the front facing Virginia Avenue. Getting to the road, she turned left heading for Main Street. There was quite a bit of traffic for this time of day, and still it didn't take her long to reach Main Street. She began to sweat and was sipping her water as she made the eight blocks to the library.

When she got to College Park library, she opened the glass door and walked in. The cold air from the air conditioner hit her in the face, which soon dried the sweat from her brow. Looking around, she could see that this was a very large library. The library had two floors and a large picture window in the front. There were two rows of computers on the back wall, and they were all occupied. Jennifer walked up to the desk where two libraries were working. The one librarian was a woman in her thirties, and her assistant was no more than a teenager. The main librarian said her name was Mrs. Getty.

"Can I help you?"

"I would like to sign up to use the computer."

"Do you have a library card?"

"No, madam, I do not. Can I sign for one?"

"Yes. You will need the card to get on the computer. It goes by the number on the card. If you fill out this application, I'll make you one, but sign the sheet or you'll lose your turn on the computer."

Jennifer took the application over to the table to fill it out. After finishing it, she brought it back, and the librarian made up her card. Mrs.

Getty said it will still be a half hour before you can get on the computer. Jennifer went to look through the romance novels while she waited. She found one by Nora Roberts and sat down to read it. She had finished two chapters before it was her turn on the computer.

She took her card the librarian handed her and went to the vacant seat and sat down. Putting the number on her card, the computer started up. She first looked at law firms to see if they needed a secretary. She found a few and put in her résumé for each one of them. Next, she found an advertising office needing a secretary and sent her résumé to them. She left her cell phone number to each one hoping for an interview. Jennifer logged off the computer and went back to the desk to check out the book she was reading.

On the walk back to the motel, she realized that she was hungry and saw a McDonald's not many blocks from her. When she walked in, she found the place was quite busy, and she had to wait a little while before she could order. The lady behind the counter asked her what she wanted. Jennifer looked at the menu and ordered a quarter pounder with cheese meal.

"That will be five seventy-five, and here's your cup to get a drink. Will call you when it's ready." She went and filled her cup with ice-cold Coke collecting a straw and napkins. Soon, they called her number, and she went up and picked up her tray. She took her tray to a table, sat down, and ate. When she finished her meal, she took her tray over to the receptacle, threw the trash away, and put the tray on top.

After leaving, she made her way back to the motel; it was getting rather hot. She was becoming quite exhausted making her way back. She drank the rest of her water as she turned onto Virginia Avenue. She hurried around the building so she could get to her room where it was cold. Soon, she opened the door to her room, taking off her shoes. She laid down on the bed turning on the TV and was soon asleep.

When she woke up, she remembered that she needed to do laundry. Going into the bathroom, she collected her bag of dirty clothes, grabbed her purse, and took them downstairs to the laundry room. She first went to the vending machine to exchange her money into quarters. Then she bought laundry detergent and fabric softeners from the machines and put her clothes in the washer plus the detergent and softener. She put the quarters in the slot for it to start. She saw how long it took and returned to her room and read her book till it was time. She then came down and put her clothes in the dryer, putting enough in to last an hour; she returned to her room. When the hour was up, she went down and folded her clothes before returning to her room.

Jennifer had just come up the stairs when the phone in her room began to ring. She rushed in, putting the clothes on the bed before answering the phone. When she answered the phone, it was June, and she was a little disappointed; she was hoping it was a call for a job.

June said, "I can tell in your voice you haven't found a job yet."

"No, I haven't, but I'm glad to hear from you."

"Well, I was taking a break from cleaning and wanted to see how you were doing."

"I am doing okay. I'm sure someone will call soon."

June said, "Jeff is out doing business and has been gone most of the day."

"Do you know what he does for a living?"

"No. He wouldn't tell me, but I will ask him tonight. I must get back to cleaning. I'll talk to you later." June hung up the phone, and Jennifer sat hers back down, putting up her clothes.

After putting her clothes in the dresser, she heard a lot of people down by the pool. She thought that would be a good thing to do. She put on her black swimsuit and a pair of sandals. She collected her key card and her cell phone in case somebody called and headed to the pool after getting a towel from the bathroom. She found an empty lounge chair and put her stuff in the chair. She headed for the diving board. When she dove into the pool, she found the water warm. She swam from one end of the pool to the other. She then returned to her chair for a suntan, and after an hour, she got up because she was starting to burn. She picked up her stuff and headed back to her room.

Jennifer put her stuff on the bed and went to take a shower. She hung up her bathing suit to dry before entering the shower. After she was done, she walked back into her room to get a pair of shorts and a T-shirt out to put on. The sun was setting, and she decided to go out on the balcony. She stood there and watched as it sunk in the wet. When it was behind the trees, she went back inside. She was becoming rather hungry and decided to eat the pizza she had left but went down the corridor to the vending machine to get a Coke. Bringing it back, she sat down to eat. Soon she was finished, cleaned up her mess, and decided to watch TV. Soon she was quite bored with the shows and decided to go to bed. Laying there, she thought maybe she would have better luck tomorrow. She changed into her nightgown and thought there may be some jobs in the paper. She turned out the light and was soon asleep.

CHAPTER 3

JOB SEARCH

Jennifer awoke to the ringing of the phone. Clearing her head, she picked up the receiver to say hello.

A woman was on the phone saying, "Is this Jennifer Wroth? This is Ms. Rose of the law firm of Jim Rhodes. We are calling about your job application. If convenient for you, would you be here today for an interview at ten o'clock this morning?"

Jennifer looked at the clock seeing it was just turning eight and said, "I would be there."

"Well, the address is 1921 Harrison Road. If you have any trouble finding it, just call us back on (678) 954-3261." Jennifer thanked her as she hung up.

She jumped out of bed and removed her nightgown and went straight to the shower. She was so excited as she washed herself. Finishing, she dried herself and went to the closet to find her best dress. She picked out her yellow dress and white high heels. First, she put on her underclothes and then the dress. She went to the vanity and started brushing her hair and decided on a little makeup. Then going back to the bedroom, she sat on the bed as she put on her shoes. It had just turned eight-thirty as she grabbed her purse and headed to the lobby.

When she got to the lobby, she saw it was George on the desk, so she headed over to the breakfast bar. She made a bowl of cereal since it would be quick. Sitting and eating, she put the address in her cell phone so it would show her where to go. After she finished eating, she made a cup of coffee to go. She left the lobby sipping her coffee and looking at her phone; she walked out to Virginia Avenue. She noticed that the road she wanted was several blocks to the right. She headed down the street hoping she would not sweat too much that anybody would notice. She figured the deodorant she had applied would help her. Finally reaching Harrison Street, she turned left seeing that it was the 1900 block. The number of that building was still two blocks away, and she began to hurry since it was a quarter to ten. She had a couple minutes to spare time before entering the building.

Going up to the desk, she said, "I am Jennifer Wroth. I have a ten o'clock appointment."

"Yes, I see. My name is Patricia Turner. It will be a few minutes. He is in a meeting. Would you please sit there? A Ms. Rose will come for you when it is time."

Jennifer sat down in the chairs looking at the receptionist; she thought she was quite pretty. She was a blue-eyed blonde with very stylish clothes. She was getting nervous the more she had to wait.

Soon an older woman came in and said, "Are you Ms. Wroth?"

Jennifer replied, "Yes."

"Well, I am Ms. Rose. We talked to on the phone." Jennifer saw that she was in her forties with light brown hair and blue eyes. "If you follow me, I will take you to Mr. Rhodes."

Jennifer got up and went with Ms. Rose. She followed her down a hallway to the third door. Ms. Rose knocked and said, "I have Ms. Wroth here to see you."

"Well, tell her to come in, and I will need you as soon as this interview is over."

She opened the door for Jennifer and said, "As you wish, sir."

"Good morning," he said as he got up from his desk and came around and shook her hand. "My name is Jim Rhodes, and you are looking for a secretary's job. Would you be seated?"

Jennifer replied, "Yes," as she sat down. Mr. Rhodes went back to his desk and picked up her résumé as he sat down. Jennifer thought he was a nice-looking man with blue eyes and curly brown hair.

"So you did not finish high school, I see, but you do have a GED?"

"No, sir, I just moved here and did not have the time to apply for classes."

"Well, I am sorry, but you must have one to work in this office. Now if you get one and come back, maybe we can work something out."

Jennifer said nothing as she got up to leave feeling quite disappointed and a little angry that he would not give her a chance and work something out.

After leaving his office and heading back to the motel, as she walked along, she was feeling a little sorry for herself with tears rolling down her cheeks. She was thinking I should see about classes, or I might not get a job. Feeling a little hungry being lunchtime, she stopped at a donut shop on Harrison Road. There were not many customers, so she was second to be waited on.

The girl behind the counter said, "May I help you?"

"I would like a dozen glazed donuts and a coffee to go."

The girl rang up her order while another girl got the donuts. The girl handed her a cup and said, "Over there is coffee plus sugar and cream." Jennifer took the cup and the box of donuts over to where the coffee was. She added the sugar and cream, snapped on the lid, turned, and left the store. She decided to wait till she got back to the room being so hot outside.

Walking along, she said, "I will not give up and go home. My father might really hurt me for running away." Thinking all these thoughts, it did not take long to get back to her motel room.

Jennifer stopped and told the housekeeper that she needed towels and to go ahead and clean the room. "I will be leaving for about an hour if that's alright?"

The housekeeper was a Spanish woman, and her English was a little hard to understand, but she smiled letting her know it was fine.

Jennifer said, "I will let you know when I am leaving."

The housekeeper replied, "Gracias."

Jennifer entered her room and sat down to eat her donuts and drink coffee, thinking she would do a little shopping and check at the library for classes. Finishing her food, she left the rest of the donuts on the table with the pizza. She changed her shoes to sandals and put on the orange T-shirt and shorts. Drinking the rest of her coffee and throwing the container in the trash, she went out to find the housekeeper. When she found her, she said, "You can clean now, but please leave my food on the table." The housekeeper, who was named Maria, said she would.

Jennifer remembered there were quite a few shops on Virginia Avenue, so she left the motel heading in that direction. She browsed through several clothing stores and found a jewelry store that had a lovely bracelet in the window. She went in to see how much it cost. The lady in the store let her examine it. It was a gold chain with different trinkets on it, and the lady said it was a thousand dollars. Jennifer knew it would break her, so she said, "I would have to put it back for now." She left the shop disappointed and thought, *Well, that did not help my spirit.*

She noticed a used bookstore and decided to go in. There were thousands of books on the shelves. She walked around the store looking for certain books and decided to go to the counter and ask. A woman in her sixties was standing there; she had quite a few wrinkles and almost white hair. The lady looked up at her with her blue eyes saying, "My name is Crystal. I am the owner. Can I help you?"

"Thanks. I was looking for more Nora Roberts novels," Jennifer said.

"Oh, we have quite a selection of her books just follow me to them." She took Jennifer down an aisle to the back of the store and on a shelf she saw many titles by Nora Roberts both in hardcover as well as paperbacks. The lady left her alone as she browsed the novels deciding on three. Taking them back up to the desk and buying them at a dollar-fifty a piece with tax it came to five dollars.

The lady took her money and said, "Come back anytime. I am sure we can get several more of her books."

Jennifer said that she would be back with a smile and walked out the door with her books, looking down the street at other shops on her way.

While she was window-shopping, she noticed a park and thought she should check it out. There were plenty of trees and flowers with benches near trees, which had lots of shade. There was a slight breeze blowing, and she decided on a delightful place to relax and read one of her books. She saw a restaurant across from the park and decided she was hungry. She walked back to the restaurant and went in, looking at the menu board deciding on a salad and ordered it with ranch salad dressing. She told the lady behind the counter it was to go. Jennifer got her drink cup and filled it with water while waiting for her order. They soon called her. She picked it up, and she left and headed back to the park.

Jennifer found a bench under a tree and sat down. First, she prepared her salad by putting it on the ranch and mixing it. She began to eat as she opened her book to read. She felt the warm sun and the breeze as she read. She heard children playing and laughing in the distance and thought there must be a playground close by. She remembered how when she was younger that she loved to get on the swings. She finished her salad and closed her book starting to feel drowsy. She decided to head back to the motel after throwing her trash in the container close to the bench.

It was a short distance back to the motel. When she got to her room, she was tired and needed to lay down for a nap. Taking off her shoes, she laid her books on the nightstand. She laid down and was soon asleep. It was not long before the phone rang in her ears. She got up and grabbed it thinking it was one of the other ones for which she had applied. When she heard the voice, she knew it was June. She felt a little disappointed until she heard her crying and felt guilty.

Jennifer said, "What's wrong? Is there anything I can do?" feeling a little frightened. June calmed down enough to let her know her problem.

June said, "I did what you told me. I asked him about his job when he got home. He blew up and started shouting at me, that it was none of my business, that if you I have a place to stay, I shouldn't complain. I wanted to know what you did for a living, was curious. He looked like he was going to hit me, but instead, he turned around and went back out the door slamming it behind him. It has been quite a few hours since he has been gone, and I could not get a hold of you till now June said. I know I was out shopping and returned and fell asleep. June said I hope he returns soon. I am worried."

Jennifer said, "He needs to cool off for a while."

June said, "I hope you are right. If he does not, do you mind if I come over to you?

"Of course, you know I am here for you," Jennifer said. "If he comes back, let me know that you are on your way here."

June said she would and hung up. Jennifer hung up the phone a little concerned for her friend.

Jennifer turned on the TV and watched the news, which told her the temperature will be in the ninety for the next seven days. After several hours of waiting for June to call, she was feeling hungry. Having leftover pizza and some donuts, she thought, *I would need a drink to wash that stuff down.* Leaving her room hoping the phone would not ring, she hurried to the vending machine just down the corridor. She got two

Cokes out of the machine and hurried back to her room. Checking the phone, there had been no calls, which worried her a little since June had not called back.

I will have to look in the paper in the morning to see if there are any more job openings.

She went over to the table taking two slices out of the box, popping them in the microwave. When they were heated, she went and sat down to eat and open one of her Cokes. She sat there looking out the window as she ate thinking things were not going too good at this time. Finishing the pizza and a couple of donuts, she got up and threw her trash away. She took her other can of soda to the bed and sat down to watch one of her favorite shows. The sun was already going down, so she went over and closed the curtains. It was not long before she began to yawn and start rubbing her eyes.

I must try June before I go to bed. She should have called back. When she dialed the number, the phone kept on ringing. Jennifer was still worried but started making excuses because she didn't call back. *Jeff must have come back and took her out. I will just try again tomorrow, and she'll tell me why she forgot to call.*

Hanging up the phone, she decided to get ready for bed. She went to the drawer and picked out a blue nylon nightgown. She took all her clothes off and slipped the nightgown on and turned down the air conditioner. She slid back the quilt on the bed and got in. She was still a little worried, so she read a while to take her mind off it. Finally, she was quite sleepy. She put the book down and turned off the light. It did not take long before she was asleep.

Jennifer had forgotten to close the curtains and woke up with the sun shining in her eyes. Getting out of bed, she noticed it was almost eight, so she had plenty of time to get to breakfast. She went and took a shower after closing the curtains. She then brushed her teeth before picking out clothes for today. She decided on a green T-shirt and matching shorts and then went to the vanity to brush her hair. She put on her sandals and headed down to breakfast. She was greeted by several people as she walked through the parking lot to the lobby. George was on duty as she walked in, and she said good morning before getting the paper out of the machine. She headed over to the dining room table and dropped her paper on the table before heading to the breakfast bar.

Jennifer first made herself a cup of coffee with cream and sugar. Getting a paper plate, she dished up eggs and sausages, carrying them all back to her table. She started to eat as she looked through the paper and noticed there was a new opening for a secretary at a church. This made her excited. *This is the job I'm looking for.* She finished her breakfast and made another cup of coffee. She headed back to her room.

Jennifer thought she should try June first before calling the church. June answered the phone after the fourth ring saying hello. Jennifer was a little angry.

"Why didn't you call me? You know, I was worried about you."

June apologized for forgetting. "Jeff came in and said he was sorry and took me to dinner to make up for it. Then he took me dancing, and it was too late to call you. Well, we are getting along good today, and he is supposed to take me shopping so I must get ready, so I will talk to you later."

When June hung up, Jennifer dialed the church. A man answered saying, "This is United Methodist Church Pastor Dodge speaking. How can I help you?"

"I am Jennifer Wroth, and I would like to apply for your secretary job."

He asked if she had any experience. "I have worked in the high school office for my school for two years," she said.

He said, "Well, can you come at six? I will be busy till then."

Quite excited, she said she would be there and asked, "Could you tell me where you are located?"

"Our church is on Virginia Avenue. The number is 1920, but I am sure you cannot miss it." Jennifer said that it was perfect; she is staying right down the road from there. "Then I will see you at six," he said as he hung up.

It was getting close to lunchtime, so she would get a bit to eat before getting ready for her interview. She decided to go down Hawthorne Avenue to the Subway restaurant. She went in the lady behind the counter to ask what she was having. Jennifer settled on a BLT six-inch sub with mayo and a drink and a bag of Doritos. She paid for her food and took her meal over to a table and went to the machine and filled her cup with Coke. She sat and ate thinking of what she should wear and feeling a little anxious. She still had a few hours since the time was only noon, so she took her time eating. Finishing, she threw her trash away and headed back to the motel. When she got back to the room, she went straight to the shower feeling quite sweaty. While taking her shower, she decided to wear her blue dress and matching heels.

Putting on her underclothes and slipping into her dress, she walked back to the vanity and looked in the mirror and said, "A little lipstick." She picked a light shade of pink and applied it to her lips and then brushed her hair. She was getting more excited as time drew nearer. She said, "I cannot stand to just sit here. I need to get out and walk." Jennifer put on her high heels and went out the door.

Looking around as she headed down the street to Walmart, which was on Main Street, it was only two when she got to the store. So she took her time walking down every aisle making a wish list as she went. The time was only three thirty when she left the store. She stopped in a quick mart on the way to get some water. The heat had already dried her out on her way back to Virginia Avenue. It was four before she made it back to the avenue.

I will look in the shops for an hour and be ready for dinner. She looked through a clothing store deciding what she would like to buy after she got a job. There were a few more shops on the way. She saw a Mexican restaurant ahead and decided she would go there for dinner. Mexican food was high on her list of favorites.

She entered La Fiesta, which was 1410 Virginia Avenue, which meant she was five blocks from the church. She found a table near the window so she could look out. Soon a server came up and asked for her order and if she would like something to drink. Jennifer looked at the menu, feeling still a little nervous, and asked for an ice tea. The server got it and returned it. Jennifer finally decided on a taco salad. The server asked her if that would be all. Jennifer replied yes for now, and the server left with her order. She knew she was going to have a slight problem eating, but she had time to eat slowly. The server soon returned with her salad and refilled her glass.

The server said, "There will be nothing else?"

Jennifer replied, "Not at this moment." She slowly ate her salad hoping that she would not throw it up. It was almost quarter of six by her watch and she better get going. She asked for the bill she paid and left.

CHAPTER 4

UNITED METHODIST

It took Jennifer about ten minutes to walk the five blocks, and she could not miss the church; it was quite big. Leaving the sidewalk and walking across a large parking lot, she entered the church. Soon as she was inside, the frigid air hit her and felt the sweat on her body drying up. She saw the pulpit way up front on a large stage, and there were chairs on the right facing toward the pulpit, which she assumed were for the choir. There were quite a few pews in the room, which would seat at least three hundred people. The carpet on the floor was light brown under the brown pews and the walls were white. There were two doors on each side of her, and she could see two more just off the stage. Jennifer was fascinated with the large speakers on the wall behind the stage. There was a window above the stage that led to a control booth. While she was looking around, someone came up behind her; and when he spoke, she jumped.

"Good evening. I am Pastor Robert Dodge. Can I help you?"

Jennifer turned a little red from embarrassment, saying, "I'm the person you have an interview for the secretary job."

"Oh, yes, I have been so busy it's kind of a slipped my mind. Oh! Yes, you're Ms. Wroth," he said as he shook her hand. Jennifer felt his hands were soft but firm. He was a lot taller than her, being about six two. He had a pleasant smile and light brown eyes. She looked up at his brown curly hair and looked thin for his height.

He said, "Would you follow me?" leading her into the door on the left. The hallway was quite narrow, but there were several doors in the long hall. When they reached the end, there was another hallway on the left, which was a short hallway with only two doors. He led her to the last door and opened it.

He said, "Would like to take a seat there please?" showing her a comfort cushion chair before his desk. He had a big oak desk, which made her wonder how they got it down the hall. Jennifer seated herself as he went around the desk and sat down. The pastor picked up her résumé from the desk that she had sent.

"Now I see you do have quite a bit of experience as a school secretary, which would be good in this job. The only problem I see is you didn't finish high school. Why was that?" he asked.

"Well, sir, it was my fault. I didn't treat the girls in my class that well. They began to hate me, thinking I was too good for them. They set me up to fail by looking like I cheated. Since there were several girls, it was my word against theirs, so the principal and the teacher believed them. I lost my job and was suspended."

"Well, why should I give you this job if you cannot get along with people?"

"Well, sir, I have learned from my mistakes, and I was just hoping for a chance."

"Well, I think I could let you have this job on a temporary basis, but you must go to class for your GED. So are you willing to work here by day and go to night classes?"

Jennifer was feeling nervous and said, "I promise I will, but will you give me a couple weeks? I will need a little money to put down for school and pay for my room at the motel."

"I think I can live with that, but in a few weeks, if you have not applied, I have no choice but to replace you."

Jennifer agreed and got up and shook his hand, saying, "You won't regret it."

"Fine. Be here at eight, and I will show you around and get you started."

Jennifer left his office in a hurry still feeling excited to have a job.

Jennifer strolled back down the street thinking things were looking up for her, and she had enough money to make it the next two weeks before she would get paid. The sun was starting to go down, and there was a light breeze blowing. The traffic was still congested from people getting off at work. It took no time to make it back to the motel. When she got to her room, she could tell that the housekeeper had already come and cleaned. She was glad to get out of those heels that were hurting her feet. She went into the closet to decide what she would wear tomorrow. She took out a beige pantsuit and a white blouse and laid them on a chair. She then looked in the dresser and found a red nightgown. Stripping off her clothes, she put it on. Then, taking her clothes, she put them in the laundry bag in the bathroom. She sat at the vanity and removed her makeup after brushing her teeth. She decided to give June call and tell her the exciting news.

June answered after a few rings saying hello, and after hearing Jennifer's voice, she asked how it went.

"I got the job on the stipulation I must get my GED, but he did give me time to pay first."

"Sounds good. I'm sure it will be rough going to school right after work," June replied.

"I know, but it will be worth it especially to keep the job."

"Well, all I can say is good luck," June said. "Me and Jeff are here for you anytime you need help."

"I thank you both, but I think there will be no problem. I see you two are getting along again," Jennifer said.

"We are. I should not have made you worry with my silly little argument."

"That's alright. That's what best friends are for." She laughed.

June laughed back saying, "You are. Well, it's getting late, so I'll say good night."

Jennifer said good night as she hung up the phone. She got into bed and turned out the lights, thinking about tomorrow before falling asleep.

The next morning, she awoke with the alarm ringing in her ears. Looking at the clock, it was six thirty, which gave her a little time, not having to be at the church till eight. Jennifer took off her nightgown after getting out of bed. She put on a green T-shirt and matching shorts to go down for breakfast. She slipped into her pink fuzzy slippers and put her key card in her pocket and hurried downstairs.

When she entered the lobby, Jean was working at the desk, and she went over and told her about getting a job. Jean said that was great and good luck. Jennifer went to the breakfast bar and poured herself a coffee and put in cream and sugar. She then got a plate and filled it with scrambled eggs and bacon. She put two slices of bread in the toaster for toast. She took the rest of her breakfast to the table and came back for the toast. After getting the toast out, she got packs of butter and strawberry jam.

Jennifer ate her breakfast and thought how nervous she was about her first day. When she finished her food, she went and put her trash in the container and got another cup of coffee before returning to her room. The first thing she did when she opened her door was to kick off her slippers. As soon as the door closed, she removed the rest of her clothes and took them to the bathroom. She dropped them in the bag and turned on the shower. Picking up her bodywash, she entered the shower, which began to relax her for what was to come. Stepping out of the shower and toweling off, she walked into the bedroom to the chair where she had left her clothes that night before. After getting dressed, she went and brushed her teeth. Sitting at the vanity, she applied a light red lipstick. Looking at her face in the mirror, she thought not to put too much makeup on working in a church. Strapping on her high heels, she got up and picked up her purse before heading for the door. It was now seven thirty, and she had plenty of time to get there since it was only a fifteen-minute walk. Leaving the elevator, she could tell it was already getting hot and thought she should get a water bottle from the lobby before proceeding. She got water out of the vending machine just inside the door and headed for Virginia Avenue. There was a lot of traffic this early in the morning, she thought, and she had to wait at the light to cross the street to the church.

Jennifer entered the double white doors. She could feel the cool air on her skin as she walked to the door on her left. Proceeding down both hallways, she knocked on the pastor's door. He told her to come in, and she opened the door.

He looked up at the clock on the wall above the door and said, "I see you are right on time". He turned off his computer on the desk and got up saying, "We need to start with a tour." The pastor led her to the next door from his and opened it. He said, "This will be your office. Mrs. Brown was the last secretary, but for the last year, I have done both. I'm sure you will fix things the way you want them," he said.

Jennifer looked in the room seeing a big brown desk and a computer and a business phone, which was the only thing on top of it.

"It's been a while since anyone occupied this room."

The room was bright with yellow walls and white curtains on the window. The beige carpet was thick under her feet and a row of gray cabinets sat on the left wall.

The pastor said, "You will find all the members in those cabinets, and all events are on the computer. You can set up your own log-in later, and there are five extensions on that phone. The first is yours. After today, I'll fix that when I return to my office, which will become the second button. The third is the treasury department and the fourth the deacon's office. The last button is the kitchen."

The pastor took her on down the hall to the first door around the bend, saying, "This is our office supply room, which also houses the printer and fax machine. You will be able to get a key from our accountant whom we will meet next."

The pastor knocked on the next door and walked in. Jennifer saw a man setting behind a computer as she walked in. The pastor introduced him as John Conner.

"He manages all our books." John got up to shake her hand and the pastor said, "This is our new secretary, Ms. Jennifer Wroth."

She noticed his blond hair and blue eyes as she shook his hand and thought he was a handsome man for being in his thirties.

Pastor Dodge said, "Give her the extra key to the storeroom."

John got the key and handed it to her thinking how beautiful she was. He was going to like her being around.

They then went on to the next door and entered.

"Mr. Roger O'Donnell, I would like you to meet Ms. Jennifer Wroth, our new secretary," the pastor said.

Jennifer noticed he was a middle-aged man with a brown mustache, which matched his hair. He smiled at her with sparkling brown eyes and told her he was the head deacon.

"If you need any help, my door is always open."

Pastor Dodge said, "He knows more about this church than I do."

Jennifer said, "Well, I guess I know who to come to if I have questions."

Roger laughed and said, "Good luck."

Pastor Dodge said, "Now we'll go on to our dining room and kitchen on the other side of the church."

She walked with him to the other door on the right, which contained a room full of tables and chairs. Each chair was wooden and the color of brown and looked to be able to seat at least a hundred. The tables had white tiled tops and brown legs. Jennifer saw a window with a steel counter attached which showed the kitchen area. She realized it was where you got your food from and saw a woman in the kitchen baking. The pastor called her to come out and introduced her.

"This is our cook, Mrs. Rita Jacobs. Ms. Wroth is my new secretary. She is starting today."

"You can call me Jennifer," she said as she shook her hand.

"Would you two like a cup of coffee? I just made a fresh pot."

Pastor Dodge said he would like one and Jennifer agreed. They took a seat at the table close to the kitchen while Rita went in for the pot. Rita came back with the coffee and cream and sugar on a tray. Jennifer went over to the table that had the dishes and silverware. She brought back three cups and spoons. Rita poured the coffee and sat down and began to fix her coffee. Jennifer was surprised that Rita was quite skinny for working in the kitchen. She looked to be in her sixties with gray hair and wrinkles, but soon found out she was only fifty-two and was a single parent with a teenage daughter named Ruby. Rita told Jennifer that she was a born-again Christian and that Pastor Dodge led her to the Lord. She admitted she still didn't know all the names of the members, being quite busy on Sunday.

Pastor Dodge said, "Well, we must get back to work, and I'm sure you have plenty to do."

Rita returned to the kitchen and Jennifer cleaned up the mess and followed the pastor back to his office.

He said as he sat down, "I am sure you would like to get started, and I will let you go and get things put the way you would like them. I have already changed the phone, so you could take over answering it."

She left his office, went into her office, and sat down at the desk. She opened the computer and began setting it up with her e-mail address and password. She looked at the roster and saw there were five hundred members that belong to this church. She checked out the events that were coming up soon, and she would have to talk them over with Mr. O'Donnell. Several hours later, she decided to see what was for lunch. She logged off her computer and headed back to the lunchroom.

Once entering, she looked for Rita who was still in the kitchen. Jennifer asked, "Do you have anything good to eat?"

"How about I make you a grilled cheese sandwich and a bowl of soup?" Rita replied.

"That would be great," Jennifer said. She sat at the table to wait for her lunch and decided on a glass of water and went to get some. Rita had just finished her sandwich and the microwave was beeping. Jennifer poured her water and said, "I will take the sandwich with me, and you can bring the soup."

Rita said, "Thanks. I will be just a minute." Jennifer went back to the table and sat down. Rita came out with the soup and brought a cup of coffee for herself. Rita said, "If you do not mind, I'll sit with you while you eat."

Jennifer said she would love that. Rita told her about starting at this church that there was no permanent cook till she took the job. She said she had helpers on Sunday since it was quite busy here.

"I bring my daughter Ruby on Wednesdays since I do not have any help that day. You will come on Wednesday night to meet her?"

Jennifer said she might though knowing she had no intention. After finishing her lunch, she told Rita thanks and returned to her office for the rest of the day. The phone never rang, and she was a little bored doing nothing.

Soon the pastor came in asking, "Well, how was your day?"

She said it was fine and she had everything under control. He smiled and left.

Jennifer logged off her computer and picked up her purse and turned off the lights as she left her office. John Conner was closing his door as she went past. He said good night and asked if she had a good day. She said that it was great, and she will see him tomorrow. They walked out to the parking lot together, and he asked her if he could drive her home. Jennifer did not want to be unkind, but she was a little leery of his advances.

"I appreciate your offer, but I am supposed to meet someone at that McDonald's over there," she said, pointing across the road.

"Well, maybe another time," he said.

She headed to McDonald's thinking she was hungry, so he wouldn't know she lied. John walked to his car thinking that he would like to get to know her better.

Jennifer went into McDonald's after crossing at the light. Looking at the menu, she decided on a Big Mac dinner. Putting her order in and paying, she collected her cup for her drink. She put in ice and Coke from the machine. Then she heard her number being called and went to get her tray. She sat down near the window facing the church.

While eating her meal, she thought, *John is a handsome man, but I don't know him.* She thought that after getting to know him it might be different since she was attracted to him. She finished her meal and threw her trash away and headed back to the motel.

When she got back to her room, she could tell the housekeeper had come in and cleaned. She removed her shoes after entering her door since her feet hurt being in the heels all day. She decided to call June to tell her about her day. She picked up the phone and sat on the bed as she dialed her number.

When June picked up the phone, Jennifer said, "How are you doing?"

June said, "I am simply fine, so how did your day go?"

Jennifer told her about everything that happened that day. June seemed not to be listening to her and was wondering what was wrong. Jennifer said, "Is something the matter?"

June said, "Not a thing. I just need to get this housework done before Jeff gets home, so if you do not mind, I'll talk to you tomorrow." June hung up.

Jennifer was worried since June never acted that way before.

She decided to watch some TV, but first, she needed to take a shower. Removing her clothes, she walked into the bathroom. After fixing the water and putting her clothes in the laundry bag, she stepped in the shower. The warm water was relaxing after her first day of work. While soaping up, she thought that she loved this job already; and with the money she had, it would be no problem till her next paycheck.

I need to find a place to get my GED before I do get paid.

Finishing in the shower, she got out and dried off. Walking in the bedroom, she went and took her yellow nylon gown out of the drawer and put it on. Then siting on the bed, she took the remote off the nightstand and turned on the TV. She finally decided on a mystery movie and laid there and watched. Soon after the movie was over, she was felt sleepy and turned off the TV and the lights. She pulled down the covers, being a little cold from the air conditioner, and covered up. She was soon fast asleep.

She awoke the next morning and thought about what to wear for work and took out a blue dress and white high heels. She put on the dress and her slippers and went down for breakfast feeling quite hungry. The elevator was full when she got to it and decided to take the stairs. There seemed to be quite a few people at breakfast, and it was hard to find a table. A young couple who was on their honeymoon offered to let her sit with them. She got a cup of coffee and a plate full of eggs and bacon and came back to the table.

"My name is Jennifer," she said as she sat down.

"We are the Carlins from Tennessee, and this is our first time in Atlanta." They said, "We are here for a couple days and hope to see you again."

Jennifer noticed the time and told them it was nice to meet them, but she had to get going before she was late for work. They said goodbye as she returned to her room to put in the final changes before leaving for work. She changed her shoes and put on her lipstick before walking out the door. On her way down the street, it was already in the seventies as she walked along. She was glad she had put on a dress and instead of a pantsuit. By the time she got to the church, she was beginning to sweat.

The cool air felt good as she entered and went left to the door that led to her office. She went in, laying her purse on the desk, sat, and logged in her computer. Soon the phone rang. Jennifer picked up the phone, pushing the button and saying, "Hello. This is United Methodist Church. Jennifer speaking."

"Good morning. I am Julie Morgan. I would like to make an appointment with Pastor Dodge."

Jennifer said, "Hold on a minute while I see what's available. I have an opening on Tuesday at two o'clock. Is this satisfactory?"

Mrs. Morgan said that would be fine and hung up. Jennifer put it on her computer and emailed it to the pastor.

Looking over her schedule, suddenly there was a knock at the door and in walked Mr. O'Donnell. He said, "I have the programs for this

Wednesday and Sunday. I need a hundred copies of each by the end of the day."

Jennifer looked at the programs and said that would be fine. "I promise to get to them as soon as possible." He thanked her and left. She first went to the pastor's office to find if he needed her.

The pastor was busy answering mail that came in and said, "Not right now. Could you come back here after lunch?"

She said that would be fine since she had to do a job for Mr. O'Donnell. She left and picked up the programs and headed to the supply room where the copier was. It was lunchtime when she finished all the programs and put them on Mr. O'Donnell's desk.

Rita had a cheese sandwich and a bowl of soup ready for Jennifer when she got there. Rita sat with her while she ate. Rita asked how her day was going. Jennifer said it was going great with no big problems.

"Everybody is so helpful," she said.

Rita said, "That is good. We are just one big family."

Jennifer finished eating and said, "Thanks. I got to get back. The pastor needs me."

"Well, I will see you later. Don't worry, I'll take care of the dishes."

Jennifer said thanks and got up and left watching Rita clear the table. She made it back to her office and picked up her pad and headed next door. The pastor told her to come in as soon as she knocked.

Pastor Dodge said, "So is everything going well?"

Jennifer said, "Fine, and I do like the job."

The pastor said, "I am glad. Now here is a letter I need you to type up to the pastor of Holy Trinity and bring it to me to sign. Somethings I do not want to email because it loses the meaning. Hope you understand?"

Jennifer said she does and will get on it right away.

Jennifer returned to her office and sat down and read the letter.

Dear Reverend Harlot,

We invite you to our meeting to discuss a tournament of baseball between your church and ours. If you will call and let us know if it can be arranged.

Yours truly,
Pastor Robert Dodge

Jennifer typed it up and got a copy from the fax machine in the other office and brought it to the pastor to sign. Going back to her office, she looked up the address and made out the envelope. She found them in her right-hand drawer with a roll of stamps. She took the letter out of the mailbox and put it in and raised the flag. She was not sure when the mail carrier would come; she would have to find out his schedule. Walking back in, she ran into John Conner who was leaving for today.

"How is it going?" he asked.

"Fine. Do you always leave this time of day?" she asked.

He said, "No. I got a dentist appointment. My tooth is giving me a fit."

Jennifer said she was sorry to hear that and walked back to her office.

The rest of the day was still boring finding little to do and no one to talk to. Soon it was time to go, and she logged off her computer and picked up her purse. She stopped in to tell the pastor good night. He said good night and he said he would be leaving soon. She walked out the door of the church and headed home.

The sun was still beating down, and no breeze was blowing. She hurried back to the motel and was sweating and quite dried out. The first thing she did when she got to her room was took off her high heels, which were hurting her feet. She removed her dress, which was soaked with sweat. She went straight to the shower using mostly chilly water to dry her sweat. After drying off, she walked back and got a red T-shirt and a pair of shorts to put on. She felt quite exhausted since the heat took everything out of her. She looked at the advertisements on the dresser and called Blimpie Sub. Ordering a steak sub and fries, they said it would be about thirty minutes. She hung up and decided to go to the vending machine down the hall. She got two bottles of Coke and returned to her room.

She walked out on the balcony to watch the people in the pool, waiting for her food. There were a lot of children playing by the pool and in the water. Most of the adults were on lounge chairs soaking up the sun. Jennifer was drinking her Coke and listening to the children laughing and having an enjoyable time. Soon there was a knock at the door, and she went to answer it. A young man stood there with her food.

"That I will be 10.95, madam."

Jennifer went to her purse and pulled out a ten and a five. Handing it to him, she told him to keep the change. He was a little surprised and told her, "Anytime you order, I will make sure to get it here quick."

Jennifer laughed and said, "Thank you." She took her food, closed the door, and went to the table to eat. She had left the glass doors open and went and closed them to keep the room cool.

She pulled out one of the books she was reading as she ate her food and sipped at her Coke. When she finished eating, she sat and read the rest of the book.

I guess I'll stop at that bookstore tomorrow for a couple more romance books on my way home. The sun had set and was beginning to get dark. She closed the curtains and turned on the lights.

"Well, I guess I'll watch a little TV before bed," she said. Taking off her T-shirt and shorts and putting on her black nightgown, she sat on the bed to watch her shows. In an hour, she was getting sleepy. She turned off the TV and lights; she laid down and was soon fast asleep.

It was a Tuesday morning, and the sun was shining in her window through the curtains. She opened her eyes and saw the alarm was about to ring. She got out of bed stretching, seeing what a wonderful day it was. She did not have to run back to her parents with her tail between her legs because she knew she would make it here. Feeling hungry, she put on a set of clothes and headed downstairs for a bite before work. When she got to the lobby, she saw her friend Jean was on duty. Jennifer went over to say hi and tell her about her new job. Jean said that was great, and she wished her good luck.

Jennifer said, "Thanks. Got to go eat and get ready for work."

Jean said, "I will be on again Sunday so we can talk then."

Jennifer said, "I'll see you then."

Jennifer got coffee and a waffle and sat down to eat. It didn't take long for her to finish and refill her cup before going back upstairs to say goodbye to Jean. As she headed to the stairs, she saw the young married couple heading to the lobby.

Jennifer said, "Sorry I missed you, but I have been busy and must get ready for work."

"Well, we are leaving today. How about I give you my number, and you can call sometime."

Jennifer said that would be great. He wrote on a card he pulled from his wallet, Mr. and Mrs. Don Carlin and his wife, Laura.

"Well, we hope to hear from you, Jennifer." They walked hand in hand to the lobby while Jennifer proceeded to her room.

First, she went to the closet when she entered her room to get out her pink dress and white heels for today. She went into the bathroom and brushed her teeth. After slipping out of her shorts and T-shirt, she put on the dress. Then sitting at the vanity, she put on a light pink lipstick to match the dress and then brushed her hair. Putting on her shoes, she got up and collected her purse and key card and walked out the door making sure it was locked behind her.

The sky was overcast, and as she walked down the street, she was thinking she should have brought a umbrella.

"I should listen to the weather report each day before I leave the motel," she said to herself. She felt it was still hot, but a breeze began to hit her, and she could tell that rain was almost here, so she hurried down the street to the church just in time. When she got to the lobby of the church, it began to pour, and she heard a crack of thunder. Making her way to her office, she hoped the storm would be over by the time she left today.

Going to her desk, she put her purse down and opened her computer. After she logged on, the first thing she saw was the appointment with Julia Morgan. She saw that a Mrs. Hope was in the hospital and saw that the pastor had nothing for the first thing tomorrow. She sent him an email to visit her. Then the phone rang. It was the pastor asking her to come to his office. Jennifer said she would be right there. Picking up a pad and pen, she walked next door. After knocking, she was told to come in.

Pastor Dodge looked at her and said, "How you like the job so far? And thanks for the email. I will be at the hospital in the morning, so if anything comes up, let Mr. O'Donnell know." She said she would. He said, "I did not need you for dictations. I already wrote the letter. Just type and send it. The letter is to a Reverend Jones. He is coming to visit on the fifth, and John Conner is going to pick him up at the airport, so would you make sure this goes out today? Let him know that his tickets are waiting at the airport for him."

She said she would take care of it right away. Jennifer took the letter and headed back to her office and typed it up and went straight to the printer to get it. She went back to her office and wrote the address on the envelope to Reverend Jones, 1020 Rush Street Chicago, Illinois. She put the letter in and stamped it and headed to the mailbox.

John Conner met her in the hall saying, "It is still pouring outside, and good morning to you."

"Oh! I need to put this letter in the box," she said.

John reached for the door of his office and handed her his umbrella. "I think you might need this," he said with a smile. Jennifer thanked him and said she would return it as soon as she got back. It was ten o'clock and the mail carrier was due, and the truck was already in the box. Opening the umbrella, she ran out and gave him the letter. He took it and reached back into the box and handed her today's mail. She thanked him as he pulled away, and she reentered the church.

Before taking back the umbrella, she took the mail to her office to sort it through. Making three piles of envelopes, she picked up the first pile, which was to the pastor and took it to him. He thanked her for the mail, and she told him his letter had since gone out. Then returning to her office, she collected Mr. O'Donnell's mail and went to his office. She knocked on his door, but there was no answer. She went in and put his mail on the desk and left. Then picking up the letters for Mr. Conner and the umbrella, she went to his office and knocked.

Jennifer said, "Here is your mail, and thanks for the use of your umbrella."

He said, "You are very welcome, and if you do not mind, if it is still raining, I can drop you off."

Jennifer was not sure of him and did not want to be impolite. "That's alright. I already have a ride," she said, which was a lie. She felt a little bad to lie to him. She returned to her office and thought he was nice-looking but was still a stranger to her. Plus, she had too much to do and needed to look up a class for her GED. She found out that Spelman College was holding classes next month, and she applied online. She logged off her computer and headed to the lunchroom.

By the time Jennifer entered the lunchroom, Rita had already had her lunch prepared. She had brought coffee and ham and cheese sandwiches for the two of them. While eating, she told Rita about John, letting her borrow his umbrella and wanting to take her home after work.

Rita said, "That is because he likes you," which made Jennifer blush.

"I am still not ready for a relationship. I need to find a place to live beside the motel, and plus, the pastor said I had to get my GED."

Rita said, "Do not worry. If it's still raining, I'll take you."

Jennifer said, "That would be great." Finishing her sandwich, she said, "I'll get back to work and see you later." Rita said goodbye and cleaned up the mess as Jennifer left.

When Jennifer got back to her office, she decided to call June and tell her about John. It took several rings before June answered the phone.

"Oh! Hi, Jennifer," she said in a sleepy voice. "I was out late with Jeff and need more sleep. How about calling me later when I wake up?"

Jennifer was a little disappointed not being able to talk to her but told her, "It's alright. Talk to you later." Hanging up, she logged back into her computer.

In a few minutes, there was a knock at her door. When she said, "Come in," an older woman opened the door.

"Hello, I am Julia Morgan. I made an appointment with you yesterday."

"Oh, yes, I am sure the pastor is waiting for you." Jennifer got up from her desk and led the attractive lady next door. She had gray hair and sparkling gray eyes, but she held her own beauty.

Knocking, she called out, "Your two o'clock appointment is here." Pastor Dodge said for her to come in. Jennifer opened the door for Mrs. Morgan and returned to her office after closing the door. Jennifer went back to her computer and noticed there was to be a fundraiser dinner in two weeks. She sent out notices to all members that the dinner would be held in the church's cafeteria, and it would be twenty dollars for couples and ten for singles. "Hope you all attend it to help the youth baseball league."

In a little while, the pastor came in and said, "Please make an appointment for me to see Mrs. Morgan again next week. I have a couples meeting at three, so I won't see you before you leave today, but have a good night."

Jennifer put in her computer for Mrs. Morgan to be there next Tuesday at ten and sent the email to her.

The time was almost four thirty as she looked up at the clock. She logged off her computer and turned off the light as she picked up her purse. Going down the hallway, she ran into John Conner.

He said, "I see it stopped raining, but I could still take you home."

Feeling ashamed of lying to him, she agreed for him to take her. There in the parking lot sat a yellow Mustang, which he opened the door for her. She told him she was in the Economy Lodge on Virginia Avenue.

He drove her there and said, "I would like to get to know you. How about going to dinner with me tonight? I promise to bring you straight back home."

Jennifer was a little reluctant at first and said she would.

"I will pick you up about seven thirty if that's alright with you."

She told him her room was 225 in the back of the building. He drove her around to the back side of the building. She got out of the car saying, "That is fine. I'll be ready." She watched as he drove off thinking to herself, *I hope things work out between us, I hate to have to avoid him at work.* Getting out of the car, she hurried on to her room.

She looked at the clock when she entered the room and saw it was near five. After closing the door, she sat down on the bed and removed her shoes. Rubbing her feet, which hurt from the heels, she said, "I know I'll have to wear a pair tonight." She went in the bathroom after closing the curtains and removed her clothes before getting into the shower. While soaping up her body, she thought, *I cannot believe I said yes.* Still, she felt a little excited and decided to wear her black dress, which was a little low cut, and she'll put back on the white heels; they do go with the dress.

Getting out of the shower, she grabbed the towel to dry off. She went to the closet after putting on her undergarments and pulled the black dress out of the hanger. She slipped it on and picked out a new pair of hose since the other already had a run in them. Walking in stockinged feet, she went back to the vanity to apply her makeup. She sat and thought about him while brushing her hair. It was only six thirty by the time she was ready. She sat on the bed and turned on the news and weather. She saw it was going to be ninety-five tomorrow.

I'll make sure to wear my lightweight dress tomorrow, and yellow won't absorb heat. The news itself was always filled with the evil that people do and not many good stories. The news went off at seven, and she just laid there and rested for the next half-hour.

It wasn't long before there was a knock at the door, and when she opened it, John was standing there.

"Are you ready?" he asked.

"Just a minute while I put on my shoes and grab my purse." He stood at the door while she got her things and led her to his car parked downstairs. He opened the door for her, and she slid into his red leather seats, which were a little warm even if the air was running. She watched as he walked around the car thinking he looked good in his navy-blue suit. He told her as they drove off that he had made reservations for eight at the Texas Roadhouse. It was a half-hour drive from there. They were soon on the interstate headed to Buford. They arrived there at almost ten till eight.

Jennifer saw the mall, which was behind the restaurant. She asked if they could look around after they ate.

He said that would be fine. "I am sure you would like it in there."

When they entered the restaurant, a host met them at the door. John told her that he had a reservation under the name Conner. She looked at her computer and said, "Yes, please follow me." She led them to a table in back and said she hope they enjoy their meal.

Soon a server came up saying, "My name is Reba. Can I get you a drink while you look over the menu?" which she handed them.

They said, "We would like two glasses and a pitcher of beer."

And she said, "I will be right back."

They looked over the menu and decided on what to eat. When the server came back with the beer, she asked if they were ready to order. John said that they were, and he would like a T-bone steak well done and a baked potato with butter and sour cream. "I would like the house salad with blue cheese while waiting."

Jennifer said she would have the same, but her steak needed to be medium well.

She took the order and said, "I will be back in a few minutes with your salad."

The server returned with the salad and said, "The food should be done in about fifteen minutes."

John spoke up after she left and said, "Would you like to hear a little about me?" Jennifer said that she would. John began by saying he grew up in Charleston, South Carolina. "My father was a factory worker named John too. I am a junior. My mother, Mary, was a stay-at-home mom, and I have a sister Laura who is older than me and a teacher back home. My parents struggled to get me into college, and being great at math, I decided to be an accountant. I looked for a job in Charleston but did not find any work until I saw in the paper that this church needed one. I moved here to Atlanta after getting the job and found an apartment to rent close to the church."

"Are your parents still living there?"

"Oh! Yes, I do go back to see them whenever I get a chance."

Soon the server returned with their food. While eating, she told John about herself.

"Have you told your parents where you are?" he asked.

"No. I wanted to be more established here, so they will not think I was being childish about running away."

They finished their dinner and John paid the bill with a sizeable tip. The server was pleased and told them to come back anytime.

Leaving the restaurant, they walked hand in hand back to the car. Jennifer felt that this might be the right guy. John helped her to the car and hurried around to get in. Driving her back to the motel, he was tempted to ask her out again but was afraid to wish him luck.

They soon arrived back at her motel, and she told him she had a wonderful evening, but she had to get to bed because of getting up early for work. John leaned over and gave her a passionate kiss, which seem quite long. She got out of the car and told him not to bother showing her to the door. He drove off, and she stood there watching him leave. She was thinking to herself that part of her didn't want him to leave, but she might regret it later. Walking up the stairs to her room, she felt full of joy. She let herself into her room looking at the time; she thought it was too late to call June and tell her about her evening. Jennifer got out of her clothes and put on her green nightgown out of the dresser and set the alarm for tomorrow. She got into bed thinking that she really felt something for John even if she was trying to stay out of a relationship. Finally, she drifted off to sleep.

Jennifer woke up before the alarm feeling good thinking about last night. It was after six, so she knew breakfast was being served. She got a red T-shirt and red shorts out of the drawer and put them on. She slipped her feet in her fluffy slippers and headed down to breakfast. Going straight to the coffee urn first, she knew she needed the coffee to wake up. While drinking her coffee, she decided on some waffles. She put the mixture in the waffle iron and went and got butter and syrup while it cooked. Getting the waffles, she stopped by the coffee urn to refill her cup. Taking everything over to the nearest table, she sat down to eat. She wasn't in a hurry since she got up so early. George was at the desk and waved hello to her, and she waved back. She finished her meal and refilled her cup again before leaving the lobby.

When she got back to her room, she took a shower and went to the sink and brushed her teeth. Wearing the towel, she went to her dresser to get her undergarments. She put them on, looking in the closet and deciding what to wear.

Maybe I'll wear this light-yellow dress today and a pair of white heels. She put the clothes on and went to the vanity to brush her hair and put on a light pink lipstick. When she opened the door to leave, the maid was before her door with the cart.

"May I clean your room today?" she asked. Jennifer said yes and held the door for her before walking down the hall to the elevator.

It seemed a beautiful morning as she crossed the parking lot. There was a slight breeze blowing, which helped with the temperature already on the rise. She felt good as she walked hearing the birds sing in the trees. When she reached Virginia Avenue, she could no longer hear the birds for all the cars. She took her time since she was early, but she reached the light across from the church rather quickly. It wasn't long before the light turned red so she could cross.

Jennifer still wanted to talk to June, so the first thing she did when entering her office was to call her. The phone rang quite a few times before it was answered. June said in a sleepy voice, "Hello, who is this?"

Jennifer said, "It's me. I just wanted to tell you about my date last night."

"I love to hear about it, but I haven't much sleep. I just got in from my new job, so can we meet later for dinner?" June said.

"I usually get out of here by five. How about we meet at McDonald's, which is right down the road from the motel? That way I can change clothes because I feel a lot more comfortable in shorts."

June laughed. "I understand. I could feel the heat when I came in this morning, but let's cut this conversation short. I need sleep."

Jennifer said, "Okay. See you later," and hung up.

She logged in her computer and knew that the pastor would be leaving soon to the hospital. She went next door to his office to see if he had any last-minute instructions. She knocked and he told her to enter. Pastor Dodge looked up from his seat and said, "Good. I was just about to call you. I have three letters that need to go out today. I'm hoping these churches have teams that our baseball team can play. Here are the letters. I'm sure you can find the addresses," by handing them to her.

Jennifer said, "I'll take care of it right away."

He said that was good. He hoped she would get them in the mail today. She said she would.

"I won't be in the rest of the day after the hospital because I have several meetings, so I'll see you tomorrow."

Jennifer said, "Have a good day," and left his office.

When she got into the hallway, John was standing there. He said, "I was waiting for you. We had such a good time last night I was wondering if you would go out with me tonight." Jennifer was filled with excitement and disappointment at the same time since she had already agreed to meet June.

"I'm sorry, John, but I already have plans tonight."

John looked a little disappointed and said, "Well, how about tomorrow night?"

Jennifer couldn't resist his charm and agreed. John took her in his arms and gave her a kiss. Jennifer was a little embarrassed thinking the pastor would walk out his door any second.

"I must get back to work. The pastor wants this done today," she said. John smiled, let her go, and headed back to his office. Jennifer knew she needed to concentrate on her letters, but it was hard since she was thinking about his hugs and kisses.

She typed up the letters to each church, and soon she had the address of each one: Providence Baptist Church on 1773 Hawthorne, Mt. Calvary Baptist on 777 Simmons, and College Park Presbyterian on Mercer Avenue.

Dear sir,

We have a team of kids who would like to play baseball and wonder if you would be interested in playing our team. Please let us know.

Your servant,
Pastor Dodge

Jennifer made three copies of the letters and addressed them with their return address. Putting a stamp on each, she made her way to the box in front of the church. She saw that the mailman hadn't come yet. She put the letters in the box and put the flag up. She went back into the church.

Seeing that it was almost lunchtime, she made her way to the kitchen. Jennifer walked in and said, "What's for lunch?"

Rita said, "I made a big pot of chicken noodle soup." Jennifer went to the refrigerator and got the pitcher of tea out to pour her some. She looked over to Rita asking if she wanted some tea too. Rita had filled two bowls and carried them out to a table and said she would. Jennifer filled another glass, returned the pitcher to the fridge, and brought them to the table.

Rita asked how her date went.

Jennifer said it was fine. "I think he likes me a lot. He not only kissed me good night last night, but he got me in the hall today."

Rita laughed. "I guess you got a boyfriend now even after you said you wouldn't."

Jennifer turned a little red while finishing her soup. "Well, I need to go collect the mail. I thought I saw him coming down the street," Jennifer said.

Rita told her to go on. "I'll clean up these dishes."

Jennifer said thanks and headed for the front door. Jennifer collected the mail from the box and met Roger in the hall going back to her office. He said he needed her to run off these bulletins for Sunday. She said she would after be sorting out the mail. She looked through the envelopes and handed his letters to him after he handed her the bulletin. Proceeding into her office, she sat down to go through the mail, making neat little piles. First, she took the one pile to the pastor's office to put on his desk since he was already gone. She went back to collect the bills to take to John. Soon as she came into his office, he was up from the desk to take her in his arms and kissing her very passionately.

"Please take your mail. I need to do a job for Roger."

He let her go with a smile saying, "You'll see me before you leave today?"

Jennifer laid his mail on the desk and said she would and hurried up and left for he kissed her again. She made her way to the supply room thinking things were moving too fast, which made her a little scared. She ran off three hundred copies and took them to Roger in his office. Roger thanked her and asked how she liked her job. Jennifer said that she liked this job very much and hoped to stay on permanently.

"He only put me on temporary, but I hope he changes his mind."

"I'm sure he will since you're doing a great job." She thanked him and returned to her office.

Jennifer looked up at the clock and saw it was almost five. She was thinking, *When things get busy, time flies*. She hoped she had time to get back to the motel and change before meeting June. Turning off her computer and heading out the door, she almost ran into Roger.

"I'm sorry. I need to meet my friend at six."

Roger said, "That's alright. I guess I wasn't watching where I was going. I'll see you tomorrow. Hope you have a good night."

Jennifer smiled and said, "To you too."

The walk back to the motel seemed long, and the heat was taking away her energy. She hurried to her room, dropping her clothes across the floor and getting a T-shirt and a matching green shorts. She put them on and put on a pair of tennis shoes out of the closet and practically ran back out the door. She knew she would be a few minutes late since it was five minutes to six. She hurried down the street hoping that June would wait for her.

Jennifer entered the restaurant at eleven minutes after the hour and saw June in a booth in the back drinking a Coke.

"I'm sorry I'm late," Jennifer said.

June said, "No problem. I didn't order and wasn't sure whether you were coming."

Jennifer said, "I'll order for us a Big Mac meal if that's okay." June said that would be fine. She went up to the counter and ordered and brought her cup back to the table. They both went over to the drink machine. Jennifer filled her cup with ice before putting Coke in it while June refilled hers. Jennifer had just sat down when her number was called. Jennifer went up and collected the trays and brought them back to the table.

Jennifer told her about work and about her relationship with John. June sat there, consuming food like she never heard a word that Jennifer said. Suddenly, June jumped up saying she had to go to the restroom. Jennifer noticed that June seemed to stagger on her way there. Jennifer hoped she was alright and continued eating. After a while, she got worried because June didn't return. She got up and headed to the restroom. When she got there, she found June passed out on the floor. She tried to wake her, but she couldn't. Jennifer wet a paper towel and wiped June face. She smelt the liquor on her breath, and when she wiped her arms, she found needle punctures. June soon woke up just as Jennifer was about to call an ambulance. June refused to let her do so as she got off the floor and staggered back to their table.

Jennifer was very worried, and June ate the rest of her food saying she would be alright. If you won't let me take you to a hospital, at least let me give you a ride home. She looked at the numbers that she had in the phone and came up with John's number. She gave him a call and asked him for a favor.

"Can you come and get us from the McDonald's on Virginia Avenue? My friend June is very sick and wants to go home."

John said he would be there in a few minutes.

John entered the restaurant and saw them sitting there. Coming up to them, he looked at June and said she should go to the hospital. June protested, saying, "Just take me home."

John helped her up from her seat and walked her out of the car with Jennifer following behind. June laid down in the back seat and said she lived on Herschel Road in the apartment complex. The number of the apartment is 4515A and passed out again. Jennifer got in the car, thanking John for coming to get them.

"I wasn't sure what to do with her refusing to go to the hospital."

He said, "That's alright. I'm glad you called." They soon arrived at the address. June woke up when the car stopped and said thanks and tried to get out of the car. Jennifer hurried and went out to help her.

June said, "I'm fine. You can go now."

Jennifer said, "I'm your best friend, and I'm going to help you in." Jennifer put her arm around her and walked her to the door. Taking June's keys from her purse, she opened the door. Jennifer led her into the bedroom, which had a queen-size bed, and laid her down and June was soon asleep. Jennifer looked over the apartment before leaving. There in the bedroom she saw a big brown dresser and a matching nightstand. She saw there was a big walk-in closet. Going back in the living room, she saw a large couch and on each side of the couch were end tables. There was a fifty-five-inch TV that fit in the large bookcase in front of the coffee table. On the other side of the room was a small dining room with a table and two chairs. Beyond that was the kitchen, but she decided not to look and locked the door when she left.

Jennifer walked back to the car and got in, telling John that June was asleep. John asked if she wanted to stop for coffee. She agreed and said, "I'm still worried about her. She wasn't on drugs before we came here."

"Well, you won't find out any more tonight, so you shouldn't think about it till you get some answers," John said.

"I know, but she is my best friend and I'm concerned."

"I understand. Let us just go to the Waffle House, and you can calm down over coffee." When they entered, the first person she saw was the waitress she met when she first came to the city.

"Hi, Jennifer. It's been a while since you have been here. I see you met someone."

"John, I'd like you to meet Molly."

John said, "It was nice to meet you."

"What can I get you two?"

John said, "Could you bring us a pot of coffee?"

"Have a seat, and I'll be there in a few minutes."

Molly returned with the coffee and stayed there while Jennifer told her what had happened to her so far. Molly said, "I'm glad for you. You were quite nervous the first time I saw you. Well, here's your cream and sugar on the table, and I got to get back to work."

After she left, Jennifer said to John, "I need to find out who did this to her."

John said, "You better be careful. It might get you in trouble."

"I'll not take any risk without your help," she said. John felt good about the fact that she was beginning to trust him. Jennifer looked at her watch; it was after eleven.

"I need to go home. We both need to get up early for work," she said. John agreed and paid the check, giving Molly a tip of five dollars.

Molly thanked him and said to Jennifer, "Don't take so long coming back."

Jennifer smiled and said, "I promise to come back soon," as they walked out.

When John pulled into the motel, he stopped the car below her room. John took her in his arms and gave her a passionate kiss. She kissed him back and was very much emotionally wanting him to come up. Knowing it wasn't a good idea, she pulled away saying, "I got to go in now." He reluctantly let her go, and she got out of the car and headed up the steps.

John drove away thinking that he felt that he was falling in love. Jennifer entered her room feeling her heart still beating fast. She tried to call June to see how she was doing. The phone rang several times, but there was no answer. She hung up the phone and got undressed for bed and put on her nightgown and picked up the clothes she left on the floor. Getting into bed, she thought about June and what to do and, at the same time, feeling quite warm inside thinking about him.

Jennifer heard the alarm ringing. Dragging herself out of bed, she turned it off. She felt tired after staying out so late. She removed her nightgown and put on a pair of red shorts and matching T-shirt. She put on her slippers and grabbed her card and headed downstairs for breakfast. She went in and made a cup of coffee and sat down to drink it. After finishing her first cup, she decided on toast. She was not feeling too hungry. She popped the bread in the toaster and made another coffee. When the toast popped, she went and got it with two packs of butter and strawberry jam. She made up the toast and ate both before getting more coffee. She returned to her room, and opening the door, she went to the glass doors to close the curtains. Picking up the clothes she had dropped in the chair from last night and this morning, she went putting them in the laundry bag before taking a shower.

After she finished washing, she dried off. Wrapping the towel around her, she went to the dresser to collect her undergarments, which were white. Putting on her bra and panties, she got a blue dress out of her closet and put it on. She went and brushed her teeth and hair then applied her makeup. Sitting on the edge of the bed, she put on her black high heels. Looking at her watch, she could tell it was time to go. She put her key card back in the purse and headed out the door. The heat smacked her in the face as soon as she came out. She decided she had better get a bottle of water before taking her walk to the church. She dug in her black shoulder bag for change for the vending machine. Getting a bottle of water, she headed to the elevator. While she walked through the parking lot, the sun beat down on her, and she began to sweat. There was a slight breeze as she reached the avenue, so it wasn't too bad on the way to the church.

Jennifer felt the cold air as she entered the church and first went to the bathroom to wipe the sweat from her face and to reapply her makeup. Then she headed to her office to start a new day. When she got to the office, she sat down at her desk and logged onto her computer. The first thing she noticed was a message from the pastor that he wouldn't be here today. He had a meeting with Mr. Watts and wouldn't be back till later that night, and there were several letters on his desk for her to take care of. She was about to go get them when John walked in.

"So have you heard from your friend since last night?" John asked.

Jennifer said, "I tried to call her but got no answer. She must still be asleep."

John said, "She must have a strong drug problem."

She said, "That's what worries me. She didn't when we got off the bus."

"So what happened?"

"I don't know, but I'm sure her boyfriend Jeff had something to do with it."

John said, "It sounds like it."

"Well, I'll try to call her later," Jennifer said.

John said, "You better be careful, and if you need any help, call me."

"I will, but I must get my work done, so I'll talk to you later," she said. She got up from her desk and walked John to the door, and he gave her a kiss before heading back to his office. Jennifer went to the pastor's office to collect the letters. She felt a warm glow from John's kiss, as she picked the letters up and returned to her office.

She typed up each letter going to the deacons of the churches asking all of them to be there on the fifth when the Reverend Harlot arrives from Chicago. She looked up in her directory to each of the ten deacons and addressed each letter. She took them out to the mailbox after stamping everyone. Putting the flag up, she returned to the church. It was almost lunchtime, so instead of going back to her office, she decided to head to the dining room to see Rita.

Jennifer found Rita in the kitchen putting up the ham that they had that last night at Wednesday service. There were two sandwiches sitting there with ham and cheese and chips.

"I thought you would like some for lunch since we had so much leftover."

Jennifer said that was fine and went and poured two glasses of ice teas. Following Rita out to a table and sitting down, Rita said, "You know I live with my teenage daughter since my husband died. I can just barely pay the bills, and we have a big house with three bedrooms. I was wondering if you would like to move in? I know it would be a lot cheaper for you, and it would help me with things I couldn't get for me or Ruby. Also, we could ride to work together. You don't have to decide now. Come with me after work today and have dinner. You can look at the house and see how we live."

Jennifer said she would get back to her before the end of the day. She wanted to go, but she remembered that she promised John and needed to find out about June. She finished her lunch and headed to John's office to tell him. She told him about Rita's offer.

He told her, "We could go out another night. I'm sure you can't keep affording that motel."

She said, "I could after I got my first paycheck but wouldn't have much for food."

"Well then go, and I'll take you to the movies on Saturday."

"Well, let me check with June before I say yes."

She went to her office to call June and a man answered. "Oh! Is this Jeff? Would you tell June I'd like to talk to her?"

"I'm sorry. She's not here right now. She went out for a little while, and I'm not sure when she'll be back."

Jennifer thought this was funny since she was sick when they let her off last night. "Well, would you have her call my cell when she gets back?"

Jeff said he would and hung up. She went back and told John.

He said, "It sounds strange. Hopefully, she'll call you back, so you are going to tell Rita yes."

"I guess I'll call you later and tell you how it went."

He took her in his arms and kissed her saying, "You better. I'll be waiting for your call."

Jennifer went back to the dining room and said, "I'll go."

Rita said, "I'll meet you here right after work."

Jennifer said okay and went back to her office.

She logged back into her computer and saw that there was a charity auction on Saturday in two weeks. She sent a notice out to all members to attend. It took her the rest of the day to email everybody. The pastor wasn't back by the time for her to leave. She logged off her computer and turned out the lights. She headed back to the lunchroom to meet Rita. Rita had just turned off the lights in the kitchen as she walked in.

Rita said, "Are you ready to go?"

Jennifer said yes as they left the dining area. Rita turned out the dining room lights. They walked out to the parking lot. Rita went over to a light blue Ford Escort and unlocked the doors and told her to get in.

Rita went out of the parking lot and turned right, going past the motel to Lee Street where she turned left. Halfway down the street, she pulled into the driveway of a two-story house. It was a red brick house with white trim around the windows and a big white door where a young girl stood. She saw that the girl looked to be about fourteen with long brown hair and sparkling blue eyes.

Rita said, "That's my daughter, Ruby." Rita got out of the car and gave her daughter a hug. Jennifer saw she was taller than her mother and rather on the skinny side. Rita said, "This is Jennifer, so she may come to stay with us. I hope you made enough for dinner for her."

Ruby smiled. "I did when you called and said there would be an extra person." Ruby said, "I got to go finish dinner. Why don't you show her the house?"

Rita smiled and said, "I knew I could depend on you."

Rita took Jennifer on the tour of the house, starting with the living room. The furniture in the room was dark brown with a tanned couch to match the carpet. There was a large TV on the stand in front of the window.

Rita said, "I know it's rather dark in this room, but it makes it easier to watch TV." She said, "Come along with me upstairs. It is a lot brighter."

Jennifer could tell she was right. The first room they went into had bright yellow walls and light blue curtains that matched the comforter on the queen-size bed. There was a brown dresser and vanity with a large mirror. A nightstand was next to the bed with a large lamp with a shade of see-through glass. The carpet had a light tan, which was wall to wall. Rita said if you stay, this would be your room. The next door in the hallway was a bathroom. It was quite large with two sinks and a white cabinet, and the tub and the shower separate. The shower curtain was pink including the rug on the floor and the toilet seat cover.

The next room she could tell was Ruby's with posters of rock groups on the walls. There was a queen-size bed with a dresser, which both were baby blue, and there was a large stereo system on the dresser.

She said, "I hope it won't bother you. The rooms are quite soundproof. Across the hall here is my room," which she led Jennifer to. Rita's room had its own bathroom to the right and a large walk-in closet on the left side and a lovely queen-size bed in the middle of the room and a large dresser with a mirror on the other wall. Ruby called upstairs that dinner was ready, so she didn't get to inspect Rita's bathroom.

They walked back down the stairs to the dining room where Ruby had the food waiting for them. Jennifer looked and saw baked chicken with baked potatoes and green beans. She said, "You did a great job. It looks delicious." Ruby smiled, blushing, saying thank you. Rita said, "If you decide to move in, I will only charge you two hundred and fifty a month."

Jennifer bit into the chicken thinking, *Wow! That is a lot less than I'm paying, and I should take her up on her offer.*

Rita said, "I won't charge you till next week when you get your first paycheck." Jennifer took a drink of her ice tea that Ruby had brought her. She thought that would be great since she had to pay the motel because between the two, she would practically be broke.

Jennifer said, "That would be great. If is it alright, I'll move in."

"Well, we could pick up your stuff after work tomorrow," Rita said.

Ruby said, "I'm sure we can get along."

Jennifer thought as she finished her meal, *I should let John bring me especially after turning him down to come here. Also, I need to settle up with the motel.*

Ruby cleared off the table and took the dishes into the kitchen. Jennifer helped her and noticed that they didn't have a dishwasher and that Ruby would have to do them by hand.

Jennifer said, "Can I help you dry the dishes? But you'll have to tell me where they go." Ruby was delighted that Jennifer wanted to help. Jennifer said, "I can help you every night if you like."

Ruby said, "She hopes you stay for a while."

Jennifer said, "I hope we can be good friends, and if you need anybody to talk to, I'll be there."

Ruby said, "That's good. It is hard to talk to Mom."

Rita entered the kitchen saying, "It's getting late, and we need to be up early." Jennifer finished drying the last plate and handed the dish towel to Ruby.

Jennifer said, "I'll be ready as soon as I can get my purse." She said goodbye to Ruby and said, "I'll see you tomorrow." She followed Rita out the door to the car.

When Rita got in, she said, "Here's an extra key to the house. If you need any help, just let me know tomorrow at work." Jennifer thanked her when they pulled in at the motel. Jennifer said, "Goodbye and see you tomorrow," as she got out of the car and headed toward her room.

Soon as she opened the door, she removed her high heels and sat on the bed and called John. Listening as the phone rang, she began to rub her feet. When he answered, she said, "Hello, John. I got great news. Rita has offered me a place to stay."

John said, "I'm glad to hear it. I'm sure that place was eating up all your money."

"Yes, it will be a lot easier on me, and I won't have to walk to work anymore."

John said, "Besides, it will get you out of heat."

"Would you do me a big favor?" she asked.

"Could it be you are asking me to help you move?" He laughed, saying, "I guess we can do it tomorrow after work."

"Well, I was hoping you would," she said.

"You know I care about you, so you knew I wouldn't turn you down."

"I'm beginning to care too and felt guilty that I had to turn you down for our date." He said that was fine since that was more important. "I must say good night. I guess I will need my strength for tomorrow," she said laughing.

"I'll see you tomorrow at work. Good night," he said.

She removed her clothes and put a black nightgown out of the drawer. She set the alarm before getting into bed. She thought about John and knew she was falling for him and was also worried about June. It took her a while before falling asleep.

Jennifer woke up before the alarm knowing that today she was moving. Pulling a T-shirt and a pair of shorts out of the drawer, she removed her nightgown and put them on for breakfast. Entering the lobby, she went first and made a cup of coffee and walked up to the counter. A middle-aged woman was on duty.

She said to Jennifer, "My name is Vera, and welcome to Economy Lodge. May I help you?"

Jennifer said, "I've been staying here and would like to settle my bill."

"Oh! Are you leaving this morning?"

"No. I'll be moving out tonight, so I'll pay through tomorrow."

"What is your full name?"

"My name is Jennifer Wroth, and I'm in room 225."

Vera found her on the computer and said that would be $211. Jennifer handed her the money, and she printed out a receipt. "Thank you for your stay here. Please return your key cards in the morning."

Jennifer left the desk and poured herself another cup of coffee and decided on a breakfast of scrambled eggs and bacon. She also picked up some biscuits and butter and grape jelly. She looked at her watch and saw she had plenty of time. She sat there taking her time to eat. Finishing her breakfast, she said goodbye to Vera before returning to her room.

Jennifer entered her room and went straight to the bathroom after removing her shoes. She threw her clothes in the bag and turned on the water. She was excited that tomorrow she wouldn't be in this room anymore. Finishing washing, she turned off the shower and grabbed a towel from the rack over the toilet and dried off. She returned to the bedroom and picked a green dress out of the closet saying she would pack everything after work. She put on the dress and went and brushed her teeth and looked at them saying they still look good. She sat down at the vanity to brush her hair and apply a little pink lipstick. She left it all on the counter to pick up later. She then went and got her white high heels and slipped them on.

Well, I guess I'm ready to go. She heard on the radio it was already seventy-five degrees. She thought, *Well, this is the last time I will be walking in this heat.* She grabbed her purse and went out the door, heading to the elevator. The sun was already beating down as she made her way to Virginia Avenue. It seemed like a long walk with the heat draining her energy. Finally making it to the church, she welcomed the cool air as she entered the building.

Making it to her office, she logged on to her computer to see what the agenda was for today. First, she sent out emails for the lunch they were having after Sunday church. It would be five dollars for adults and three for children. She also saw that next Saturday they were holding an auction for gowns for the choir. That all the items were at Mrs. Dascal's house and needed to be picked up before Friday. She began to look through the list of members to go and get the items, finally coming across a Mr. Drax who owned a construction company with his sons. She figured he would have the trucks to deliver the stuff. Making the call, it wasn't long before someone answered.

"Good morning. This is Drax's and sons, construction. My name is Jamie. How can I help you?"

"This is Ms. Wroth. I am the secretary for United Methodist. They are holding an auction here next Saturday, and we were hoping that you could pick the stuff up for the auction."

"I'm sure my father would be delighted to do so. Just give me the address."

"She lives at 1025 Washington Road, and we need you to pick it up by Friday if it's convenient."

"I'm sure I can get several of our employees to help and just tell her to be there at ten on Friday morning."

Jennifer thanked him and called Mrs. Dascal back and told her the time they would show up. Mrs. Dascal was very thankful and said she would be waiting for them.

After hanging up with her, she got up and went next door. She knocked on the pastor's door and was soon invited in. Jennifer told him about what she had taken care of. He was happy and told her he had three more letters that needed to be done before the mail arrived. The three letters were to different churches about the baseball team, and she addressed the letters after looking up each one's address. Putting stamps on the letters, she walked them out to the mailbox just in time. The mailman had just arrived at the box and was putting in letters.

He looked at her and took the letters from her saying, "You must be new."

"I'm Jennifer. I'm the pastor's new secretary."

"Well, I'm Bob and glad to meet you, and I'm sure we'll meet again since I'm on duty here Monday through Friday."

She said it was nice to meet him and took the mail out of the box. "Well, I'll be seeing you. I got to get back to work."

Jennifer returned to her office to sort out the mail. There were several letters for the pastor and several bills to give to John. After making stacks of each including a few for Roger O'Donnell, she decided to take the pastor his pile of letters first. Knocking on his door, he told her to come in.

Jennifer said, "Here's your mail, and I did get your letters out in time."

"Thank you, and how do you like your job so far?"

She said she liked it a lot and now she had it easier since she'll be moving in with Rita.

"I'm glad to hear it, and if you get your GED, I think you will be here permanently."

She said, "Thank you, sir, and I've already applied to Spelman College." She left his office and went to Roger O'Donnell's office and knocked.

"Good afternoon, Ms. Wroth. What can I do for you?"

"I just brought your mail for today," she said, handing it to him. "I would like it if you would call me Jennifer since we will be seeing a lot of each other."

"I'm sure we can be friends, and you can call me Roger. I hope to see you at the Sunday service, and I will introduce you to my family."

Jennifer said, "Thank you, but I'm not sure if I will be here."

"You must come. My wife would love to meet you."

Jennifer left his office and headed to John's. When she opened the door, John got up and hurried to her. He took her in his arms and kissed her. She put her arms around him and dropped the letters on the floor. She suddenly pushed him away to pick up the letters. John laughed and said, "Don't worry. I'll pick them up."

Jennifer blushed and said, "I got to get back to work."

John gave her another kiss and said, "I'll see you after work."

She returned to her office and decided to call June. After a few rings, she picked up.

"Hi, Jennifer. How's your day?"

Jennifer said, "I see you are in a better mood."

"Well, Jeff took me to dinner last night, and I had a really nice time," June said.

"I was wondering if you would go to church with me Sunday and talk to Pastor Dodge."

"I don't see a problem. I'll make sure with Jeff."

"That's good. Me and John know where you live so we could pick you up. Oh! By the way, I'm moving in with Rita Jacobs and her daughter."

"I'm glad for you. It will be a lot less expensive for you."

"Yes, and John is helping me move right after work."

"Well, maybe someday you will invite me over to see where you live."

"When I get settled in, I'll ask if I can invite you to dinner one night."

"That would be great."

"Well, I'll need to get my housework done, so I'll talk to you later and let you know what Jeff said." Jennifer said goodbye, and June replied goodbye and hang up the phone.

She looked up at the clock. Seeing it was lunchtime, she logged off her computer and left her office. She stopped by to tell the pastor that June would be there Sunday, so he could talk to her after services.

Pastor Dodge said, "That would be alright, so where are you headed?"

"I'm going to lunch. Would you like to come?"

"Thanks. I'll probably go later after I finish my sermon for this Sunday."

Jennifer left his office and went down the hall heading to the dining room. When she got there, Rita had already had lunch waiting for her. There was ham and cheese sandwiches with chips and a glass of ice tea. Jennifer sat down across from Rita and began to eat. Rita said a prayer of thanks before eating.

"I got John to bring me after work," she said.

"Well, I'll have dinner ready for both of you when you get there. Ruby is excited that you're moving in, and she hopes you two will be good friends. I worry about her since she finds it hard to make friends."

"Well, I'm sure we'll get along, and I do love the room you picked out for me. I was wondering if you don't mind, I could cook some nights."

Rita smiled and said, "That would be great. It would give me a break from cooking."

After Jennifer left, she was glad that Jennifer had come because hardly any of the staff, including the pastor, ever comes to lunch.

Rita cleaned up their plates and glasses and returned to the kitchen. Jennifer went back to her office. Jennifer was watching the clock and seemed that time stood still. A Mrs. Reed called and wanted to know if she knew when the little league would start.

Jennifer told her, "They are having tryouts next week if you want to bring your son."

She said that she would be there. "Do you know the time?"

"This Saturday is the auction, and the following Saturday will be the tryouts. It will be from ten o'clock in the morning till noon."

Mrs. Reed thanked her and hung up. A few hours later, it was time to go. Just as she was logging off the computer, John walked in.

"Shall we go?" he said.

She got up from the desk and kissed him saying, "Thank you for helping me."

"You know I care about you, so you knew I wouldn't turn you down."

Jennifer laughed and said, "You always repeat yourself."

He laughed and said, "Let's go."

John got to the car and opened the door for her before getting in. They left the church and headed to the motel to collect her stuff. Walking hand in hand to her room, she took out her key card and opened the door. Dragging out her suitcases, she asked him to take out the clothes from the dresser. She went to the closet and filled it with her shoes first and laid her dresses on top. Soon the whole room was packed, and John carried the two suitcases down to his car while she came behind with the bag he had filled from the nightstand. Jennifer put her bag on the back seat while John put the suitcases in the trunk. Jennifer walked back into the lobby to return her key cards and found her friend Jean working.

Jean said, "I'm sorry to lose you as a customer, but here is my phone number if you ever need a friend to talk to."

Jennifer put the number in her purse after handing Jean the key cards. Jennifer said, "I will call you, and maybe we can go out together some night." Jean said she would like that.

John drove her to Rita's house and brought in her suitcases. Rita met them at the door, saying, "Drop your stuff in the room because dinner is ready."

Jennifer and John went up to the room and returned to the dining room where Rita and Ruby were waiting. Jennifer introduced John to Ruby. She said, "I have seen him at the church several times."

John said, "Well, it's nice to have a name to go with the face since I saw you several times too." He said, "I can see why you were named Ruby with that red hair of yours."

She laughed and said, "My mother had red hair too. I took after her. Even our blue eyes matched. They always made fun of her saying she spit me out."

They all sat down to dinner and told stories about each other while they ate. It was soon getting late, and John had to go. Jennifer walked him out to the car, and they stood there and kissed for a while before she came back in.

Ruby had just walked out of the kitchen and said, "I finished the dishes. Would you like me to help you unpack?"

Jennifer said she would, and they headed to her room. Ruby helps her put her things away and said, "I'm glad you are here."

"Well, I am too, and I'm sure we'll have great times together."

Ruby said, "Well, I got to get ready for bed and got to be up early for school." Jennifer watched as Ruby left the room feeling great and feeling so lucky.

Jennifer took her nightgown to the bathroom next door and took a shower. While showering, she thought about John. After drying off, she put on her gown and carried her dirty clothes to her room. She put them in the bag she brought from the motel. She got in the bed and was thinking of her love for John and hoping that their relationship would work out. She soon fell fast asleep.

Jennifer suddenly awoke and saw she was still in the bus station. The door opened to the left, and she saw Pastor Dodge walk in with her friend June. They seemed not to notice her and headed to the other side of the room where the people were making hymns. She wondered why they were ignoring her. It seemed to hurt her feelings, and she didn't know why her friend didn't say anything to her.

Jennifer returned to her office to sort out the mail. There were several letters for the pastor and serveral bills to give to John. After making stacks of each including a few for Roger O'Donnell. She decided to take the pastor his pile of letters first. Knocking on his door, he told her to come in. Jennifer said here's your mail and I did get your letters out in time. Thank you and how do you like your job so far? She said she liked it a lot and now she had it easier since she'll be moving in with Rita. I'm glad to hear it and if you get your GED, I think you will be here permanently. She said thank you sir and I've already applied to Spelman college. She left his office and went to Roger O'Donnell's office and knocked. Good afternoon, Ms. Wroth, what can I do for you? I just brought your mail for today, handing it to him. I would like if you would call me Jennifer since we will be seeing a lot of each other. I'm sure we can be friends and you can call me Roger. I hope to see you at the Sunday service, and I will introduce you to my family. Jennifer said thank you, but I'm not sure if I will be here. You must come, my wife would love to meet you. Jennifer left his office and headed to John's. When she opened the door, John got up and hurried to her. He took her in his arms and kissed her. She put her arms around him and dropped the letters on the floor. She suddenly pushed him away to pick up the letters. John laughed and said don't worry, I'll pick them up. Jennifer blushed, and said I got to get back to work. John gave her another kiss, and said I'll see you after work.

She returned to her office and decided to call June. After a few rings she picked up. Hi Jennifer, how's your day. Jennifer said, "I see you are in a better mood. Well Jeff took me to dinner last night and I had a really nice time, June said. I was wondering if you would go to church with me Sunday and talk to Pastor Dodge. I don't see a problem I'll make sure with Jeff. That's good me and John know where you live so we could pick you up. Oh! By the way I'm moving in with Rita Jacobs and her daughter. I'm glad for you it will be a lot less expensive for you. Yes, and John is helping me move right after work. Well maybe someday you will invite me over to see where you live. When I get settled in, I'll ask if I can invite you to dinner one night. That would be great. Well, I'll need to get my housework done, so I'll talk to you later and let you know what Jeff said. Jennifer said goodbye and June replied goodbye hanging up the phone.

She looked up at the clock, seeing it was lunch time, she logged off her computer and left her office. She stopped by to tell the pastor that June would be there Sunday, so he could talk to her after services. Pastor Dodge said that would be alright, so where are you headed? I'm going to lunch would you like to come. Thanks, I'll probably go later after I finish my sermon for this Sunday. Jennifer left his office and went down the hall heading to the dining room. When she got there Rita had already had lunch waiting for her. There was ham and cheese sandwiches with chips and a glass of ice- tea. Jennifer sat down across from Rita and began to eat. Rita said a prayer of thanks before eating. I got John to bring me after work, she said. Well, I'll have dinner ready for both of you when you get there. Ruby is excited that you're moving in and she hopes you two will be good friends. I worry about her since she finds it hard to make friends. Well, I'm sure we'll get along and I do love the room you picked out for me. I was wondering if you don't mind, I could cook some nights. Rita smiled and said that would be great, it would give me a break from cooking. After Jennifer left, she was glad that Jennifer had come because hardly any of the staff including the pastor ever comes to lunch.

Rita cleaned up their plates and glasses and returned to the kitchen. Jennifer went back to her office. Jennifer was watching the clock and seemed that time stood still. A Mrs. Reed called and wanted to know if she knew when the little league would start. Jennifer told her they are having try-outs next week if you want to bring your son. She said that she would be there, do you know the time. This Saturday is the auction and the following Saturday will be the try-outs. It will be from ten o'clock in the morning till noon. Mrs. Reed thanked her and hung up. A few hours later it was time to go. Just as she was logging off the computer John walked in. Shall we go he said. She got up from the desk and kissed him saying thank you for helping me. You know I care about you, so you knew I wouldn't turn you down. Jennifer laughed and said you always repeat yourself. He laughed and said let's go.

John got to the car and opened the door for her before getting in. They left the church and headed to the motel to collect her stuff. Walking hand in hand to her room. She took out her key card and opened the door. Dragging out her suitcases she asked him to take out the clothes from the dresser. She went to the closet and filled it with her shoes first and laid her dresses on top. Soon the whole room was packed, and John carried the two suitcases down to his car while she came behind with the bag he had filled from the nightstand. Jennifer put her bag on the back seat while John put the suitcases in the trunk. Jennifer walked back into the lobby to return her key cards and found her friend Jean working. Jean said I'm sorry to lose you as a customer but here is my phone number if you ever need a friend to talk to. Jennifer put the number in her purse after handing Jean the key cards. Jennifer said I will call you and maybe we can go out together some night. Jean said she would like that.

John drove her to Rita's house and brought in her suitcases. Rita met them at the door saying drop your stuff in the room because dinner is ready. Jennifer and John went up to the room and returned to the dining room where Rita and Ruby were waiting. Jennifer introduced John to Ruby. She said I have seen him at the church several times. John said, "Well it nice to have a name to go with the face since I saw you several times too. He said I can see why you were named Ruby with that red hair of yours. She laughed and said my mother had red hair too. I took after her even are blue eyes matched. They always made fun of her saying she spit me out. They all sat down to dinner and told stories about each other while they ate. It was soon getting late, and John had to go. Jennifer walked him out to the car, and they stood there and kissed for a while, before she came back in. Ruby had just walked out of the kitchen and said I finished the dishes would you like me to help you unpack? Jennifer said she would, and they headed to her room. Ruby helps her put her things away and said I'm glad you are here. Well, I am too and I'm sure will have great times together. Ruby said Well I got to get ready for bed and got to be up early for school. Jennifer watched as Ruby left the room feeling great and feeling so lucky.

Jennifer took her nightgown to the bathroom next door and took a shower. While showering she thought about John. After drying off she put on her gown and carried her dirty clothes to her room. She put them in the bag she brought from the motel. She got into bed and was thinking of her love for John and hoping that their relationship would work out. She soon fell fast asleep.

Jennifer suddenly awoke and saw she was still in the bus station. The door opened to the left and she saw Pastor Dodge walk in with her friend June. They seemed not to notice her and headed to the other side of the room where the people were making hymns. She wondered why they were ignoring her. It seemed to hurt her feelings and she didn't know why her friend didn't say anything to her.

CHAPTER 5

THE PASTOR

Pastor Dodge was walking across the bus station not knowing why he was here. He looked behind him, and June and Sarah were following him. He looked across the room seeing Jennifer sitting over there and wondered why she wasn't with the rest of the church family. He called over to her, but she never answered. He noticed that several members weren't there with them. He tried to remember what happened, but the answer alluded to him. He asked June why Jennifer was over there, but she didn't know. He sat on the bench thinking about his life and hoping that would give him a clue what was happening.

He remembered that he was Robert Dodge and grew up in the small town of Riley Wisconsin found in Dane county. They lived in an individual house, which was quite small, but had three bedrooms. It was a white wooden house and was quite old. They had an outside toilet and got water from a well. His father worked for Middletown National Hardware almost all his life. His name was Robert too and had brown hair and brown eyes just like him. He watched as his father struggled to make ends meet. His mother Martha was a homemaker who took care of him and his sister, Leslie. His mother was kind of short which also had brown eyes and hair, so Leslie had almost the same features as her mother. They were a Christian family and always went to church on Sunday. They both rode the bus to Middletown Elementary. Since Leslie was only a year younger, she was a grade behind him. Robert always helped his sister with her homework, and since he was well built, the kids knew not to pick on him or his sister. When he went to Middletown Junior High, he went out for the football team. He always played guard till his graduation from high school.

One day, they were returning on the bus from a game and were hit by a truck, which flipped the bus. Many were hurt, and there was no one around. Everybody was scared and was worried that some would die with no help. Robert began to pray for someone to come, and soon many of the boys joined him. It wasn't long before they heard a voice calling them. A highway patrol officer came upon the wreck and started helping the boys off the bus. He said the rescue squad was on the way to the injured. It wasn't long before more police cars arrived and ambulances. It changed his life right there; he decided to go into ministry.

He began to help in the Riley Baptist Church, and the Pastor Raymond Garth helped him apply at the North Central Christian College. He quit the football team in high school to get a job in a grocery store after school to help pay for his tuition. His father helped as much as he could, but the church was the most helpful. After graduation, he went to Minneapolis to college while his sister attended Globe University Madison West.

After four years, he graduated and was ready to find his own church; but for a while, he helped preach at Riley Baptist. Leslie graduated and got a job as a science teacher at Middleton Elementary. Robert put in his résumé online hoping it would happen soon. He prayed every day, and after three months, he got an offer in Atlanta, Georgia. He wasn't sure if he wanted to travel that far from home. One day, he got a call from Roger O'Donnell who was deacon of United Methodist in Atlanta.

"Our pastor has died, and we have looked at your résumé. Would you be interested?"

Robert knew in his heart he was going, and he said he would come. He told his parents that he would come back to visit, but he had to go.

Roger called him saying that he had made all the arrangements. Robert packed his clothes and noticed it was about five. He drove over to Middleton where his sister had an apartment. She had moved there after getting the job as a teacher. Robert knocked on her door and soon she came to answer it.

"Robert! What are you doing here?"

"I wanted to say goodbye. I'm taking a job in Georgia."

"I will miss you and glad you came to see me."

"Well, you know I love you, sis, and will miss you also and hope you will give me a call at times."

"I love you too, Robert. You know I will," she said with tears in her eyes. "Have you eaten yet? I was going to order a pizza. Would you stay for a little bit?"

Robert said he would, and she called Papa John's and ordered a pepperoni pizza to be delivered. They sat and talked about their childhood together waiting for the pizza to be delivered. When it came, Leslie paid while Robert went in the kitchen to get two glasses of tea.

After they finished eating, he said, "I better get home to be ready for tomorrow."

Robert gave his sister a hug and kissed her goodbye. She held the door for him saying goodbye with tears in her eyes.

Roger O'Donnell called Robert the first thing in the morning and said, "Your plane is leaving at eleven o'clock, and I'll be here at Atlanta Airport to pick you up. Your ticket is at the airport in Middleton, so I hope to see you soon."

Robert's father and mother insisted on driving him to the airport. Robert was happy to go with them. They arrived at the airport about ten minutes after ten, which gave him plenty of time to collect his ticket and check his luggage. When his plane was called, tears fell from Martha's eyes and she said she would miss him. Robert choked up a little when he saw a tear in his father's eye.

"I promise to call and come visit when I can," he said.

His father said he wouldn't forgive him if he didn't. Robert gave his mother a hug and kiss and hugged his father. They watched him get on the plane and didn't leave till it left the ground.

Robert looked out the window seeing them standing there and said he would call them when he got there with tears in his eyes.

It was a long flight from Wisconsin to Hartsfield's Jackson International in Atlanta. When he got off the plane and headed into the terminal, he saw a man holding a sign for Robert Dodge. Robert walked up to him saying that he was Robert Dodge.

"Welcome to Atlanta. I'm Roger O'Donnell who you talked to on the phone."

"I'm glad to meet you," Robert said.

"Well, let's go get your luggage. Just follow me," Roger said. They made their way to the train that took them to the luggage department and was just in time for the carousel of luggage.

Robert saw his suitcase and grabbed it and said, "I'm ready to go."

"You only have one suitcase?" Roger said.

"Yes, that's all I brought."

"Well, we'll have to take you shopping after you get settled in."

They made their way to the parking lot and headed to a big white van with United Methodist Church printed in big black letters across the van. When they got in, Robert noticed the seats were red upholstery and the carpets were black. Roger started the van and headed for the ticket booth. After paying the attendant, they got on the road heading for downtown Atlanta.

Roger said, "We are in College Park on Virginia Avenue."

Soon they pulled up to the church. It didn't look like a church except the steeple on a large red brick building. There were a few white columns next to the white double-door entrance. Roger asked Robert if he wanted a tour of the church or go to the parsonage to get settled in.

"If you don't mind, I would like to unpack first, and I promised to call my parents to let them know I got here safely."

Roger drove around to the back of the church where a red-brick house with rosebushes on each side of the door. Robert saw that it was quite big and must have been built for a family.

Roger got out and grabbed the pastor's suitcase, saying, "Let me introduce you to Mrs. Marie. She is the caretaker, also the one who looks after the pastor." They walked into the kitchen where they found her cooking.

Roger said to Mrs. Marie, "This is Pastor Dodge." Mrs. Marie shook his hand.

She was a medium-sized woman with clear light brown eyes with a few wrinkles around them. He could tell she was in her sixties even with her hair dyed brown. Roger said she ran the parsonages doing all the cooking and cleaning. After her husband died five years ago, she moved in here in a room just off the kitchen.

Marie said, "I hope it won't be an inconvenience, but my two children and their families come to visit at Christmas."

"Oh!" said Robert. "Where are your children now?"

Marie said, "One lives in New York and the other in San Francisco."

Robert said, "That's alright. I was intending to go home for Christmas."

Mrs. Marie took an instant liking to him and thanked him for his suggestion. Mrs. Marie gave him the keys to the parsonage and the church, asking if he wanted anything to eat.

"Well, not really at this time. I would like to unpack and get a shower."

Mrs. Marie led him upstairs to the master bedroom, and he noticed several other bedrooms on the floor.

She said, "This bedroom has a bathroom while the three bedrooms use the one at the end of the hall. Would you like me to help you unpack?"

Robert said, "I'm sure I can handle unpacking after my shower. Maybe I'll let you make me something after I take a nap."

She said, "I understand plane rides are quite tiring." She went back downstairs.

He shut the door and took a pants and shirt out of his suitcase. He headed to the bathroom. It was a rather large one with a tub and a shower stall. The bathroom was done in blue, which had a large mirror above the bathroom vanity, and the toilet lid had a light blue cover, which matched the bathroom rug. Robert undressed and turned on the water; he had brought his little case in the bathroom and removed his soap. Being under the shower, he could tell he was quite tired and would rest before putting his clothes away. Drying off, he put on his clothes and went straight to his queen-size bed and laid on top of the covers. He pulled out a pillow from the quilt and was soon asleep.

When Robert awoke, he went in the bathroom and wiped his face to wake up. He returned to the bedroom and began noticing the bedroom. It was rather plain with brown furniture but had a large walk-in closet. He put his clothes from his suitcase on hangers and put his underwear and socks in a drawer in the dresser. Robert put his empty suitcase in the closet and headed down to the kitchen. Roger was sitting at the table drinking coffee when he came in. Robert asked Mrs. Marie if there was any more. She told him there was and if he takes it with cream and sugar.

Robert said he did and asked, "Could I get a few pieces of toast with that?"

She said, "Coming right up," and went to make his coffee after dropping two pieces of bread in the toaster.

"Well, are you ready for the tour of the church?" Roger spoke.

Robert said, "Soon after a few cups of coffee."

Mrs. Marie brought him his coffee and toast and he ate while Roger sat there sipping his coffee.

After Robert finished his coffee, Roger said, "Are you ready for the grand tour?"

Robert told him to lead on. They left the parsonage and walked around to the double white doors and went in. The first thing he saw was the stage up front, which was rather large with two big speakers hanging from the ceiling. On the right side of the stage were many seats for the choir and one in front was for him. The pulpit sat in the middle of the stage, and there were musical instruments on the left side.

Roger said, "If you look behind us, you'll see a large window above us that is the control room. On your left there is the door to our dining area, but we will go through this door on the right."

It was a long hallway, which had three doors, and then it angled to the right at the end. Roger explained that the first door was his office and would head to the second which was their accountant. Roger knocked at the door before entering.

"John Conner, I would like you to meet our new pastor, Robert Dodge."

John got up from his desk and came around to shake his hand. "Glad to meet you and hope you will find this place to be your home." Robert said he was sure he was going to like it here. "If you need anything, I'm here to help," John said.

Robert said, "Thank you."

Roger said, "Let's get going," and led him down the hall. He took out his key and opened the third door saying, "This is where we have our office supplies and copy machine."

Robert looked it over, and they went down the right corridor with two doors. Roger knocked at the first saying, "This is Mrs. Brown, your secretary."

Mrs. Brown opened the door, saying, "Welcome." She looked quite old, nearly seventy with long gray hair and crystal blue eyes. She was rather thin but still attractive in her long blue dress.

Roger said, "She does a fantastic job of keeping this church running."

Mrs. Regina Brown blushed at these words. Robert said that he looked forward to working with her.

Roger led him on to the last door saying, "This is your office." It was not much to see being vacant for almost a year. It had a desk and a chair with a computer and phone, but not much else. Roger said, "You can have this room made up anyway you would like. I'm sure you can talk to John. He can have it done the way you want."

Roger said, "Shall we go and look at the dining room area next?" He took him back down the hall and over to the other door on the other side. Roger entered the dining room and introduced Mrs. Julia Morgan. "She is the cook for this week. We don't have a permanent cook, so each of the members' wives take turns."

After looking over the kitchen and dining room, they returned to the middle of the church.

Robert asked, "Where does that door lead behind the stage?"

"Oh! It's just an empty room. We had no use for it, and we were thinking of building a building next to the parsonage for Sunday school since it's all held here in the church."

Robert said, "We could get more members if we turn that room into a nursery."

Roger thought that might be a good idea, and he would take it up with John to see if they had enough in the budget. Roger returned to his office, and Robert went and checked out the back room and could tell it would be perfect.

Being there for several years, a lot began to change. The nursey was added and the woman who had worked in the kitchen took over the nursery. After leading Rita Jacobs to the Lord, she became the permanent cook. It was now five years since he came here; and with the members' help, the church had grown, and the Sunday School building came into existence. Jennifer Wroth had taken over for Mrs. Brown who had died over a year ago.

Robert was done for the day and needed some food and rest. He stopped in Jennifer's office to see how it was going. Jennifer told him everything has been taken care of.

"So you are headed home?" he asked.

"I'm waiting on John. He is helping me move."

"I'm sure you'll be glad to get out of that motel."

"I will, sir, and I already have applied for classes for my GED."

"I'm glad to hear that," he said.

Just then, John walked in. "Excuse me, sir," John said, "should I wait outside?"

"No, it's alright. I was leaving." Robert headed back to the parsonage where Mrs. Marie had a meal waiting for him. Robert thought that the church should have a birthday party for Mrs. Marie who was turning sixty-eight. He would talk to Roger about this idea. He finished his meal and said he was retiring to his room and working on his sermon for Sunday.

"So I bid you good night."

Mrs. Marie said, "Good night. I'll have breakfast ready when you get up."

Robert really appreciated her for all her hard work.

It was Saturday morning, and he had the day off. He had already written his sermon for tomorrow. He went downstairs. Mrs. Marie saw him coming and poured him a cup of coffee and brought it over when he sat down. She made him two fried eggs with several pieces of bacon and asked if he wanted toast. He told her everything was fine.

"Why don't you sit down and have a cup of coffee with me?"

She poured a cup and sat down.

Mrs. Marie said, "This job is getting too hard for me, and my daughter in San Francisco wants me to come and live with them."

Pastor Dodge said, "I would hate for you to leave, but if you could give me a little time to find a replacement for you."

Marie said, "I will stay on till you do."

He thanked her and said he would get right on it. Finishing his coffee, he got up and left the parsonage, going over to the church.

Pastor Dodge knocked on Roger's door and walked in.

"Good afternoon, sir, what can I do for you?"

"Mrs. Marie's birthday is Monday, and I thought we should give her a party."

Roger said, "That's a good idea, and I will take care of that."

"Another thing. She wants to retire. Do you know anybody who would like the position?"

Roger thought for a minute, saying, "Not that I know of, but I'll talk to some of the members about it."

"Well, I will talk to you later. I was going to do a little shopping today."

They said goodbye and Robert left.

It was Sunday morning. Pastor Dodge walked in the church, and seeing Jennifer, he walked over to her.

"Good morning, Pastor. I like you to meet my best friend, June."

Pastor Dodge looked at her and the bruises that were visible and thought how many he couldn't see. "I'm glad to meet you, Ms. June Rodgers. Jennifer has told me all about you," he said.

June blushed and said, "Nice to meet you too."

The choir began to sing, and Robert headed to his seat on stage.

After the prayer and a few more songs, it was his turn, and he felt confident of his sermon.

"Welcome, everybody, to United Methodist. And for those who don't know me, I'm Pastor Dodge. I could read your scripture, but I would like to do my own version of this story. If you look at Exodus, I haven't taken anything away from the scripture, but first I want to ask you a question. If you had a precious gift and shared it with your best friend, he would think it was trash. Would it hurt your feelings and, in anger, keep the gift that you gave him? That's the story I'm about to tell.

"The Egyptians made giant statues for burial places. The blocks were each enormous, and the Jews were made to put these blocks together to form pyramids. Many Jews died doing this work in the burning sand. They were whipped excessively when they slowed down, and a few were left to die. Moses came to the elders and said that God wanted to free his people. At first, they thought he was crazy, but after showing them miracles, they began to believe. Moses then went to the Pharaoh and told him to let his people go. The Pharaoh refused until the seventh plague, which took his first-born son. He told them to leave, but he felt in his heart revenge. He waited till they were trapped, but Moses raised his rod and the sea parted. Taking three million Jews through the Red Sea on dry land took several hours. The Pharaoh gave chase, but when the last Jew reached shore, the water came together and drowned them. Soon everyone was praising God.

"Then they made camp and God called Moses to the top of the mountain where he was there for forty days. The Jews thought he wasn't coming back, so they returned to their evil ways, making a golden calf to worship. God was angry with them. He had gave them freedom and made a promise to lead them to a land of milk and honey. Moses talked him out of destroying them, but he still made them wander through the desert for forty years. They murmured and complained, but God was still gracious, making sure they had water and food. He even put a cloud over them, so they were not so hot and made a fire in the sky at night to guide them, and still they were unhappy. Moses sent spies into the land of promise, but only Joshua and Caleb told of great God's gift. They were still afraid to go since the ten spies returned saying that the enemy was too strong to fight. Moses wasn't allowed in the promised land for taking his anger out on the Jews. Soon, Joshua leads them into the promised land, but of the original men who crossed the Red Sea, only Joshua and Caleb were left. When they crossed the Jordan River, God parted the river and three million Jews crossed. God had spared all the women and children, which many had grown up.

"Now God is offering you that special gift to make it to the promised land. You can either accept it or be left to the fires of hell. All can receive this gift by saying, 'Lord, I'm a sinner, and I believe he died on the cross for my sins and was resurrected in three days.' I'm calling you to this altar if God is speaking to your heart. Will you accept his gift of eternal life? Just get up from your seat and walk this aisle for Jesus."

Soon there was twenty men and woman coming down the aisle. The ten deacons came to help to pray with these people. June soon got up and followed them, and the pastor prayed with her. He told her he wanted to talk with her after church in his office.

"Jennifer will show you the way."

Pastor Dodge stood in front of the congregation with tears of joy in his eyes saying he was so happy that this many were saved today. He gave a thanks to Jesus in a prayer before dismissing them. He shook hands with everybody at the door, saying, "Hope to see you here soon."

Jennifer took June around to the pastor's office to wait for him. Pastor Dodge came in ten minutes later and said, "I'm glad you came to see me, Ms. Rodgers." Pastor Dodge could tell she was high, but he believed she gave her heart to the Lord. "So how did you get hooked on drugs?" he asked.

June said she was sound asleep one night and felt a prick and woke up to Jeff injecting a needle into her. "Jeff told me it was heroine and that eventually I would crave it, as he laughed at me. He kept injecting me every night, and if I tried to stop him, he would knock me out with his fist. He told me that he had great plans for me, which I was very frightened of."

Pastor Dodge said, "There are shelters for abused women, and I can get you in one. We can also take you to a rehabilitation center. We will fix it so Jeff will never know where you went."

"I'm afraid he will hurt Jennifer to find out where I am."

"Don't worry. Jennifer will be protected not only by me, but Mr. Conner too."

Jennifer said, "See, you have nothing to worry about."

"Well, I'll think it over and get back to you," she said, knowing she was really scared of Jeff.

Jennifer thanked him for his time.

Pastor Dodge said, "I wouldn't take too long. It will be harder to get off the drugs the longer you wait."

They left his office, and he hoped that she would come back and get help. He prayed for her and decided to head to the parsonage for lunch.

Mrs. Marie had made him burger and fries for lunch. He sat down and ate. He was still thinking about her and didn't hear what Mrs. Marie said.

"I'm sorry I didn't hear you. I had something on my mind that was troubling me."

Mrs. Marie said, "That was a great sermon and got plenty of responses."

"Yes, it did. I thank God for bringing this to my mind and hope he will help me with another great sermon next week." He finished his lunch and retired to his room for a nap.

Pastor Dodge suddenly woke up from his daydream when June asked him why they were there and why Jennifer was not with them. Robert looked around coming out of the fog a little confused. He had no answers for her. June wasn't sure what was happening either, just sitting on the bench with quite a few members of the church. The last thing she remembered was being in the church on Sunday. Soon she began to think about her life.

CHAPTER 6

JUNE ROGERS

June remembered that she grew up in Torrington, Wyoming, with her parents. Her dad worked in a factory for eleven years and was pronounced with stage four cancer.

When she was younger, he would always come home and pick her up with a hug and kiss. He was quite strong, being six-foot and two hundred pounds. When she was ten, he dropped a lot of weight and was always sleeping. One day he came home from work and passed out at the door. Her mother got scared trying to wake him and called 911. The ambulance came and rushed him to community hospital. He died a few hours later, and her mother fainted when the doctor came out and told her he was gone. A nurse came with some smelling salts after the doctor laid her in the seats. June began to cry not knowing what was going on. She was ten years old, and now her father was dead. The next three days were kind of confusing with relatives she never saw before, and the house was filled with people. She was really upset that her father died, but people wouldn't leave her alone. The house cleared up the day after they buried her father. She still felt the urge to cry almost every day. After three weeks, she came out of her depression. All her friends in school helped her to feel better, and she was able to get back on track in school.

Her mom was dating one of the male nurses that took care of her father. His name was Jack, and he was always telling her that Wade went peacefully. It took her a while to figure out that he meant her father. She never knew her father's first name until he was buried; her mother always called him dad. Getting curious, she asked what her mother's name was, and Jack told her it was May. She finally realized that she was following her mother. They both had blond hair and blue eyes, and she looked a lot like her, so she got the reason for her name. About a year later, her mother married Jack Dalton. He still worked in the hospital, and her mother took a job in Hardee's. They got along, and he would bring little presents and he was very handsome, being quite tall and muscular with brown hair and his blue eyes, and she had a small crush on him.

When she was thirteen, she began to blossom, and Jack would take her shopping for new clothes, and some were tight and a little revealing. The boys in school all wanted to take her out, but Jack would stop them. Jack would flirt with her, and she would go to her room embarrassed. Soon, she was sixteen and decided to join the cheerleading squad, and Jack was there at every game. One day her mother was in a car accident leaving work. She was rushed to the hospital, and they called the school to let her know. She was excused, and one of the teachers drove her to the hospital. Her mother was not too bad off, but they wanted to keep her overnight for observation. Jack was off that day and didn't even come when he was called home. June was angry at him and was going to tell him off when she got home. She stayed with her mother for a few hours.

Her mom said, "Go home. I'll be alright. You need to get ready for school tomorrow, and I'll be there when you get home." June gave her mother a kiss and left the hospital and walked home.

June was sweating by the time she reached the house. Jack was watching TV when she came in. She yelled at him saying, "Why didn't you go see my mother?"

"It wasn't that bad of an accident, and I see enough of that in the hospital every day."

"Well, did you call to see if she was alright?"

He didn't answer her, which made her madder. She went on to her room cursing him under her breath. She went to her room and took off her clothes and got in the shower. Suddenly, the bathroom door opened, and Jack walked in. She screamed at him to get out, and he just laughed at her. She grabbed a towel and tried to get out of the bathroom, but he wouldn't let her. He raped her there on the floor of the bathroom as she screamed and cried. She finally got loose and ran into her room and locked the door. She spent the night crying and scared he would break in.

The next morning when she got out of bed, no one was home. She was glad he went to work and felt a little safe. She went to school just to be away from there, being afraid he would come home. Her mother was home when she got there, and she told her what happened. Her mother went and talked to Jack, and he said that nothing happened; she was just trying to get back at him for not going to the hospital. May knew that June left the hospital angry at Jack, so she believed his story.

She had been talking to a boy online named Jeff, and she told him what happened.

He said, "If you want, you can come and stay with me." June thought that it was a good idea to be afraid of Jack's actions. Jeff said, "Do you have an ID?" She said she does. He told her he would wire her the money to Walmart to get a ticket to Atlanta.

The next day after school, she walked to Walmart, which was just down the block from the school. She showed them her ID, and they gave her the money. She then went down the street to the bus station to find out when the next bus left for Atlanta. The next bus didn't leave till seven in the morning. June bought a ticket and walked home. She went straight to her room. She emptied her book bag and filled it with her bathroom items and put her books under the bed. She filled her suitcase and slid it under the bed too. She knew that both of her parents would be gone by six that morning. She went down to dinner like nothing was happening. She hardly talked to either one of them; they seemed to ignore her too. Her parents sat down to watch TV and left her to clean up the kitchen. She soon went to bed and locked the door behind her.

June woke up feeling a little nervous and excited. She went downstairs. It was six fifteen, and she noticed that both were gone. She went back up and collected her book bag and suitcase. She knew it was a half-hour walk to the station, so she left without eating breakfast. The bus was pulling in when she got there and went straight over to the driver to hand him her suitcase and ticket. It wasn't long before they pulled out of the station, and she began to relax.

She had met Jennifer on the bus, and they became best friends. They shared their troubles all the way to Atlanta. When she saw Jeff at the bus station, he was just what she thought he was until later. He was nice, even finding Jennifer a motel and taking her there. The first month was like a dream come true, which made her very happy.

When she started to ask questions, her world came tumbling down. He was angry with her for asking and walked out, and he hadn't returned when she went to bed. Suddenly, she felt her a prick on her skin and woke up and saw Jeff with a needle in his hand. June yelled at him saying, "What did you do to me?"

He laughed and said, "You'll feel really good in a few minutes." She started to feel strange and dizzy. "There. That's what you get for asking questions."

This made her angry, and she got up from the bed swaggering. She grabbed hold of him, and he slapped her down. She was angry and humiliated and couldn't believe this was happening. For a week, all she could do was sleep, and her friend kept calling her, but she denied her problem. Jeff was coming in each evening administering more drugs into her system. Soon, she looked forward to being high.

One evening, he came in and said, "No more shots. It's getting too expensive."

She looked at him confused, not knowing if she could get along without them. The next day, she woke up feeling sick and didn't know what to do. She tried to sleep, but it wouldn't happen, and she began to vomit and sweat. She turned the air conditioner down, and it still didn't help. Jeff saw her when he got home and laughed.

"Well, have you come up with the money for your drugs yet?"

"You know I couldn't," she said.

"Well, if you need it that much, I have some buddies that will pay to be with you." June was suddenly in shock and became quite scared. Jeff just laughed at her and said, "Don't worry. I'll take care of you." Jeff said as he walked out the door, "Don't worry. My buddies will pay enough for quite a few. You'll be good after tonight."

Soon as he left, she began to pack. She knew that she needed to get away. She left the apartment and headed down the street toward the church. She didn't have any money and couldn't call for help. She just knew that Pastor Dodge would help her.

It was about midnight by the time she reached the church and went around to the parsonage. All the lights were out when she banged on the door. It seemed to take forever before a light came on, and Mrs. Marie came to the door. Looking at June, she didn't know whether to call the police but felt sorry for her and said, "What do you want?"

June said, "I must talk to Pastor Dodge. It's very important."

Mrs. Marie brought her into the living room and said, "Sit here while I go wake up the pastor."

June was still scared and didn't know what to do and was afraid the pastor wouldn't help her. Soon Pastor Dodge came in with Mrs. Marie and said, "Would you put on some coffee?" Mrs. Marie left them and headed to the kitchen.

June told him about what happened to her and said, "I felt in my heart that you would help me."

"Well, I will do everything I can for you. Let's first pray that God will guide us both in the right direction." Soon as the prayer was done, Mrs. Marie arrived with the coffee. "Mrs. Marie, can you make up the spare bedroom? She will be staying the night." He said, "In the morning, I'll make some calls, and you can stay here with Mrs. Marie. No one knows you came here, so they won't be looking for you."

June said, "Thanks, but please tell Jennifer. She'll be worried when she tries to call."

He said he would let her know. "But for now, you need to get some rest and turn off your cell phone."

In the morning, Pastor Dodge had breakfast with June and said, "I will let you know later what we'll do." June spent the day with Mrs. Marie. They got a long fine, and she told her about what had happen to her.

She said, "You need to watch who you met online. Most of them don't tell the truth."

Pastor Dodge came back at lunchtime and said, "After church hours today, I will be taking you to a Mrs. Ranch. She heads up the abuse center. She has some naltrexone that will help you with your problem, and I also talked to Mrs. Thompson, and soon as they get an opening, you'll be going to a rehabilitation center."

June was happy to hear this because she was afraid Jeff would come to the church looking for her.

"I told Jennifer where you were at, but for her own protection, I'm not telling her where you'll be going."

June understood and agreed. She spent the rest of the day with Mrs. Marie and told her that she was saved last Sunday, and she would like to work in the church.

Mrs. Marie said, "I want to retire, and if you like, you can take over my job when you get back." June was excited and said she would love it too. Mrs. Marie said, "It's settled, and I'll tell Pastor Dodge of our decision."

Pastor Dodge came back at four. "Are you ready to go?"

"Yes, and Mrs. Marie said I could have her job if it's okay with you."

Pastor Dodge said, "That will be great, but you know it will be at least three months."

"I know I just want off these drugs, and hopefully, Jeff will leave me alone."

"If he gives us any trouble, we can get a restraining order, but we hope we don't have to go that far. Well, let's get you over to the abuse center, and I'll be back in a week to take you to the rehabilitation center."

She went out to the church parking lot where the Pastor's Ford Focus was. It was a white car with blue seats, and he already had the car running to cool off. "Don't worry," he said, "the seats are just a little hot since it almost hit a hundred degrees today."

June got in and was happy she wore jeans and not a skirt. They drove out of the parking lot with the air conditioning on full blast. It took them over thirty minutes to reach the other side of town. The building looked like a plain red-brick building, and as they entered, they had to use an intercom to announce who they were. After the door buzzed, they walked into a reception area where a young lady sat all alone.

"Good evening, I am Robin. How can I help you?"

"We're to see a Mrs. Ranch," the pastor replied.

"I will tell her you are here," and she made a call on her switchboard.

June had to sit down while they waited feeling kind of tired and sick to her stomach. To June, it felt forever before Mrs. Ranch showed up. June was feeling quite sick at that moment but got up when she was introduced. June could tell this lady was nice-looking, being in her thirties. She had dark brown hair and light brown eyes and was wearing a beige pantsuit.

She said, "You can call me Betsy, everyone does, and if you follow me, I can give you an injection that will help with the pain. Today, we will excuse you from our session, but while you are here, there will be one once a day. You have nothing to worry about. No one is allowed in here, and if you have a cell phone, you must hand it over."

June took her phone out of her purse and gave it up.

Pastor Dodge said, "you are in good hands, and I'll be back next week to transfer you to the rehabilitation center."

June thanked him and followed Mrs. Ranch through the door after Robin buzzed them in. June was given the injection and went with her to a room with eight cots in the room.

Mrs. Ranch said, "Yours is the last one on the right. You get some rest and I'll introduce you to the other seven women tomorrow."

June set her suitcase by the bed and laid down and slept right through dinner. She only woke up once when the other women came in. She soon closed her eyes and went back to sleep.

June woke up rushing to the bathroom down the hall. She barely made it to the bathroom before throwing up. Mrs. Ranch came in and asked if she was alright. June was feeling quite weak and achy. After washing her face in the sink, she said she was alright.

Mrs. Ranch said, "Breakfast is being served in the dining room, and you should try to eat something."

June said she would be there when she got dressed. Mrs. Ranch left and June headed back to her dorm room. *All the other women must be down to breakfast,* she thought, getting dressed. Entering the dining room, she saw quite a few women and thought, *Besides the other seven women, that must be the staff also.*

Mrs. Ranch came up to her and said, "We will have a conference in an hour and introduce you to the others, but for now, eat something."

June didn't feel like eating a thing, being a little sick to the stomach. She went and got some toast and a cup of juice and sat down eating and drinking quite slowly. June felt a little better after finishing her food and was not looking forward to their talk session.

Mrs. Ranch led them all to a room with chairs in a circle and told them to be seated.

"Now we are not going to be formal, so everyone will be called by their first name. I'm a Betsy and welcome to our class, and now each one please let us know your name going around the circle."

Betsy pointed to the first woman who said, "My name is Sarah."

The next woman introduced herself as Regina and followed by Laura. The next in line was Lisa and then Mona and then followed by Tonya and Dawn. June was the last in the circle to say her name.

Betsy said, "Now that we know each other, tomorrow we will begin with Sarah sharing her story with the class."

Sarah was not much older than June and rather pretty. She had long blond hair and blue eyes but was quite skinny. She looked quite nervous about having to talk tomorrow, and June though maybe she would be a friend and help her. June told Sarah why she was there and that she was a Christian, and she would like to be friends. Sarah said she would like that; she didn't have any friends since she left school. Sarah was happy she had someone to back her up the next day.

After breakfast the next day, they went into the counseling room. Betsy told Sarah to stand up and tell her story to everyone. Sarah made it short saying she was abused by her father, and he was in jail for child molesting. Everyone was sorry and said she was not alone. Three of the women said they were also abused by their father and two by their husband. Only Dawn and June were abused by their boyfriend.

Betsy said, "Now that you know about each story of abuse, you can start healing."

When the meeting was over, June told Sarah to come with her. They went into the entertainment room where there was a Bible. June told her about Jesus and that he forgave her of her sins.

"If you can, find it in your heart to forgive your father and ask Jesus to forgive your sins."

Sarah said, "It's hard to forgive my father, but you're right, he's had enough punishment."

June said, "If you believe in Jesus, you will be saved." Sarah went with June on Sunday to church and was saved by Pastor Dodge, and they were voted into the church as members.

June went up to her friend Jennifer and gave her a hug, saying, "I like you to meet my friend Sarah. She will need someone while I'm in the rehabilitation center." Jennifer said that she would look out for her. June was starting to feel bad and needed to get back to the shelter for her daily shot. Pastor Dodge asked Roger if he would mind taking them back.

He said it would be fine. "I'll take your car, and Tammy can take the kids home."

Pastor Dodge told them, "This is my head deacon. He's my right hand."

Roger went over to his wife and told her what's happening and that he would be home after he dropped them off. Roger took them out to the car and told them to get in. June was a little nauseated and threw up in the parking lot. Roger reached in the glove department and gave her a few tissues to wipe her face. June apologized, but Roger assured her it was alright.

"Pastor Dodge has informed me of your problem." June felt a little embarrassed and quite sick. Soon they made it to the shelter, and Roger said, "Hope we see you next Sunday."

They said that Sarah would, but she thinks that Pastor Dodge is to put her in the rehabilitation center by then.

Roger said to Sarah, "If you don't mind kids, I can get you next Sunday." Sarah said she would be happy to go.

June left Sarah behind and had Robin buzz her in heading straight to Mrs. Ranch's office. Betsy saw how she looked and prepared her shot. After administering it, she asked how the two of them did in church. June told her the topic was about Jesus ministering to the people and both of them had applied to be a member. Betsy said that was good and maybe she would go with them sometime.

June said, "I've got to lay down a while if you don't mind."

Betsy told her to go ahead and said, "We don't hold sessions on Sunday."

June returned to the dorm and laid down feeling like her stomach was in uproar. After going to vomit few times, she finally drifted off to sleep.

Sarah came in at dinnertime to wake her, saying, "You need to eat something." June rose feeling a little better and followed Sarah to the dining room. They were having ham and sweet potatoes with green beans. June ate a little and had two glasses of ice tea before going back to her room to rest.

Sarah stayed by her side the rest of the week. June's craving for the drug was strong, and she tried to get Mrs. Ranch to give her more injections, but she refused telling her it would do her more harm than good. Sarah was there to comfort her and prayed with her that God would help. Finally, the day had arrived for her to go. Pastor Dodge showed up to take her, and she asked if he wouldn't mind if Sarah rode along with her. He said it would be alright since Jeff didn't know her. The three of them got into his car after June had packed all her belongings. It was another half hour before arriving at the center.

June looked at the building, which was green-colored stone with two columns in the front entrance. Entering the lobby, it looked like any other doctor's office with a receptionist, expect you saw the only other door was a heavy metal one.

"Good morning. I'm Bret. How may I help you?"

Pastor Dodge said, "This is Ms. Rogers. She has an appointment with Dr. Jones."

He called him and soon he came out with a nurse.

"Welcome to our rehabilitation center. This is Nurse Brown. She will be taking care of you."

June shook her hand, which was cold.

"Dr. Jones said we will be weening you off your drugs, and it may take up to three months. You will have to join group sessions plus you'll also have meetings with me once a week. I'm sorry, but for the first two weeks, you can have no visitors and must give up your phone." He asked if there was, any questions.

June hugged Sarah and said goodbye. Sarah said, "Don't you worry. I'll come to see you."

June followed the nurse through the steel door. Pastor Dodge shook the doctor's hand and said thanks.

Dr. Jones said he would let him know of her progression. "I'm sure you'll be checking on her in two weeks."

Pastor Dodge said he would and told Sarah, "We better go." He took her back to the abuse center and prayed with her before heading back to the church.

Dr. Jones took her into his office to get her background. June could tell he was in his fifties with his gray hair and light blue eyes. He looked kind of thin for his height of five eight. June told him of her growing up and why she left home and about Jeff. He told her maybe she looked at Jeff as a way out but ended up going from the frying pan to the fire.

June said, "I never thought he would do that to me."

"Well, you met him online, so you only knew what he told you." June agreed. He picked up the phone and soon Nurse Brown appeared. "Now I want you to go with the nurse, and tomorrow we will start your treatment."

June followed the nurse to a room where she was to remove all her clothes and put on a dressing gown. Nurse Brown said, "Everything will be returned to you when you leave. There are two beds in a room, so I will introduce you to your roommate."

June followed her down the hall to the fifth door on the right, and they went in. There was a frail-looking woman with brown hair and brown eyes.

"Ms. Mary Ann, this is your new roommate, June. I hope you two can get along."

June said, "Hi. Have you been here long?"

Mary Ann said, "Only about a week. Ms. Brown, I still feel quite sick."

"Well, you had your shot for today, so you will have to wait until tomorrow," the nurse said. Mary Ann was not too happy with this answer and complained. "You know what will happen if you keep complaining." She got scared and shut up; she didn't want to be tied down.

Mary Ann took June down the hall saying that there were twenty women in here. "This large room is our entertainment room with games and TV. On the other side of the hall is the cafeteria. Beside the ten rooms, there is the nurses' station and the doctor's office. We are meeting here in the entertainment room for group sessions. The last room was a gym with exercise equipment. We must work out for an hour each day in here. Well, that is the tour. We should be called to lunch soon. All doctor's visits are done in the morning, and we are up by six and must be in bed by ten." Mary Ann said, "We had better go back to the room, so we won't be last for lunch because if you're not in your room, they will skip you and go to the next."

An orderly came in and told them it was their turn for lunch. They followed the orderly to the cafeteria. Mary Ann said, "They only serve six people at a time, and when we are done, the next set will come. The staff doesn't want a big group at one time, so they can take care of our needs. There are only three attendants who work here and two nurses. Nurse Bennet is the night nurse and only one orderly at night. They only have one cook on staff, so you can't get anything after eight. Some of these girls can be aggressive, so watch yourself. You will meet all the girls tomorrow at the group session."

They were given a sandwich of ham and cheese with potato chips. They were also given water to drink, and Mary Ann said, "They don't want us to have too much sugar." Mary Ann said, "In the morning after breakfast, we must go to the gym." When they finished their food, they were ushered back to their room. "I'm sure your body aches, so we should take a nap before going to the entertainment room."

June agreed and laid down. When they awoke, they headed down the hall to watch TV. In the room was one large TV, and a woman named Shirley was controlling the remote. Shirley was over six feet tall and quite muscular, and everybody was afraid of her.

They returned to their room because it was almost time for dinner and didn't want to get in a fight with Shirley. Just as they got back there, an orderly named Bob told them they could go to dinner. When they entered the dining room, Mary Ann said, "This is our group, and Shirley isn't in ours."

June said, "I'm glad. I felt like punching that bully in the nose."

They went and got their trays of roast beef and potatoes and sat down together and ate. Finishing and returning their trays, they returned to their room.

Soon as they got into the room, somebody knocked at the door. Mary Ann went to the door, and one of the women in their group asked to come in.

"My name is Laura, and I was wondering if I could hang out with you two."

June and Mary Ann said sure and told her their names.

Laura said, "I had been here longer than you two, and no one would talk to me since I wouldn't be part of Shirley's group."

June noticed that Laura was younger than her and had long straight black hair and blue eyes. She looked rather skinny probably from her addictions. Laura told them she hoped to get out of here soon after having already being here for four months. June thought she must have had it bad to still be here. The three related their stories to each other, not realizing the time.

An orderly came in saying, "It's time for bed lights to go out in ten minutes."

Laura said, "I'll see you guys in the morning," and left. They both got changed and just got into the bed when the lights went out.

The next morning, June got up and looked out the window. The sun was shining brightly. She knew it would be a hot day in the middle of August. They both had brushed their teeth and got in their sweats for their hour in the gym. They both decided to work out on the treadmills. In a few minutes, their new friend Laura came in, followed by three others in their group. Laura came over to them and said good morning and they said it back.

Laura started whispering, "You see that blonde over there? She is my roommate, Vicki. Watch what you say in front of her. She is part of Shirley's gang."

June noticed that she had muscle working out with the barbells. The other two were doing aerobics. When the hour was almost up, Bob came in and said, "You women need to hit the showers. Breakfast is in ten minutes."

The showers were next door in the locker room. The six women undressed and took a shower and returned to the locker room to dress. The other three woman were finished by the time June and Mary Ann got dressed. Laura was last and they waited on her. The three headed to the dining room and got their trays. The food consisted of scrambled eggs, bacon, and toast. June noticed that the other three were talking about them. She ignored them and went to get her Sweet'N Low for her coffee, which already contained cream. When June sat back down, she gave them a dirty look before turning around.

June said, "I was wondering, Laura, me and Mary Ann go to church on Sunday. Would you like to come?"

Laura said, "That would be great to get out of here for a while."

June said, "I'll phone Pastor Dodge to let him know you're coming."

After breakfast, it was time for group sessions. The six of them went in and took their seats while waiting for Nurse Brown. When she came in, she said, "Now I want you each to tell who you are and why you are here."

Each identified themselves. June didn't know that the other brown-haired woman was Dot and the black-haired one was Jan. When they were finished, Nurse Brown made an announcement that Laura would be leaving them in September. Everyone congratulated her, except Vicki who made a snide remark, "Hope I get a better roommate."

The meeting broke up, and Laura went back with June and Mary Ann. June said, "Don't let her get to you. It won't be long."

To Laura, it seemed a long time before she got out, but soon the day came. Her parents came and got her and took her home. She said goodbye to June and Mary Ann; they hated to see her go. She said she would stay in touch with them.

The next day, Jennifer and Sarah came to visit. June was happy to see them. They both gave her a hug and said, "You are looking a lot better."

Jennifer told June that Jeff had come to the church looking for her. "We let him know that you returned home, but we were not sure he believed us. He hasn't been back." June felt a little shiver at the mention of his name. Jennifer said, "The police is looking for him, so I don't think he will ever show up."

Mary Ann said, "I'm glad you have good friends. My friends are all drug addicts, so I'm going back home when I get out. My mother has agreed."

Sarah said, "Pastor Dodge is looking for us an apartment, and he said that we could share Mrs. Marie's job. Right now, I'm staying at the parsonage until you get out. I just got my driver license and getting a car next week. If you like, I will teach you to drive, so one of us can be there in the morning and the other in the afternoon." June said that would be great.

The end of October came, and her and Mary Ann were ready to leave. Mary Ann's mother showed up and thanked June for helping her daughter. June gave Mary Ann a hug and said, "I hope you stay in touch." She said she would and gave June a hug before leaving. June got her stuff ready to leave. Jan came in to tell her goodbye and told her that Dot died of an overdose.

June said, "Where did she get the drugs?"

Jan suspected Shirley, but her group refused to talk. Sarah showed up to take her and carried her bag out of her car.

June said, "Wow! A candy-apple red Chevy Impala."

"I like it even if the payments are a little high." Sarah said, "Pastor Dodge will be showing us our new apartment, so we are headed to the church."

When they arrived, Jennifer was there waiting with a hug and said, "Glad you're here."

June hugged her back saying, "It's great to get out of there."

"Pastor Dodge is waiting for you in his office."

The three went there, and Pastor Dodge got up and gave her a hug saying, "Glad you're back. When you get settled, you will be taking over the parsonage in the morning cooking and cleaning and Sarah in the afternoon since she will be taking a few hours a day to train with Jennifer."

June said, "Why? Are you leaving?"

"No, but I will be gone for a month on my honeymoon."

June said, "What!"

Jennifer said, "I am engaged to John, and we will be married in March. I was wondering, since I have no one here, would you give me away?" June said she would be honored.

"Well," said the Pastor, "shall we go look at your new apartment?" They all agreed. "Well, you three head out to the parking lot while I let Roger know we are leaving."

When Pastor Dodge got to the parking lot, he said, "Roger's wife will meet us there if you will follow me." They left Virginia Avenue and got on the Perry J. Parkway, which took them fifteen minutes to get to Garden Walk Apartments. He pulled up in front of the B-building saying, "Yours is on the second floor," as he got out of the car. Walking up the stairs, he handed June a set of keys. June unlocked the door and saw that the apartment was completely furnished. The living room had a tan carpet, which matched the drapes to the sliding glass door. There was a small balcony. Next to that was a kitchen, which had a table for two but had all the modern appliances. Off the living room there were two bedrooms with a joining bathroom. Both bedrooms were decorated with queen-size beds and dressers. The closets were both walk-in. In the bathroom, there was both a shower and a tub with a large vanity and mirror. Pastor Dodge said that Mr. and Mrs. O'Donnell live just around the corner from them.

Both June and Sarah were impressed by the apartment. Pastor Dodge said the church paid the deposit and the first month rent. "If it's alright with you, we will take twenty dollars a month out of your paychecks till you repaid the amount. We also paid the utilities, which will be included in the payment. Then next month, you two can take over the bills for the rent and utilities. The rent will be 929 a month if that's satisfactory." June and Sarah both were very thankful for the church's help. "So if you two are finished looking at the apartment, we are invited to dinner at the O'Donnells. Mrs. O'Donnell said she would go with you shopping tomorrow to get groceries and other items you would need," Pastor Dodge said. "Now we'll walk around to their apartment."

When they got to 1C, the pastor knocked on the door. The door was opened by an eleven-year-old boy, which had brown hair and brown eyes. Pastor Dodge said, "Hello, Timothy. Your mom invited us to dinner, and I'd like you to meet Ms. Rogers and Ms. Wright. They will be your new neighbors."

June shook his hand and said, "Glad to meet you."

"Nice to know you, madam," he said.

She said, "You don't have to be so formal. Just call me June"

Sarah told him he could call her by her first name too and said, "I'm glad to meet you, Timothy."

He led them into the living room where the O'Donnells were sitting. Roger got up and shook hands. "I'm sure you two saw me in the church. My name is Roger, and this is my wife, Tammy."

Tammy got up and was quite tall and was beautiful with red hair and large green eyes. June shook her hand and knew that Timothy took after his father.

Roger said, "Dinner is almost ready, and don't worry, my wife is a very good cook and she won't poison you." Tammy punched Roger in the arm, which made him laugh. She said to Tim to go set the table. Timothy rushed into the kitchen to get the plates and soon had all the table setting done.

Tammy said, "Very good, Tim. Let's go get the food now."

June jumped up and said, "Do you need any help?"

"No, thank you. We have it handled," she said. Tammy brought in the platter of roasted ham, and Tim brought the potatoes. He then rushed back into the kitchen for the green beans. Roger brought in the pitcher of ice tea and sat down asking Pastor Dodge to lead them in a word of pray.

"Thank you, Lord, for this food and this family that made it for us. Please help Sarah and June as they are starting a new life together and in the church. We ask this in your name. Amen."

The meal was delicious, and Robert complimented Tammy on a good meal. They laughed and had a good time together at the table and were soon finished eating. June offered her and Sarah's services to clean up.

Tammy told them, "No way, me and Tim have this job down pat." They all went into the living room and soon Tammy and Tim came in saying everything was put away and the dishes were in the dishwasher. Tammy said, "Tomorrow after I put Tim on the bus, I'll show you around and will collect what you'll need."

June said, "Thanks. We welcome the help."

Pastor Dodge said, "You two can get settled and wait a few days to come to work."

Tammy said, "If Sarah needs help, we can take you to the church if you need a ride."

June was happy about the help and was glad to have a few days to get everything settled.

Leaving the O'Donnells, the three walked back around to their building where the pastor said good night and got in his car and left. June and Sarah took their suitcases that they had got from the pastor's car and headed upstairs. June decided on the smaller bedroom since Sarah had a lot more clothes.

June said, "When we get paid, I'll have to go clothes shopping."

Sarah said she would go with her to her room to unpack. June put her clothes away in the dresser and closet. She took a shower and put on her nightgown of blue and waited on Sarah to get done. Sarah had on a green nightgown, and they sat in the living room to watch a little TV.

Sarah said, "If we are going with Tammy tomorrow, we shouldn't stay up too late." June agreed and went and clicked off the remote before saying good night. They soon went to their separate bedrooms and got into bed. June thought she was glad to be out of that place but was still a little afraid of Jeff.

June woke up the next morning feeling hungry and needing coffee. Going into the kitchen, she found the coffeepot was already set up with two cups sitting on the counter. She turned it on and looked in the fridge, finding a carton of eggs. She looked under a cabinet finding pots and pans and plates in the cabinet. There on the counter was a loaf of bread, so putting some in the toaster, she looked in the fridge for butter.

She found some and a small jar of grape jelly. She went and prepared her and Sarah's breakfast and thanked Tammy all the time. Sarah came into the kitchen and was surprised when she saw breakfast.

June said, "Tammy must have looked out for us. We must thank her." Sarah agreed while she poured herself some coffee. It was after eight thirty when Tammy knocked at the door.

"So I see you found what I left, and you two have nothing to worry about. Pastor Dodge gave me the church's credit card, so you would have enough food and other items till you are paid." June and Sarah said that they were grateful for the pastor's help.

They left Tammy in the kitchen while they went and got ready to go shopping. Tammy washed up the dishes while she waited. June came in saying, "You didn't have to do that."

Tammy said, "It's fine. I hate waiting anyway."

Soon Sarah arrived, and they went out the door locking it behind them. They decided to go in Tammy's white Toyota van, which gave them plenty of room for groceries. Tammy drove them to the nearest Walmart saying, "You need to get enough for at least two weeks since that's when you get paid." They filled up their cart with groceries and household cleaning supplies. Sarah went and got some personal items plus toilet paper. June got a mop and broom, and Tammy said, "You can borrow my vacuum cleaner when you need it." June had enough personal items from the rehabilitation center to last her the next two weeks. Tammy paid for it all with the credit card, and they loaded it into her van. So now that was another four hundred that they would have to pay back to the church. June thought it would take them a while to pay it back at twenty each paycheck. June was smiling to herself at how good they were taken care of.

The two of them put away the groceries and began cleaning the apartment, and soon, Tammy brought the vacuum cleaner over so they could do the rugs. She helped them until it was time to go get her son who was in elementary school. June put on the lasagna that was in a box, which took over an hour to cook, while moping the kitchen floor. Sarah had washed all the sheets off both beds since she noticed that they hadn't been done for a while. They finished cleaning as the lasagna was done, and they sat down to eat.

Sarah said, "If you like, you can go with me tomorrow, and I'll show you what to do." June said that would be fine. Sarah gave the blessing and began to eat after June poured the tea. Sarah said that she likes to cook and would take over that job since June believe in TV dinners. They both began to laugh and fill their plates. June picked up all the plates and put them in the dishwasher just as soon as they finished eating. They retired to the living room to watch TV and was soon ready to go to bed. Sarah decided to take a shower in the morning and got out of her blue nightgown and got undressed. She picked up the book she was reading, which was a murder mystery. It didn't take long before her eyes closed, and she woke up to find the book on top of her. She laid it on the desk and turned out the light. June lay in her bed after taking a shower and putting on her black nightgown. She was thinking how lucky she was to have such good friends. She was excited to take over the job in the church's parsonage and hoped that Jeff had stopped looking for her. She turned off the light and lay on her side and fell asleep.

CHAPTER 7

TAMMY O'DONNELL

Tammy was happy as she headed back to her apartment thinking this must be what God called her to do. Roger had plenty to do in the church, but she had little beside going to services. She felt that the Lord was putting those two in her path for a reason. She got in her apartment and fell to her knees and prayed. "Lord, let me know what you need for me to do, Amen."

She then picked up her keys and headed to pick up her son. After leaving the elementary, she asked him how his day went, and he told her it was exciting. "We were doing finger paints." Timothy showed her his hands, which were blue, and said he was turning into a Smurf. Tammy laughed and said, "We will have to give you a bath when we get you home."

When she got home, he went and took a bath. Her mind raced back to when she was growing up with her two sisters. She remembered the pretty blue house they grew up in. It only had two bedrooms, so all three sisters shared a room, which was crowded. Her father was a farmer in Ogden, Utah, and couldn't afford a bigger house. They all worked in the field after school. She was the oldest, so she helped her sisters with their homework. Her mother Mabel had her hands full with the house, so she would help whenever she could. The two sisters, April and May, were a little jealous that Tammy looked like their mother, but they looked like their father. Both had black hair and blue eyes, thinking that Tammy got all the boys because she was better-looking. May was the more jealous since she was a little overweight, and everyone made fun of her. Her father Burt was a little overweight too and was always taking up for May. Tammy had quite a few boyfriends through high school and so did April.

When it was time for college, Bert had saved enough for his daughters to go. Both the youngest were going to Salt Lake City College, but Tammy wanted more with computers and had applied to Omnitech Institute in Atlanta, Georgia. She got in and worked part-time at McDonald's to be able to go. She promised her parents that she would come back afterwards, and that was before she met Roger.

Roger was attending Getaway Christian Academy and working in the church to help pay his tuition. Tammy met her best friend Megan in college, and they were sharing a dorm room. Megan was a tall blonde with blue eyes, and her parents were well off, so she wanted for nothing. Megan always tried to get her to go parties, but she never had the time.

"Well," she said, "since you never go out, how about going to church with me on Sunday?" Tammy was surprised that Megan wanted to go to church but found out her boyfriend was in the choir. Tammy agreed to go that Sunday where she met Roger.

When she walked into the church, Roger was staring at her.

Tammy asked, "Who is that guy over there?"

"Oh! That's Roger. He works here in the church but doesn't talk to no one except the pastor. If you like, I can introduce you to him," Megan said.

Tammy said she would like that. "He is a really handsome guy."

Megan went over to Roger and said, "My friend would like to get to know you."

Roger was so fascinated with her he tripped over the carpet. Tammy held back her laugh and told Roger she was glad to meet him. Megan told Roger that they went to school together. Roger asked Tammy if he could take her out next week for dinner, and she accepted. On their way back to the dorm, she said, "He is cute with that mustache he's trying to grow."

Megan said, "Well, if that's what you like, I wish you good luck."

Tammy sort of forgot about the date having a week of test. Friday came and a knock at the door of her dorm; the housemother said there was a boy outside saying he had a date with her. Tammy realized that she had forgotten and told the housemother to tell him she would be right down. It took her about a half-hour to get ready hoping he would wait. Tammy put on a nice red dress and white heels and headed downstairs.

Roger was waiting and wearing a blue T-shirt to match his jeans. Roger said, "Wow. I'm sorry I'm underdressed, but I hope you don't mind I can't afford a fancy restaurant, and I hope McDonald's will be alright." Tammy said that was fine wishing she hadn't got so dressed. He led her to an old Ford Focus, which was starting to rust. The seat was a little worn, but she didn't say a word. The evening turned out to be quite nice, and he told her about wanting to become a minister. He told her he had one more year of college and loved working in the church. She said she only had six months to graduation and was thinking of returning to Utah. He said he hoped she would stay here. When he took her back to the dorm, he kissed her good night. Running up the stairs to her room, she got that warm feeling and hoped he would ask her out again.

Roger met her in church the next Sunday and asked if she would date him on a regular basis. "If it is alright with you, I could take you out every Friday night. That way, we won't be interfering with our schoolwork." Tammy agreed to the arrangement and was excited that their relationship was progressing. Roger took her out each Friday, and her affection for him grew.

On the day of her graduation, in front of everyone, he asked her to marry him with a small gold diamond ring. In a way, she was embarrassed and excited, but she said yes. The whole graduation class applauded her, and he asked her if she would wait the next six months for him to graduate. Tammy said she would, but she had to go home for a time, and they could keep in touch by phone. Roger agreed and said on spring break he would come to Utah to meet her family. She said, "That would be great, but I'm leaving tomorrow with my sister April." Tammy introduced him to her sister who came all this way to see her graduation. Roger took them both to dinner that night and said he would drive them to the airport tomorrow. Tammy jumped at the chance saying that would be fine.

The next morning, Roger showed up in time to help them with their suitcases. When they got to the airport, Tammy asked April to go and get the tickets. April took both suitcases to check in so Tammy could be alone with him. Roger said he would miss her and took her in his arms and gave her a passionate kiss. Tammy felt much love for him and was hesitant to go, but she knew he had to finish college first. She asked him to leave because she didn't want to say goodbye in from of all those people, and said, "You already embarrassed me once."

Roger laughed and said, "Call me, and I'll see you at spring break." He kissed her one more time, and she turned and walked away with tears in her eyes. Roger hated to let her go, and he didn't want to cry in front of her, but he left the airport with tears streaming down his face.

Timothy broke her train of the thought, calling, "Mommy, I'm done." She went in to check if he was dressed.

Tammy said, "Why don't you go play in your room until dinner." Tammy went into the kitchen to make fried chicken knowing it was Roger's favorite meal. Tammy felt a warm feeling remembering how they first met. When Roger showed up at five, he asked if she got those two squared away. "Yes, they are both good and be able to start work soon." Roger saw what she was cooking and asked what the special occasion was. "I was thinking about how we first met, and I thought you might discuss our wedding after dinner."

Roger said, "If you thought I forgot our anniversary, I didn't. I do have a surprise, but I'll tell you after our discussion."

"Oh! I see how you are punishing me because I thought you forgot."

He laughed and said, "But of course." The three sat down to dinner and had a good time, and Tammy was feeling the love from her two boys. Roger helped with the dishes and put Timothy to bed after helping him with his homework. She brought two glasses of tea in the living room so they could relieve their marriage.

CHAPTER 8

ROGER O'DONNELL

Roger knew Tammy wanted to talk about the wedding, but he remembered his childhood. He grew up on a farm in Marietta with his mother and father and sister. Before school, each day he had to feed the chickens and the cows. His father, Roger Senior, would be out tending to the crops before he even got out of bed. He was a husky man with the same color eyes and hair as him. Mary his mother was a short blonde with blue eyes and so was Faith, his sister. She was five years younger than him, so she didn't have to do chores except help Mommy cook at night. Roger kept up with his grades all through school, but Faith was still smarter; and when she graduated, she went into law school. He told his dad he wanted to be a preacher, not a farmer. His dad said he would be proud of him no matter what profession. When he graduated, he went to a college for the Bible. He did alright, but he just wasn't cut out to be a preacher. Pastor Evans got him to take over as head deacon, which made him happy.

While in Utah with Tammy's parents, he got along fine and agreed to their marriage. It was June before he graduated, and the pastor would marry them after they went through marriage counseling with him. He told Tammy about it and said, "I decided with my sister, Faith, for you to stay at her house." Tammy said that April had to come back with her to get ready for the wedding. He called Faith, and she said it would be alright for her to come and stay too.

Roger met the plane from Utah to take them to his sister's. His sister had a large home and was rather expensive. Faith became a corporate lawyer and brought home a hundred thousand a year. She had a five-bedroom house in Cobb County with a large circular drive inside a gate. She also had a maid and cook and also a butler and gardener. The butler brought in their luggage when Roger parked in front of the house. Tammy was really impressed with the house looking like a small mansion. Faith was just inside the door to greet them, telling the butler which rooms to store their luggage.

"I was wondering," Faith asked, "I'm between cases, if it would be alright if I helped plan the wedding with you?"

Tammy said, "I would be honored with your help, and we thought maybe you would want to be a bridesmaid with my sister."

Faith said with a great big smile, "I would love to. I'm sure for now you would like to get some rest, and maybe we can talk at dinner, which is at five."

Tammy said, "That would be great," and took Roger by the hand saying, "Will you be here?"

Roger said, "I have a little work at the church. I can be back by five thirty, I think." Faith said she would make sure to save him a plate. Roger kissed Tammy goodbye and said, "I'll see you later," and left.

Roger suddenly heard what Tammy was saying and stopped thinking about his childhood and leading up to the wedding.

Tammy said, "It took about five sessions with Pastor Evans before he agreed to marry us. I was very happy that Sunday you walked the aisle with me to be saved and give yourself to Jesus. It was hard to find a place for the venue, but your sister Faith found one for us. I was happy when she joined me and April to pick out the wedding dress. She arranged all the flowers and was there to help pick out the cake. I really appreciated that she took time off to help us and gave us a honeymoon in Niagara Falls.

"The church was full of our family since all your family flew in from Utah, which your sister had found hotel rooms for them. I was very proud of my father giving me away, and I even saw a tear from his eye. Megan was my maid of honor since she is the one that brought us together. My sisters and yours were the bridesmaids, and I laugh when May caught the bridal bouquet. Roger's father stood up for you since you had no brothers. I enjoyed the party afterwards, cutting the cake and dancing with my new husband. I was excited about a week in that motel in New York and the falls looked great. I especially was happy to be

Mrs. O'Donnell and being with you a whole week with nothing to worry about. It was even more exciting when I found out I was pregnant when we got back."

Roger said, "I couldn't wait to get out of my sister's house and move into this apartment." Roger worked hard under Pastor Evans and took over most of the programs. Pastor Evans was almost seventy years old and was happy that Roger took over. He only had to plan sermons. It took Roger almost six months of saving before he had enough to rent his own apartment. Faith had mothered over Tammy the last six months of her pregnancy and was sorry for them to go. Faith had helped them to move into Garden Walk. Since the apartment came furnished, they only had to buy baby furniture.

Faith insisted on helping Tammy pick it out and helped pay for it saying, "This is my only nephew." She couldn't wait to be an aunt. Tammy got the landlord to move the furniture out of the one bedroom so they could make it a nursery. Her and Faith assembled the crib together and bought a bassinet and changing table, which was all in blue knowing already that it was a boy. Faith also went out and bought a dresser in blue to match the rest. Tammy got a knock at the door and got up slowly from the couch feeling so big.

When she opened the door, a man was standing there saying, "We have a dresser for you."

Tammy didn't understand at first, saying, "I didn't order a dresser."

"You are Mrs. O'Donnell?"

"Yes."

He said, "Well, another Ms. O'Donnell sent this to you."

"Oh! I guess you should bring it in."

Once they put the dresser in the room and took the box and trash out, he had her sign for it. Tammy called Faith and told her she shouldn't have.

Faith said, "You needed it for the boy." Tammy thanked her and had to hang up since Faith was in a meeting. Tammy showed it to Roger when he got home.

Three months later, her water broke and she called Roger at his office, and he rushed home. Tammy got her suitcase out and made a quick call to Faith after calling the doctor. Tammy met Roger at the door, and he ushered her to the car and headed for Well Star on Cleveland Avenue.

It took him twenty minutes to get to the hospital, and her contractions were coming closer apart. The doctor was waiting for her; she was Dr. Dorothy Lament who had been with her the whole pregnancy. Roger noticed that she was a small woman and looked like a teenager, but she was in her thirties.

It wasn't long before Faith showed up from her office. Faith said, "What's happening?"

"The doctor is examining her now."

Dr. Lament came out and said to them, "It won't be long. She is already six centimeters."

Faith said to Roger, "There is nothing to worry about. She's been my doctor for years."

Dr. Lament smiled with her full lips and sparkling brown eyes and said, "All fathers for the first time are nervous."

Faith laughed and said, "I guess that's true."

"Well, I must get back in there with your wife," the doctor said. Roger and Faith sat down to wait.

The nurse soon came out and said, "Congratulations! You have a baby boy. You can go see your wife now, and the baby will be in there shortly after the pediatrician exams him."

Roger and Faith went to the room to see Tammy. She looked tired and she asked if he had seen the baby. He said no. They said they would bring him in soon. There was a knock at the door, and a nurse rolled in the bassinet. Roger looked at his son for the first time with much love and being very proud.

Roger took the child in his arms and said, "I will raise him in the church and hope he will take my place someday."

Faith wanted to hold him also, and when she took the child, she said he was beautiful. Faith said, "I'll be there to help you raise him."

Tammy left the hospital the next day with Timothy John O'Donnell who they named after the disciples of Jesus.

***

Faith was true to her word, always buying Timothy new clothes, and was there whenever Tammy needed a babysitter. Roger was always reading to his son every night from the Bible. When Timothy was five and starting school, he was saved at the church.

Roger was proud of his family and especially that his sister was going to church with them. Pastor Evans was preaching on Romans by Paul. Who wanted to go to Rome but went there under arrest by Nero? Roger introduced Faith to the pastor who hope she would come back again.

The next day while Roger was working in his office, he got a call from Mrs. Marie in the parsonage. She was hysterical and crying saying she found Pastor Evans on the floor of the kitchen. Roger said he would be right over after he called 911. The ambulance was pulling up when he made his way to the parsonage. The ambulance driver checked him out and declared him dead.

"Do you want to take him to the hospital or call the funeral home to come get him?"

Roger said, "You need to take him to the hospital since the medical examiner is there. I'll be along in a little while to sign the papers, but I must first check what he will. Roger checked the papers to find out that he had a nephew in Nebraska, and he wanted to be cremated. When the nephew found out all his money was going to charity, he wanted nothing to do with it. Roger called Dennis Smith Funeral Home to have the pastor cremated, and he would be over tomorrow to sign the papers right. Now he was on the way to the medical examiner's office.

The director said, "We can hold services here for him in two days, so we'll have the hearse here by Wednesday at noon." The funeral director said, "Can you come tomorrow and sign papers and pick out an urn for him?"

"I have other papers to sign, but is three o'clock good for you?"

The director said, "We will see you then," and hang up the phone. Roger called the other deacons for them to send out that there would be a funeral service at ten on Wednesday. Roger also went down to Mrs. Brown's office to let her know about the service. Roger left and went home telling Tammy what had happened. She could tell he was stressed, and they both kneeled prayed to ask God to help them through the next few days.

The next day, Roger went to Well Star and found out that Pastor Evans had a heart attack. He left there and went to the funeral home to arrange for the coffin and for them to pick him up and hold the viewing on Tuesday and services on Wednesday. The funeral director said that he would have him picked up Tuesday morning.

Roger signed all the papers and thanked him. Roger went back to his office to call the insurance company and said they would bring the papers tomorrow for him to sign. Roger went home with a headache and was worried about who would preach this Sunday.

Tammy told him, "Rest. Tomorrow you can get it all done."

Roger said, "I know that you are always here to calm me," and he took her in his arms and kissed her. Tammy had a wonderful meal prepared for the three of them, and Timothy told his father about pre-K. They sat at the table giving the Lord the blessing and then eating the roast beef and potatoes. Roger tried not to worry about it and relax. They watch TV for a while deciding to go to bed early having a busy day tomorrow.

The next day when he got to the funeral home, the coffin had already arrived and the other deacons had set everything up for the view, which Roger was grateful for. There were lots of church members coming in to view the body all day, and all agreed to be there for the funeral services tomorrow. Roger went back to the church to find a pastor calling all the friends from school, but most had already had a church of their own. He was almost at the bottom of the list when his friend Jack Borden said it would be a month before he moved to his new church. He would be happy to serve for a month and maybe they'll find someone by then. Jack also said he would do the service tomorrow since he knew he won't have time to prepare. Roger said he would be grateful and hope to see him before the service to let him know a little about Pastor Evans.

Roger noticed that time had flew, and he needed to get back to the funeral home soon. There was a knock at his office door and he said, "Come in."

A man in his forties caring a briefcase came in. "My name is George Dart. I am here with the life insurance papers you need to sign. I have already talked to Mr. Lyons, your lawyer, and found out the will, so you are having him cremated. So we can go and take care of it all at one time."

Roger said that would be terrific and rose from his desk after signing the papers. The two of them walked back out of the church and Roger said, "Let's go in my car, and I'll bring you back to yours."

They were soon at the funeral home and were brought into the director's office.

"Mr. O'Donnell, are you satisfied with the coffin? And we'll be there tomorrow to pick it up in the urn after the cremation." Roger said that was fine and signed his papers and the director signed the insurance papers and took the check for his services. They shook hands, and Roger brought the insurance guy back to the church. Roger shook hands with him and took the check for the church before Mr. Dart left.

Roger walked back into the church; many members came up to him to shake his hand, and Roger returned to his office. Everything looked good for tomorrow, and he was relieved. Roger spent the rest of the day answering the phone of people calling with their condolences. He was glad when it was time to go home and slipped out before he was stopped by any more people.

Tammy said, "You look exhausted. It must have been a trying day."

Roger said, "I hope you are ready for tomorrow."

Tammy said, "I have everything laid out and have already let the school know that Timothy won't be there tomorrow."

Roger said, "You are a good wife, and I love you. And what's for dinner?"

Tammy laughed and said, "Some romantic you are. Well, I baked a ham and sweet potatoes.

Roger said, "That sounds great."

"Well go wash up and change out of those wet clothes. You sure perspire a lot."

Roger said, "Now who's being romantic?" smiling.

Timothy came in and said, "Dad, are you preaching tomorrow?"

"No. son, a Pastor Dart is. He will be taking over the church for a month."

Timothy said, "I hope he isn't boring."

Roger said, "You know better to judge people before you meet them."

"Sorry, Dad," he said as he looked down at the floor.

"Go wash up. Mom's got a great dinner for us."

The next morning, they got dressed to go to the services and Timothy complained about wearing a suit.

"Now, young man, you must be on your best behavior today."

"Yes, sir, I'll try," he said.

"That's all I can ask, and sit up straight, so you won't fall asleep." Timothy laughed knowing his father was joking with him.

When they got to the services, it was very crowded, and they made their way to the first seats, which were reserved for them. Pastor Dart stood to the right of the casket and waited till everyone was seated.

Pastor Dart started by saying, "We are here to rejoice and moan the passing of our beloved Pastor Evans. He has been with this church almost forty years. I'm sure a lot of you know him and know he is with the Lord. Reading from Romans 8:35, 37–39. Who will separate us from the love of Christ? Will hardship or distress or persecution or famine or nakedness or peril or sword? Know in all these things we are more than conquerors through him who love us.

"For I am convinced that neither death nor life nor angels nor rulers nor present things nor things to come nor powers nor height nor depth nor anything else in all creation will be able to separate us from the love of God in Christ Jesus our Lord. Now we say goodbye to Pastor Evans and hope to be with him in heaven. Roger got up and said he was going to the crematoria and the urn shall be placed over there on the stage of the church, so we can remember him always."

Roger went to the crematory and found out they would deliver the urn sometime today. He went back to his office at the church to wait. Pastor Dart knocked at his door, and Roger told him to come in. He said, "That was a nice sermon, and I appreciate you doing it."

Pastor Dart said, "Thanks, and I'm here to let you know I am working on Sunday's sermon."

Roger said, "I know you will be great." Pastor Dart said thanks as he left Roger's office. They arrived at four o'clock with the urn, and he signed it. Roger then put it on a base on the side of the stage. He decided it was time to go home. Closing the church, he left.

Roger scheduled many part-time pastor through the year and finally settled on a Pastor Dodge from Wisconsin. Roger talked to this pastor on the phone and was convinced that he was the perfect candidate for the church. Pastor Dodge said he had prayed for a church and now God has answered his prayer.

"I must have a few more weeks to take care of everything here."

Roger said that was fine. "Just let me know when you are to be here, and I'll meet you at the airport."

Suddenly, Roger woke up to see his wife sleeping next to him and Timothy who was beside her.

"Son, where are we?" he asked.

"I'm not sure, Dad. I just woke up too, but it looks like a bus station."

Roger saw most of the members of the church around him, but none could answer him on what was going on. He looked across the room and saw a few of the members there, especially when he saw Jennifer who seem to be waiting for someone.

Tammy woke up and was confused and asked her husband if they were going on a trip with other members. Roger asked Pastor Dodge, but he had no clue either.

"All I know so far is we are waiting for a bus."

CHAPTER 9

JENNIFER'S COURTSHIP

Jennifer couldn't understand why John hadn't arrived yet and worried that he might not come before the bus left. Feeling quite tired, she fell back asleep and dreamed of her time with John.

Jennifer woke the next morning to the smell of bacon frying and made her way downstairs. Rita was cooking breakfast telling her she needed to get ready for work. Jennifer thought for a minute and realized she must still be half-asleep. She rushed back upstairs and got in the shower to clear her mind. She remembered that she had just moved in with Rita, and she was expected to be at the church in an hour. After getting dressed in her light blue dress, she went down to breakfast feeling a little hungry. Rita had bacon and eggs on her plate, and Ruby brought over the toast. Jennifer poured herself a cup of coffee before sitting down.

Rita told Ruby she needed to hurry up because the bus would be coming soon. Ruby had on a pair of jeans and a T-shirt of some band that Jennifer didn't know. Then a horn honked outside, and Ruby grabbed up her books and rushed out the door saying, "See you, Mom and Jennifer."

Rita and she finished their breakfast, and Jennifer went to collect her heels. Rita had on a black skirt and a white button-down shirt and was wearing tennis shoes. She asked Jennifer if she was ready to go, and she replied she was. They made their way out of the car and headed to work.

Jennifer saw Mrs. Reed and her son standing in the doorway of the church.

"Good morning, Ms. Worth, when will the rest of the players be here?"

"Oh! They won't be here for another thirty minutes, and did you see Mr. Conner come in? He is coaching the ball team this year."

Mrs. Reed said, "I saw him going to his office."

"Well maybe you should go see him since he has all the answers." Mrs. Reed left Jennifer and headed to Mr. Conner's office. Jennifer went on to her office after telling Rita, "I'll see you at lunch." Jennifer opened her office and went straight to her desk. She logged on to her computer and saw there were no big appointments, and suddenly there was a knock at the door.

Pastor Dodge came in and said, "We all are going out to watch the tryouts. Would you like to come with us?"

Jennifer said, "That would be nice. Let me put some sunscreen on since I burn easy." She went in the bathroom, which was between her office and the pastor's office. Most people didn't know about the bathroom, which was mostly for the staff, and she had overlooked it until now since the pastor told her it was there. Coming back out of the bathroom, she picked up her purse and followed him out the door. The baseball field was on the left side of the church. When they got there, she put on her sunglasses and noticed there were thirty kids with their parents. John was standing out by the pitcher's mount calling all the kids out there.

He said, "First, we'll check your hitting, so everyone on the benches as I call your name step up to the plate, so I can pitch to you." When he had pitched to each one seeing who could hit the ball, he then tried them out in the field. When he said, "That's it now. I'll send you a text on who the nine players will be with five relief players tomorrow. Right now, everybody head for the lunchroom. We are serving hotdogs and Gatorade."

Jennifer started to walk back in when John hurried over to her and asked if she was busy tonight. She said, "I got my first class tonight at eight o'clock."

John said, "I can give you a ride, and I can be there at seven thirty."

Jennifer said, "That would be fine since it's only about ten minutes away. Do you know where Sky View High School is?" she asked.

John said, "Isn't that the one on Old National Highway?"

"Yes, it is, and I'll be there for an hour."

John said, "That's alright. Maybe we can stop for a cup of coffee afterwards. There's a Waffle House just down the street."

Jennifer said she would like that feeling more and more affection for John. She walked back into the church with him. She left him in the lobby and went back to her office. John headed into the lunchroom to be with the team.

Jennifer got busy with answering letters for Pastor Dodge and stopped a few minutes to call June. Jennifer told her how she and John were getting more involved. June told her Jeff was being nice to her, and he brought her flowers after being so mean to her.

Jennifer said, "You will still go with me on Sunday?"

June said she was, but she had to go to Jeff. He wanted this place clean before he gets home. When June hung up, she thought that June would be hurt if it wasn't done. She was still worried about June especially taking drugs.

When work was done, she headed to the lunchroom to go home with Rita. Rita was still cleaning up after the baseball party. Jennifer said, "Let me give you a hand, so we can get out of here."

Rita said, "Thanks. I heard about your class tonight, so I told Ruby to have dinner ready when we get there." Jennifer puts the last of the dishes in the dishwasher while Rita cleans each table in the dining room. When Jennifer walked back in, Rita said, "You ready to go?" They both walked out of the church and got in the car heading home.

Ruby met them at the door, saying, "I made beef stew, and we can eat anytime."

Jennifer said, "Let me take a shower first and change clothes for school, and I'll be right down." She hurried upstairs to her room, taking off her clothes and jumping into the shower. When she got out, she put on a pair of red shorts and a T-shirt. She found a pair of her tennis shoes and slipped them on heading back downstairs. The other two were at the table, and Ruby gave the blessing.

They began to eat, and Ruby said, "Would you like some bread?" which she held on a plate. Jennifer took two and so did Rita. Rita told Ruby that a few of the players were in her school.

Ruby said, "I know. I was the one that told them about the team."

Jennifer said to Ruby, "That stew was great. You are a good cook."

She said, "That's because of my mom, and she always bakes at the church on Wednesdays."

Soon they were finished eating, and Rita said she would help Ruby since she'll be leaving for class soon.

Jennifer hurried out when John was outside honking his horn. He got out to open the door for her before getting back in the car. It took about ten minutes to get to the school. When he got to the school parking lot, he saw there were a few minutes before she had to go in.

John said, "I'll wait for you to get out of class. I have quite a few e-mails to send to the parents of whom I have picked for the team. Hope the parents are not mad at the ones I eliminated. I should be done by the time you get done."

John took her in his arms and kissed her. Jennifer got out of the car and headed into the school.

"Good evening, class. My name is Lee Sterling. I will be your teacher for the next eight weeks. Finally, I hope you have learned enough to pass the test for your GED. You ten students will have to attend every Wednesday to be able to take the test and must buy your book, which is 14.95. I will expect the money at the end of class. Anyone who can't afford the money today can decide after class. Before we get started, I would like each of you to interduce yourself to the class." Mr. Sterling pointed to the first person and said, "Tell us your name."

"My name is Tom and I'm eighteen." The next in line was Margret who was twenty. The third was Jennifer who was nineteen. The fourth was who was next to the oldest being forty. Then followed by Julia being eighteen. The next four were Bob, Roy, Reba, and Ken who was the oldest being sixty. The last one was Tim who was shy and whispered his name.

Mr. Sterling said, "I didn't hear your name."

Reba said his name was Tim, and he turned red in embarrassment. Everybody laughed. Mr. Sterling taught them for an hour after handing out their books that they needed for the class. Nine students brought their money at the end of class except Tim. He asked if he could make payments and was told that was fine. He handed the teacher five dollars before leaving.

Mr. Sterling said, "Study in your books the first chapter for next week, which is history, and have a good night."

When Jennifer got out of the car, John was still on his computer. She got in and asked if he was done.

John said, "I had just finished my emails," closing the computer. He asked how her night went. She said she saw no problems in passing and said if she had any trouble, "I'm sure Ruby would help."

John said, "I could use a cup of coffee. How about you?" Jennifer agreed when he started the car. John drove to the Waffle House just down the street. He held the door for her to get out of the car, including the one into the restaurant. They took a booth in the back seeing that the place was almost deserted. The waitress brought a pot of coffee and filled their cups on the table. She left some cream on the table saying, "Are you ready to order?"

John looked at Jennifer and said, "Are you hungry?" Jennifer said no. John told the waitress, "We are just having coffee."

She said, "If you change your mind, let me know."

When the waitress left, Jennifer said, "Did you have any trouble?"

John said, "Only one parent was not happy. I think the boy's father tried to push him into playing."

The waitress soon returned and said, "Here's your bill. If there isn't anything else?"

John said no and went up and paid. They left the restaurant and headed back to Rita's. Before going in the house, John gave her a kiss goodbye and said, "I'll see you tomorrow."

Ruby was waiting for her and asked how it went. She said, "It was fine, but you need to go to bed. You have school tomorrow, and I must get up early too."

Ruby said good night and headed up the stairs to her room. Jennifer went on up and changed into her nightgown before going to bed. Getting to bed, she thought about John and realized it was becoming serious. Soon closing her eyes, she was fast asleep.

The next morning, Jennifer awoke with Rita calling her. Rita opened the door saying, "There was a storm last night, and we lost electricity and we were running late. We will pick up something on the way to work after we drop off Ruby."

Jennifer got dressed in her pink dress and went to the bathroom to brush her teeth and hair. Going back to her room, she grabbed a pair of white heels and headed downstairs. Both Rita and Ruby were headed out the door. Jennifer slipped on her heels before following them. After dropping off Ruby, they stopped at McDonald's. They got two coffees and two egg McMuffins from the drive-through.

Rita parked her car and went straight to the dining room. Jennifer headed to her office and was stopped in the hall by Roger. "I see you're late this morning," he said.

Jennifer said, "The clock didn't go off because of the storm."

Roger said, "That's why I have a battery-operated one."

Jennifer said, "I might get one."

Pastor Dodge heard them talking in the hall and stuck his head out of his door. He said, "When you get settled, please come in. I have a few letters I need to go out today."

Jennifer went into her office and put her breakfast on the desk before opening her computer. She went into the pastor's office, and he told her that the letters were inviting other teams to come and play against our team. She said she would get them out right away, taking the letters back to her office. She took a little time to finish her breakfast. Suddenly, the phone rang. Picking it up, there was a Mr. Price on the line saying his wife was in an accident. After finding out which hospital, she went in and told Pastor Dodge.

He said, "I'll head for there right away."

She said, "I hope she is alright," and they both left his office. Jennifer returned to her office to take care of the letters. Finishing them, she dropped them in the mail before returning to her office to call Mrs. Price's family to tell them what happen. At lunchtime, she saw John in the hall, and he asked if he could take her home after work.

Jennifer said, "I'll let Rita know that I will be leaving with you." She finished lunch and told Rita, "I'll see you at home."

The rest of the day was quiet with nothing happening, and the pastor hadn't got back by her time to leave.

Jennifer met John in the parking lot, and he drove her home. When they arrived, Ruby was just getting off the bus. Ruby hurried over to the car to say hi to John. "Why don't you both come to dinner with me?"

Jennifer said, "It was alright," wanting to be with John.

Ruby said, "Let me drop my books and write my mom a note." They waited in the car while she went inside. Ruby dropped her books on the kitchen table and got a piece of paper out of her notebook.

"Dear mom, went to dinner with John and Jennifer. They said they would bring you something back."

In the car, Jennifer asked how she was doing in school. Ruby said she was making straight A's. Jennifer said that was great. Ruby said, "The only thing is I have no friends. They are always picking on me calling me the teacher's pet. The only one who doesn't pick on me is Susie, but they make fun of her too."

Jennifer said, "They are just jealous, and teenagers are somewhat cruel." Jennifer said, "You should invite Susie to your house. She needs a friend just like you."

Ruby said, "You are probably right, and I'll ask her tomorrow."

The traffic was quite heavy, and John said, "Shall we stop at McDonald's since it is closer to the house?" They said it would be alright. He pulled into the parking lot and helped both of them out of the car. John went up and ordered him and Jennifer a Big Mac meal and a Quarter Pounder meal for Ruby. They gave him a number and three cups after paying. He brought the cups to the table, and each took turns filing their drinks. Soon they called his number, and John went up and collected their trays. After finishing eating, he went an ordered a Big Mac meal for Rita. When he got her food, they went back to the car headed home.

Ruby went on into the house, and Jennifer and John stayed in the car. Rita started screaming at her saying, "Where have you been?"

Ruby sat Rita's food on the kitchen table looking for her note. She found it on the floor and picked it up; she handed it to her mother. "I'm sorry, Mom, it must have fallen off the table."

Rita gave her a hug after reading the note. "I'm sorry for screaming at you. I was just scared and worried."

When Jennifer entered the house, Rita noticed that her cheek flushed and said, "I see you two are getting serious."

Jennifer remarked, "I think so too."

Rita followed Jennifer up to her room, saying, "I'm sorry for that. I do worry about her a lot."

Jennifer said, "Don't worry. I'll protect her, and it's nice that we became friends."

There was a knock at her door, and Ruby walked in and said, "Mom, I finished my homework. Is it alright if I invite my friend Susie?"

"Sure, dear, I would like to meet your girlfriend."

Ruby said, "It was Jennifer's idea, and I thought it was a good idea." Ruby went back to her room.

Rita said, "I'm glad you are getting her out of her shell. I couldn't get her to go nowhere. She always wanted to stay at home."

Jennifer changed in her nightgown of blue and said, "Let's go watch some TV since I'm not tired, and it's too early to go to bed." The two made their way downstairs and turned on the TV. Rita decided to make some popcorn; the smell brought Ruby downstairs. The three sat watching and eating popcorn. Soon it was eleven and the news was coming on.

Ruby said, "I need to go to bed. I have school tomorrow." She left after the weather report, which was still in the nineties and no rain.

Jennifer said, "Good night. See you tomorrow." Rita watched the rest of the news before turning it off and headed to bed.

Jennifer opened her eyes the next morning to the smell of coffee, noticing that she had plenty of time to get ready for work. She brushed her teeth and took out a white blouse and black skirt. Putting them on, she made her way barefooted downstairs to the kitchen. Ruby was eating cereal and Rita was drinking coffee when she walked in.

Rita said, "There's a cup on the counter to make you a cup of coffee, and there's some donuts next to the pot if you are hungry."

Jennifer went over, made herself some coffee, and took a glazed donut and sat down. Soon the bus honked. Ruby grabbed up her book bag. She said goodbye to Jennifer and gave her mom a kiss before rushing out the door. Rita was surprised saying she hasn't done that in a long time, so I guess it's a good thing for you to be around.

Jennifer laughed and said, "I guess we better get ready for work. Rita headed upstairs to take a shower and get dressed. Jennifer got up and put on some lipstick and bushed her hair. She slipped on her red high heels, as Rita came out of her room wearing a blue pantsuit saying, "You ready to go?" Jennifer said that she was, and they headed to the car.

When they arrived at the church, Rita headed to the kitchen, and Jennifer went the other way to her office. In the hallway, she ran into Roger, and he said, "Good morning, Jennifer. So how's the new place? I'm sure it's better than that motel."

Jennifer smiled and said, "I like it a lot being with Rita and her daughter." Jennifer went on to her office and logged on to her computer.

John stopped in for a minute for a kiss and to tell her he loved her. Jennifer sat there after he left and realized that she was falling in love too.

Suddenly, Jennifer woke up when someone said hello, looking around; she didn't know where she was and saw Jim Rhodes standing over her.

"I'm sorry if I woke you. I was just wondering why I was here in this bus station. The last thing I remember was we were at Sunday services."

Jennifer thought about that for a minute and sort of remembered seeing him there with his wife and suddenly it faded away. Jennifer noticed his wife was over on the other side of the room with Pastor Dodge, which confused her even more and wondered why John was there.

CHAPTER 10

JIM RHODES

Jim said, "I thought you would be next to the pastor instead of your best friend."

Jennifer said, "I'm mostly waiting for John, and I tried to go over there but something stopped me. The ticket man said my bus was over here not over there."

"Well, I guess we're on the same bus, and I can't understand why Lottie is over there with them. You know I'm great friends with Pastor Dodge and attend church with you every Sunday. I know you if you remember, you turned me down for a job."

Jim laughed. "Yes, now that I remember, it's been a while." Jim said, "You weren't born here in Georgia. I was up north in Athens with my parents and brothers and sister."

Jennifer said, "I was an only child," and turned away from him and went back to sleep.

Jim sat there watching her sleep and wanting to be with his wife, but when he called over to her, it seemed like she wasn't listening. Sitting there alone, he started remembering growing up. They had a white wooden house on the outside of town that their father bought working as a firefighter. He remembered that he was a little afraid of him, always towering over him with his rough voice. He was six-foot-two and weighed at least over two hundred pounds. His father had brown curly hair and blue eyes, and when he was mad at them, Jim swore that shark swam in them. Jim thought it was funny that his parents were obsessed with the letter J since his father's name was John, and his mom was Janet. My brothers' names were James and John, and his sister was Jenny. He was the youngest in the family. Jenny his sister was beautiful and looked a lot like her mother with blond hair and blue eyes. The two older brothers were very tall like their father and with the same hair color and blue eyes. He was a little different only in size being as short as his mother being five-three and skinny.

He didn't have much to do with girls and was embarrassed when Jenny kissed him. He knew that the other two boys were playing around with her and was told if he said anything, they would beat him up. They were a little jealous of him because Jenny paid him more attention. Maybe because he didn't take advantage of her. She would never let them pick on him all through elementary. James turned eighteen and join the Army and didn't see his family again till his father died. It was a sad day when he died in the line of duty, and they gave his mother a medal. He had entered a burning house and rescued a small child, but he passed out after getting the child to safety. Between smoke inhalations, his heart gave out. They rushed him to the hospital, but it was too late.

Mom took it hard even after they said he was a hero. The next tragedy broke her, and she died of a heart attack when she found out that James was missing in action. Johnny had applied for the Police Academy in Los Angeles and went back after their mother's funeral. Jenny stayed in Athens becoming a nurse in St. Mary's. The fire department paid for his tuition to University of Georgia School of Law. So he had to find a place to live in Atlanta and spent nights working in Burger King to pay the rent.

After three years, he graduated, and his sister Jenny was there at his graduation. She spent two days with him before returning to Athens. It took another four years working for the district attorney before he could open my own office. While working with the district attorney, he lost his first case, which was laughed at by the staff. The district attorney's name was Devon James. He was very understanding but said maybe he should try something else. He applied with a corporate law firm of Thomas, Forrester, and Associates. They started him as an intern and gave him a secretary that was a gold digger. Her name was Velda Adams; she was very beautiful with long blond hair and blue eyes.

She was always wearing short skirts and low-cut blouses. She was tempting, but he ignored her advances. She finally flirted with Mr. Forrester. Tom took to her advances and asked the trade secretaries with which he agreed. His new secretary was Ms. Rose and helped him a lot to win cases.

Jim soon found a one-room apartment at the Embarcadero club. There were a lot of better places, then the ones had lived in, and now that he had a better income becoming partner in the firm. The apartments were on Sullivan Road, not far from work and had quite a lot of extras. The buildings were light tan, and each had their own balcony. Jim had bought some patio furniture, so he could sit out there when he got home. His parents hadn't taught him to cook so he would have food delivered from different restaurants in the area. Before, all he had was TV dinners and was glad to get away from them. Some nights he would go to the gym and workout and swim in the pool.

The first thing he did when he got his raise was he went out and bought a car. Jim went to a Ford dealer and got a gray Ford Focus, which he made a sizeable down payment on and got low monthly payments. The building had underground parking that the law firm was in. He had to pay a monthly fee to park there. The only bad feature was there no elevator from the garage, and you had to walk out front to the lobby. Jim had just arrived at work and said hello to Bob, the parking attendant, after walking back to the street. Bob was a rather old guy in his fifties, but he was very friendly and loved to talk to everyone.

Jim walked into the lobby seeing a beautiful woman waiting for the elevator. While they waited for the elevator to arrive, Jim couldn't keep his eyes off her. He knew that he had to know her. She had long red hair and bright green eyes and could tell she had a lovely figure. When they finally got on the elevator, he spoke up, "My name is Jim Rhodes. I'm a lawyer on the fifth floor."

She looked at him and smiled, saying, "My name is Lottie Sherman. I'm the accountant for Regis Inc. on the sixth floor." There wasn't much time to say anything else since the doors were opening on the fifth floor.

Jim said, "I hope to see you around again sometime."

Lottie laughed and said, "That wouldn't be hard since we're a floor apart."

He laughed saying, "That's true. See you later." The doors closed, and he headed to his office still thinking about her.

Each morning, they would meet, and he hadn't got enough nerve up to ask her for a date. He knew she wasn't seeing anybody at the time.

One day he was called into Mr. Thomas office. Jim knocked at his door and was asked to come in.

"Mr. Thomas, did you want to see me?"

"Yes, Mr. Rhodes. Take a seat," he said.

"Do you know about Regis Inc. on the sixth floor?"

"Yes, sir, it's an accounting firm."

"Well, it has come to our attention from the manager, Mr. Brown, that they are being sued by Mrs. Westcott, and I would like you to handle the case. You have a meeting with Mr. Brown in about a half-hour, and he will give you the details."

"Thank you, sir. I'll get right on it," he said and returned to his office. While preparing to go to the appointment, he was hoping that he would have a moment to see Lottie.

He told Ms. Rose where he was going, and he told her to look up anything she could find on a Mrs. Westcott.

She said, "I'll get right on it."

He said, "Good. When I get back, we'll go over the details."

Jim walked to the elevator a little excited hoping he could ask Lottie for a date. The first person he ran into was Lottie, and he smiled and said he had an appointment with Mr. Brown.

She said, "I was the one to suggest your firm to look over the problem and was surprised that they sent you. Well, come this way so we can talk to Mr. Brown since it involves me."

Walking into Mr. Brown's office, he got up from the desk and shook hands telling him to take a seat.

"Now, Ms. Sherman, would you tell him the particulars of the case?"

"Well," Lottie said, "Mrs. Westcott came to us and wanted us to invest some of her money in stock. We said we could, but she insisted that we go through this certain brokerage. We advised her not to and that we could find a better one. See, Roberts & Sons had pulled some shady deals in the past, giving them a bad reputation. We did what she requested, and they advised her of a bad stock. Because going through us, she made it our fault instead of the brokerage firm. She came in here with her lawyer accusing us of steering her wrong and upsetting me. So, are you willing to represent us?"

Jim said, "This is an easy case since she insisted on doing it her way, and you did get her to sign papers to that. I will get my secretary to file a case with Judge Roland. You know, Ms. Sherman, you will have to be in court and testify."

Mr. Brown said, "I'm sure Ms. Sherman will help in any way she can."

Leaving Mr. Brown's office, they walked together to the elevator. Lottie said, "I appreciate your help in this matter."

"Well, there is one thing you could do," he said, "would you have dinner with me?"

Lottie smiled and said, "I was wondering how long it would be before you asked me out, and yes, I will." She went over to the receptionist's desk and wrote down her address saying, "I'll see you at eight." He laughed as she handed him the paper on the way to the elevator.

When he got to his floor, he told Ms. Rose, "We will need information on Roberts & Sons." He then went into his office and looked at the paper. The address wasn't far from here; it was 860 Glenwood Ave. He called up Arias and made a reservation. Jim sat there glad he finally got a date with her and spent time going over the details Ms. Rose had found out about Mrs. Westcott.

After reviewing the case, he called Robert Shaw, the lawyer that was representing Mrs. Westcott. "Hello, Mr. Shaw, I'm attorney Jim Rhodes. I represent Regis Inc. Going over your case, I'd advise your client to try to sue Roberts & Sons because this firm recorded their interview with your client, and she gave them no choice in the matter. If you take this to court, you will end up paying court costs."

Mr. Shaw said, "You are right, so I'll get Mrs. Westcott to change her suit to them instead. I appreciate you bringing this to my attention."

Jim said, "No problem. I hope it will give you less paperwork."

Mr. Shaw laughed. "Well, thanks. Maybe we should have lunch sometime."

Jim said, "That would be fine. I would like to see how you made out."

Mr. Shaw said, "Call me Robert, and I'll give you a call when it's over."

Jim got on the intercom and told Ms. Rose, "You can stop your research. Her lawyer withdrew his suit with us. You can wrap things up and can go home a little bit early."

Ms. Rose thanked him, saying, "My daughter was waiting to go shopping."

"Oh! Is she here?"

"Yes, sitting here waiting for me."

Jim came out and Ms. Rose introduced her daughter Cilla. "Nice to meet you. I didn't know she had a daughter."

Cilla said, "She adopted me from the orphanage when I was ten."

Jim was impressed with Ms. Rose, and he told Cilla how much. "Well, you too run along. Hope you have a good evening." When they had left, he was even more glad that Mr. Forrester had changed secretaries. Jim packed up his stuff and headed home.

When Jim got home, he headed straight to the shower after dropping his sweaty suit in the laundry. He thought this was the hottest month yet while he washed himself. Walking naked into the bedroom, he pulled out a nice blue suit out of the closet. He ran his electric razor over his face and put on some Brut cologne. It was just turning seven when he put on his suit and a pair of black shoes. Grabbing his keys from the living room table, he headed out the door.

Jim arrived early, and Lottie invited him in to wait for her to get ready. He started looking around her apartment. The first thing he saw was the yellow couch in the living room, which didn't match the green rug. The apartment seemed small to be a one-bedroom. There was a kitchen in front of him, which had a small table with two chairs. Jim wandered into the bedroom. It had two twin beds on either side of a nightstand. There were two doors in the room, and he could hear Lottie in one door, which must be the bathroom. Jim opened the other door, which was a small closet stuff with clothes and shoes. Jim returned to the living room and saw a small TV on a stand on the other side of the room. There was a coffee table in front of the couch and that was all the furniture in that room. There was only one window in the living room and one in the bedroom.

When Lottie came out of the bathroom, she was dressed in a short-sleeved blue dress. She went to the closet and got a pair of black heels and put them on. She went out to the living room where Jim was waiting.

Jim said that she looked lovely and asked, "Who lives here with you?"

Lottie said, "This is really my sister's apartment. We are just sharing the rent."

Jim led her out the door to his car, which he opened for her. Soon they were on their way to the restaurant.

It took fifteen minutes to get there through heavy traffic, and they had little to say on the way. When they pulled up to the restaurant, a valet was waiting. Jim got out, opening the door for Lottie, and handed the keys to the valet. Walking hand in hand, they entered the restaurant. The maître d' was waiting, asking if he could help them. Jim said he had a reservation under Rhodes.

He checked his list and said, "Very good. Please follow me." He led them to a table with a white tablecloth sitting almost in the center of the room and said, "A waiter will be here shortly."

The waiter showed up and handed them the menus and said, "What would you like to drink?" Jim replied saying they would like a good red wine. The waiter said, "Would you like any appetizer with your wine?"

Jim said, "No. That will be all for now." The waiter left, returning shortly with the wine, pouring Jim a little. Jim tasted it and said it was good, and the waiter filled both of their glasses.

"Now, sir, what can I get you?"

Jim said, "We would like the lobster dinner with baked potato and salad."

"What would you like for your salad, sir?"

Jim said he would like blue cheese. "Is that alright with you, dear?"

Lottie said that would be fine except she wanted ranch on her salad. The waiter said it was very good, taking the menus and heading to put in their order.

While she sipped her wine waiting for dinner, Lottie said, "My sister Helen was out when you got there, or I would have introduced you. We were born in Valdosta. I was attending college in Athens while my sister got a job with Regis Inc. here in Atlanta. When I graduated, she begged me to come live with her. She was having a hard time keeping up the rent and said she could get me a job with the company. That way we could share the rent and be close to each other."

Jim said, "It's funny that we haven't run into each other since I was born in Athens."

Soon their food arrived, and they began to eat. The lobster was delicious, which seemed to melt in his mouth. Jim watched her eat and was thinking how beautiful she was, and he felt very attracted to her and hoped their relationship would go further. When they finished, Jim asked for the bill. The waiter returned with a packet with the bill inside. Jim slipped his credit card in and handed it back to the waiter. Jim finished his wine while waiting and when the waiter returned, Jim put a sizable tip on the paper. Jim got up and held the chair for her to get up.

Lottie was thinking he was quite a gentleman and hoping he would ask her out again. Jim took her hand and led her outside and asked the valet for his car. When the valet brought the car, Jim opened the door for her and took the keys from the valet, giving him a ten-dollar tip. The valet said, "Thank you, sir, and hope you come again."

Jim got in the car and headed back to her apartment. When they arrived, he walked her to the door, giving her a kiss before leaving. Lottie enjoyed the kiss and wanted to have him come in but knew her sister was probably home. Jim drove away knowing he wanted to see more of her.

Jim woke up the next morning in a good mood remembering about last night. He was a bad cook, so after getting dressed, he headed to McDonald's for breakfast. He went through the drive-through and got a coffee with cream and sugar plus an egg croissant. Jim made it to the office in plenty of time. He met Ms. Rose at the entrance to his office and she said that Mr. Thomas wanted to see him. That made Jim rather nervous wondering if he had done anything wrong. He knocked on Mr. Thomas's office and was told to come in. Mr. Thomas told him to sit down. Jim knew Mr. Thomas had been a lawyer for thirty years and was in his sixties. He wore his gray hair with pride, not ever thinking of dyeing it.

Jim said, "What can I do for you, sir?"

He told him not to worry. "I just have a new case for you and a question, but you been here long enough you can call me Randy."

"Thanks, sir—I mean Randy," Jim said, correcting himself.

"The first thing is the question. You see that when you traded secretaries with Mr. Forrester, his practice went downhill. She was a big distraction for him and got him in hot water with his wife. Mrs. Jane Forrester came to me to complain. I told Tom he would have to let her go. He reluctantly agreed, especially to save his marriage. The problem is he wants his old secretary back."

Jim said, "I'd rather not, sir. She's a big help."

Mr. Thomas smiled, looking through his glasses with a sparkle in his blue eyes and said., "I told him you would not. I interviewed another lady who had quite a lot of experience and is an older lady. I sent Mrs. Murray to take over as his secretary, and seeing her, he requested yours."

Jim laughed. "I suppose she's not a beauty to look at."

Randy said, "Between you and me, she is quite plain, but she will be efficient at her job, which he needs."

"Are you done with the Mrs. Westcott case?"

"Yes, Randy. Her lawyer decided to sue the brokerage instead."

"Well, I'm glad since I have a new case for you. There is an employee of Capstone that got hurt on the job, and I need you to investigate to see who is at fault. They are hoping not to have a big lawsuit. They want you to check it out and see if they can come to a settlement without bringing dragged through court."

Jim said he would get right on it. Jim left and returned to his office. Going up to Ms. Rose's desk, he said, "I need the address of Capstone and for you to get in touch with the manager."

Soon, Ms. Rose called on the intercom saying, "Mr. Mosley is on line three."

Jim picked up the phone and said, "I'm Jim Rhodes from Thomas, Forrester, and Associates. I have heard about your problem, is it alright if I come out and talk to the people involved?"

Mr. Mosley said that would be fine. Jim hung up the phone and told Ms. Rose he would be out of the office for the rest of the day. Jim said, "I wanted to ask you if you would like to work for me, or would you want to return to Mr. Forrester? Before you answer, I told Mr. Thomas that you were a great help, and I really didn't want to lose you."

Ms. Rose got a tear in her eye, saying, "I like working with you and rather stay."

Jim smiled, saying, "Thank you, and I'm sure I'll see about getting you a raise."

Ms. Rose said, "You don't have to go to that trouble. I'm satisfied."

Jim said, "I'm still going to."

Ms. Rose thanked him as he turned and walked out of the office. Jim seen that the company was on Sullivan Road, which was about fifteen minutes from the office. It took him almost twenty-five minutes because of traffic. Jim first went into the warehouse to find the supervisor who was in charge. It took him some time to find Mr. Robertson; he was telling a worker to get that truck loaded.

"Hello, Mr. Robertson, I'm the attorney assigned to this case. I would like to know the details about the accident and how I can get in touch with your employees."

"Well, sir, it was a stupid mistake on Bob's part. He needed to adjust his forks on the forklift, which he left running. The forklift slipped out of gear and ran over his foot crushing it. One other person jumped on the forklift and stopped it."

"Well, I will need you to testify in court and need someone to check that forklift for problems." Mr. Robertson said he would get the maintenance to look at it over right away.

Jim warned him, "If there is something wrong with it, do not fix it or there will be a bigger lawsuit than there is now. If something is wrong with it, we may be able to settle out of court." Jim left him standing there and walked back to his car.

It was time for lunch and decided to take the rest of the day off. There was a park nearby, and he decided to take a walk and think about Lottie. There was a hot dog stand in the park, and he went up and bought two and a drink. He sat down at the nearest bench and began to eat. It was a warm day, and the birds were singing in the trees and a squirrel was watching him to see if he dropped any morsel for him. Jim was starting to realize how much he cared about Lottie and hoped someday to make her his wife. He got up and strolled around the park for an hour seeing all the children out there playing, thinking, *Someday I'll have a boy to play ball with*, which brought a smile to his face. It was now time to go home and thought he might like to have a steak for dinner. He got in his car and headed to LongHorn.

When he got there, it seemed everybody had the same idea and had to wait almost an hour before he got a table. He ordered a rib eye dinner with a salad and baked potato. He had ordered a beer and sat there thinking about that day. When the waiter arrived with his dinner, he ordered another beer. He sat there eating his dinner and drinking his beer. When he was done, he thought of ordering another beer but thought against the idea. He sure didn't want to be pulled over on his way home knowing that he would get a DUI. He gave the waiter a healthy tip after paying the bill and headed back to his apartment.

When he got home, he removed his clothes and showered the sweat of the day from his body. He got into a pair of light blue pajamas and gave Lottie a call. Her sister Helen picked up the phone and asked who was calling.

"This is Jim Rhodes. Is Lottie at home?"

Helen said, "Just give her a minute. She'll be right with you."

Jim said, "Thanks and hope to meet you one day."

Helen said, "I would too after all the things my sister has to say about you."

Jim laughed just as Lottie picked up the phone. "Were you laughing at me?" she said.

Jim got defensive and said, "No. I'm sorry. I was laughing at something your sister said. I was calling to ask you out tomorrow night. I'd really like to see you."

Lottie said that would be fine. What did you have in mind?"

"I thought we could go bowling and you could bring your sister."

Lottie said, "Just a minute. I'll go ask her," and she left the phone. She was back in a few moments saying, "She would like to meet you and bowling sounds fun."

Jim said, "That will be great. I'll make it for eight, and we can go to dinner beforehand."

Lottie said, "So what time are you coming for us?"

"Well, I thought a little before six thirty." Lottie told her sister and she said that would be fine. Jim thought about her for a while and then brushed his teeth and went to bed.

The next morning, he woke to the alarm. He went in the kitchen and got the coffeepot perk. He went into the bedroom and put on his gray suit with a red tie. Before he put on his shoes and socks, he went back in the kitchen. There were some jelly-filled donuts on the counter; he got two and ate them with his coffee. He got up and went into the bathroom and brushed his teeth and hair. Putting on his shoes, he went out to the parking attendant to get his car to head to the office. Jim had made friends with the attendant who saw him coming rushing to get the keys and bringing the car around.

Jim said, "Hello, George. How's it going?"

George got out of the car and smiled and said it was a nice day. Jim handed him a five-dollar tip and got in the car and said goodbye and drove off. George watched him go thinking he was a good man; most of the tenants never even gave him the time of day let alone a tip. George always went out of his way to make sure that Mr. Rhodes' car was clean.

When Jim got to the office, Ms. Rose told him there was a call from Mr. Mosley. Jim told her he would call him back. Jim called back and a woman answered the phone saying, "This is Capstone. May I help you?"

"You can. I'm returning a call from your Mr. Mosley."

She said, "Hold on a minute." There was a click on the phone, and Mr. Mosley picked up.

"I was calling to tell you that Mr. Robertson checked, and the forklift was faulty. We would like to make a settlement with Mr. Bradley. We will fax over the proposal and Mr. Bradley's address and phone number. Soon Ms. Rose brought in the fax.

Jim looked it over and said, "Can you make an appointment with Mr. Bradley?" She copied down his phone number and said she would call. Ms. Rose soon returned and said he'll be here at ten o'clock tomorrow. He was having a doctor's appointment today.

Jim said, "That is fine, and you can go to lunch now." Ms. Rose thanked him and left. Jim thought about asking Lottie to lunch, but he would see her tonight and he didn't want to push her. There was a Subway on the first floor and decided that would be fine. Making his way to the first floor, he entered the restaurant. He ordered a BLT sub and chips and a drink and sat there eating till it was time to go back to work. The rest of the day was kind of slow, nothing to do but read over the fax. At four, he told Ms. Rose to go home and he would close up.

She said, "I already made the reservations at the bowling alley and Outback." He called to thank her as she walked out the door. Jim turned off the computers and lights and locked his door. He headed down to the garage to go home.

Jim was home about five, and he went and took a shower to get ready for tonight. He had plenty of time and went into the kitchen and sat and relaxed with a glass of ice tea. It was almost six when he decided to leave and went and got his car from James since George had already left for the evening. Jim drove to Lottie's apartment and was there by six fifteen.

A woman came to the door when he knocked who had to be Helen. She had the same red hair and green eyes as Lottie but was much older. She looked him up and down and said, "You must be Jim. Come in." Helen said, "Lottie will be here in a minute." Helen had on a pair of blue jeans and a T-shirt saying, "Is this alright sort of modeling it?"

Jim smiled and said, "You look fine."

Lottie walked in and said, "You flirting with my sister?" Jim turned a little red and the girls laughed. Lottie had on jeans and a T-shirt too saying, "Shall we go?"

He told them they had a reservation at Outback at six forty-five. They walked out to the car, and Jim held the doors for each of them.

When they got to Outback, it was quite crowded, and he was saying thanks to Ms. Rose. It was only a five-minute wait before they were ushered to a table. They decided since they were going bowling that they would drink ice tea. After the tea was served, Jim ordered a sirloin steak with French fries. Both Helen and Lottie got a rib eye and baked potato. Jim told Lottie that the case on her was dropped. She was quite happy to hear that, which made her evening more enjoyable. The waiter returned with helpers to serve their food and asked if they needed any steak sauce. Jim said no but Lottie asked for A1. The waiter returned with it saying, "Enjoy your meal." They had finished eating by seven thirty, and Jim asked for the check. Jim paid with his credit card and gave a nice tip. They left the restaurant and headed to the bowling alley.

The attendant of the bowling alley gave them lane four and asked their shoe sizes. Jim got a ten in men's while Lottie got an eight in women's and her sister a seven. They played several games and Helen, being a better bowler, beat them both. Jim felt he hadn't done bad with an advantage of 190. Leaving the alley and returning the shoes, Jim paid the bill. Walking out of the car, Helen was picking on them saying how bad they did against her. They were all laughing as they got in the car.

When they got home, Helen made an excuse to hurry in knowing that they wanted to be alone. When she left, Jim took her in his arms and gave her a passionate kiss, which made her feel warm inside. She knew it took everything in her power not to bring him into the house. Lottie knew she had to go; after a few more kisses, she would give in.

She said, "I must get some sleep for tomorrow," and Jim knew it was true, but he was reluctant to let her go. Jim walked her to the door, giving her one last kiss before letting her go. He went back to his car and drove home and thought seriously of looking for an engagement ring for her.

Jim had gone home and straight to bed. The next morning, he felt great and got up with a smile remembering his date last night. He went and started the coffeepot before taking a shower. He put on his gray suit for today with a green tie then headed back to the kitchen for a cup of coffee. He sat down and drank his coffee and thought how beautiful Lottie was and so was her sister. He finished his coffee, put on his shoes and socks, and he headed to the parking garage. George was on duty and said good morning. Jim said it was a lovely day as he took the keys from George. George thought it was too hot already this morning and didn't make a comment to Mr. Rhodes. Jim tipped him more than usual, so George's mood improved. He told Jim to have a great day as Jim drove out of the parking lot.

When Jim got to work, he was a little disappointed since Lottie wasn't standing at the elevator. When he got upstairs, Ms. Rose greeted him and said, "Don't forget Mr. Bradley will be here in an hour."

He called Lottie and said, "How about lunch at eleven?" Lottie said she would come downstairs at eleven. He told her he loved her and hung up.

Just before ten, Ms. Rose called him on the intercom to inform him that Mr. Bradley was there. Jim told her to show him in. Mr. Bradley was on crutches and followed Ms. Rose into the office. Jim got up and shook hands, offering him a seat.

Jim said, "I have reviewed your case, and the company will offer you five thousand and pay for all your medical expenses. They also said if you agree to this term that you will be able to return to work after your recovery. If you rather you pursue your suit, they are pretty sure you'll end up with nothing since it was your negligence for leaving the forklift running."

Mr. Bradley said he would accept these terms only if they were in writing.

Jim said, "I will have the proposal write up and signed by tomorrow if you would stop in tomorrow. I'll hand the papers to you signed and notarized." Mr. Bradley got up and offered his hand and said he would see him tomorrow. When Mr. Bradley walked out, he called Ms. Rose to come in.

Jim told her, "Write up the agreement and take it to Capstone and have Mr. Mosley sign it, but first find out if they have a notary public. If not, take ours with you. When you get that done, just drop them at the office and take the rest of the day off." Ms. Rose said she would get it done and thanks for letting her off for the rest of that day. He heard Ms. Rose finishing typewriting and left. Jim looked up at the clock and saw it had just turned eleven. He was turning off his computer when Lottie walked in. Jim noticed she had on a purple dress and white heels and commented that she looked good. She laughed and said, "You ready to go?" Jim got up from the desk and gave her a quick kiss before heading to lunch.

They headed down to the first floor to the Subway, which was in the building. The temperature outside had reached the nineties, and so it was wise to eat in the building instead of going any place else. Lottie ordered a BLT meal, and Jim ordered an Italian sub with only a drink. They sat and talked about their date last night.

Lottie looked down at her watch and said, "I need to get back to work." They finished up their food, and Jim walked her back to the elevator and rode upstairs together. Jim got off at the fifth floor and headed to his office. There were no more appointments for that day, so he left early.

Jim got home and saw the morning paper sitting at his door. He forgot a boy came around and told him to getting it. He went inside and sat down and looked over the paper. He looked in the entertainment section to see that *The Amazing Spiderman 2* was playing at the theater. Jim thought that he wanted to be with Lottie, and this would be a good excuse. He noticed that she wouldn't be home for a couple more hours. Jim went and took a shower and sat down and watched a Steve Martin movie on TV. He looked at his watch and saw that she must be home by now.

Jim called her on the phone and said, "Do you have anything to do tonight?"

Lottie said, "Not really. Helen has a date tonight."

He said, "How about we go and see the new Spiderman movie?"

Lottie said, "Sure. What time is it playing?"

Jim said, "We can go to the eight-thirty showing and maybe grab a bit to eat before we go."

Lottie looked at the clock, seeing it was five-thirty, she said, "Give me an hour."

Jim said, "That would be fine, and I love you," before hanging up. Lottie said she did too and put down the receiver, heading to the bathroom for a shower.

Jim showed up at her door at six forty-five, but she still made him wait for about fifteen minutes. He told her she didn't have to get dressed up because he was wearing jeans and a blue polo shirt. Lottie wore a white blouse and a black skirt, which was barely above the knees, and wore a pair of blue tennis shoes.

She said, "I'm glad. My feet were hurting from those heels."

"I thought we would stop and get a burger from Wendy's since it's right around the corner from the movies."

Lottie said, "I think that's a great idea. Don't want my stomach growling during the movie."

Jim laughed and said, "Shall we go?" He led her out to the car and held the door for her. It took them a half hour to get to the restaurant because of the traffic. Since the movie didn't start for an hour, they decided to eat inside the restaurant as also it was still quite hot outside. Lottie ordered a double cheeseburger meal since she had not had anything since lunch. Jim did too, but he wasn't that hungry since he had a snack before picking her up. They had a conversation about work and ate. Seeing it was eight, they said they should get over to the movie since there may be a line. Walking over to the theater, they saw that they were right. By the time they got the tickets and a box of popcorn, the movie was already showing previews. Jim found them two seats in the middle of the theater. Lottie held the popcorn on her lap since Jim wouldn't let go of her hand. He laughed because she kept feeding him popcorn with her other hand.

Lottie made sure he didn't distract her from the movie. After the movie was over, she said, "It was good, but when I go to a movie, I want to see the picture. Lots of people never see the picture spending all their time making out." Jim understood and didn't get his feelings hurt. Lottie said as they got in the car that she would make out with him, but that was all. Her parents raised her a Christian and nothing would happen till they were married.

Jim thought to himself well that was what was on his mind, so he would look for an engagement ring soon. When they got to her apartment, they sat in the car a while kissing. Lottie soon told him she had to go in, and Jim got out of the car. He opened the door for her and walked her up to the door. He gave her a hug and kiss saying good night. Jim went back to the car feeling warm all over and knew she was the one for him. He got in his apartment and feeling a little lonely without her and went straight to bed.

Jim entered the office the next day still thinking about getting a ring. Mr. Bradley was in the waiting room.

Jim said, "Give me a few minutes, and I'll be right with you. And, Ms. Rose, will you come with me?" Ms. Rose followed him into the office, and he said, "Did you get the documents and check?"

She said, "They are on your desk, and you have an eleven o'clock appointment with a Pastor Dodge."

"Did he tell you what he wanted?"

"No, sir, all I know he's from the United Methodist Church."

"Well, you can send Mr. Bradley."

He came in and sat down, and Jim handed him the agreement, which Mr. Bradley looked over before signing. Jim took the papers and handed over the check. Mr. Bradley smiled looking at the check saying he was glad to do business with him and would recommend him to his friends. Mr. Bradley got up and Jim went over and shook his hand and opened the door for him to leave.

At eleven, Ms. Rose buzzed him saying, "Your appointment is here."

Jim came out and shook hands with the pastor, saying, "How can I help you?"

Pastor Dodge followed him into the office and took a seat across from Jim, saying, "My church would like to hire you for legal advice on a permanent basis."

Jim asked, "Who recommend me?"

"We have an accountant who met you in college. He said your law school was on the same campus as his Christian college. You might remember him. His name is John Conner."

"I do. We were always hanging around together. He was one of my best friends."

"Well, would you consider being our lawyer? You don't have to make up your mind right away, but come out to our church and look around."

Jim said, "I'm free Monday morning if that's alright with you, and I would like to see John again."

Pastor Dodge said, "That will be great. We'll see you Monday." He got up and shook hands and left. Jim went out and told Ms. Rose he would be out of the office on Monday. Jim called upstairs to ask if Lottie was free for lunch. Lottie got on the phone and said she would be right down.

They had lunch at Subway again ordering the same thing from the other day. Jim told her about his visit from the pastor. Lottie said, "If you don't mind, I'll go with you. I was looking for a church to attend." He said he would love to have her go with him. After lunch, there wasn't much to do but a lot of paperwork. When he was finished, he looked up at the clock and it was time to go.

Jim stopped at the drive-through of Burger King on the way home. He got two Whoppers with cheese to take home for dinner and got a Coke for now, being thirsty from the heat. When he arrived at his apartment, he handed over the keys to George and took his stuff upstairs. Jim decided to take a shower first and put on a pair of shorts. He made himself a glass of tea and sat down on the couch to watch some TV. After about an hour, he put on his whoopers in the microwave and ate, watching one of his favorite shows. He called Lottie to say a good night, and he loved her and would see her in the morning. She said that she did love him too. After hanging up, he returned to his show. After a while, he was ready for bed. He turned off the TV and he headed to the bedroom. It didn't take him long to fall asleep.

When he woke up in the morning, it was Friday, and he had the whole weekend off; and he would go shopping for an engagement ring. Lottie was waiting for him when he got to work and he asked, "Do you have any plans for the weekend?"

"Me and Helen thought we would pack lunch and go hiking at high falls tomorrow."

"Well, I did want to do some shopping, but I think I can do it after work."

"Well, we are leaving at nine, and it takes about an hour to get there."

Jim said, "Well, why don't we go in my car, and I'll come and pick you two up."

Lottie said, "I'll ask Helen and tell you at lunch."

Jim said that will be fine, getting off the elevator at his floor. Jim went to his office and

Ms. Rose said, "Good morning. There is a Mr. Kelly in your office who wanted to talk to you."

Jim entered the office and saw a young man about twenty. He was about average built with brown curly hair and light blue eyes. He said, "Are you Mr. Rhodes?"

And Jim replied, "I am."

"Well, you see, I represent a clothing factory, and we heard what you did for Capstone. We would like you to represent us in a civil suit."

"Well, sir, I'll have to look over the case and get back to you."

"I was hoping you would take the case today because we don't have much time before it goes to court."

"Well in that case, you should talk to Mr. Forrester because he can do something more quickly than I. See, any case I take up I must get approval, and he is one can take care of it right away. Do you want me to introduce you to him?"

"Yes, I guess that would be good. By the way, my name is Mr. Jim Lore."

"Well, nice to meet you. Just come with me and we'll go to his office." Jim took him over to next door and introduced them and headed back to his office.

Ms. Rose said, "I see you gave that one to Mr. Forrester."

"Yes, I couldn't do him any good. Plus, I had a feeling I wasn't going to like it."

"Oh! You think something shady is going on?" she said.

He smiled at her. "We will see, won't we?"

At lunchtime, Lottie came to his office and said, "It's alright with Helen, so we'll see you tomorrow. I'm sorry about lunch today. We were asked to skip it. Too much work before closing for the weekend."

Jim watched her go, saying, "See you in the morning." He called Ms. Rose into his office. "I was wondering if you know anything about jewelry stores."

Ms. Rose smiled. "So you are thinking of getting engaged?"

"I am wondering if we can take the rest of the day off and you help me pick out a ring."

Ms. Rose said, "It will be an honor, and I could get some of my shopping done too."

"Well," he said, "close the shop and let's go."

After Ms. Rose turned off the computers, she was ready to go. "But I have one request. Out of the office, can you call me Julia?"

Jim smiled and said, "On that basis, I guess you should call me Jim."

They traveled together to quite a few jewelry stores and finally found the ring they were looking for in Jared's. The ring was 14k gold with a large diamond in the middle and little ones around the large one. The lady said it was three thousand with tax. Jim made an agreement of a thousand down and two hundred a month. The saleslady said that they can do free sizing and did he want to take out insurance. Jim added insurance and free cleaning every six months. After leaving the jewelry store with the ring in a red box, he said to Julia, "Thanks for helping me."

She said that it was fine. "I guess I'll have to shop tomorrow since we took too long finding the perfect ring."

Jim said, "Let me take you to dinner to show my appreciation." Jim took her in his car to Olive Garden for dinner, which was a sixteen-minute ride. They were led to a table where they ordered shrimp scampi and wine to drink and had breadsticks while waiting for their food. Julia said while sipping wine that she was glad that he had switched secretaries.

She said, "You treat me with more respect and not make passes at me."

Jim said, "I do appreciate that you work so hard for me to make my job easier." Soon their food arrived, and while eating, they talk about when he should propose.

Julia said, "You have an interview on Monday, so if you let me, I can have it all set up for you on Tuesday."

He said that would be great. "I'll come on Monday before I go to pick her up. Is ten all right?"

Julia said that should work. "I'll be in at nine and have talked to everybody by then, and I'll give you the details." Julia was enjoying her food and enjoying the fact that she had no intention of telling him everything. She wanted to surprise him too. Julia told him that she was an only child and her parents lived in Virginia. She goes to see them at least twice each year. Jim said his parents were a lot closer, and he saw them quite often. They finished their food, and Jim paid the check and took her home. Tomorrow he would act like nothing was going on, he thought on his way home.

When he got home, he handed over his keys to the attendant and went to his apartment. He decided to call Lottie, and he told her he had all his shopping done and he would be there at eight-thirty. She said that would be fine and said, "You don't have to bring anything. Me and Helen went shopping. When we got home, we prepared everything for tomorrow. Well, you have a good sleep. I'll see you in the morning, and I love you."

Jim said he loved her as he hung up the phone. Jim went in and took a shower putting on his pajamas. His mother always brought him pajamas, so he always wore them to bed. He sat down on the couch and turned on the TV for a while. Jim fell asleep in the middle of the show and didn't wake up till twelve and went in the bedroom to bed after setting the alarm for seven in the morning.

Jim awoke to the sound of the alarm and forgot for a moment because it was ringing. He went into the kitchen and prepared the coffeepot that he forgot to set last night. While it was perking, he went into the bathroom and splashed cold water on his face to be awake. He then brushed his teeth, and seeing his hair was a mess, he combed it. Going back into the kitchen, he made himself a cup and sat down, thinking he needed to act naturally so they wouldn't suspect him to be up for anything. He finished his coffee and put on a pair of khaki shorts and a blue T-shirt. He found his old hiking boots and put them on and went to get his car. He left the garage at eight so he knew he would be early.

Jim knocked at the door, and Helen let him in. Jim saw all the picnic stuff sitting on the table. Helen said, "We are almost ready. Would you put the food in your car?"

Jim said he would and started collecting stuff. Soon he had the car loaded and the two girls walked out. He held the door for them. Lottie had on a red tee and green shorts, and Helen had on blue shorts and a green top. Jim got in the car and made the hour trip to the park.

When they arrived, it cost them five dollars to park near the number one picnic pavilion. They unloaded the car with food and charcoal, and Jim started up the grill. Lottie and her sister spread out the table with assorted food and condiments for the burgers and hot dogs. The cooler had the meat and drinks, which Jim had carried being too heavy for the girls. Jim looked around at the trees, and he could hear the birds singing. There was a slight breeze to help with the heat from the sun.

Helen said, "I would like to go hiking after lunch. Will you two come along?" They both agreed and Jim said that the grill was hot enough to start cooking. Lottie brought over the burgers and hot dogs to put on the grill. Jim stood there cooking and thinking how peaceful it was out here with the birds singing, and he could hear children laughing and playing down the road a piece. Jim loved being here with Lottie thinking someday it would be his children playing here. Lottie came over to see if any were done yet and suddenly Jim took her in his arms and gave her a passionate kiss.

Helen hollered over saying, "Don't burn my burgers you lovebirds."

They laughed as they parted, and Jim went back to attending the grill. In a little while, they sat down to eat. The conversation was light, not discussing anything pertaining to their work. Cleaning up, they sat everything on the table and decided to hike through the woods while the grill cooled down. Each of them took a bottle of water and started down the trail. The trail was kind of shaded from the trees, and they did a mile before seeing deer taking off when they saw them coming. In about an hour, they came back to the camp, eating a little more before packing up the car. Jim was a little disappointed that it was almost time to go. He wished that he could stay out here forever not worrying about anything, just being with the one you love. The grill had cooled down, and Jim cleaned it out and put it in the right container.

He drove them back home, and he could tell they were exhausted since both women were fast asleep on the way back. Both Lottie and Helen woke up as he pulled in front of their apartment. He helped them empty the car, and before he left, they had made him a plate to take with him. He held Lottie in his arms telling her what a great day it had been and how much he loved her. She replied that she did too, and he gave her one last kiss and said, "See you Monday." She said she would be ready. Jim headed home.

Monday morning, Jim went to the office before going to pick up Lottie and found Julia and Helen talking together. She looked up at Jim asked if there was anything important.

"No. Julia just stopped by to see if you're arranged for tomorrow and if anything was pressing today."

Julia said, "We have taken care of everything. The only thing you need to know is the elevator will stop between floors, which will give you time to propose marriage, and when it starts up again, go up to the six floor with her."

He said, "Thanks. I didn't know that Helen knew."

Helen laughed, saying, "I knew since Friday night. I just didn't say anything."

Jim said, "You keep it secret well." He said, "Well, I got to go get Lottie. If I hang around here, I'll be late."

Julia said, "See you tomorrow." He smiled at both women and left the office and returned to his car.

When Jim got to Lottie's apartment, she wasn't outside waiting, so he got out of the car and went to the door. He knocked and she yelled at him to come in. "I'll be ready in a few minutes. There's some coffee in the kitchen."

Jim went in the kitchen and poured himself a cup, looking at his watch thinking, *Women are never on time*. Jim had just finished drinking the coffee when Lottie walked in. She had on a long black dress and matching high heels. He saw the dangling gold earrings and remarked how beautiful she was.

Lottie felt grateful and gave him a kiss saying, "Shall we go?"

Jim walked her to the car and helped her in. He got in and headed to Virginia Avenue. The traffic was heavy, and they made it just in time.

When they pulled in the parking lot of the church, a man was standing at the door. He came over to the car saying, "Are you Mr. Rhodes? My name is Roger O'Donnell, and I'm the head deacon of the church."

Jim got out of the car and shook hands before helping Lottie out. Jim said, "This is Ms. Sherman. She is an accountant in our building."

Roger shook her hand, saying, "Nice to meet you, Ms. Sherman." He said, "Follow me and I'll take you to the pastor's office."

In the lobby, they took the door to the right, which was a long hallway. When they made the turn at the end of the first hallway, there was a woman coming toward them. Roger stopped, saying, "Good morning, Mrs. Brown. I would like you to meet Mr. Rhodes and Ms. Sherman."

Mrs. Brown said, "Nice to meet you. I'm the pastor's secretary."

Roger said, "Right down here is the pastor's office," and he went up to knock on the door. Roger opened the door saying, "Mr. Rhodes is here and brought a Ms. Sherman with him."

Pastor Dodge got up from the desk and came and shook hands saying, "Glad to know you, Ms. Sherman."

Jim said, "She came with me to look over the church. She was looking for a church to attend."

Pastor Dodge said, "Well, we would be glad to have you. Now let me show you the rest of the church, but we must stop at Mr. Conner's door or he'll never forgive me."

Pastor Dodge knocked on Mr. Conner's door saying, "I'm sure you want to come out and say hello to this couple."

John opened the door to see Jim. He rushed over and gave him a hug. "I haven't seen you in almost three years since college, and now you're a big-time lawyer."

Jim laughed and said, "Maybe not that big. I would like you to meet my girlfriend, Ms. Lottie Sherman."

John gave her a hug and said, "You shouldn't let this one get away."

Lottie laughed and said, "I have no intention to."

Jim said, "You might see a lot of her. She is thinking about going to this church."

John said, "I hope you do. It is a fine church, and most of our congregation are friendly and will be there if you need help."

"Well," Lottie said, "I'll be here Sunday. Will you be here?"

John said, "I'm here every Sunday unless I have an errand for the church." John said, "I have got to get back to work. How about you and Jim having dinner with me soon?"

Jim said, "I'll hold you to it. We need to catch up."

Pastor Dodge led them to the lunchroom after checking out the main church with its large stage.

Lottie said, "It's quite large and magnificent."

Pastor Dodge felt a little sad when he said it holds nearly five hundred people, and some Sundays it's almost filled. In the dining room, there were quite a bit of tables and chairs and there was a service window that you could see in the kitchen where a few ladies were working. The pastor said, "We don't have a permanent cook. Maybe you would like the job?"

Lottie was a little embarrassed saying, "I'm sorry, but I'm not a very good cook."

Pastor said, "That's alright. Each of our ladies in the church take turns. Why don't you go talk to those ladies while me and Jim talk over business and we'll meet you back here for lunch?"

Jim followed Pastor Dodge while leaving Lottie behind. Then they went to his office and sat down. Jim said, "I'm impressed with your church and would be glad to take over the legal matters of this church."

"I'm glad to hear that, and please call me Robert since we will see a lot of each other."

Jim said, "Call me Jim and just send the contract over to my office with a check for five hundred dollars for a retainer. Put in care of Mrs. Rose. She is my secretary."

Robert said he would get it out soon. "But right now, let's go back to your charming lady for lunch."

They returned to the lunchroom, and Lottie served them a ham and cheese sandwich and chips and Ms. Ross brought out glasses of ice tea. Lottie said, "I enjoyed talking to the ladies, and I'm sure I will like attending this church."

Pastor Dodge said, "I'm glad to hear that."

They sat and ate their lunch, and Jim told Lottie that he was now working for this church, and she said, "Good, and you can come with me Sunday."

Jim looked at them and said, "I see I have no choice," and all three laughed. After lunch, they shook hands with Pastor Dodge and left. Lottie said on the way home, "I like him a lot."

Jim said, "He is a very good person, and I'll be glad to work with him." Jim dropped her at her apartment, giving her a hug and kiss before leaving.

It was Tuesday when he woke up the next day, which he was very excited about. He knew that Helen would make sure that Lottie would be at the elevator waiting. Jim picked the ring out of his dresser drawer and put it in his pocket. He remembered that Julia said to propose in the elevator, but he didn't know what those two had planned. He dressed in his best suit of gray with a red tie and drank his coffee. He headed down to the garage, saying good morning to George.

George said, "You seem to be in a very happy mood today."

Jim smiled and said, "I'm expecting it to be a great day."

George handed him the keys and said, "Good luck."

Jim handed him a five-dollar bill and said, "You have one too."

George said, "Thank you, sir," and Jim got in the car and drove off.

Jim got to the office, and Lottie was waiting by the elevator for him. She said, "My sister said you had something important to talk over."

Jim said, "I'll tell you when we get upstairs," and they entered the elevator together. One of the maintenance men watched while they got on and called in on his walkie-talkie to the guy in the control room. The elevator suddenly stopped between the five and sixth floor.

Lottie said, "Something had happened to the elevator," turning around to Jim, and she saw he was down on one knee.

He said, "Lottie, ever since you came into my life, I have loved you and more each day. I would be honored if you would be my wife," opening the red box in his hand.

Lottie began to cry and said yes when he slipped on the ring on her finger. He got up and started kissing her, and the elevator began to move. When the door opened on the sixth floor, people were crowded all around. Jim was totally surprised that his office workers were there. Helen and Julia were standing in front of the crowd saying, "How do you like your engagement party?"

Lottie was very excited and showed everyone her ring. There was plenty of food and an open bar. They were wished happiness by everyone, and they had pushed back the desks for dancing. Mr. Thomas had engaged a DJ for the party. In a few hours, quite a few were sent home being quite intoxicated.

Jim finally found Lottie on the other side of the room and yelled, "Are you ready to get out of here?"

She immediately came to his side saying, "I was hoping you would." They said goodbye to everyone and left, and the party was still going strong.

They arrived at her apartment, and she asked him to come in and discuss their plans. He came in, and they sat on the couch together. Jim put his arm around her and kissed her passionately.

She said, pushing him away, "I would like a church wedding and have Pastor Dodge reside over it." Jim said he would call him when he got home. Lottie said, "I would like to plan the wedding if you don't mind."

Jim laughed and said, "You go ahead. I would be lost."

Lottie said, "I should have it done in two months. See if he has an opening in May."

He started kissing her again and felt that urge and knew he had to stop. "Lottie, I love you and know you want to wait till our wedding so I must go."

She said, "I understand. I do want to wait."

He gave her one last kiss and got up from the couch and went home.

When Jim got home, he called Pastor Dodge and asked if he could make appointment to see him tomorrow.

Pastor Dodge said, "I checked with my secretary. I have an opening at one o'clock if that's convenient?"

Jim said, "I can take my lunch break then. I'll see you there." Jim said goodbye and sat up thinking how great it would be to be married to Lottie. Before he got up from the couch, he called and ordered a pizza from Papa John's. They said it would be there in about thirty minutes. Jim decided to take a shower before they got there and get out of the suit he was wearing. Getting out of the shower, he put on a pair of shorts just as the doorbell rang.

When he opened the door, a man said, "I have a pepperoni pizza for a Mr. Rhodes."

Jim said it was him, taking the box and handing over a twenty and saying, "Keep the change."

The guy smiled and said, "Thanks. Enjoy your dinner." Jim carried it to the kitchen table and got a beer from the fridge and sat down to eat. He thought while he ate after he got married Lottie would cook for him, and he wouldn't have to eat out every night. He hadn't had a home-cooked meal since his mother Janet had died. He sat and watched TV for a while and went to bed.

Next morning when he got to the office, he went over and gave Julia a hug and a kiss on the cheek saying, "You're the best. The party was great, and your plan was excellent. I was even surprised."

Ms. Rose smiled. "I'm glad you enjoyed it."

Jim said, "Lottie has already decided that you will be one of the bridesmaids. I'll be out of the office after twelve thirty going to see Pastor Dodge about the wedding."

"Well, good luck. Just let me know when it is."

When Jim pulled in the parking lot of the church, he met Roger coming out the door. Roger said, "I heard that you are setting up your wedding with the pastor. Me and my wife would be honored to attend."

Jim said, "I will let you know when it is. I would love for your family to attend."

Roger went on to his car, and Jim entered the church, making his way to Pastor Dodge's Office. Jim knocked and was told to come in.

Robert got up from his desk and said, "I'm pretty sure what you're here for since I didn't send for you."

Jim said, "I guess it was obvious from the other day."

Robert laughed and said, "So when did you want to do this wedding?"

"We were wondering if you could have our wedding in the month of May."

"Well, it would have to be in the middle, you know, having Mother's Day and Memorial Day. Do you think the week of the twentieth would be alright?"

Jim said, "That would give Lottie plenty of time."

"Well, there is one stipulation in all marriage couple. I like to do counseling before the event. Talk it over with Lottie and see what meeting we can set up and tell Mrs. Brown, and she'll see if it's available."

Jim said he would. Robert said, "I have one request growing up in Wisconsin. I never got a chance to see the Milwaukee Brewers, but I have two tickets to the Braves on Saturday. Would you like go?"

Jim said he has never made it to a Braves game either. "I would love to go."

"It's settled. Meet me here at eleven thirty on Saturday. It starts at one."

Jim said he would be here.

"Will you let Roger know of the date of the wedding? His family wants to come." Robert said he would inform him and shook Jim's hand as he left.

Jim returned to the office hoping to catch Lottie before she left for the day. He met her just coming out the door with two women from work.

"Hi, Jim, I would like you to meet Jean and Betty. We were headed to the Sonic to get a shake since Helen had to work over."

"Well, can I go with you girls? I wanted to tell you about seeing Pastor Dodge."

They said sure since they are going to be at the wedding too. Jim walked with them down the street saying, "Why don't you call your sister and tell her I'll drop you at home?" Lottie made the call and told her just when they got to Sonic. Jim paid for their milkshakes, and he told them it will be held the week of the twentieth of May.

Lottie told the girls, "We'll have to get to work on this wedding real soon." The two women agreed and finished their shakes and said, "See you tomorrow." She and Jim were left there alone at the table. She said, "I can't wait to be your wife."

Jim grabbed her hand, looking in her eyes, and said, "Neither can I." They walked back hand in hand to the car. He told her as they drove home, "Pastor Dodge said we had to meet him for marriage counseling for several weeks before the ceremony."

Lottie said, "I can only be off on Wednesdays and Saturdays."

"Well, I'll talk to Mr. Thomas to set up my schedule to work a half-day on Wednesdays, and I will call Pastor Dodge and see if it is alright with him." Jim gave her a hug and kiss before she got out of the car. Jim said, "I'll let you know tomorrow."

Lottie walked into the apartment thinking about all she had to do for the wedding. Jim stopped at a convenient store on the way home and picked up a ham and cheese sub. He also got a Cola and chips. He paid, got in his car, and headed home.

Jim had his head full of thoughts about everything that was happening while he ate his food. He finished eating and cleaned up his mess and set the coffeepot for tomorrow. He went and took a shower and decided to call Pastor Dodge. His call was transferred to the parsonage where Mrs. Marie answered and said she would get him. Pastor Dodge came on the phone and said hello.

"This is Jim just calling to let you know we can do your counseling on Wednesdays, mostly in the afternoon."

Robert looked at his schedule saying, "Will three be good for you?"

Jim said that would be perfect, and he would pick him up on Saturdays.

Robert said that would be great and said, "I'll see you then." Jim hung up the phone. He sat and watched TV till it was time for bed. He had a hard time falling asleep thinking about the wedding.

The next day as he got off the elevator, the receptionist, Patricia Turner, said good morning to Mr. Rhodes. She said, "Mr. Thomas wants to see you in his office right away." Jim headed down the hall, and when he got there, he told Mrs. Murray that he was there to see Mr. Thomas. She ushered him into Mr. Thomas's office. Jim had never paid attention to her before noticing her reddish-brown hair and green eyes.

She said, "Mr. Rhodes is here."

Mr. Thomas said, "Come in and sit down, and you may leave, Mrs. Murray. First, I want to congratulate you on your engagement, and I need you to take the case that has come up."

"Well, sir, before you tell me about it, I was wondering if I could have Wednesday afternoons off? The pastor wants us to do marriage counseling."

Mr. Thomas said, "That can be arranged. To tell you the truth, I should have done that before my marriage. Anyway, it has come to our attention that there was a case involved with embezzlement, and I would like you to look it over."

Jim said he would, and Mr. Thomas said, "I'll send all the materials over to Mrs. Rose."

Jim returned to his office and stopped by Ms. Rose's desk and told her about the assignment. Ms. Rose said the file was just being downloaded to her computer now. She said she would check it out and let him know when she had all the details. He thanked her saying, "The wedding is scheduled in May, and I hope you attend." She said that she would be there. Jim went on into his office and sat down and went over other cases that were pending.

Ms. Rose came in and said, "What I found out was that Ms. Hill was an accountant for East Pebble incorporated, and they began to see their profits disappearing, so they wanted her to be examined."

Jim called upstairs to Mr. Rivers, saying, "I have a client who needs their finance audited. I was wondering if I could have you search for them."

Mr. Rivers said, "It would be our pleasure. Just have them give me a call."

Jim thanked him and said that he would recommend them to him. Jim hung up and called the company. They said that they would give Regis Inc. a call.

"Good. When they bring me the report, we can decide where to go from there." They said thanks and hung up. Jim left the office and returned home.

Jim woke up the next day, Saturday. He went and had breakfast at Waffle House. He then returned to his apartment to get ready for the game. It had just turned eleven, and he hurried out the door to collect Robert from the church. When he saw Robert, he laughed because he was in blue jeans and a Braves T-shirt. Jim said, "Where did you get that shirt?" as Robert entered the car.

"Oh! I picked it up at a sport shop not far from here."

The traffic was heavy, and it took a while to get there. When they arrived at the stadium, Jim asked, "Who's playing?"

Robert said, "The Pittsburgh Pirates are hard to beat, so it should be an exciting game." It took them a half-hour to find their seats. Jim went and got them each a hot dog plus a drink. The first pitch was played when he returned to his seat. During the game, there were plenty of home runs, and the Braves were up to bat in the ninth and a run was scored, which they won 9 to 8.

Jim said, "That was a good game."

And Robert said, "Stop over here before we leave." Robert got two seasons pass so they could attend all the home games. They became good friends and would be out at the ballpark every chance they could.

Suddenly, someone touched Jim's arm, and he woke up and looked at his surroundings. He realized that he had fallen asleep in the bus station. Jennifer was still beside him, and he thought for a minute that Lottie had touched his arm, but it was Helen sitting down beside him.

She said, "I'm sorry I woke you. I just wanted to know why we were here."

Jim said, "I haven't figured it out. I just know we are scheduled to be on a bus soon."

Helen said, "To me, it seems like a dream. I could have sworn I was in church with you and the family."

He said, "That is the last thing I remember too."

Jennifer said, "I'm still waiting on John. I hope he gets here before the bus arrives."

Jim still couldn't figure out why his family was across the room. He called Lottie, but she didn't answer like she couldn't hear him.

CHAPTER 11

LOTTIE

Lottie woke up in a strange place. She saw she was in a bus station and did not know how she got there. She noticed she was surrounded by church members, including her two daughters. She asked Pastor Dodge, "Why are we here?"

He said, "I'm not sure, but we all have tickets for the same bus. Now on that side of the room, I heard them waiting on another bus."

"Do you know why my husband is on the other bus?"

"I'm not even sure why my secretary is over there. I guess it will all be explained later."

Lottie was confused and afraid even of her children, but Rita calmed them down. She decided to review her life hoping to find the answer.

Lottie remembers that she grew up in a house in Valdosta with her parents and her one sister, Helen. Her father's name was Don. He was tall but skinny with brown hair and blue eyes. He worked as an insurance salesman at a nine-to-five job. Her mother Betty was a stay-at-home mom who they had looked after with red hair and green eyes. She always thought that her mom could be a model. The finance was rather tight, so getting new clothes was only at Christmastime. She always looked up to her sister, who was three years older. When things got tight, Mom started cleaning houses part-time to help them get through school. When they would get home from school, Helen would always help her with her homework. Mom was always there before their father got home to have the meal prepared. Everyone got along in the house, and it seemed there was never an unkind word spoken.

Lottie's worst time came when she was thirteen. Her father had got a raise and decided to take their mother out. Helen was told to babysit, and Mom had ordered a pizza and gave Helen the money to pay for it. They left and soon the pizza man came while Helen was helping her study for a test. Helen paid for the pepperoni pizza; it was their favorite. They finished the pizza and the homework, and Helen suggested they watch a movie, and she would make the popcorn. Lottie sat down and turned on the TV and waited for her sister to bring the popcorn. Halfway through the movie, a large thunderstorm started and the electricity in the house was cut off.

Lottie became really scared and started to cry saying, "I hope Mommy comes back soon."

Helen said, "Since it is dark here, we might as well go to bed."

Lottie said, "I'm too scared to go to bed by myself." Helen said she would lie with her till she fell asleep. They got ready for bed, setting the alarm to go to school and seeing that their parents hadn't come back yet; they fell asleep.

Lottie woke up with the alarm ringing in her ears and went into her sister's room to wake her. They went through all the procedures to get ready for school but didn't hear their mother fixing breakfast. Lottie ran downstairs and found no one in the kitchen. She got scared and ran back up to her sister to tell her, and they rushed to their parents' room, but nobody had slept in their bed. Their parents were not there, and they were really scared. Someone was knocking at the door downstairs, and they went down to answer it. When they got there and opened the door, they found two police; there was a man and the other a woman.

Helen said, "May I help you? We thought you were our parents who forgot their keys."

"Are you the Sherman children?" the man asked. Helen said that they were. "We hate to inform you, but your parents were in a car wreck last night. The rain was so heavy a truck drifted into their lane, and they were killed instantly."

Helen looked at them like they were crazy, and Lottie began to cry.

The woman said, "Do you have any relatives to take care of you and make the arrangements for your parents?" Helen didn't answer right away, but Lottie spoke up saying that they had an Aunt Melody. She said, "I'm Officer Harriet, and if you want, I can call your aunt for you." Helen went into their address book to find her aunt's number.

Officer Harriet called and said, "Is this Ms. Sherman?"

Melody said, "Yes. Who is this?"

"I'm Officer Harriet. I'm here to inform you your brother is dead and also his wife. We would like to know if you will take custody of your two nieces." The officer explained to her what happened, and she said that she would be there in a half hour. Officer Harriet said that they would be waiting for her.

Melody came in and wondered what happened to her brother. Officer Harriet said to Ms. Sherman, "We are sorry for your loss," and went on to explain the circumstances. Melody said she would have to make several calls before she could make funeral arrangements for the couple. She said that Betty's parents were dead and had no way to get in touch with her relatives. Making her calls, she found out there was a large insurance policy on both, which would pay for the funeral and have enough to take care of the children. It was hard enough on the two girls to attend a funeral, but they had to leave their school and start a new one. Melody had gone to identify the bodies while they were left to pack their clothes. The funeral was quite fast, and they were in the limousine with Melody to the cemetery called Sun Hill.

Both girls were crying while the minster did the eulogy, and Melody had to drag them away when the services were over. Melody was well-to-do and had a big house and servants. Both girls spent more time with the servants than Melody. She wasn't a loving person and very strict. John the butler let them get away with a few things. Molly made them feel at home being the maid and cook. She treated them like her own and helped them through school. Melody sold their house, which helped pay for college, and Helen got a part-time job at Arby's to pay for her books. Helen was going to night classes for math, which she was going to for a degree in accounting. Lottie took courses in math and science; and after graduating, she had wanted a job at NASA, but they wouldn't be hiring for five more years.

Helen, after graduating, found a job in Atlanta with a firm called Regis Inc. and moved there to find an apartment. It was tough going at first, and she started dating Joe Rivers who was her boss. She called up Lottie and said, "I got you a job here since you got to wait five years, and I miss you. You can work here and share this apartment, and you'll have money to save when NASA calls." Helen had convinced her, so she packed her things and said goodbye to Molly and John who seemed like her parents. She told Melody about leaving who said it sounded like a good idea. Melody drove her to the Greyhound station and said goodbye with hardly any emotion. She bought her ticket and called her sister to tell her when to pick her up.

When Lottie got off the bus, Helen was there waiting. Lottie ran up to her and gave her a big hug, and she started to cry. It seemed like forever since they saw each other. They walked back to the building together to collect her suitcases. When they got out of the parking lot, Helen hit her key fob, which surprised Lottie for Helen to have a red Chevy Nova.

Lottie said, "Wow! How could you afford this?"

"Well with your help paying half of the rent, it will be no problem."

They put the suitcases in the trunk and got in and headed to Helen's apartment. Helen asked how Melody was.

Lottie said, "She's fine and mean," and they both laughed.

Lottie saw the name on the street, which was Glenwood Avenue. Helen pulled up in front of the apartment building, saying, "Welcome home."

Walking into the apartment, Lottie said, "I can see why you could afford that car." She looked around and said, "That's some ugly furniture. Where you get it, Goodwill?"

Helen laughed and said, "No. It came with the apartment. If we get rich, we can buy better."

Lottie said, "I won't hold my breath," and they both laughed.

She said, "You'll have to sleep on that ugly yellow couch until you can afford a bed. I cleaned out some drawers in the dresser in the bedroom for your clothes and half the closet. When you get settled in a few days, I'll decide, so you can talk to my boss."

Helen said, "My supervisor is Joe Rivers, and we have been going together for a few months. I'm sure he can get you on without talking to Mr. Brown." She said, "I haven't been to the store lately, and tomorrow is my day off, we can go to the grocery store. If you don't mind, there's a McDonald's around the corner. I'm sure you're tired, so tell me what you want, and I'll go pick it up."

Lottie said that she would like a Big Mac Meal with a Coke. Helen collected her keys and said she would be right back. Lottie looked around the apartment. The carpet was green, and the walls matched the couch—a sick yellow. She thought to herself that when she got some money, she would repaint the walls. The kitchen was small with a refrigerator and stove and a small table with two chairs. The counter by the sink had a microwave and a coffeepot and not much room for anything else but a drain rack for the dishes.

Lottie then went to the bedroom and saw there was just enough room for two single beds next to the brown nightstand and the brown dresser was next to the closet. On the other side of the closet was the door to the bathroom. Nothing special about the bathroom, just a sink and a toilet and a stand-up shower. There was a large mirror over the sink but still not much counter space. The whole room was in white with green tile on the floors. Lottie heard the front door open, and Helen came in with the food. Helen took the food in the kitchen and called Lottie to come and eat. Lottie came in and sat across from her sister and began to eat her burger.

After eating and cleaning up their mess, Helen said, "I'll get you a pillow and a blanket for the couch, so when you're ready for bed." Returning with the items, they sat and watched the TV, which sat on a stand. The TV was a nineteen-inch, which was rather small. Soon, Lottie got up and went in the bathroom and took a shower and put on her pajamas. Lottie came back in the living room saying, "If you don't mind, I would like to go to bed."

Helen said, "That's alright. I have a book I haven't finished." Helen got up and dressed for bed and lay in the bedroom reading her book. Lottie made up the couch, and after laying down, she was soon asleep. Helen finished her book before turning out the light.

When Lottie got up, Helen was already in the kitchen saying, "Good morning. Did you have a good sleep? I hope that couch wasn't too uncomfortable."

Lottie smiled, taking the cup of coffee her sister handed to her.

Helen said, "We are going to take you on a tour of the city and then do some grocery shopping for the week since this is my only day off besides Sunday." Helen cooked eggs and bacon for breakfast and Lottie made the toast, and they sat and ate, talking about their childhood and how much they missed their parents.

Helen said, "Go take a shower since we will be gone all day." Lottie got a pair of brown shorts and a green top and headed to the bathroom. Just when she got out, her sister walked in naked saying, "My turn." Lottie went into the bedroom to get dressed away from the steam in the bathroom. Helen came out and put on her cargo shorts of blue and a "Welcome to Atlanta" T-shirt.

Lottie laughed, saying, "You advertising?" They both sat on the bed and put on their tennis shoes.

Helen got up from the bed saying, "You ready to go?"

Lottie said, "I guess so. Where to first?"

Helen walked out to the car saying, "We would look at the city and the Turner Stadium. After going through the streets of the city," she said, "you have a choice—the aquarium, the zoo, or Six Flags."

Lottie said, "I need to get out and walk, so I guess the zoo."

Helen said, "On another day, I'll take you to Stone Mountain, and I can guarantee you'll get plenty of exercise."

Lottie said, "I'm definitely not up to that." She and Helen spent quite a few hours looking at the animals. It was starting to get hot, and most of the animals went inside.

Helen said, "I guess we might leave and go to lunch since there is not much to see now."

Lottie said, "That would be a good idea to get out of this heat." Before leaving the park, they bought T-shirts of the zoo and water since they were both dried out.

They found a Burger King close by and went in not only to eat but to cool off. Lottie got goose bumps from the cold since they had the air condition on low. Lottie ordered a chicken sandwich and a cup of coffee to warm up. Helen ordered a Whooper with cheese meal and a Coke. They sat and ate their meal quietly thinking about all the animals they had saw.

Lottie said, "If you don't mind, let's go to the grocery store and home. It's getting quite hot outside to roam around."

Helen said, "That is fine since the heat took away most of my energy." They went to Kroger, which was close to their apartment. Helen got enough for a week spending over a hundred dollars. Getting home, they put the groceries away and decided to take a nap before preparing dinner.

Helen was up first and got two steaks out of the fridge to cook. She marinated the steaks in a bowl with A1 and put two potatoes in the oven to bake. She then made up a salad before waking Lottie. She walked into the kitchen saying, "You should have woken me to help you."

Helen said, "We will take turns cooking," and Lottie agreed. They sat and ate the salad while the rest of the food was cooking. Helen got a phone call and told Lottie to watch the food. When she got back, she said to Lottie, "It's all set. You need to go with me to work tomorrow. Your interview with Joe is the first thing in the morning."

Lottie said, "That was fast."

Helen laughed, saying, "It helps when you know the boss. Tomorrow night, you will be by yourself since I have a date." They sat down to eat since Lottie had removed the food from the oven.

Lottie said, "I haven't had this good food for a while since you know how well Aunt Melody cooks."

Helen laughed between bites saying, "I remember her bland food." They finished and cleaned the dishes before watching TV before bed.

Lottie said, "I got my résumé out," and set it on the table and need to go to bed early.

Helen said, "I still have my book and I still haven't finished. See you in the morning."

Lottie went into the bedroom collecting her bedclothes before changing for bed. She went and made up the couch and walked back into the bedroom to give Helen a kiss. Helen had already changed and was reading when Lottie kissed her and said, "Thanks and good night."

Helen said, "That's what sisters are for plus I need the money." Lottie laughed and punched her sister in the shoulder. Helen said, "See how mean you are?" laughing. Lottie returned to the living room and laid down. It was a tiring day and soon was fast asleep.

Helen woke up with the alarm going off and got up and headed to the kitchen to put on the coffeepot. She headed back to the bedroom to take a shower, calling Lottie, and it was time to get up. Helen brushed her teeth and then took a shower. She came back in her bedroom to get dressed putting on a blue pantsuit. Lottie went into the closet and picked up a red dress and headed on into the bathroom. Helen went back to the kitchen and poured a cup of coffee waiting for Lottie. Lottie soon arrived in her red dress and grabbed a cup of coffee and sat down. She said to Helen that she was quite nervous.

Helen said not to worry. "I told them about your math degree, and they were quite impressed. And because I have influence with the supervisor, you're a shoo-in."

Lottie laughed. "You always did know how to make me feel better."

"That's what big sisters are for now. Finish getting dressed. You don't want to be late." Lottie went back to the bathroom to brush her teeth and hair and applying a little makeup. Helen came in and said it was time to go. Lottie went into the bedroom, slipped on her black high heels, and said, "Let's go." Helen locked the door behind them and punched the key to open the car. They got in and headed downtown to work.

When they arrived at the building, they went into the underground car park for the building. The only trouble was there no elevator from there, so they had to go back up to the front of the building to enter the lobby. Helen told her that Regis Inc. was on the sixth floor while heading to the elevator. They got in the elevator when it arrived at the bottom floor.

Lottie's nervousness increased as the elevator began to rise, and she felt like her stomach would let loose its contents when the doors opened. Helen saw how nervous she was.

"I know you got this. Just calm down and announce yourself to the receptionist. I got to get to my desk before I'm late," she said and kissed her on the check and went through a door on her left.

Lottie walked up to the receptionist and said, "I have an appointment."

"Hi, my name is Judy, and welcome to Regis Inc. Just take a seat, and I'll let Mr. Rivers know you're here." Lottie watched this short-haired brunette as she called Mr. Rivers. She looked up with her brown eyes, which sparkled when she smiled. "He said he'll be with you in a few minutes." Lottie decided to take Judy's advice and sat down. It seemed like forever before she was called back up to the desk. Judy said, "He will see you now. Just take the door to the right and his office is five doors down."

Lottie opened the door to the hallway and walked to the fifth door and knocked. Someone told her to come in, and she opened the door.

When she walked in looking at him, she could tell why her sister liked him. He was very handsome with black curly hair and blue eyes. He also was very muscular and could have been mistaken for a wrestler. He had a firm handshake but not too hard to hurt.

He said, "Would you sit down, Ms. Sherman?" He said, "After looking over your résumé you sent in and your sister vouching for you, I see no problem of you joining our firm. I hope that you'll change your mind about leaving us if NASA does call, but it's a while before that happens. Would you like to begin in the morning?"

Lottie said that would be great and got up and shook his hand.

"Well, we will start you at nine-fifty, and after a month of evaluating, we will raise you to ten-fifty. If that is agreeable, I'll see you in the morning and have one of my assistants help you get settled in."

She left his office excited and couldn't wait to start tomorrow. Judy asked her as she came out how it was.

Lottie said, "I start here tomorrow."

Judy smiled. "Glad to have you here and good luck. And if you need any help, I'm here."

Lottie said, "Thanks. It's always good to have a friend."

Lottie didn't want to go home. She was excited to tell Helen she got the job. She went window-shopping till it was lunchtime for Helen and headed back to the building. She got there just when Helen was getting off the elevator.

She went up to her sister giving her a hug, saying, "I got the job, and I start tomorrow."

Helen said, "Congratulations. I told you there wouldn't be a problem."

Helen said, "I'm hungry, and I like to get something to eat before my time runs out."

Lottie said, "I'm sorry. Let's go to Burger King. It's only a block away." They left the lobby and headed down the street. Once they made it in the restaurant, Helen ordered a Whooper with cheese meal since she hadn't had any breakfast. Lottie ate only a cheeseburger off the dollar menu and a small drink. She was still excited and couldn't eat much.

When they were through eating, Helen handed Lottie her house key saying, "You need to go make a copy for heading home." She walked Helen back to work and headed to Walmart to get the key made. She found the key machine in the lobby of Walmart and used her bank card, which still had some money from her college loan. After making the key, she called a cab and soon was back at the apartment.

Lottie went in and decided she would make a lasagna dinner with garlic toast. She went in the freezer and got out the lasagna package and preheated the oven. Once she put it in, it would take two hours, which would be in time for Helen to get home. She popped it in the oven and went to pick out an outfit for tomorrow. She went into the closet and pulled out a light green dress and her white high heels. She then got undressed and took a shower and put on a pair of brown shorts and a white tee after drying. She did a little cleaning around the apartment including dusting the furniture. Noticing the time, she went and got out the garlic bread and put it on a pan. She then put it in the oven next to the lasagna knowing that Helen would be home soon.

When Helen arrived, Lottie put the garlic bread in the oven and said, "Dinner would be ready in twenty minutes."

Helen said, "I'll take a shower and be right down." Helen walked into the kitchen just when Lottie pulled out the bread and lasagna. Helen had changed into a pair of blue shorts and a red top. Helen poured two glasses of tea while Lottie brought the food to the table. When they sat down to eat, Lottie asked how the rest of her day went.

Helen said, "Busy work seems to pile up, and thanks for dinner. I really like the fact that you are here with me. It was quite lonely without you."

Lottie said, "I really missed you too. You know it's hard to talk to Aunt Melody, and I could never find a friend I could relate to. Well, we are back together, and I'm sure things will begin to look up."

When they finished dinner, Helen put the food away while Lottie washed the dishes. Helen came over and dried them and said, "Why don't you go get changed and we'll sit and watch some TV together before bed."

Lottie said alright and went into the bedroom and changed into her black silk nightgown. Helen came in and said, "I guess I'll change too." Lottie turned on the TV, and Helen went and changed to her red silk nightgown. They watched a few programs before going to bed. Helen went into the bedroom and collected the pillow and blanket for Lottie, which she would need. It gets chilly here at night with the air blowing.

Helen gave her sister a kiss on the cheek saying, "I'm happy you are here. Good night."

Helen went back to the bedroom and picked up her book and read quite a while. Lottie was already fast asleep when she went in to check on her. Helen turned off the TV and the light. Returning to the bedroom, she got in bed and was soon asleep.

Lottie was the first one up and went and made up the coffeepot. She went into the bathroom and showered and brushed her teeth before waking Helen. Helen looked at the time as she got out of bed and noticed she had overslept. She hurried and got ready, put on a blue pantsuit, and went to the kitchen for a cup of coffee. She saw that Lottie was already dressed and ready to go.

Helen said, "Give me a minute, and I'll put on my shoes, and we can stop on the way for breakfast."

Lottie said, "I'm too nervous and I can't eat a thing."

Helen said, "Well, I'll eat this granola bar for now, and we'll get a big lunch." Lottie said that was a good idea. In a few minutes, they walked out of the door heading to the car.

When they arrived at work, they walked to the elevator in the main lobby. When they reached the sixth floor, Mr. Rivers was there waiting for them.

"Good morning, Ms. Sherman. You go on ahead, Helen. I will show Lottie her new workspace." Helen proceeded to the left door, and Lottie and Mr. Rivers followed her. There were many cubicles in the room, and Helen went left while Mr. Rivers led her right. The last cubicle on the right was hers, and there was a desk with a phone and computer.

Mr. Rivers said, "This will be yours. I have an assignment for you after you get settled. You see that room over there in the back of the building? That is the break room plus it also has our copy and fax machine. When you log on to your computer, there will be a file on a Mrs. Westcott. Read it over."

She said, "Yes, sir. I will get right on it."

He said, "That's what I like to hear, and get back with me on thoughts of this assignment."

Lottie logged in to the computer, putting in her username and password, and began reading up on the file. Mr. Rivers left her alone and went back to his office. She saw that she was sixty years old and was not too far from retirement. She was CEO of an advertising firm making over fifty thousand a year and would retire with over three quarters of a million dollars. She also saw that she had a few million in the bank and quite a few properties and stocks.

Lottie said to herself, *This may be quite difficult taking over her taxes and investments. I see that if I handle this right, I'll be a shoo-in, so I better not mess up.* Lottie noticed that in some cases that this woman had made some bad choices in stock and Lottie said, *I'll have to get her to discuss some of her investments, so I better call and make an appointment to see her, so I can move forward with her finances.* She looked up the number at the advertising agency.

Lottie called the number and a male voice answered saying, "This is India Marketing. May I help you?"

"This is Ms. Sherman with Regis Inc. I would like to talk to Mrs. Westcott."

He said, "Just a moment please."

Mrs. Westcott came on the phone. "Yes, can I help you?"

Lottie said, "I'm the accountant that is assigned to your case. I would like to have a meeting to discuss your finances and what way I could be of service in the future."

Mrs. Westcott said, "I have time next Tuesday if that is alright with you."

Lottie said, "That would be fine. Will ten o'clock be convenient? Which will give me time to make a presentation."

Mrs. Westcott said, "That would be fine. See you then," and hung up.

Lottie thought she wasn't going to like her; she was very abrupt and unfriendly.

The week went fast, and today was Tuesday when Mrs. Westcott was to come in. She went over everything before she arrived and was just logging off Mrs. Westcott's account. She looked up into the face of Mr. Rivers.

Lottie said, "Can I help you? Is something wrong?"

Mr. Rivers said, "Not at all. You have done such a good job this past week that our boss would like to meet you. Would you come this way?"

Lottie got up from her desk and followed him out that door and past the receptionist to the hallway, which led to Mr. Rivers' office. They went past it to the next doorway, and he knocked. Mr. Rivers opened the door to a man in his fifties whose hair was turning gray mixed with the brown. When he stood up, he was just as tall as her but was a little overweight. He shook her hand with a sparkle in his blue eye saying, "Glad to meet you. Ms. Sherman, I have some good reports on you and your sister. You are both hardworking. I have already met your sister and wanted to get to know you. If you need anything, just let Mr. Rivers know. And if he can't solve it, I'm sure he'll let me know. Mr. Rivers said he would, and I'm sure you need to get back to your desk since it's almost time for your appointment."

She said, "Thank you, Mr. Brown, and I'm glad that you appreciate my services." She left them two there and returned to her desk to wait for Mrs. Westcott.

When Lottie arrived at her desk, a lady in her sixties was waiting. Lottie said, "You must be Mrs. Westcott."

She said, "I am," and took a seat after shaking her hand.

Lottie could tell she looked good for her age. Her hair was gray but not a wrinkle except around her blue eyes, and she had the figure of a young woman. She had an expensive taste, having diamond studs in her ears and a gold chain around her neck. She hadn't taken off her mink coat that she was wearing. Lottie could see this woman was a little arrogant.

"Well, Mrs. Westcott, I see no trouble taking over your finances. And if you have any questions, let me know."

"Well, I want to invest my money in a new company called Rite." Lottie looked up the company online and strongly advised her not to buy stock in this company. She said, "I still want to buy a hundred shares in this company, and if you won't do it, I'll find someone that will."

Lottie called Charles Schwab and had them send over a hundred shares of stock and transfer ten thousand dollars out of Mrs. Westcott's account. She got up and said, "Thank you. I'll let you know if I need you for anything else." She turned and left before Lottie could say anything else.

Mr. Rivers came over and saw that Lottie looked a little upset. He asked what was wrong. She told him, "Mrs. Westcott wouldn't listen and made me buy stock that was a mistake."

He told her not to worry about it. "You are there to satisfy the customer whether they are right or wrong. So you did what she wanted, so it's her problem."

Lottie said, "Yes, sir, but I do have a bad feeling about that."

He said, "It's lunchtime. Why don't you go and not worry? This company will back you up." Lottie told Helen that she would meet her in McDonald's she would be there soon.

Lottie hurried down the street to Ashley Furniture to get a single bed so she wouldn't have to sleep on the couch no more. When she got to the store, she told the saleslady what she wanted. The lady showed her different styles of single beds and decided on a Hollywood bed. She put a hundred dollars down and would make similar payments each month. She couldn't get it delivered till tomorrow night. She said to herself, "One more night on the uncomfortable couch." She then hurried back down the street to McDonald's where Helen was waiting. Helen had already ordered her a quarter pounder meal. Lottie sat down and began to eat. She told her about the bed that would come tomorrow. Then she told her about Mrs. Westcott.

Helen said, "Don't worry about it. I've had a few customers I didn't like." They walked back to work talking about how to change the bedroom to fit her bed.

Lottie returned to her desk and the phone rang. She picked it up saying, "Regis Inc. May I help you?"

"Yes, I'm Mr. Lawrence. I would like an accountant to take over the companies' taxes and payroll."

"Well, if you come tomorrow, I will be happy to help. Just ask for a Ms. Lottie Sherman. Will ten o'clock be convenient for you?"

He said that he would be there and hung up. Mr. Rivers heard that she would have another appointment tomorrow and told her what a great job she was doing. The rest of the day went quickly, and they headed home.

When they arrived home, Lottie said, "You go take your shower, and I'll start the hamburger helper." Lottie went in the kitchen to find the hamburger defrosted in the sink this morning. She pulled out the skillet under the sink and began to brown the hamburger. While it was cooking, she went over to the cabinet next to the fridge and pulled out the four-cheese meal. She drained the hamburger in a jar they had under the sink and put the hamburger back in the skillet including the stuff from the box. She got water and milk from the fridge to pour in the skillet and let it cook. Helen had already showered and put on her blue nightgown and walked into the kitchen barefooted.

Lottie said, "It will be done in less than five minutes."

Helen went to the fridge and got a pitcher of tea and poured each a glass before sitting down. Lottie said thanks and sipped her tea while waiting. Soon it was done, and Lottie filled to big bowls and brought them to the table. Helen got some silverware out of the drawer, and they began to eat.

Lottie said, "Tomorrow no more sleeping on the couch. I hope Mrs. Westcott knows what she's doing. I wasn't too happy with her decision."

Helen said, "Don't worry. This isn't the first time someone made a bad decision. The firm won't hold it against you if it doesn't work out." Helen finished her food first and said, "You go take your shower, and I'll clean up in here." Helen said, "When you get done, we'll move the bedroom around."

Lottie finished her shower when Helen came into the bedroom. She grabbed her red nightgown and put it on and began by moving Helen's bed toward the closet and putting the nightstand next to it.

Helen said, "See, there's plenty of room for your bed."

Lottie began to smile. "You were right all along." They then went and turned on the TV and watched programs till bedtime. Lottie went and collected her stuff for the couch and said, "See you in the morning." Helen went into the bedroom and turned on the reading light to read her new romance novel. Lottie had been asleep a while needing to use the bathroom, she made her way through seeing that Helen hadn't turned off the light and had her book lying on top of her. Lottie used the bathroom, went in, and turned off the light and went back to the couch. She was soon asleep too.

The next morning, Lottie opened her eyes and smelt the aroma of coffee in the air. Lottie looked at the clock on the coffee table and saw that she had overslept. She jumped off the couch and went and put on a blue pantsuit before heading to the kitchen for coffee.

Helen was already dressed in a dark blue dress and black high heels and was sipping her coffee. Helen said, "We don't have a lot of time.

We'll have to stop at McDonald's drive-through on the way to work, so you got about five minutes before we leave."

Lottie hurried and drank her coffee on the way to the bathroom. She brushed her hair and teeth, put on her deodorant, and picked up her white heels. Helen had already headed to the car, and Lottie ran to the car in her stockinged feet carrying her shoes. In the car, Lottie applied her makeup and finally slipped on her shoes when they made it to McDonald's. Helen ordered each of them two egg sausage biscuits with cheese and coffee. Helen handed Lottie the food and the drinks before going on to work. When entering the garage, Helen looked at her watch saying, "We got about ten minutes before going upstairs."

Lottie handed Helen her food, and they sat and ate their biscuits. They got out of the car and took their coffees with them. Walking around to the front door, Lottie looked toward the elevator and saw a handsome man standing there. She asked her if she knew him.

Helen said, "He's one of the lawyers on the fifth floor." He had already went up by the time they got to the elevator. Lottie hoped he was single because she would like to get to know him.

When they got off the elevator, Lottie hurried to her desk and logged into her computer. She looked up Mr. Lawrence's business so she would familiarize himself with his business. He was the owner of a life insurance company called Family Heritage and did most of their policies in Georgia. He was there at ten and she told him all that she could do for his company. When she finished her presentation, he signed a contract with Regis. She was filing all the paperwork when the phone rang.

Lottie said, "This is Regis Inc. May I help you?"

"Hello. This is Mrs. Roberts. I own a flower shop downtown and would like to know if you are available to take over our finances."

Lottie said, "Can I expect you here tomorrow?"

Mrs. Roberts said, "Will three thirty be too late?"

Lottie said, "That wouldn't be a problem. See you then." Looking up at the clock, she noticed it was almost lunchtime. She looked up the flower shop, which was called Bouquet on Virginia Avenue.

Helen came up to her desk and said, "You ready for lunch?"

Lottie said she was very hungry. She said, "Let's just go to Subway, which is downstairs," and Helen agreed.

They went up to the counter and Helen got an Italian sub with everything on it and a bag of chips and a Coke. Lottie got a BLT with just mayonnaise with a cookie and a Coke. They paid for their food and sat down, and Lottie said she got a new client and maybe another tomorrow. Helen said, "I knew you would be good at this job." Helen said, "I have two clients that I'm working with, and Jim is proud of us both."

They soon returned to work. There were no more phone calls that day for her but a few for the other girls in the office. She was glad when it was quitting time, being a little bored. Lottie turned off her computer and left her desk for the day and met Helen in the lobby. She told her sister, "I thought the day would never end. All I did was spend these last hours doing nothing but watching the clock."

Helen said while they headed to the car, "It is that way some days." They pulled out of the parking garage and headed home.

When they pulled up at the door, the Ashley Furniture truck was waiting for them. Helen went to unlock the door while Lottie headed over to the truck. She told them that she was Ms. Sherman, and two guys got out of the truck opening the back. They carried the big box, which contained her bed. They set up the bed in the bedroom, took away the box, and said, "Would you please sign here for the bed?"

Lottie signed the paper and the two guys left. Helen looked at the bed with the white plastic headboard saying it looked good. Helen said, "I forgot to take out anything for dinner. Would you settle for a pizza?"

Lottie said, "Only if it's double pepperoni and cheese."

Helen laughed. "Getting picky, are you?" Helen called Dominos and ordered the pizza and was told it would be about thirty minutes. Lottie went and took a shower while Helen sat reading on her cell phone waiting on the pizza. Lottie had just got into her pink nightgown, knowing it was transparent. She waited for the delivery guy to leave before coming out of the bedroom.

Helen said, "I need a shower before we eat. I am sweaty from the heat outside." Lottie waited for her to come back and went into the kitchen and got two glasses of ice tea. Helen soon returned dressed in a blue nightgown, and they sat down to eat. They spent the rest of the night watching TV before going to bed. Lottie loved her new bed and was happy to be back in the same room with her sister since they had always shared a room growing up.

Lottie opened her eyes as the alarm sounded. She smiled to see Helen waking up. Helen said, "You go start the coffeepot. I need a shower to get the sleep out of my eyes." Lottie headed to the kitchen and filled the pot with water and filled the basket with three scoops of coffee. Turning it on, she headed to the bathroom to brush her teeth. Helen had the bathroom steamy, and it was hard to clear the mirror to see.

Lottie hollered at her saying, "Save some hot water for me."

Helen shut off the shower and walked out of the stall saying, "Hand me that towel, and I didn't take it all." Helen dried off and wrapped the towel around her and headed to the bedroom. Lottie took off her nightgown and got in the shower and found it was just warm. She hurried up and washed knowing it would get cold soon. She dried off and went and got her light pink dress out of the closet before getting her undergarments out of the drawer. She got dressed and headed barefooted to the kitchen. Helen was already dressed in a blue navy pantsuit sipping coffee and eating the donuts they got on the way home.

Lottie said, "You took almost all the hot water, and don't you think that is a little too hot to wear?"

Helen laughed, saying, "I did leave you some, and you know how cold it is in that office." Lottie ate her donut after making her a cup of coffee. Helen said, "I'm going to finish getting ready," and left the kitchen. Lottie finished eating and went to the bedroom to find her black heels. Helen had already applied her makeup and grabbed her white heels saying, "We needed to go." Lottie put on her shoes and followed her out the door, locking it behind her.

When they arrived at the office, Lottie logged into her computer, and checking on Mrs. Westcott, she saw that her stocks were going down fast. She called her to let her know and asked if she should sell them.

Mrs. Westcott said, "You'll do no such thing. It will go up, and I'm very busy. I'll talk to you later," and abruptly hung up. Lottie was worried even if Mrs. Westcott was rude. She went back to the paperwork of Mr. Lawrence's finances and concentrated on them, forgetting Mrs. Westcott. She looked up at the clock and saw it was lunchtime but had too much to do before Mrs. Roberts showed up. Helen walked over and said, "You going to lunch?"

"Not today. I'm running behind. I'll eat a snack when I get time." Helen left and came back after lunch with a Coke and a Nutri-Grain bar. Lottie said thanks and sipped and ate while strolling through the computer.

She had just finished her paperwork for Mr. Lawrence and noticed it was almost three thirty. She looked up and saw her sister ushering a lady to her desk. Lottie stood up saying, "You must be Mrs. Roberts who owns Bouquet."

She shook Lottie's hand saying, "I see you did look up my store."

Lottie smiled and asked her to sit down. When she first walked up, she thought that she was a child, but her gray hair with brown tints gave her away. Mrs. Roberts was only five foot and probably didn't weigh a hundred pounds. She sat across from Lottie looking at her with her blue eyes.

She said, "I have a small shop with two employees. I need you to do our taxes and handle the payroll, which I seem to never have time to do. My two helpers don't mind too much that I'm always late with their pay, but I don't want to lose them. I sure don't want the IRS after me since I don't know all the rules, so could you help me?"

Lottie said, "I can for sixty a week if that's acceptable." Mrs. Roberts said that would be fine. Lottie drew up the contract and printed two copies out. Mrs. Roberts signed the papers and gave her access to her account. They shook hands, and Mrs. Roberts took her copy and left.

Mr. Rivers came over to congratulate another new account saying she was doing a terrific job and was glad he had hired her. Lottie thanked him and went back to the paperwork on her two accounts. Soon it was time to leave. She shut down her station and grabbed her purse and met Helen in the elevator.

Helen said, "You are envied by the boss, and he told me he should never doubt me."

Lottie said, "I'm sure that made you happy," just as the elevator arrived. They traveled together to the first floor saying good night to other employees.

Walking out the door to the garage, Helen said, "I wonder how long it will take before they connect the elevator to the garage."

Lottie said, "You must be wishful thinking."

Helen opened the car doors with the button saying, "You are probably right." They got in and headed home.

When they walked in the door, Lottie said, "It's your turn to cook, and I'm headed to the shower." Helen went in the kitchen preheating the oven while she prepared her broccoli casserole. She put it in the oven and sat and searched her cell phone. Lottie decided to wash her hair while she was showering so it took her a little more time, and she figured that dinner would be ready time she was finished. She dried off and wrapped her hair in a towel and sat down at the vanity to use the blow dryer. After her hair was dry, she pulled a green nightgown out of the drawer and put it on. Putting the towel on the rack to dry, she walked to the kitchen.

Helen was still looking at her phone when she walked in asking about dinner. Helen looked up saying, "It's another fifteen minutes, and you can watch it while I take a shower."

Lottie poured herself a glass of tea and said, "Go ahead." Helen left and went straight to the bathroom. She took off her clothes, dropped them in the hamper, and turned on the shower. She laid her phone on the counter by the sink and stepped in the shower. The warm water felt good after a hard day at work. Knowing she was spending too much time, she hurried up and soaped her body. She rinsed herself off and turned off the shower as she stepped out. She dried herself and hurried and put on a pink gown and headed back to the kitchen.

Lottie had already pulled it out of the oven and brought it to the table, which was already set. Helen said thanks and sat down and saw a glass of tea was sitting in front of her. They each loaded their plates and began to eat.

While they ate, Lottie said, "Sometimes I miss Aunt Melody."

Helen took a bite and said, "I do too even if she was strict."

Lottie was about to eat her last bite saying, "We should go visit her sometime," and Helen agreed. They washed up the dishes and went out to the living room to watch TV before bed. Time seemed to move fast, and soon, they were ready for bed. Lottie went and turned off the TV, and they headed to the bedroom, which it was long before they were both asleep.

Lottie sort of jumped forward in her dream remembering how she met her husband, Jim Rhodes. It was the very next day when Mrs. Westcott rushed into her office screaming it was all Lottie's fault that she had lost so much money. Lottie tried to reason with her, but she was determined to sue the company. Mr. Rivers rushed over trying to calm her down, but she stormed out saying, "You will hear from my lawyer."

Mr. Rivers said, "You know the guy you are talking to, you should see if he will represent us." Jim had solved the problem, which eventually came to them being engaged.

Lottie saw in her dream that Helen was excited to be the wedding planner with Mrs. Rose's help. Lottie let them decide who in the office would be bridesmaids. Half the guys in Jim's office were planning a bachelor party. Helen told Lottie they had an appointment after work to pick out dresses for the wedding. They drove from work to North Highland Avenue, but there wasn't a parking spot near 853. They parked several blocks away and walked back to the store after feeding the meter. When they entered the store, a lady walked up to them.

"Good afternoon, I'm Maryann. Welcome to La Rime's Boutique. How can I help you?"

Helen said, "We have an appointment to try on the bride's dresses."

She went and showed off at least a dozen gowns. It was the last one that they both agreed on. The dress fit perfectly with a low-cut in the front and low in the back. It was a beautiful white gown reaching just above the floor. Helen also put on layaway six pink ruffles gowns for the bridesmaids and made an appointment for the girls to come in and try them on for alterations. They decided after work at 4:30 next Tuesday and Maryann agreed.

Helen put down a deposit and said, "Mr. Jim Rhodes will come and pay for the gowns." Before getting back to the car, they walked into Little Caesar's for a pizza to take home. They ordered a pepperoni and a liter bottle of Coke. Twenty minutes later, they made it back to the car and headed home.

Lottie called Jim from the car and gave him the address of the boutique, and he said he would take care of it tomorrow.

"Well, I love you, and we're almost home, so we'll talk later after we eat and get settled."

Jim said, "I love you too, and we'll talk later since I'm in the car headed home." They hung up just as Helen pulled up to the apartment. Lottie carried the pizza into the dining room while Helen got two glasses of ice for the Coke.

While eating, Helen said, "After you leave, I'll have to find someone to take your place. You know it's too hard to pay the rent here and have food."

Lottie said, "Take your time and find the right one since you have over a month to figure it out." Lottie said, "I guess after we eat, we need to call Aunt Melody to see if she wants to attend the wedding."

Helen said, "I hope she doesn't give us a hard time."

Lottie said, "I'm headed to the shower after we clean up the kitchen."

Helen said, "I guess you want me to call," and Lottie laughed and said, "You're the wedding planner."

Helen said to herself, "Lucky me for putting my big foot in my mouth." Helen picked up the phone and called, and after a few rings, it was picked up.

Aunt Melody said, "Who is this? And if you're selling something, you might as well hung up."

Helen said, "It's your niece, and I'm calling to say that my sister is getting married next month wanting to know if you'll attend."

"Well, I haven't heard from you girls since you left and was kind of heartbroken that you didn't call to tell me how you were doing." Helen didn't know what to say knowing she was wrong. Aunt Melody went on saying, "I would be honored to attend the wedding, and if you need any help, just let me know."

Helen said, "I will call you with details by next week."

Aunt Melody said, "You need to call more often and tell your sister to call too." She said she would and said, "I love you feeling quite humiliated for not calling." Aunt Melody said she loved her and couldn't wait to see them both next month.

Helen hung up and headed to the bathroom to tell Lottie. She was just getting out of the shower when Helen walked in. Helen told her all that was said, and Lottie felt a little embarrassed that she hadn't called before. Lottie dried off and Helen stripped and entered the shower. Lottie got a yellow gown out of the drawer and put it on. She heard the shower turn off and got a blue nightgown for Helen.

She handed it to her and said, "I'm going to call Jim and see you in the living room when I'm done."

Helen went on and walked barefooted to the living room and turned on the TV. Lottie sat down on her bed and called Jim. Lottie said,

"Helen is going to take care of the flowers tomorrow, and we need to schedule a time with the bakery for the wedding cake."

Jim said, "We have plenty of time, and I love you too."

Lottie said, "Oh! I'm sorry. I love you too. Just got caught up in the arrangements. Well, I'll see you tomorrow."

He said, "Why don't we have dinner tomorrow and talk over our plans?" She said that would be great and blew him a kiss good night. Lottie then went and joined her sister on the couch.

Lottie said, "I have a date tomorrow night with Jim." They watched TV till ten before going to bed. Before turning out the light, she told her sister, "Good night and I love you."

The next morning before work, Helen told Lottie that she had several places to go after work. Lottie said she was having dinner with Jim. "I'll let you know where it is so you can have dinner with us."

The day seemed to last forever, and she couldn't wait to see Jim that night. Helen dropped her off at home before doing her errands. Helen first stop was at the College Park Florist where she looked over the flowers in the shop and decided on yellow roses for the wedding, which was Lottie's favorite. She had them make up six bouquets for the bridesmaids and yellow boutonniere for the men. She said, "Bill it to Mr. Jim Rhodes, and they must be at the United Methodist Church on May the twentieth."

Helen then found a photographer in Midtown who worked out of Photograph Studios. The guy was Mr. Raymond. He said that he could do the photos and also said, "If you were looking for a place for the wedding party, I could rent you this place cheap."

She said, "I'll get back to you on that but want you for the picture taking." Helen also went to a catering service called Affairs Of-Pine, and they agreed to cater and to just let them know where it was. Helen called her sister asking where they were. She had a lot to talk about. She found that they weren't far from her, a place called Malones. She told Lottie she would be there in ten minutes.

Jim pulled in the lot at Malone's and helped Lottie out of the car. She had on a light blue dress with nylons and red heels, and Jim had on the same blue suit. Walking in, he let them know of his reservation. They seated them at a table in the middle of the room.

A woman named Marsh came up saying she would be the waitress. She handed them their menu and said, "Anything I can get you?"

Jim ordered a pitcher of beer, and she went to get it. She returned in a few minutes asking if they were ready to order.

Jim said, "No. We are waiting for another person." It wasn't long before Helen showed up. The waitress brought another menu and glass to pour her some beer. Helen told them all she had done and told Jim she sent all the bills to him.

Jim said, "No problem."

"And you can call the Photograph Studio back and say we agreed to hold the venue there."

Jim said, "I have a friend who is a baker, and I'll call her for us to go taste a few cakes for the wedding." Jim said, "Since all that is settled, let's order," and he motioned for the waitress. Jim said, "I would like a rib eye steak and baked potato and a salad with blue cheese."

Lottie ordered the salmon plate with fries and a salad with ranch dressing. Helen decided on a baked chicken with baked potato and a salad with ranch.

Marsh said, "I will return soon. Shall I get you another pitcher of beer?"

Jim said that would be fine as he finished the pitcher. They sat and discussed the wedding, sipping their beer. In about twenty minutes, they returned with their meal. After the meal, they sat and drank some more beer before calling for the check. Helen said to Lottie, "See you at home," and left while they waited for Marsh to return with his credit card. When she returned, he put on a sizeable amount for a tip. They got up and headed to the car.

Jim let her out at her apartment saying, "After work tomorrow, I'll pick you up."

Lottie held him and gave him a kiss. She said, "So I'll see you tomorrow," before getting out of the car and walking in. Jim smiled while she walked to the door, loving her more each day. He drove away when she closed the door and headed home.

Monday afternoon he was standing in the lobby just waiting for her to get off work. When she came out of the elevator, he gave her a hug and kiss saying, "Are you ready to go?"

Lottie said, "Where are we going?" Jim said to my friend's bakery to taste cakes and led her to his car. It was a fifteen-minute ride to Wright's bakery, and he helped her out of the car and walked in.

The lady behind the counter asked, "Can I help you?"

"Tell Martha we are here for the cake tasting."

She called Martha from the back and said, "HI, Jim. Is this your fiancée?"

Jim said, "This is Lottie. And this is my friend Martha." The girls shook hands, and she ushered them over to a table and said I'll be back with the samples. Martha returned and put five pieces of cake before them and stood back brushing her blond hair out of her eyes, which were blue. Lottie and Jim tasted each one of the cakes and decided on a white chiffon cake with white frosting. Martha said that was a good choice, and we can put a bride and groom on the top of the cake with a blue trim on each of the three layers.

Jim said, "That will be fine, and we won't need it till the third week in May."

Martha said, "We can have it ready."

Jim handed her a fifty-dollar bill for a deposit and said, "You remember my secretary Ms. Rose? She will be here that week to pick up the cake and give you the money then."

Martha said, "That will be fine. It will be ready." They left the bakery walking hand and hand back to the car.

Arriving back at the apartment, they sat in the car for a while kissing, and he said, "I can't wait till you're Mrs. Rhodes." She kissed him back and said, "I couldn't either, but I got to get in and help Helen with dinner."

"See you tomorrow at work."

"I'm sorry, but if you remember that the bridesmaids' fitting is tomorrow."

"That's right," he said. "We can go out Wednesday."

She kissed him again and said, "That's fine. See you then, but you better call me tomorrow night so I can tell you how it went."

Jim laughed and said, "You should know that I would," and gave her one last kiss before getting out of the car to help her out. Jim drove away feeling an urge and knew how much he loved her.

Tuesday afternoon after work, Helen got all the five girls together. Helen said, "We are going to La Raines to have your dresses fitted. It isn't a problem for any of you?"

"Holly told me Mary-Ann can go."

Helen said to Ruth, "Are you able to?"

She said yes and so did Doris and Peggy. Helen led the four girls to her car and drove them there. Holly and Lottie followed them in Holly's car. Holly asked if she had a flower girl and Lottie said no.

"Well, my sister is five, and when she heard about the wedding, she begged me to ask if she could be the flower girl."

Lottie said, "What's her name? It's Rose."

"That will be a perfect name to be a flower girl. Tell her I would very much like her to do the job."

Holly said, "She'll be excited."

When Lottie and Holly got there, the others were already in their dresses. The lady said, "Only these two so far need to be altered." Ruth's dress was too tight, and Mary-Ann's was too short. Holly went and tried on her dress, which fit perfectly. The manager said that we'll have all six dresses ready by next week. Lottie called Jim and told him, and he said he would send Ms. Rose with a check to pick up the dresses next week.

"Tell them next Friday to stop in my office and pick up their dresses."

When they got out of the boutique, Lottie told the girls that she was taking them to dinner. She led them to the LongHorn, which was right down the street. There was no use taking their cars, so all seven girls walked together to the restaurant. Lottie went in and told the greeter that there were seven in her party. The greeter said it will be a few minutes to wait.

Soon she came back and led them to a table in the back of the restaurant and said, "Your waitress will be here very soon." A woman came up to the table saying, "Welcome to LongHorn. I'm Regina and I'll be your waitress."

Lottie ordered two pitchers of beer while everybody decided what they wanted. There was a lot of gossip while they sat and drank. The waitress came back to take their order all except Holly ordered a rib eye and baked potato and salad. The waitress said she would bring several different salad dressings for them to choose from. Holly ordered a salmon meal with fries and a salad. The girls went back to talking about their different cases and especially about Mr. Rivers and how Helen got him wrapped around her finger.

Helen said, "That's not true," but everybody laughed at that.

The celebration lasted quite a while, and Lottie said, "I hate to break this up, but I think it's time to go." Each girl came and gave her a hug, which left her and Helen. She called Regina over for the check and paid with a nice tip. They left and returned to Helen's car. They drove home talking about that. It was great having all the girls together. When they got home, they took turns taking a shower and getting ready for bed. Lottie talked to Jim on the phone and told him about Holly's sister wanting to be flower girl.

Jim said, "I guess we'll have to find a ring bearer."

Lottie said, "Maybe one of your relatives."

"I'll ask my parents." Jim said, "I love you and good night." Lottie said she did too before hanging up. When the two sisters got in bed, they went over all their plans.

Finally, May arrived and the weather was still good—not too hot or not too cold. It was one of those springs where you'd rather be outside and not cooped up in the house. Helen had everything completed on the first week with help from Ms. Rose. Helen came downstairs after work to catch up with Ms. Rose.

"We are going to hold a bachelorette party at the Photograph Studios, and I need you to get the girls together and take them there ahead of me and Lottie." Helen gave Ms. Rose the address and said, "I will take Lottie for dinner and meet you there. Don't worry, the girls already know they are waiting for Lottie to leave before coming downstairs to you."

Helen got back in the elevator and went back upstairs just in time for Lottie to come. Helen said, "I'm holding the elevator for you not," expecting that Helen had already been downstairs. Helen said as Lottie entered the elevator, "I thought we should stop and get something to eat since I feel very hungry."

Lottie said, "I guess, but I'm not that hungry yet."

Helen said, "Well if you want, you can get something to drink, and we'll get you something afterwards to take home."

Lottie said, "That is fine. Where are we going?"

Helen said, "McDonald's is closed, and we can come back for the car." They walked the few blocks and went in. Helen ordered a Big Mac meal and a Coke extra for Lottie. They sat at the table while Helen ate her dinner, and Lottie sipped her soda.

Lottie said, "I thought you were hungry. You sure are taking your time."

Helen said, "I didn't know you were in a rush."

Lottie replied, "I'm not really. It's just you made me think you were starving to death. I'm finished. Why don't you go order your meal?" Lottie went up to the counter and ordered a quarter-pounder meal to go and stood there waiting for it after paying. Helen was cleaning up when she got back and saying you ready to go. They walked out of McDonald's and headed back to the parking garage to collect the car.

Helen said, "Everything is ready except you picking up your wedding gown."

Lottie said, "We got two more weeks. I have plenty of time."

Helen said while getting in the car, "Would you like to check out where the reception is going to be held? It's on our way home."

Lottie agreed to see it. When they stopped in front of the building, Helen said, "We got this hall and the photographer to go with it."

Lottie said, "Wow!"

Helen said, "It's a big hall. Let's go up so I can show it to you."

Lottie agreed as Helen parked the car, and they went up the stairs. When entering the room, the lights came on and everybody yelled, "Surprise!" All the girls were there in the office and Ms. Rose Jim's secretary.

Lottie went up to Ms. Rose and said, "I should have known that you had a hand in this." There was an open bar and a buffet table with different fixings for sandwiches. All the girls were having a good time, and each had a wedding gift for her.

Helen said, "You know Holly. She is going to move in when you leave."

Holly said, "It's about time I get out of my parent's house and share a room with my little sister. By the way, I told her you agreed to let her be flower girl and she was ecstatic, and my parents went out and bought her a dress for the occasion."

Helen said, “The flower shop agreed to give her a bucket of rose petals to drop on the aisle.”

Holly said, “I’m sure she’ll love that.”

The party lasted for hours, and several girls helped Lottie to take all her gifts to Helen’s car.

Lottie asked, “Can we go home now? I’m quite tired.”

Helen said, “That will be fine. Ms. Rose agreed to clean up.”

Lottie went around thanking everybody and giving each other a hug and a kiss on the cheek and especially Ms. Rose. Lottie said to Ms. Rose, “I enjoyed this a lot,” and turned and walked down the stairs. Lottie was happy it was Friday and she did not have to go in early and could sleep for a while. When they made it to the apartment, Lottie was so tired; she took off her clothes and slipped into her nightgown and went to bed. Helen brought in all the gifts and took a shower before retiring.

Finally, the day arrived, and both offices were closed because they were all at the wedding. Johnny came on a plane from Los Angeles, and Jenny drove down with Lottie’s Aunt Melody to the airport to pick him up. The church was full when they arrived, and Aunt Melody went to find Lottie. Jim hugged his brother and sister and led them to a place up front. Jim had rented a tuxedo for the event and so did Mr. Thomas, the best man. Pastor Dodge told the pianist to begin the wedding march. Rose the flower girl started down the aisle dropping rose petals. Mr. Thomas’s grandson was the ring bearer; he was five years old, and his grandfather was proud of him walking down the aisle. Helen followed him and the rest of the bridesmaids in their pink dresses. Lottie was last holding her aunt Melody’s arm. Jim watched her walking down the aisle and thinking how beautiful she was.

Pastor Dodge told everyone to be seated over the click of the camera off to his right. He asked, “Who gives this woman away?”

Aunt Melody said, “I do,” and went to her seat. Pastor Dodge went through the vows and asked Jeremy for the rings and handed them to each of them. After putting on the rings and saying, “I do,” Pastor Dodge said, “I now pronounce you man and wife. You may kiss the bride,” and everyone got up and cheered. They all went to the cars to make it to the Photographer Studios downtown.

When they entered the hall, there were tables set all around the room with white tablecloths, and the side table was full of food from the caterers plus an open bar. The wedding cake was on the other side with the photographer snapping pictures. Jim and Lottie were led to the table at the front of the room, which was reserved for the wedding party and even Pastor Dodge was there being Jim's friend. Each table contain flowers and a bucket of champagne, which to make toast. There was music, and Jim and Lottie had the first dance. There were quite a few toasts made to the bride and groom. The party lasted several hours. Jim and Lottie left soon on their way to their honeymoon. Helen took charge of the rest of the party and cleaned up.

The Rhodes went on to Miami Beach, Florida, and stayed at the Ramada Inn right on the beach. They had a glorious week there on the beach, but Lottie had to see a doctor there because she got sun poisoning. They were both red as lobsters and stayed in their room till she was better before heading home.

On the way, they stopped at Helen's to collect Lottie's stuff, but Helen was at work. Holly let them in saying, "You guys are surely red. I was off today, and I heard you were coming so I went ahead and boxed up your belongings if you didn't mind."

Lottie said, "Thank you. It would have been hard with this sunburn." Holly helped Jim carry the boxes out to the car. Lottie looked around and thought she would miss this place. She and Jim made it to his apartment.

The attendant George felt sorry for her and said, "Don't worry, Mrs. Rhodes. I'll bring the boxes in." Lottie went on in and got ready for a bath. George brought all the boxes in before returning to his job.

She called Jim saying, "Everything is here and he's gone."

Jim said, "Everything is fine."

"I'm glad you didn't decide to carry me over the threshold. I've might have hit you."

Jim started to laugh saying, "Did you need me to rub you down in aloe vera lotion?"

Lottie got out of the tub and dried off gently and said, laying on the bed, "Yes, please." Jim came into the bedroom with the lotion and lightly applied the lotion to her skin. She fell asleep, and he covered her up.

Jim and Lottie took about three days before their skin cleared up, and Jim told Mr. Thomas that he would be returning Monday. Lottie, on the other hand, took longer to heal but eventually returned to work.

Lottie was back at her desk the next week, and all the women in the office welcomed her back.

Helen took her out to lunch that day, missing her that whole ten days. She asked, "Was your vacation worth it?" She laughed. Lottie said it was great even with the sunburn.

When Jim returned to work, he had opened a savings account and started adding to it more each week. He worked hard for the next six months, and when Lottie got pregnant, he knew it was time to look for a house. Jim found a house on West Forsyth and went to the credit union to take out a loan. He hadn't told Lottie, wanting it to be a big surprise. Jim had saved up ten thousand dollars and put it down on a two-hundred-thousand-dollar house with a twenty-year mortgage at twenty-five hundred dollars a month. After the deal was signed, he couldn't wait to tell Lottie. At first, he was afraid she would be mad at him.

Jim said, "I thought we could go look at this house I found since we will need more room."

Lottie said, "You're right," and he drove her over to a house. Lottie saw it was a two-story brick house with regular-size front yard.

Jim said, "I got the keys. Let's go in." Lottie walked in the house seeing a large living room with a sliding glass door leading to the backyard, which was quite large, and Jim said it has a privacy fence and big enough to get a swing set for the kids.

Lottie said, "You sure there'll be more than this one?"

Jim said, "That's why this house has three bedrooms," which made her laugh. When she saw the kitchen with all the appliances, she fell in love with it. Jim took her upstairs and saw the three bedrooms, and the master bedroom had a large bathroom and the other bathroom was at the end of the hall with the other two bedrooms on either side of the hall facing each other. All three bedrooms were quite big, and Jim said, "We could get three or four kids in them."

Lottie looked at him and said, "I might have something to say about that."

"Well, what do you think?" he said.

She thought only a minute and said, "We need to put a deposit down on this house."

Jim smiled at her and said, "It's too late. It's ours." Jim told her all about it. "And we can move in anytime."

She was excited and gave him a big hug and kiss. "We must go furniture shopping tomorrow."

Jim said, "I got to work. Why don't you see if your sister is off and you two go?" Lottie called Helen immediately to see if she could go shopping with her tomorrow.

Helen asked, "Aren't you going a little too early for baby clothes?"

Lottie said, "We are going shopping for furniture. Are you off?" Helen said she could get off tomorrow after Lottie explained that Jim bought a house.

The next day, Helen came over and helped her pack to move. Then Helen took Lottie to Ashley Furniture in town and met with the saleslady. First, they looked at living room sets and decided on a five-piece sectional sofa with matching coffee table and two end tables. They also got a large bookcase with a forty-inch TV set in. Moving on to the dining room, they got a mahogany table, which had six cushioned chairs. They also got a large China cabinet that matched the table. Moving on to the bedrooms of the master bedroom, she found a king-size bed with his and her dressers and a nightstand. The furniture company give them a thirty-two-inch TV to be mounted on the wall. In the other two bedrooms, they decided to leave them till Lottie had children but bought twin beds for each room in case of overnight guests. The total came to just under five thousand dollars. Lottie put down a deposit off two thousand and drew up a contract to pay two hundred a month. They said they would have everything delivered by tomorrow.

Helen and Lottie went to lunch at the subway in the building so Jim could join them to tell him what they bought. Lottie got a BLT meal with chips and a drink and ordered a duplicate one for Jim. Helen got Italian sub with chips and drink. They just sat down when Jim walked in and came over giving Lottie a hug and kiss. During lunch, she told him everything she bought, and he couldn't wait to see it.

Jim said, "We must invite your sister and Holly over next week when everything is done."

Helen said, "She would like that. I'm sure Holly would too."

Jim said, "It's settled. I'll have Lottie call and tell you when we're ready."

The following week, Lottie invited them to the new house for dinner that night and had a big surprise. Both Helen and Holly came and looked over the new house before sitting down to a dinner of spaghetti and garlic bread. They each had a glass of wine, and Jim made a toast.

"To you two and to my wife who is going to have our first child." Helen got up and went to Lottie to give her a big hug and congratulated her. After the two of them left, they decided to talk to the rest of the girls in the office. They were planning a baby shower with everything to fill the nursery including furniture. The next day, they went downstairs to Ms. Rose and told her what they planned and for her to get Jim to stop Lottie from buying anything.

Ms. Rose also involved the other secretaries in the office and had their bosses contribute. They decided that Helen would get Lottie out of the house so they could bring everything in to surprise her. Everything was ready by the time Lottie was in her sixth month. Lottie was feeling a little depressed since Jim kept putting off setting up the nursery. When Helen came over, Lottie told her she couldn't understand why Jim kept putting it off like he didn't want the baby.

Helen said, "I'm sure he will be ready soon, and you know he loves the baby."

"I guess," she said, being depressed.

Helen said, "Why don't we go window shopping for the baby? I'll buy you a present for the baby. Now, not another word. Get dressed so we can go out."

Lottie got up from the couch and went into the bedroom, removed her gown, and put on a pair of jeans and a maternity top. She got a pair of tennis shoes out of the closet and put them on with a little trouble over her large belly.

Helen saw her walking out and said, "Let's go."

Helen led Lottie to the car and helped her in as Ms. Rose sat in her car across the street watching them leave. Ms. Rose called both offices letting them know it was time. It took several trips for the elevators to empty all the women out of both offices and all the males carrying all the gifts to the ladies' cars. Soon they were all headed to Lottie's. Ms. Rose got the furniture people to unload the baby furniture and set it up in one bedroom after moving the one twin bed and dresser into the other room. The furniture men were just finishing up as the women began to arrive. Each lady brought their gift to the nursery and looked at the furniture saying what good taste Ms. Rose had never being married. After unloading their gifts, they parked in the next block so Lottie wouldn't be suspected.

Soon Helen returned with Lottie, and everybody was up in the nursery. Helen said, "Why don't you lay down? I'm sure you're exhausted." She followed Lottie up the stairs, and Lottie saw a light in one of the bedrooms and the door closed. Lottie said, "I swear I left that door open," and went and opened it. Soon as the door opened, everyone hollered in surprise. Lottie saw everyone there and her nursery complete; she began to cry. Everyone gathered around her giving her a hug and kiss and showing her what they bought. Lottie had never seen so many newborn diapers before. The nursery had a bassinet and a crib and a changing table and dresser. They thought since she didn't know the sex of the baby, a lot brought gift cards. Others brought onesies and blankets to bring the baby home. Several brought baby cereal and formula and jars of baby food. Lottie was surprised at how much stuff was there. Mrs. Thomas came late bringing a baby tub and bath supplies. Lottie was filled with joy and hugs and kissed everyone before they left.

Helen asked if they were still on for dinner and Lottie said, "I'll start when everybody leaves, and you and Holly can help me." Lottie got chicken out to fry and Helen made the mashed potatoes.

Lottie told Holly, "You can set the table and make tea and green beans."

They worked together to finish dinner and soon Jim arrived. Jim said that that chicken smelled good. Lottie told him to go take a shower and it should be done by the time he gets done. When Jim returned, the four of them sat down to dinner.

Lottie said after dinner, "I'll show you all things that everyone had brought." While they ate, Lottie told them the doctor predicted that it would be in March. "My due date was the tenth." Lottie was already beginning to show and could feel the baby kicking. They all had an enjoyable time talking about the baby shower. After they finished eating, Helen and Holly cleaned up while Lottie took Jim upstairs to show him everything.

Jim was amazed at how much stuff was there and especially from his firm. He hugged and kissed her saying, "We're ready anytime you are." Lottie laughed and punched him in the shoulder. They went downstairs and everything was cleaned up.

Lottie told them, "Thank you very much, and glad you two are always there for me."

Lottie had taken maternity leave in her ninth month, and on March 1, her water broke. She called her doctor, and he said, "I'll meet you at the hospital."

She then called her sister who was at work and told her to tell Jim. She picked up her bag for the hospital and headed out to her car that Jim had bought for her. She was overjoyed when he had driven up in the fire red Toyota Camry and his friend from the office came behind with their car. It was the best Christmas present that year. They had a wonderful Christmas together, and now know there will be more than us two next year. When the pain subsided, she started the car and headed to the hospital. Helen had already told her boss she was leaving and headed downstairs to tell Jim the news.

Ms. Rose saw her coming and got on the intercom and said, "You better come out here. I think it's time." Jim grabbed his jacket off the back of his chair and came out of the office. He saw Helen standing there and he said, "Let's go." Ms. Rose said she would close up the office and meet them there.

They headed to Well Star feeling quite excited. When they arrived, they were told to go to the second floor to Labor and Delivery. At that time, no one was allowed in the delivery, so they were showed to the waiting room. They sat there for quite a few hours, and soon, Ms. Rose arrived and soon followed by Mr. Rivers and Holly.

James said, "You two must be hungry. Why don't we go down to the cafeteria and get something to eat? It's my treat." The five of them went downstairs, and Jim informed the nurse where they were going. Jim had a soda and a ham sandwich but was too nervous to eat, leaving half on his plate. Just as they returned to the waiting room, the nurse came out with the news that she had a baby girl who weighed seven pounds and eight ounces. The nurse led them to the nursery window where they showed him his child. She didn't have any hair but had green eyes like her mother. Jim thought it was the most beautiful baby in the world.

Soon they could visit Lottie in room 212, and James took Helen downstairs to get flowers while the rest went to Lottie. Jim came in and walked to the bed and kissed his wife while the others too congratulated her. Jim said it was a beautiful baby.

"Have you given her a name?"

"I have, but I want Helen here before I say."

Helen and James soon returned with a bouquet of yellow roses, which was Lottie's favorite.

Lottie said, "Thanks and, now I'll tell you all what my little girl's name is."

"I decided with Jim. Her name will be Beth Ann, which is your middle name Helen, also our mother's middle name. Jim agreed long as I let him name the next girl."

They all laughed.

"I want you, Helen, to be more than an aunt. I'm hoping you'll be her godmother." Helen broke down in tears and said she would be honored.

The next day when Helen left work, she headed back to the hospital. Lottie was feeding the baby when she got there.

"When you're done, if you don't mind, the girls in the office wanted me to send them pictures of the baby." Helen took the pictures and sent them to the girls in the office. Soon Jim came in asking to let him hold the baby. Helen passed it over to him, and the baby opened its eyes and smiled at him. It filled his heart with so much love for his first child. Jim held the child and went over and kissed Lottie.

Lottie said, "They are releasing me and the baby tomorrow. I hope it won't be any trouble for you get off work early."

Jim said, "Don't worry, but I must go out and get a car seat for the baby since no one brought one to the baby shower." Jim handed the baby back to Helen and kissed Lottie and left.

Jim went to the Walmart, which wasn't far from the house and got the best baby car seat they had. When he got home, he parked the car and opened the back door to attach the seat after removing it from the box. He cooked a frozen pizza and ate before watching TV before bed.

When he got to work, Lottie called and said, "I'll be released at eleven." Jim told Ms. Rose that he would be leaving early. About ten thirty, he left for the hospital. When he got to the room, the nurse said we ordered a wheelchair, and you should bring your car up to the front. Jim went back out to collect the car. The nurse wheeled Lottie and the baby out and took the baby and hooked it in the car seat before helping Lottie into the car.

After a few days at home, Lottie said, "We'll have to get someone to watch Beth Ann for me to return to work."

Jim said, "I been thinking that I'm making enough. You should quit and stay home with the baby."

After a complete discussion, she agreed to do that and called Mr. Rivers. Lottie told him and he said that she could come back to work anytime she wanted. Several girls from the office would drop by on their days off to see her and the baby. She heard a knock at the door thinking it was one of the girls but, when she opened the door, found Pastor Dodge standing there. She invited him in and asked if he would like a coffee since she was just sitting down with a cup.

He said, "I've been meaning to get here to see you and the baby. We missed you in church and wonder when we can expect you back." He said, "There is no problem with the baby since we have a nursery."

Lottie said that she and the baby would be there Sunday. "Let me get the baby so you can see it." Lottie left the room and returned in a few minutes with the child. "Pastor Dodge, I'd like you to meet Beth Ann."

Robert picked up the baby and said she was a beautiful girl. "Now I'd like to pray for her." Robert prayed for the baby and then Lottie before leaving.

After she finished cleaning the house, she looked at the clock and saw that Jim would be home soon. She went and started frying pork chops and put water in a pan for the instant potatoes and opened a can of green beans that she put in the microwave. She had just finished dinner when he walked in and came into the kitchen to give her a kiss. Lottie told him to wash up because dinner was ready.

When they sat down to dinner, Lottie told him of the pastor's visit and that she would attend church on Sunday with the baby. She said, "I wanted to know if you'll go with us."

Jim, taking a bite, said, "We have a new client, and I might have to work. I also have a little more paperwork to get done. I'll join you in the living room when I'm done." He got up and carried his plate to the kitchen and came back giving Lottie and the baby a kiss before going to the study.

Lottie cleaned the dishes and finally put Beth Ann down for the night. She had just turned on the TV when he came to join her.

That Sunday, she showed up at church with one of her friends from the office since Jim didn't go. Lottie walked up to the pastor and said, "I'd like you to meet my friend Polly who worked in the office with me."

Pastor Dodge shook hands with her and looked down at her who was very short but had nice long black hair and crystal-clear blue eyes. His sermon that day was on Romans 6:23, "For the wages of sin is death, but the gift of God is eternal life through Jesus Christ our Lord."

Pastor Dodge said, "The choice is yours. You can either accept Jesus and go to heaven or accept the devil and follow him to hell."

When the invitation was called, both Lottie and Polly came down the aisle, and Pastor Dodge prayed for them, and they were both saved that day. Pastor asked them if they would like to become a member of the church and they agreed. He said, "We'll have it set up, and by next week, you can be voted in." Lottie and Polly said they would be there.

The next Sunday, they were made members, but Jim still refused to go saying he had important work he had to finish. Polly joined the choir, and being very attractive, she began to get quite a few men trying to date her.

Pastor Dodge asked Lottie about Jim, and she said he was very busy with his work. Pastor Dodge said he would talk to him. "I was wondering about your sister."

Lottie said, "I had asked her to come, but she hadn't answered me."

"Do you think you could call her and see if it is alright for me to visit her?"

Lottie said that she would talk to her sister and let him know. Robert thanked her and continued to shake hands with the members at the door.

Lottie called her sister when she got home and told her that she and Polly were now members of the church.

Helen said, "That's nice, and how is Beth Ann doing?"

"She is fine, and Pastor Dodge wanted to set up a meeting some night with you and Holly."

"Well, maybe tomorrow night since we have nothing planned."

Lottie said she would tell him.

Helen said, "If you ever need a babysitter, you know you can count on me."

Lottie said, "I know. And I love you and talk to you later."

Helen said, "I love you and goodbye."

Lottie called the pastor after hanging up and said, "Tomorrow night would be fine," giving him the address.

Robert said, "Thanks I'll. make sure to be there." Lottie hung up and went to take care of her baby who was crying.

Pastor Dodge showed up at Helen's that next night about six. When he knocked at the door, a young lady opened it. He said, "Good evening, I'm Pastor Dodge. Is Helen here?"

Holly smiled and said, "She is in the kitchen cooking dinner."

"Oh! Then you must be Holly, her roommate."

She said she was. "If you have a seat here in the living room, I'll tell her you're here."

Pastor Dodge sat on the couch while Holly went on into the kitchen. Holly came back and said, "Helen had just finished dinner and is hoping you would like to join us." He said he would and got up and followed her into the kitchen. Holly had set a third chair in front of their small table and told him to be seated. Helen brought over the pork chops she had fried. Holly brought over the baked potatoes and peas and asked what he would like to drink. Robert asked for some tea and Holly went and got the pitcher out of the fridge and filled his glass. When the women sat down, he asked if he could give grace.

He said, "Oh, Lord, bless this food that we are about to eat, and I pray that both Helen and Holly will come to know you, and I ask it in Jesus's name. Amen."

Before dinner was over, he had told them to come in next Sunday. He prayed for them before leaving. They both shook hands and said, "We'll see you then." They went to clean up the kitchen, and the pastor got in his car and left.

The two of them began to attend church regularly. Holly was saved after a few weeks. Helen took over the nursery so she could be close to Beth Ann. Lottie was happy that the four of them would be there and was still hoping that Jim would eventually come.

In September Lottie found out she was pregnant with her second child. In March, they celebrated Beth Ann's birthday with only Helen and Holly. Helen said she would babysit anytime she was needed. Lottie only had three months to go. On June 22, she had another girl named after the middle names of Jim's mother and sister. Jim's sister showed up for the baby. She heard the name would be Audrey Jean.

She told Jim, "I'm glad you didn't give her two J's like me. Mom is the only one who didn't have two J's." She told her brother, "I never told anybody my middle name. I always put Jennifer J. Rhodes, and I noticed that no one knows your middle name is John."

Jim said, "Only Lottie knows and that's because it's on the marriage license." He and Jenny were standing by the nursery window when the nurse came over to show them the baby. Audrey weighed seven pounds and two ounces and had little curly black hair with blue eyes.

Jenny said, "Looks like this one take after you, especially since Beth Ann took after her mother." Jenny stayed a week and got Beth Ann a doll since they were paying more attention to Audrey. Jenny told Beth Ann, "With this doll, you'll know how to protect your sister. Since you're older, you'll be the one she looks up to." Beth Ann felt proud that she had a sister to take care of.

When Beth Ann turned six, she gave Audrey the doll that Jenny gave her since she had so many of them. Lottie kept them in church, and Helen was always there in the nursery to take care of them and was sad when Beth Ann moved to her Sunday School class.

On Audrey's fifth birthday that Sunday, she told Beth Ann that she wanted to give her heart to the Lord. Beth Ann realized that she should go to the altar with her. They left their mommy in the pew and when down the aisle to Pastor Dodge and said that they wanted to be saved. Pastor Dodge prayed with them, and they were saved that day. Lottie saw what was happening and began to cry with such joy that her girls made their decision to follow the Lord. Telling Jim afterwards, he agreed to start attending church. Lottie said her prayers have been answered.

She heard someone talking to her and awoke to see Holly sitting down beside her and Polly next to her.

"Lottie!" Holly said. "I thought Jim and Helen would be here with us."

Lottie remembered how her sister had betrayed her by having an affair with Jim behind her back. If it wasn't for Ms. Rose, she might never have known. It took her a long time to forgive them and only with Pastor Dodge helping her and lots of prayer. Several times her two girls tried to go to their father, but something was holding them back, which kind of scared them. Jim was a little sad too but was glad Helen sat next to him.

CHAPTER 12

RUBY

Jennifer said to Jim, “I hope John gets here soon. I’m so afraid that he’ll miss the bus.”

Jim said, “I’m sure he’ll make it. Look isn’t that your friend Rita?”

Jennifer saw Rita and Susie walk into the bus terminal and her daughter trailing behind. They two of them went and join the pastor with all the other members of the congregation.

Ruby walked over to Jennifer and said, “For some reason, I couldn’t follow my mother but at least you are here.”

The ticket master walked over to them saying, “Are you Ms. Ruby Jacobs?”

She looked up at him and said that she was; he handed her a ticket and walked back to the booth. Ruby said, “That was strange.”

Jennifer looked at her ticket and said, “We are on the same bus.”

Ruby said she was glad but asked, “Where are we going?”

Jennifer said, “That’s the one thing I haven’t found out yet. I’m hoping John knows when he gets here.”

Ruby said, “I was glad when you moved in with us but sad when you left.”

Jennifer said, “We saw each other every Sunday, and I always called to check up on you.”

“I know and I was glad.”

Jennifer said, “You are still my little sister and always will be.”

Ruby said, “I’m happy that I could always come to you with my problems, and I especially am glad since I’m confused and quite nervous.”

Jennifer said, "Whatever happens, I got your back."

Suddenly, John walked up and leaned down and kissed Jennifer. She said, "I was afraid you weren't coming."

He said, "I wasn't sure either, and do you know why we are here?"

"No. I was hoping you had the answer." He looked over to Ruby and said, "Hello, and why aren't you over there with your mother?"

Ruby said, "I can't get there."

John looked over to the other side of the room seeing everybody from church. John was called over to claim his ticket, and he asked what was happening. The ticket master didn't give him an answer. John walked back to Jennifer saying, "Why is no one saying what's happening?"

Jennifer said, "I don't know, but I'm scared."

John sat down and put his arm around Jennifer.

Ruby felt that no one wanted to talk to her, and she started remembering her life. She was born here in Atlanta with her mother and father. Her mom was thirty-eight and her father was in the military and was stationed in the Middle East. She never met her father because he was killed in action. Ruby found out he had come home to see the baby born but was sent back almost immediately. She had a vague image in her mind of a man in uniform who had brown hair and blue eyes like her. Her mother raised her alone, and she only saw pictures of her father. She was happy when Jennifer came to live with them because she treated her like a little sister. She could always go to her if she had a problem.

She didn't have a problem in elementary, but now she was in middle school and was alienated by almost all her classmates except Susie who seemed to be in the same boat as her. Her mother just wouldn't understand, and she was always complaining that she wouldn't go to church with her. Only one time they caught a student picking on her. She had got her lunch and was walking to the table when Judy Moore tripped her and made her spill her tray all over the floor. Mrs. Smith, the lunchroom lady, saw Judy deliberately stick out her foot. She got on the intercom and called the principal to come to the lunchroom. When Mrs. Lamore got there, Mrs. Smith was cleaning up the mess. She told Mrs. Lamore what happened.

Mrs. Lamore said, "Ms. Moore, you will have detention after school, and you will be charged for Ms. Jacobs's lunch." She turned to Ruby and said, "Go get another lunch. You won't be charged."

Ruby went and got another lunch but had a hard time eating it after being embarrassed and laughed at by everyone in the cafeteria. Susie was at the same table asking if she was alright. Still feeling angry, she lashed out at her saying leave me alone. Susie looked down at the table feeling quite hurt. The rest of the day everybody left her alone, and when she calmed down, she was sorry; she talked to Susie that way.

When she got home, she hoped that she would get a chance to talk to Jennifer without her mother being around. She went upstairs and changed out of her school uniform and put on a T-shirt and blue shorts to match. Ruby went down to the kitchen and saw her mother leave out chicken to fry. She got out the skillet and the oil and saw the batter made up on the counter. She warmed up the skillet with the oil and rolled the chicken in the batter before putting it in the pan.

She heard her mother and Jennifer come in, and soon her mother came in the kitchen. "Have you done your homework?" she asked.

Ruby said, "No. I was going to do it after dinner."

Rita said, "I'll take over dinner. You go do your homework." Ruby asked where Jennifer was. Rita said, "Probably taking a shower." Ruby hurried upstairs to the bathroom door and knocked.

Jennifer called out, "Who is it?"

Ruby said, "It's me. Can I talk to you?"

Jennifer said, "Come on in. The door is unlocked."

Ruby entered a steamy room and said, "Today a girl named Judy made me lose my lunch. She said this isn't the first time. It's every day someone is picking on me." Jennifer turned off the shower and walked out. Ruby handed her a towel.

Jennifer asked, "When they pick on you, do you fight back with words?" Ruby said that she did. Jennifer said, "There's your problem. When you fight back, they think it's funny. If you didn't fight back after a while, they'll get bored and leave you alone. Now let me get dressed before dinner, and I hear your mother calling you."

Ruby hurried out of the bathroom and headed downstairs thinking maybe she was right. When she got downstairs, her mother said, "I need you to set the table and make the sides." Ruby put on a pot of water to boil while she got the plates and silverware. By the time she finished setting the table, the water was boiling. She got out a can of corn and opened it and put it in the microwave. Getting out packages of instant potatoes and, with the water, started mixing it in a bowl. The microwave beeped, and she put the corn in a bowl with a little butter. Ruby then carried the sides to the table, and her mother came behind her with the chicken.

Jennifer came downstairs in a red T-shirt and matching shorts. She saw that dinner was ready and got glasses and the pitcher of tea. She filled the glasses, and everybody sat down. Rita said grace before they ate.

Rita fixed her plate before asking Ruby how her day went. Ruby told her what happened, and her mother said, "I'm glad the principal took care of it." Ruby felt that she wouldn't see her opinion, so she kept quiet. She knew not to ask her mother to take her out of school, but she really wanted to quit. After dinner, Jennifer helped her clean up while Ruby loaded the dishwasher. She told Jennifer her only friend was Susie, and she screamed at her today being so mad.

Jennifer told her, "You should call your friend and apologize."

Ruby felt bad about it and went to her room and called Susie before doing her homework.

Susie picked up the phone and Ruby said, "I want to say I'm sorry for today."

Susie said, "I understand why you were mad. I would have been too. I can't talk right now. My parents are fighting, and I must go to my room. I'll talk to you tomorrow," and hang up.

Ruby heard her screaming in the background and felt more sorry for Susie. Ruby sat at her desk in her room doing her homework and watched a little TV before getting sleepy. Ruby grabbed a pink nightgown out of her drawer and headed to the bathroom. She took a shower and put on the gown after she dried. She dropped her clothes in the hamper and headed back to her room saying good night. Her mother came into the room after she got into the bed. She came and gave her a kiss and said, "See you in the morning," and left the room. Ruby turned off the light and thought about what Susie was going through and was glad she didn't have that problem. It wasn't too long before she drifted to sleep.

The next day at school, she took Jennifer's advice. When they started on her, she ignored them and went on to class. They couldn't understand why she didn't holler at them and say she was no fun. They gave all their attention to Susie who would go away crying. Ruby thought that they were so cruel and would never be friends with them. She tried to tell

Susie not to pay attention to them, but she was too upset to even talk to her. By the end of the week, no one was picking on her, and she could tell that Jennifer was right and she suddenly had friends.

Feeling great about herself, she cooked dinner for Jennifer and her mom before they walked in the door. Ruby came and gave her mother a hug and told her dinner is ready. Rita was totally surprised since Ruby always waited on her to take over dinner. Ruby then went and hugged Jennifer and said, “You were right. Nobody bothers me anymore.” They walked into the dining room and the table was set with a plate of pork chops and each had a bowl of salad next to their plates and even a tall glass of ice tea. Rita was impressed and sat down to give the blessing.

Rita said, “You have done a great job, and I’ll clean up after dinner.” Jennifer gave her praise too. After eating, Ruby went to do her homework, and Rita and Jennifer cleaned up. She said to Jennifer, “I have never seen her so happy, and I appreciate what you did.”

Jennifer went in to check on Ruby before going to take a shower. Ruby was writing at her desk when she walked in. Ruby looked up and said, “I owe you big time, and how can I repay you?”

“Well, you could make your mother happy by attending church with us on Sunday.”

Ruby said she would call Susie to see if she would go with her. Ruby went upstairs to her room and made the call. After five rings, Susie came on the phone saying hello. Ruby said, “It’s quiet there. Aren’t your parents at home?”

Susie said, “I convinced them that they needed to go out together. Hopefully they’ll stop arguing all the time.”

I was glad to hear it. “I’m sure it will work. “Oh! By the way, I’m sorry that you are still getting picked on in school. You need to take Jennifer’s advice and ignore it. It worked for me, and I’m sure it will work for you.”

Susie said, “You are probably right. I notice nobody bothers you anymore.”

“Well, it took a little while for them to give up.”

Susie said, “I will try it and see what happens. I’m tired of them making me cry, which seems to make it worse.”

"I know they get off on your tears, so you need to stop crying." Susie said she would try. "One more thing. Because Jennifer helps me, I promise to go to church with her and wonder if you would go with me."

Susie thought for a moment. "I'm sure my parents would let me go, and I guess I would." Susie said, "I only live a few blocks from you, so I'll come over about eight thirty if that's alright."

Ruby said that was perfect before saying, "Goodbye, and see you in school."

Ruby went and got her nightgown of pink and headed to the bathroom to take a shower. When she got there, Jennifer was coming out the door in her blue nightgown. Ruby said, "Susie said she would go with us Sunday."

Jennifer said, "I like that. Do we have to pick her up?"

"No. She is going to walk over here."

"I'm sure your mother will be surprised, so we won't tell her."

Ruby said, "I like that idea, and I'll be down when I'm finished in the shower." When Ruby was dried and dressed for the night, she joined her mother and Jennifer on the couch. Her mother asked what they were talking about upstairs in the hall. Ruby said she asked Jennifer if she would help her with her art project.

Rita said, "I see. Since I have no artistic ability, just let me see when you two are done."

Ruby said she would and sat quietly the rest of the night. Rita got up in a little while and made them some popcorn to eat. The three share it while watching one of their favorite shows. A few hours later they turned off the TV and headed to bed.

The rest of the week was uneventful since Susie took Jennifer's advice, and by the end of the week, they stopped picking on her. Ruby said, "See it worked."

Susie said it did, but it was hard not to cry. "Well, it's over, and I'll see you in two days from now since it's the weekend,"

Susie said, "You forgot we are supposed to go to church Sunday."

Ruby said, "Oh, yes, I was hoping to forget I made that promise. Well, I'll see you Sunday morning."

Susie said, "Don't worry. I'll be there. My parents said it was alright."

They left school Friday, and Susie was looking forward to going, but Ruby wasn't. She knew she had made the promise and wished she could of back out, but with Susie going, she had no excuse.

Sunday soon came, and Rita heard a knock at the front door and went to answer it. When she opened the door, she saw a young lady standing there. Rita could tell it was a teenager standing there dressed like a woman. She had on a red dress and black high heels and said to Rita, "Hi, I'm Susie and was invited by Ruby to go to church with you."

Rita almost spilled the coffee she was holding and said, "Come in. I'm sure Ruby will be ready soon. Would you like something to drink?"

"No, thank you, Mrs. Jacobs. I already had breakfast."

Rita closed the door and called up Ruby and said that Susie was down there.

Ruby said, "Good. Were you surprised? I'll be down in a minute."

Jennifer walked in the room saying, "You must be Susie."

Rita looked at her and said, "You knew she was coming?"

Jennifer grinned and said, "It is a surprise. They are both going to church with us."

Rita said, "I am surprised since I could never talk Ruby into going and now Susie too." Rita had Susie sit up front with her while Ruby and Jennifer sat in the back.

Soon they arrived at church, and Pastor Dodge came up and shook hands. Rita introduced her daughter to him and Ruby's best friend Susie. "If you remember, she helped me several times on Wednesday night."

Pastor Dodge told the girls, "Welcome to the church," and said, "I saw her but was never introduced to her." They found an empty pew and sat down before the service began.

After the choir had finished with the song "Amazing Grace," the pastor went up to the pulpit and said, "Today we are reading from John 15–21. For God so loved the world that he gave his only begotten son, that whosoever believeth in him should not perish, but have everlasting life. For God sent his son into the world not to condemn the world, but the world through him might be saved. He that believeth on him is not condemned, but he that believeth not is condemned already, because he hath not believed in the name of the only begotten Son of God. And this is the condemnation, that light is come into the world, and men loved darkness rather than light, because their deeds were evil. For everyone that doeth evil hate the light, lest his deeds should, reproved but he that doeth truth cometh to the light, that his deeds may be made manifest, that they are wrought in God."

When he was finished, Pastor asked if anyone there would like to be saved. The spirit came over to Susie, and she made her way to the altar and Rita followed her down. Susie told the pastor that she wanted to give her heart to Jesus, and he prayed with her and Rita. She was saved, and the church welcomed her to the congregation. Rita gave her a hug and said, "You are welcome to come with us every Sunday."

Susie, with tears in her eyes, said, "I would love to be with you here." They walked back to their seat while the choir sang their song before closing the service with a prayer. Pastor Dodge stood at the door shaking hands and said congratulations to Susie.

On the way home, Susie was still sitting up front, and Rita was talking to her and ignoring everyone else, which made Ruby jealous. She became mad and wished she had never talked Susie in going. Ruby thought to herself, *I'll never talk to her again, and at least I still have Jennifer.*

When they pulled into the driveway, Ruby jumped out of the car, and saying nothing, she went into the house and slammed the door behind her. Susie was wondering what she did wrong, and tears fell from her cheek.

Rita felt ashamed of the way Ruby was acting. She told Susie, "Don't worry about it. She'll get over whatever is wrong. You will be here next Sunday, won't you?"

Susie said she would as she headed home. Rita was angry and wanted to yell at Ruby, but Jennifer stopped her and said, "She's jealous because you made a fuss over Susie. You never showed her affection like you did with Susie today. Don't worry, I'll talk to her and straighten her out." Rita told Jennifer thanks and went into the house.

Jennifer went in the house and on up to Ruby's room and knocked. Ruby called out with a sniffle to come in. She ran to Jennifer crying saying, "She liked her more than me just cause I don't like church and Susie does. I'll never go with them two again."

Jennifer said, "You made too much out of it. She was just happy for Susie. She loves you very much and has told me so. I think you should apologize to your mother and especially Susie since you hurt her feelings."

After calming down, she went down and told her mother she was sorry.

Rita told her, "I love you very much, and you shouldn't think that I don't."

Ruby said, "I love you too, Mom, and I'm sorry for acting like a spoiled brat."

Rita gave her a hug and kiss and said, "You should apologize to Susie and tell her you're happy for her."

Ruby returned to her room and called Susie, but her mother answered. Ruby said, "Please, Mrs. March, may I talk to Susie?"

"I'll see. She is very upset and crying in her room and won't talk to me."

Ruby said, "It's my fault. I was calling to apologize."

Mrs. March said, "You know you're the one she talks about saying how you two are best friends." She said, "Just a minute. I'll see if she'll talk to you."

Ruby waited feeling that much worst.

When Susie came on the phone and said hello, Ruby said, "I'm sorry. I was mad at my mom and took it out on you. Can we still be friends?"

Susie said, "I'm glad you are not mad at me because of what I did."

Ruby said, "No. You have more courage than me. I couldn't have stood in front of all those people. I congratulate you on being saved."

Susie said, "Next week I am going to ask to be a member."

Ruby said, "I am happy for you, but I didn't want to go in the first place. I owe Jennifer for helping me, and I hope you don't hold it against me if I don't go."

Susie said, "As long we are best friends, it'll be okay."

Ruby told her that will never change and said, "See you in school." Susie said goodbye and hung up.

Ruby and Susie spent all their time together in school as well as home. They would hang out in Ruby's room listening to the radio when they weren't doing homework. Ruby was up to an A average with Susie's help. The only day they were apart was on Sunday since Ruby refused to go to church. Susie told her mother to go to church, and she was saved so the arguing stops.

Then their relationship started to drift apart when Molly Summers transferred to their school. Ruby started hanging out with her because she was the most popular. Molly came from Chicago and was a very beautiful girl on the outside but not on the inside. She was built like a model with long brown hair and hypnotic green eyes, and every boy in school was falling for her. Molly soon formed a gang of girls and Ruby wanted in. Molly told her she had to drop Susie.

"We don't want no Christian girls in our group. She's just a loser." Ruby joined the gang, leaving Susie behind. Susie was hurt when Ruby started talking badly about her. Ruby's grades went down quickly even to the point of almost failing. She stayed out late and even sneaked out a few times in the middle of the night. In school, she was too exhausted to pay attention in class and was sent to the office several times to sleep in class. Rita was called into the principal's office for skipping class. Rita tried to talk to her, but she didn't listen.

She told Ruby, "You are now punished. You'll come straight home and do your homework, which I will check." Ruby was quite mad but knew talking back would only make it worse.

That Friday, Molly told Ruby in school that she was having a party tonight. Ruby said she was punished and couldn't go nowhere.

Molly said, "Well, Johnny Apollo will be there, and he especially wanted to meet you."

Ruby knew he was the quarterback for their high school football team. Ruby had a big crush on him, having brown curly hair and dreamy brown eyes. That temptation was too big, and she told Molly that she would be there. "But it will be late. I'll sneak out when everyone's asleep."

Molly said, "No problem. The party won't be till ten anyway."

Ruby came home and did her homework for Monday, which Rita checked and said, "I see you're doing better in school now." Ruby acted like it was a big deal that she pleased her mother. Ruby was finally allowed to go downstairs and watch TV with Jennifer and her mother. It was after ten when they went to bed, and Ruby waited till everyone was sleeping. She listened at both doors and heard no sound then went to her window in her room and climbed out. The porch was right under her room. It was easy to get on the porch roof and slide down the pole. Molly must have told Johnny because he came out of the darkness when she made it to the ground. Johnny told her his car was parked around the corner, and they headed to it. Johnny's car was a red Toyota Corolla, and he opened the door for her and then got behind the wheel and headed to Molly's party.

They walked into the party hand in hand, and Molly came over and said she was glad she was here. Molly handed her a drink. It smelled sweet, and as soon she took a drink, it burned going down her throat. Ruby said, "What is this?"

Molly told her it was a strawberry daiquiri and laughed.

Johnny told her, "It won't hurt you. Drink up."

At first it didn't bother her, but after a few hours, she was feeling dizzy. Johnny got her on the floor to dance to the music, but she couldn't. He led her over to a couch and started kissing her, and soon he was touching her. Ruby suddenly knew what he was doing and jumped up from the couch saying, "No!" She was quite drunk and staggered to the door saying, "I'm going home."

Johnny came after her saying, "You'll never make it. Let me take you."

Ruby gave in, and he helped her out to the car and took her home. When they got there, she got out, and he pulled away fast leaving her there. Ruby started to climb the rail but hit the ground a few times before reaching the roof. She made it to her window and fell on to the bed and was out like a light. In a little while, she became cold and went and closed the window before returning to bed.

In the morning, Rita came to wake up Ruby with the news she had heard on the TV. Rita found Ruby on top of the cover still dressed in clothes, which were wrinkled. When she shook her, she could smell the liquor on her breath. Rita shouted at her saying, "You went to that party last night."

Ruby looked at her saying, "I'm sorry, and I know I was wrong for going."

"How did you get out of being arrested?" Rita said.

Ruby said, "What are you talking about? I left early."

Rita said Molly Summers was arrested for underage drinking plus quite a few of her friends.

Ruby said, "I was with Johnny, and he got fresh, so I made him bring me home."

"You know you are still punished for sneaking out, and what do you mean he was getting fresh?"

Ruby said, "He put his hands where I didn't want them."

Rita said, "Then you shouldn't see that boy again."

"I don't think you have to worry. He was very mad at me when he left."

"Then go take a shower and get dressed for school. Ruby took out her school clothes and walked barefooted to the bathroom. The first thing she did was brush her teeth since her mouth tasted so bad. Taking off her clothes and sticking them in the hamper, she jumped into the shower. She washed quickly because it was getting late. She dried and got in her clothes and brushed her hair that was a total mess from last night. She grabbed her sneakers out of her room and headed downstairs. She didn't have time for breakfast. Putting on her shoes and socks, she grabbed her book bag and went out the door.

When she got to school, everyone ignored her while walking down the hall. She felt that she went from Ms. Popular to Ms. Zero. Johnny was hanging onto a girl named Sharon who was known for giving out to boys. She could hear them whispering as she headed to class. It went like that the whole day except at lunch Susie came to sit with her.

Ruby said, "I'm sorry for acting the way I did. Do you know why everybody is ignoring me?"

Susie said, "The rumor is that you left the party early, and you must have called the cops."

Ruby said, "I didn't because Johnny took me home and I passed out in my bed."

Susie said, "I'm glad you didn't get arrested."

Ruby said, "Thanks. You're the only friend I can count on. Can we start over hanging out together?"

Susie said, "I would like that."

"I know I'm punished, but maybe I can talk my mother into letting you come over." Ruby was glad when that day was over, especially not having to face Molly and her friends.

Ruby got home without anybody bothering her and decided to cook dinner herself hoping that her mother would forgive her. She fried pork chops and made mashed potatoes. It was almost done when Jennifer walked in.

Ruby said, "You're early. Where's Mom?"

There was a funeral today for an old member of the church, and your mother attended with the pastor. She should be home shortly, and I heard you got yourself in trouble last night. Ruby told her about it while Jennifer opened a can of green beans to put in the microwave.

Ruby said, "What's worse is they think I called the cops. I think I'll be in more trouble when Molly comes back."

Jennifer said, "I'm proud of you not giving into him, and you can see by the other girl was that was all he wanted from you."

Rita soon arrived and said, "I'm glad you made dinner since I didn't have time." Sitting down to eat, Rita said to Jennifer, "Do you know Mrs. Brown from church? She was the one you replaced as secretary. It was her funeral we attended. She didn't live too long after retirement. She was working in her garden and had a heart attack. Her family was at the funeral and told me she had refused their help. Her daughter Libby will get the house."

Jennifer said sorry that she's gone. "I only saw her a few times in church and the pastor introduced her to me. Rita was still upset with Ruby but was glad that she hadn't ended up in jail. Ruby told Jennifer she was a little scared of what would happen tomorrow. She asked her mother if Susie could come over to help her with her homework tomorrow.

Rita said, "It will be alright, but you will come straight home and you won't be leaving here after school for a long time." Ruby told her mother that she was sorry and wouldn't ever do it again. Ruby finished up the dishes and stayed the rest of the night in her room.

The next day when she got to school, the gang was waiting for her. Molly wanted to know why she snitched on them.

Ruby cried saying, "I didn't. I was sick from the drinks, so Johnny took me home."

"Yea, I know you're just a goody two-shoes. I'm sure every boy in this school won't have nothing to do with you and you're no longer part of our gang. If we find out that you did, you'll be in big trouble. All our parents are picking us up after school since the poor things had to pay our bail. Don't think we can't get you, so you better be right."

They soon found out it was a neighbor who saw a teenage couple staggering on their lawn making out. Mr. Summers was very hostile to them for not calling him first. Ruby was reduced back to only Susie as friend since everyone acted like she didn't exist. With Susie's help, her grades began to improve, and she was taken off restriction.

From now on, Susie always walked home with Ruby in case she needed help from being attacked by the other kids. She always stayed and did homework together so that Ruby's grades would improve. Rita came home and saw them working, and Ruby stopped to help her mother with dinner. Rita said, "That's okay. I'm ordering pizza tonight, and I hope you'll stay, Susie." She said she would.

Jennifer soon arrived since she was with John most of the time and not coming home with Rita. Jennifer came in breathless saying, "Look, everybody, I'm engaged." Jennifer showed all three girls her ring and we set a date in June, and I've talked it over with John. Ruby, I would like you to be my maid of honor. And, Susie, you will be a bridesmaid."

Both girls were quite excited about it.

She said, "Rita, if you don't mind walking me down the aisle since my father has died, my mother is too upset missing him. I called her to say she will come but doesn't want to be at the wedding." Rita said she would be honored. "John has asked me if I would let his sister be a bridesmaid and I said I would, and he wants to know if she could stay a few days in June. His mother and father have also been notified and his father will be his best man. They were excited too and already booked a hotel room in Atlanta."

Rita said, "She can stay. What's her name?"

Jennifer said, "Her name is Laura, and it won't be a problem for her to come since school will be out." Jennifer said, "Well, Ruby, are you up to the challenge? That means we will be plan the wedding and you won't have much time after school except homework."

Rita put it in, "And it had better come first."

Ruby said, "It will, Mom, don't worry, and I'll keep my grades up too."

Rita said, "Then it's alright. I give my permission for her to do it."

They sat around eating pizza and discussing what they needed to do. Ruby said, "I'll miss you when you leave here."

"Don't worry, I'll talk to you on the phone, and you all will have to come to dinner." They laughed and had a good time that night. Ruby walked Susie home since it was getting dark and came straight back.

That morning when she got to school, she was still alienated except Johnny and his new girl Sharon harassed her every chance they got. Ruby was upset with them but had to take it. She was afraid to complain since the other kids might think she had turned them in.

Susie told her at lunch, "He's only jealous since you wouldn't give in, and she's only doing it to look good to Johnny."

Ruby did her best to ignore those two the rest of the day. She walked home with Susie saying, "Can you help me with dinner after we do our homework? I want to get started on this wedding right away."

Susie said, "You know I will. I can't wait to get started too."

Every day after school they made calls to quite a few people and couldn't find a hall for the venue since everybody seemed to get married in June. Rita suggested that they held it in their backyard. Jennifer told the girls it would be alright. They could rent tables and chairs for the event. Making quite a few phone calls, the girls finally found a caterer to do the wedding. Jennifer went with the girls to a bakery down the street where they decided on a wedding cake. The cake would be three tiers of yellow cake with white and blue frosting, and they could pick it up a day before the wedding. John didn't have anything to do with the preparations and left it to the girls—only paying for the bills they handed him.

June arrived and the girls ordered the flowers last, wanting them to be fresh. On the day of the wedding there would be golden parade tulips on each table and a bouquet of yellow roses for the bride. Pastor Dodge dropped over to see how the girls were doing. He was amazed at what they had accomplished. He told the girls if he ever got married, he would call them first to plan it. Both girls were excited that he liked what they did.

After he left, Jennifer said, "I'm with him. You two are the best."

Ruby and Susie gave her a hug saying, "We loved doing the planning."

Rita said, "When Laura gets here next week, we'll have to go and get your dresses for the wedding."

Jennifer said, "Don't worry. I already got the wedding dress. Me and your mom went out and got it while you two were too busy to notice. We thought we would surprise you, so you won't see it till the wedding. Ruby, I'm leaving it up to you what color the bridesmaid dresses will be."

The next week there was a knock at the door. Rita went to the door and opened it to a lady in her forties who had short brown hair and blue eyes. She could tell right away that it was John's sister.

She said, "Hello. My name is Laura, and I thank you for letting me stay here." The two girls rushed out to meet her. Ruby told her that she would be staying in her room, and she'll sleep on the couch. Laura said, "I didn't want to be a problem."

Ruby said, "It won't be. I hope you don't mind the music posters."

Laura said, "Don't worry, I'm a big music fan too."

Rita said, "Are you hungry? We were about to sit down to dinner." Laura said she was, and they sat a plate out for her. That night it was fried chicken and mashed potatoes with gravy and corn. They told Laura that they were going out with their mother to pick out dresses and if it was alright with her to come along to get her dress.

Jennifer told her, "These two have been too busy. They had to wait on you to get their bridesmaid dresses." Laura said it would be alright and she would go along as long that the dresses weren't too crazy.

Jennifer said, "You got no problem. Susie is a Christian, so she won't let that happen."

Laura said, "Oh! I understand so no problem."

The girls took Laura's luggage to Ruby's room for her and showed her where the bathroom was. Susie had to go home, and Rita said to Ruby to walk her. Susie said good night to Laura and said, "See you tomorrow." Rita was proud of Susie especially since she had helped Ruby to end up on the honor roll. They would be junior's next year when school started again.

In the morning, Ruby went and made coffee since school was out for the summer. She wanted to be helpful around the house, which would get her back in her mother's good graces. When she heard everybody getting up, she began breakfast by frying eggs and bacon. Jennifer was the first to arrive since she and Rita had to go to work.

Rita came in and said, "Good morning and thank you for breakfast." She said, "Tell Susie to be here at five thirty so we can go to the bridal shop. Laura heard when she entered the room and said she would be ready.

Susie was there at five fifteen, and Laura came downstairs and the three waited for Rita to get there. Rita came in and hurried to her room to change clothes and said, "I made us an appointment for six." She was soon back downstairs in a pair of black shorts and a red tee saying, "It's nice to get out of that uniform being so hot out there." She said, "If you guys are ready, let's go."

They all went out to the car, and Ruby told Laura to take the front seat. They arrived at the bridal shop with five minutes to spare. The lady in the shop came over when they entered.

"May I help you?"

Rita said, "I called you earlier about bridesmaid gowns."

"Oh, yes, you must be Mrs. Jacobs," she said.

"Well, Ruby tells her what color gown it should be," her mother said. Ruby told the lady, who was named Marsha, that the gowns should be a light blue since all the flowers will be yellow.

Marsha went to the back of the store saying, "Follow me." She said, "We have quite a few gowns in that color." Marsha showed them six gowns of different styles in that color. They narrowed it down to two since four of the gowns were too revealing. Ruby tried them both on and decided on one. It was a chiffon with puff-up sleeves and was ankle length. Susie said she liked it a lot.

"Do you have three in that style?"

Marsha said they did and went and got the other two. Susie and Laura tried them on and found they didn't fit well. Marsha measured them and said, "We can have them ready by next Tuesday."

Rita said that was fine and put a deposit down on the three dresses and said, "A man named John Conner will pay the rest when we come back to pick them up."

Marsha said, "That will be fine. See you all on Tuesday."

When they arrived back at the house, they noticed John's car there. Rita said, "Jennifer must be home." When they walked in, she and John were sitting on the couch. John got up and came over to his sister to give her a hug.

John said, "It's been a while since I saw you last."

"I know," she said, "you haven't been home since last Christmas. Mom and Dad wonder how long you would stay away until you told them about the wedding."

Jennifer said, "John hasn't talked that much about your family, and I can't wait to meet your mom and dad."

Laura said, "If you want to hear about our family, if you all sit here in the living room, I'll tell you our story."

Susie called her mother saying she would like to stay a little while longer so she could hear the story. Her mother gave her permission to stay. John sat between Jennifer and Laura while Rita sat in a chair across the room and the two girls sat on the floor.

CHAPTER 13

LAURA CONNER

We lived in the suburbs of Charleston, South Carolina. Laura's father worked at a vending company and brought a house with her mother on Glendale Drive. It was a two-story house with three bedrooms. Her mother was pregnant with her at the time they moved in, which they were living with his parents. She attended Springfield Elementary. She was ten in the fifth grade when John was born. One day when she was in school, her mother was cleaning the house when her water broke. She called Dad, and he rushed home from work to take her to the hospital. By the time they got to the university hospital, her labor pains were every five minutes, so they took her straight to labor and delivery.

She had the baby at one o'clock in the afternoon while she was at school. Her teacher said to Ms. Conner, "Your father is in the office, and you need to go home."

When she got to the office, her father said that Mom had the baby. They went straight to the hospital, and when they entered, they went up to the information desk to find what room she was in.

My father said, "I'm John Conner. Could you tell me what room Mrs. Mary Conner is in?"

The receptionist looked at her computer and said, "She is in 312."

He said thank you, and they headed to the elevator and pushed the button for the third floor. When they got to her room, she was feeding the baby; and when she was done, she let her hold him. Holding him in her arms, she always felt she had to protect him.

After they left, Dad said they needed to go to the store to get things for the baby. They went to Walmart to buy a car seat and baby clothes and blankets since it was March and cold outside. The next day, he brought John home. They were still young; my father being thirty-two on February 23, and Mom just turned twenty-nine in January. Her father worked hard most of his life to put them both through school.

Laura graduated from West Ashley and went on to college for her teaching degree. She went for four years to Southern University while working at McDonald's to help her father pay for her education. When she graduated, she applied for a job as a six-grade teacher. Springfield was delighted for her to take over their class especially since most of the teachers knew her. John had already graduated elementary and was in junior high when she began to teach.

Laura had been there teaching for six years when John graduated from West Ashley High. He was very good at math and decided to go on to business school. She and Dad paid his way through Trident Technical College. When John graduated, they threw a big party inviting all their friends.

John was going with a girl from college, her name was Roberta Lewis, but they broke up when she heard he was moving to Atlanta. They had a big argument at the party, and she left. He never heard from her again. They were all sad when he left, but he couldn't find a job around them. John always came home for Christmas, and they hope that when he gets married, he'll keep up the tradition.

Jennifer said, "If we can bring my mother, it wouldn't be the same without her."

Laura said, "Don't worry. I'm sure it would be no problem."

Jennifer said, "Thanks for sharing your story, and I can't wait to meet your parents."

Laura said, "They'll be in town Monday. They're checking in at Economy Lodge not far from the church."

John said good night to his sister, giving her a hug and kiss. Jennifer walked him to the door, and they stepped outside for a minute.

Ruby said, "Let me get my pillow and blanket from my room. I'm sure you'll be ready for bed soon." Ruby returned in a little while in a green nightgown with her bedclothes.

Laura said, "Good night to everybody," and made her way upstairs. She got her red gown out of her suitcase and went in the bathroom to shower and brush her teeth. Putting on her gown, she carried her dirty clothes back to her room and put them in the laundry bag she had brought. She was very tired and got into bed and was soon asleep.

Sunday morning, they all got ready for church, which Laura agreed to go to. She put on a nice white dress and matching heels and made her way downstairs.

Jennifer said to her, "Good morning, and don't worry we have room since Susie's mother started to church, she rode with her and Ruby went with them, so it's just us three." They sat and drank coffee and had donuts that Rita had gotten that morning. Soon it was time to leave, and they walked out to Rita's car. It only took about fifteen minutes to get there and had a hard time finding a parking space. Susie and Ruby were waiting at the door for them. Laura exclaimed that it was a big church as she walked through the doors. Pastor Dodge came over to greet her saying, "I hope you're having a nice visit." He said it was nice to meet John's sister.

The next people they met were Sarah and June, who greeted them. Rita said, "We will find your seat," and led Ruby and Susie to a middle pew.

Jennifer turned to Laura and said, "This is my best friend, and she'll be taking over my job till I get back."

Laura said, "How do you do, and how come you're not the maid of honor?"

June replied, "Me and Jennifer talked it over with Ruby. Going through so much, we decided to let her do it. We figured if she was kept busy, she wouldn't get depressed by the school kids. Don't worry, we are bridesmaids too. We went in the bridal shop, and Jennifer already let them know that we needed the same dress. Ours had to be altered too, so when John picks them up Tuesday, there will be five. Plus, I haven't been long out of rehab, so I would have been rushed."

Laura said, "Ruby had done a great job."

June said, "I know and I'm proud of her."

Ruby came back and said they're getting ready to start and blushed at what June said. "We were going to tell you on Tuesday that these two were also at the wedding."

Ruby said, "I guess I better let the caterers know." They went and sat down with Rita.

The choir started their song and had everyone rise to sing and going through several selections before Pastor Dodge walked up to the pulpit. He said, "Good morning. It's a nice day to celebrate our Lord. Please open your Bibles to Mathew 22, the parable of Jesus. The kingdom of heaven is like a certain king, which made a marriage for his son and sent forth his servants to call them that were bidden to the wedding, and they did not come. Again, he sent forth to other servants saying, tell them which are bidden, behold I have prepared a dinner. My oxen and fatling are killed all things are ready come unto the marriage, but they made light of it and went their own way. One to his farm and another to his merchandise and the remaining took his servants and entreated them spitefully and slew them, but when the king heard thereof, he was wrath and he sent for his armies and destroyed the murderers and burned their city. Then saith he to his servants the wedding is ready, but they which were bidden were not worthy. Go ye therefore into the highways and as many as ye shall find bid to the marriage, so those servants went out into the highways and gathered together all as many as they found, both bad and good and the wedding was furnished with guests and when the king came in to see his guests, he saw there was a man which had not on the wedding garment and he saith unto him, friend, how camest, thou in hither not having on a wedding garment and he was speechless. Then said the king to his servants, bind him hand and foot, and take him away and cast him into outer darkness. There shall be weeping and gnashing teeth. For many are called, but few are chosen."

Pastor Dodge finished his sermon saying, "You need to come to Christ before you are cast in the fires of hell. You that are saved must join the other servants to invite people to the wedding feast. If you haven't, maybe you should look in your heart to see if you are the Lord's child. I call the ones who don't know Jesus to come, and if you are ones that have doubt, I call you too. Being saved means you do more than keeping it to yourself. You need to spread the good news about your survivor. While we sing 'Just As I Am,' you come."

Laura felt the calling and ventured down the aisle to the altar.

Pastor Dodge prayed with her, and she begged forgives of her sin and asked Jesus to come into her heart. Pastor Dodge said, "Here is a new sister in Christ." Several more had come down the aisle and were forgiven for their sins. When Laura returned to her seat, Rita was there to congratulate her. The pastor had Roger led them in a song as he made his way to the door. He shook everyone's hand as they left the church. They returned home to Rita's house where they were proud of Laura. John drove up with Jennifer and came to praise Laura saying she always had more courage than him.

John said, "I only work at the church not buying into it." When he left, Rita said she felt sorry for him. Laura kept silent not knowing what to say. Ruby didn't want to get involved and went upstairs to her room. Ruby and Susie talked on the phone for a few hours before dinner. When she came downstairs, John had already left, and the other three were sitting at the table eating.

Rita said, "I called you a few minutes ago, but you didn't answer."

"Oh! I was on the phone with Susie." Ruby sat down at her place and began to eat. Laura said the pork chops were great with mash potatoes and peas. Everybody else was finished by the time Ruby started.

Ruby said, "I'll take care of cleaning up," and Rita said thanks and went upstairs. The other two went into the living room to talk. Ruby finished eating and cleared the table and put the dishes in the washer and turned it on. Ruby went into the living room where Jennifer and Laura were. Jennifer was telling her how she had come to Atlanta. Ruby sat down to listen since she didn't know the whole story herself. Rita returned in her blue nightgown and turned on the TV. Ruby went on to her room and got a green nightgown out of her drawer and went and took a shower. After drying off, she went back to her room, and Laura was there already changed into her blue nightgown. Ruby collected her pillow and blankets and said good night. She went downstairs to the couch where the room was deserted. Ruby figured everyone had gone to bed. Making up the couch and setting the alarm for the morning, she laid down and was soon asleep.

Ruby woke up to the alarm and went in the kitchen and started the coffeepot. She had just returned to the living room when the phone rang. Ruby went over and picked it up and said hello.

"Is there a Laura Conner there?"

Ruby said, "Yes. Can I ask who's calling?"

"This is her mother. Would you have her come to the phone?"

Ruby told her to hold on a minute and ran upstairs to her room and knocked. Laura called out, "I guess you need to get ready for school to come over and unlock the door."

Ruby said, "That's true, but your mother is on the phone."

Laura said thanks and went by Ruby and headed downstairs. Ruby went into her room to get dressed. Laura picked up the phone and said to his mother, "Where are you?"

"We already checked into the motel and wonder if you'll be over soon."

"I should be there in an hour. I must get dressed and have some breakfast while waiting in a cab. Well, me and your father are going to breakfast now and should be back in our room time you get here."

Mary said, "The room number is 122, and you do remember where it's at?"

"Sure, Mom, you know I was there when you made the reservations."

"I know, dear, but maybe you forgot."

"No, Mom. I'll be there. Goodbye and love you."

Mary hung up saying love you too.

Ruby came downstairs dressed for school while Laura was drinking coffee in the kitchen.

"I guess you're going to see your parents and won't be here when I get back."

Laura took another sip of her coffee and said, "I won't be back till late. Jennifer and John are supposed to meet us at the motel after work, so it will be you and your mom for dinner."

"I guess that's good since with everybody here, I haven't got to talk to her for a while." Ruby said, "I hope I get to meet your parents before the wedding."

Laura said, "I'll make sure you do," and gave Ruby a hug.

Ruby said, "I got to go before I miss the bus. See you later."

Laura said bye as Rita and Jennifer walked into the room. Rita went and poured some coffee and said goodbye to Ruby, giving her a kiss. Ruby ran out the door while saying goodbye to Jennifer as she brushed by her.

Jennifer smiled and said, "See you later." Laura told them that her parents had called and were at the motel. Jennifer said, "We'll be there, and I know where they are since I was staying there before moving here."

The two left, and Laura called a cab to take her to Econo Lodge on Virginia Avenue. "I'm at 104 Lee Street." The dispatch said it would be about forty-five minutes. Laura said that would be fine and hung up. She made a quick breakfast of scrambled eggs and toast and eat and went and got dressed. She brushed her teeth and put on her makeup. She just slipped on her shoes and looked in the mirror at her blue dress to make sure it was not too short. Her nylons were beige with her white high heels, and turning around, she heard the horn blowing. She grabbed her purse and rushed downstairs and saw the cab. She went out the door and locked it behind her. She walked out to the street and got in the cab.

The Diamond cab driver asked where she was going as he flicked down the meter. Laura said she was going to the Economy Lodge. They were soon there. She paid the driver and looked for 122. It was a short distance from the lobby, and she walked to the door and knocked. Her mother opened the door and hugged her and ushered her in.

Her father came over and gave her a kiss saying, "So have you seen his fiancée?"

Laura replied, "I've spent a few days with her getting to know her. She is very kind and smart."

Mary popped up and said, "I heard she was the pastor's secretary."

"That is true. The church is just down the street from here."

"I called John and told him you're here, and he said he would be here after work with Jennifer."

"Everybody I've met since I have been here is quite nice and made me feel welcome. On top of that, Dad, I've become a Christian and will look for a church of my own when we return home."

Her father said, "I'm getting hungry. Know any place we can have lunch?"

Laura said, "There's a Waffle House just down the street." Her father said, "Well if you are ready, Mary, let's go."

Laura said, "It would be easier to walk there." Her parents said that was fine.

When they got to Waffle House, they entered and was greeted by a nice-looking woman.

"Welcome to Waffle House. My name is Molly. I'll be your waitress. Please follow me." She led them to a table handing each a menu. "What would you like to drink?" she asked.

John Sr. said, "Bring us some coffee and lots of creamers." Molly soon returned with a pot and filled each of their cups. John Sr. said, "Leave the pot and give us a few more minutes." When Molly returned, all three decided on the breakfast special of two fried eggs and hash browns and toast. John and Mary wanted sunny-side up while Laura wanted over easy. Molly soon returned with their food and heard them talking about the wedding.

Molly said, "If you don't mind, I think I might know the couple."

John Sr. said, "You might. They both work just down the street at that United Methodist."

Molly said, "You're not talking about Jennifer who is a secretary there?"

Laura said, "Yes. She and my brother are getting married on Saturday."

Molly said, "I'm surprised I wasn't invited."

Laura said, "Well, I don't know if you know a girl named Ruby. She planned the whole thing and forgot to let you know."

"Well," John Sr. said, "I'll tell my son you're coming if that's okay with you."

Molly said, "I'll be there." After they finishing eating, John went and paid the check, handing Molly a ten-dollar tip.

She said, "Thank you, but you need not give me that much."

"You're a friend, and we always look out for our friends."

She smiled and said, "See you Saturday." They left and returned to the motel.

John and Jennifer made it to the motel around five. John had dropped her off at Rita's while he went home to shower and change. Jennifer had showered and put on a navy-blue dress and black high heels and sat in the living room waiting for John to get back. He soon arrived in a nice black suit and red tie and said, "You were ready to go." Laura answered the door of the motel room, and the two walked inside.

John said, "Mom and Dad, I'd like you to meet Jennifer."

Mary came over and gave her a hug saying, "Glad to meet you." John Sr. held out the hand, which Jennifer took. Mary said, "We heard a lot about you and hope we'll see more of you in the future. You two must come for Christmas, John always does." Jennifer said that would be a marvelous idea since they won't have decorations this year being too soon. John Sr. came over and hugged John and saying he was very happy to be his best man.

John said, "I need you two to get ready. We have dinner reservations. Well, you'll have to give us a little time. We were not prepared."

Laura looked over at Jennifer saying, "You wouldn't know a bookstore close by. I want to get a few books to read, and we got to wait on them anyway."

Jennifer said, "There is one just about four blocks from here across from the park. If you want, we can walk there because with the traffic, it would take less time."

Laura told her mother they would be right back, and the two left the room. Walking down the street, a breeze was blowing, which kept it from being too hot. Laura said, "This is a nice walk, and I hate being cooped up in a hotel room." They soon made it to the Used and New Book Store. When they entered, Jennifer went straight up to the counter and said, "Good evening, Mrs. Lambert. I'd like you to meet me soon to be sister-in-law, Laura Conner."

Mrs. Lambert said, "You're getting married?"

Jennifer said, "This Saturday."

"Well, congratulations. What can I help you with?"

Laura said, "I'm into mystery novels and would like a few before returning to South Carolina."

Mrs. Lambert said, "Which part are you from?"

Laura said, "Charleston where I'm a teacher."

"Well, there is a whole aisle devoted to mysteries, the third aisle, and it's in alphabetic order according to the author." Laura went down that aisle browsing and found three novels by John McDonald and brought them back to the counter where Jennifer was waiting. Mrs. Lambert rang them up and charged her two dollars, giving her the third book for free. She said, "If you have time before going back, I might have some more of that author in the back."

Laura said, "I'll try," and they left.

On the walk back, Laura told her about inviting Molly to the wedding. Jennifer said, "Thanks. I forgot to tell Ruby about her." When they made it back to the room, her parents were ready. They all piled into the car with Jennifer up front and Laura between her parents in back. It took almost thirty-minutes before getting to the Texas Steak House. John went into the restaurant and said, "I've a reservation for five."

"Mr. Conner, it will be a few more minutes. We're in the process of cleaning that table." It wasn't long before the hostess led them to a table. The waiter soon appeared with a menu and asked them what they would like to drink.

John said, "Bring us two pitchers of beer for now."

The waiter said, "I'll be right back. There are two buckets of peanuts on the table for you to enjoy." The waiter returned with the beer and asked if they were ready to order.

John sipped his beer and said, "Can you give us a few more minutes?" They all looked over their menu before calling the waiter back. John told the waiter that he would have a rib eye medium rare and fries plus the house salad with ranch dressing. John Sr. ordered just like his son, and Mary ordered a sirloin steak with baked potato and salad with blue cheese. Jennifer and Laura ordered a barbecue chicken breast and ribs and a salad with French dressing.

While waiting for their food, John asked his dad if he had a suit for the wedding. John Sr. replied, "When we heard about you wanting me to be your best man, your mother made me go out and buy a new suit, and you know she had to go with me to pick it out."

John laughed saying, "You know you wouldn't get away with picking it out."

John Sr. said, "You know being married for forty years that you can't get away with any secrets. We went to the Men's Warehouse and picked up a blue suit with a light blue tie and she made me buy a new white shirt to go with it. I didn't want to argue that I had plenty of white shirts." They all laughed and toasted the wedding.

Soon the waiter returned with two helpers to serve the food. The waiter asked if there was anything else and was told to bring more beer. They sat and ate talking about weddings and old times. Jennifer listened to learn more about John from his parents. The waiter returned and started clearing the plates while they were sipping their beer after finishing eating. John asked for the check and put a healthy tip.

They went out to the car and drove back to the motel to let his parents out. He got out of the car and gave them both a hug and kiss before getting back in.

"We'll see you tomorrow," he called as they drove away. It wasn't long before he pulled up to Rita's house, and Laura knew they wanted to be alone so she said to Jennifer, "See you inside." It was almost half an hour later before Jennifer came in. Laura looked at Jennifer and said, "You must have had a lot to talk over." Jennifer said good night with a smile on her lips and headed upstairs. Laura walked into the living room where Rita and Ruby were watching TV.

"Well, I just wanted to say good night, and Jennifer was a big hit with my parents."

Rita said, "That was good, and I'll see you in the morning." Laura went on up to Ruby's room.

CHAPTER 14

THE WEDDING

That Friday night, Ruby made sure all the tables and chairs were set up in the backyard. Rita followed by Susie came to help her and soon Laura came out too. There were several guys sitting up a table with sound equipment for the DJ that Ruby had hired for the wedding celebration. Ruby told Laura that the caterer's called and said they would be here early tomorrow to set up. She said she would have to get up early because the florist was bringing all the flowers in the morning.

"I wonder if you could ask your mother, Susie, if you could stay over and help me. The couch rolls out to a bed so we both can sleep there."

Susie said she would go call her mom and went inside to use the phone. Susie returned and said it was alright with her.

Ruby said, "That's great, and I'll walk you to your house to get some things to stay overnight."

When they got to Susie's house, her mother asked Ruby how it was going.

"We are almost done, Mrs. March, and as soon we will get everything arranged. Susie will be back to get ready."

"Well, we'll see you at the wedding tomorrow," she said.

Ruby said, "I can't wait, and I'll have the usher save you two a seat."

"Thank you, Ruby. I'll be very proud to see my daughter walk the aisle." Susie soon returned downstairs with her backpack and asked if Ruby was ready to go. Ruby said yes and said goodbye to Mrs. March.

Susie ran over and gave her mother a hug and a kiss saying, "See you in the morning." Mrs. March stood at the door watching the two girls head down the street before closing the door.

Ruby and Susie took turns taking a shower, and both put on their blue nightgown that they had gone out and bought together. Rita told them they better get some sleep for tomorrow. Ruby pulled out the couch bed, and Rita brought pillows and blankets for them. Rita said good night and headed upstairs to bed. She got dressed for bed in her green nightgown and heard the girls laughing. She called down to them to be quiet or they'll wake up Laura. Laura laughed since she was excited too, which made it hard to go to sleep. The two girls whispered to each other about the wedding and finally drifted to sleep.

The next morning, Ruby woke up hearing the front doorbell ring. She got off the couch to answer the door. When she opening it, a guy was standing there saying he was from the florist with her delivery.

Ruby said, "Could you put them on a table in the backyard? And I'll take care of it."

He said he would but asked, "How about the bouquet of yellow roses?"

Ruby said, "You can give them to me and put the rest in the back."

The delivery guy went out to the truck and brought back the roses and handed them to her. Ruby signed the flowers and closed the door, and the delivery guy went to collect the rest of the flowers. Rita had come downstairs asking who it was.

Ruby said, "It's the flowers. Can you take care of these roses while I get dressed?" She handed the flowers to her mother and went to wake up Susie.

After folding up the bed and folding the covers, she went upstairs to her room to get dressed. She knocked on the door saying, "I need my clothes. The flowers are here." Laura got out of bed and opened the door. Ruby went straight to her closet and got a pair of blue jeans and a red T-shirt. She then went across the hall to the bathroom and took a quick shower before getting dressed. She met Susie in the hall coming from her mom's bathroom. They both headed to the backyard to arrange the flowers. Laura got dressed and headed downstairs with Jennifer close behind her. Rita was already making breakfast when they entered. Jennifer saw the roses and said they were beautiful.

Rita said, "Have a cup of coffee, and breakfast will be ready by the time Ruby and Susie are done in the backyard."

While they were putting flowers on each of the tables, the caterers showed up and began to set up their table and grills. When the two finished, they returned to the house and found a plate of eggs and toast waiting for them. They both got a cup of coffee with cream and sugar and sat down to eat.

When they were done, Susie said, "I've got to go home and get ready for the wedding, and my mom is fixing my hair."

Ruby said, "I'll see you at the wedding."

She said, "My mom, Jennifer, Laura, and me have an appointment at the Beauty Bar for a manicure and a pedicure. We are leaving very soon."

Susie left and the four of them got in the car and headed up to the salon. They were taken in right away, and there were four beauticians to do their nails. It took about an hour before they returned home. Ruby looked out in the backyard and saw that the caterers were almost completely set up. She also saw guys bringing in sound equipment for the DJ they hired. When she turned around, she saw her mother in the same exact dress that the bridesmaids were wearing.

Ruby said, "Wow! I didn't know you got that dress."

Rita said, "If you remember June and Sarah had to get their dresses so we three went and got our dresses at lunchtime since it's not that far from the church. By the way, Mrs. Marie delivered your dress the other day with Laura's. I guess you didn't see them in your closet."

"No, Mom. I was rushing around to take care of the backyard, and don't worry, Susie already has her dress."

Ruby said, "She didn't tell me."

"I guess she thought you knew what her mother said. Laura is upstairs ready to help you get dressed."

"Thanks, Mom. I'll get going," she said as she rushed upstairs.

June and Sarah arrived at the house for Jennifer. She went and got her gown and handed June the bouquet. Jennifer said, "I'll see you girls at the church," and left. Rita was trying to hurry up Ruby and Laura.

Rita said, "There is nothing else you can do when we get there and you, being the maid of honor, should already have been there."

Ruby said, “Okay, Mom, I understand,” grabbing her shoes and heading out to the car in her gown barefooted. When they got to the church, Roger O’Donnell was waiting at the door and directed them to the room that was being used for the bride and her maids.

Ruby saw as she entered that June and Sarah were helping Jennifer to get ready. She realized that was part of her job and felt a little upset that she wasn’t there in time to help.

Rita said, “You couldn’t do it all, so you should be glad for the help.”

“I guess you are right, Mom. I should go over and thank them for their help.”

Ruby went over to Jennifer and said, “You look beautiful in your gown, and thanks, June and Sarah, for helping me.”

They all said, “You did a fantastic job of setting up this wedding, and we are glad to help any way we can.” Ruby smiled with a tear falling from her eye.

June said, “Don’t cry. You’ll mess up your makeup.”

Ruby laughed and said, “I better finish getting ready.” She walked over to a desk, and Susie arrived with her mother. The last person to enter the room was John’s mother, Mary, who asked if there was anything she could do. She went and helped Sarah and said that both the men were very nervous waiting for this to start that’s why they send her in here.

Everyone in the room laughed and said, “You can go tell Mrs. Marie to get ready to play.”

Susie was the first to leave the room and to walk the aisle. The organ was playing, and she saw the preacher and the two Johns waiting upfront. Right behind her came Sarah followed by June. Just as she made the front, she saw Laura enter and right behind her was Ruby. When Ruby made it to the front, the music changed to the “Wedding March” as Jennifer entered with Rita.

When Jennifer made it to the front, all the bridesmaids took their seats except Ruby. Rita took the front seat after been asked who was giving her away.

Pastor Dodge began by saying, “We are gathered here to unite this couple in holy matrimony. He said if any here have a reason for this couple not to be joined, speak now. Do you, Jennifer Wroth, take John here to be your lawfully wedded husband?”

“I do,” she said.

"Do you, John Conner, take Jennifer here to be your lawfully wedded wife?"

He said, "I do."

Pastor Dodge turned to Ruby and asked for the rings, and she handed them over before sitting down with her mother. Pastor Dodge gave John a ring, and John recited, "With this ring I do thee wed," placing it on her finger. Pastor Dodge then gave Jennifer a ring and she recited, "With this ring I do thee wed."

When she had put it on his finger, Pastor Dodge said, "I now pronounce you husband and wife. You may kiss the bride."

While they were kissing, Pastor Dodge said, "I'd like to introduce you to Mr. and Mrs. John Conner." Everyone got up and applauded as they walked back down the aisle.

Rita got up and said, "The party is at my house. See you there."

Rice was thrown as John and Jennifer walked out the door of the church. Everyone headed to their cars, and it was like a caravan headed to Rita's house. Rita and John parked in the driveway while the rest parked up and down the street. The caterers were busy passing out drinks and had a buffet table prepared. The DJ was already playing music as they entered, and the wedding cake had already arrived and was sitting in the front of the bride's table. There were several toasts made and then they cut the cake. John and Jennifer were brought to the dance floor to have the first dance.

Mrs. Marie came over and wished them happiness and told Jennifer when she got back from her honeymoon that she wouldn't be there. She said, "I've taught Sarah how to do my job, and I'm going to retire and take a long trip through Europe."

Jennifer said, "I trained June to take over my job while we are in Niagara Falls."

John's mother and father congratulated him and said, "We'll be expecting you at Christmas."

Jennifer said, "We'll be there since June can take over for me those few days, and I'm sure John will have all the church bills taken care of."

Mary said they were heading home tomorrow with Laura; she had to get back to work at the school.

Ruby came over and Jennifer said, "I knew you could do a good job."

Ruby was a little embarrassed and said, "Thanks, but I'm going to miss you."

"Don't worry. I'll come and visit and call you."

Jennifer gave her a big hug, and tears were in Ruby's eyes. Jennifer said, "When I get back, we'll go out just you and me to catch up."

Ruby said she would like that. She left and headed back to her mother's table.

Susie said, "Alright."

Ruby replied, "I'm happy for them and sorry for her to go."

"Well, we can still hang out together," Susie said.

"I know. I'm glad you're my friend," she said, giving Susie a hug.

When the party was over, Jennifer collected her bags, and she and John said goodbye to everyone. They stopped out of his apartment and collected his bags and headed to New York.

Ruby and Susie spent the rest of the day cleaning up after the caterers and the DJ left. Most people had gone but a few also stayed and helped clean up, including Mrs. March. When they were done, Susie left with her mother.

Ruby went in the house and her mother said, "I see you're finished."

"Yes, Mom, but I'm sure tired."

"Don't worry. The rental place said they would pick up the chairs and tables tomorrow. Why don't you get dressed for bed? I'm sure you would like to get out of that gown and high heels. Laura has already changed and has packed her suitcase, so tomorrow night you'll be able to sleep in your own bed."

"I know, Mom, and I'm going to sleep in Jennifer's tonight." Ruby went upstairs and knocked on her bedroom door and went in. She collected a red nightgown out of her drawer and headed to the bathroom.

Laura stopped her for a moment and said she could move to Jennifer's room.

Ruby said, "Thanks. I'll help you after I get a shower."

Ruby bathed and put on her nightgown and brought her gown back in her room to hang up. She then helped Laura to move in Jennifer's room and said good night. Ruby padded barefoot downstairs to the living room where her mother was.

Rita saw her and said, "No slippers?"

Ruby said, "No. My feet hurt from wearing those high heels all day."

Rita laughed. "It's something you have to get used to." Ruby told her mother that Laura moved so she could have her own room. Rita said that was nice of her.

"It sure will be quiet when it's only you and me."

"Rita gave her a hug. I know you were getting used to having everyone around, but you still have Susie." They sat together for several hours before retiring to bed. Ruby was glad to have her room back but missed Jennifer already.

When Ruby woke up the next morning Laura had already left, and the tables were gone like nothing ever happened. Her mom was getting ready for church and asked if she was going.

"Not today, Mom. I'm tired, but I promise to go next week." Ruby was all alone after her mother left and decided to eat a bowl of cereal. The house was quiet, and she could even hear the clock ticking. She went upstairs and soaked in the tub for a while and dried off and went to her room to dress for the day. She put on a pair of jeans and a blue shirt while listening to music on the radio. She got cleaner out and cleaned her room and even vacuumed the carpet. She heard her mom come in, and a little while, she called her downstairs.

Ruby said, "I'm coming," turning off the music. She made her way downstairs. Her mom had made sandwiches of ham and cheese with glasses of tea.

Rita said, "We had a nice service, and I made lunch for us." Ruby sat at the table and ate with her mother.

"I cleaned my room, Mom, and I'm not standing this peace."

Rita laughed. "I know. It will take a little time to get used to. Maybe Susie can come over and keep you company today. She and her mom were there in church today asking about you."

"After I clean up here, I'll give her a call." Susie told her she was spending the day with her mother and would see her in school tomorrow. Ruby spent the rest of her day watching TV.

CHAPTER 15

THE HONEYMOON

Jennifer leaned over and gave John a kiss, accidentally bumping Ruby sitting right next to her. Jennifer said, "I'm sorry. I didn't mean to wake you up."

Ruby said that it was alright. "I was dreaming about your wedding."

Jennifer said, "You did a great job, and we were both happy for you to do it."

Ruby said, "You never got the chance to tell me about your honeymoon when you got back. I guess we will be here awhile. Can you tell me about it in detail?"

Jennifer said, "I guess I owe you that much. After the party, we headed up 85, and we turned on to 20 to take us over to 95. I always wanted to stop at South of the Border, and John was kind enough to take me. We got there in time for dinner around six thirty. We went into the restaurant there and ordered tacos and had a few beers. John took me into the gift shop there, and we looked around a while. John bought me a sombrero. We left there and headed to Petersburg, and it was about ten thirty when we got there. John saw a Country Inn and Suites and decided to stop there for the night. I waited in the car while he went in an register. He soon came back out and helped me out of the car before collecting the bags. We went through the lobby and took the elevator to the third floor. John found our room, room 306, and opened the door with a key card. John put a suitcase in front of the door to keep it open. He then picked me up and carried me across the threshold before retrieving our luggage. Once inside, he took me in his arms and began to kiss me. I became a little dizzy with the excitement. I felt so much love in that moment, and we shared each other on the bed for hours.

"The next morning, we arose early and took showers before getting dressed and going downstairs to the lobby for breakfast. John went and made us a cup of coffee. We sat there drinking our coffee and talking where we were going next. We decided we would stop in Atlantic City. And after finishing our coffee, we went to make a plate of food. I got some eggs and plenty of bacon since I love bacon a lot. John got some sausage with his eggs. I had put several pieces of bread in the toaster and went up when they popped up. I collected several butter and strawberry jams. John, at the same time, refilled our coffee cups. We sat there staring at each other while we ate our breakfast in silence."

After breakfast, John went up to the desk to checkout. Jennifer went on up to the room to pack. John paid for their one-night stay and got a receipt.

The man named Randy said, "I hope you had a nice stay with us and come back again."

John said, "Thanks, and we'll bring the key cards down when we leave. John returned to the room, and Jennifer had everything packed. They picked up their luggage and made their way back to the lobby. John dropped off the cards and had Jennifer wait at the door while he went and got the car. John pulled up, opening the truck and storing the luggage. He then went and opened the car door for Jennifer. John stopped at a gas station right outside of the city and filled up. He also got change from the attendant for the tolls ahead. They headed up 95 through Washington and Baltimore to New Jersey. Jennifer watched the buildings in Washington and wished that they would stop at the White House. She thought that she would get John to stop on their way back.

A little after one they made it to Atlantic City. John pulled up to the Hard Rock Hotel and Casino. John got out of the car, handing his keys to the valet. John helped Jennifer out of the car before the valet drove away. Entering the lobby, they found their way to the Colonial Oak Restaurant. John went up to the maître d' asked for a table for two. He told John it would be a few minutes and if he could wait over there and pointing to seats. John and Jennifer sat down to wait and were soon called to follow a young lady.

"Welcome," she said, "my name is Ariel. Right this way. A waitress will soon be with you." Once they were seated, Ariel left and bought back another woman saying, "This is Rachel. She will be serving you."

Rachel said, "Can I get you anything to drink?"

John asked her to bring them a pitcher of beer. Rachel returned with two glasses and a pitcher of beer asking if they were ready to order.

John said, "Could you give us a few minutes to look over the menu?"

Rachel poured them beer into a glass and said, "Call me when you're ready."

Jennifer looked around while they sipped their beer, and John was looking at the menu. John said, "I think I'll have steak and turf. How about you?" Jennifer asked what kind of seafood comes with it. John said, "I don't know, but I can ask for an assortment." She said that would be fine.

John called the waitress over and told her what they decided. Rachel asked how he wanted his steak. John said medium rare, and Jennifer said medium well. She took their order and left.

John said, "I want to exchange a hundred dollars for the casino, and I'll be right back." Jennifer sipped her beer as he left. John soon returned just as they bought out the food. Jennifer, seeing the large steak, didn't know if she could eat all that besides the lobster and crab legs and other seafood.

Rachel said, "Can I get you another pitcher of beer? There is melted butter for your lobster plus other condiments for your food."

John thanked her and told her to bring another pitcher. They sat eating their food with music playing in the background.

Jennifer said, "I'll never eat all of this," and John called Rachel over to bring them doggie bags. After paying her with a credit card and adding a nice tip, they collected their food and headed to the casino.

Jennifer saw all the different slot machines and card tables in the room. There was plenty of noise from the machines, especially when one paid off. John made his way to the slot machine and put in his card. The first time he got back about five dollars but continued to lose. Jennifer played one and won twenty dollars and quit. When John had lost everything on the card, he wanted to get another, but Jennifer talked him out of it. They left the casino and headed out to the valet to collect their car. When the valet brought their car around, John gave him a tip as he collected the keys.

They were soon on their way to Buffalo going 76w. Jennifer asked him to stop at a rest area for it seemed the beer went straight through her. Going to the bathroom, they came outside and looked around holding each other's hand. They looked at the map to see how far they had to go. John called the Marriot telling them that they would be late.

The clerk said, "No problem. We will hold your room."

John said thanks and hang up. They sat on a bench under a tree. There was a slight breeze blowing, and he reached over and gave her a kiss and said, "I love you, and I'm glad you talked me out of gambling more money." Soon they returned to the car and headed to Niagara Falls.

It was almost ten thirty by the time they made it to Buffalo and took another fifteen minutes to find the hotel across the bridge on the Canadian side. John showed them their passports to enter into Canada. John let Jennifer out in front of the hotel with the luggage. He was directed to the parking garage half a block away. After parking the car, he walked back to the hotel and helped Jennifer inside with the luggage.

John went up to the desk and said, "We have a reservation here for three nights."

The clerk looked up on his computer. "Yes, I see Mr. and Mrs. Conner have the honeymoon suite. My name is Ralph and welcome to the Marriot. Good thing you made the reservation because we are booked solid until next month." Ralph called a boy and a bellhop arrived.

He told him, "Take this couple to 2305," handing the key cards to him.

The bellhop picked up the luggage and said, "Follow me," taking them to the elevator. After getting off on the twenty-third floor, it was a short walk down the hall. The bellhop put down the luggage to open the door before ushering it in. He asked if they wanted him to unpack.

John said, "We can take care of that." Handing the guy a tip and taking the key cards, he showed the guy out and closed the door. Looking around the room, it was spacious with a clear view of the falls. The room was soundproof, and they couldn't hear the rushing water till they opened the balcony doors. Before unpacking, they stepped out on the balcony to look at falls, which had plenty of floodlights shining on the falls. They stood there a half-hour holding each other admiring the falls.

John gave her a kiss and said, "It is wonderful to be here with you, and I love you."

Jennifer looked at him with love in her heart, saying, "I love you too." It was getting late and both were tired. They walked in and unpacked before getting ready for bed. They got in bed, but it was several hours before they went to sleep.

John went down to the lobby and used the phone against the wall to make several reservations for that day. It was almost an hour later before getting off the phone. John then went into one the shops to buy a surprise for Jennifer. Taking his two bags, he headed over to Starbucks to get two coffees before returning to the room. John quietly entered the room so he could put away his present before waking Jennifer. John brought the cup of coffee over to the bed telling Jennifer she needed to get up. Jennifer opened her eyes when he bent down to give her a kiss. She smiled when he handed her the coffee.

John said, "You need to get up, sleepyhead. We have a whole day of things to do."

She looked at him saying, "What have you planned?"

John smiled and said, "It's all a surprise, so after you drink your coffee, go take a shower and get dressed. We are having breakfast soon."

Jennifer rose and took a shower, putting on a matching red T-shirt and shorts. She brushed her hair and teeth and said she was ready.

They left the suite and headed to the elevator where they descended to the mezzanine. They went in the Terrapin Café where a waitress ushered them to a table. The food was buffet-style, so they ordered coffee before making their way to the breakfast bar. Both filled their plates with scrambled eggs, bacon, and muffins. John picked up butter and jelly before returning to the table. The waitress named Joy had already returned with coffee, cream, and sugar. When they sat down, she poured the coffee in their cups and asked if there was anything else they needed.

John thanked her and said, "That's all for now." They soon finished eating and John called the waitress over to pay. After paying and giving her a tip, they made their way back to their room.

John said, "You need to put on your tennis shoes," and handed her his present. When she opened the bag, she found a big yellow raincoat. He had one too and said, "We have a reservation at Journey Behind the Falls."

Jennifer grabbed her tennis shoes and put them on and was excited, jumping up and give John a kiss and hug. John smiled and said, "Let's go." They left the room and went down to the lobby before walking the block to the parking garage. After paying the attendant, they turned left on to Fairview Boulevard. After a few miles, they turned into Murray Street and then made a circle around to the left on Niagara Falls Parkway. John pulled up to the booth to get their tickets before parking the car. John got out of the car and put on his raincoat before helping Jennifer out. Jennifer put her raincoat and walked to the boardwalk. Walking hand in hand, they got splashed from the falls and soon entered the tunnel, which led under the falls. On the other side there were shops for memorabilia where John bought Jennifer a T-shirt of Niagara Falls. After looking around a while, they made their way back through the tunnel to the parking lot.

It was almost noon by the time they got in the car. John told her he already had a place reserved for lunch. They headed back up Niagara Falls Parkway to Falls Avenue and on to Clinton Hills Road. Not far from there, they pulled into the parking lot of The Rainforest Café. John helped her out of the car, and they headed into the restaurant. The first thing Jennifer noticed was the glass wall containing every kind of fish. She walked over to it fascinated by the giant aquarium. John went and talked to the waitress who showed them to a table next to a gorilla display. Jennifer noticed three gorillas in the trees, which looked like it was raining. After looking at the menu, they ordered hamburgers with fries and a Coke. Jennifer looked around; while waiting in other parts of the forest, she saw giraffes and elephants. Soon their food arrived, and they had a good time sitting there and eating. When they were finished, John paid the bill, and they walked back to the car. Getting back in the car, John looked at his watch and said, "We'll just make it to the boat tour of the falls."

They arrived at the Hornblower's boat tours and put back on their raincoats. They headed to the pier. John paid for their tickets just as the boat pulled in. They got on and sat down waiting for the other people to get on before traveling along the falls. When they got back to land, it was 5:30. Getting off the boat, John said, "I hope you're hungry. We have a reservation at Skylon Towers at six." Jennifer couldn't believe all that John had done for her and felt quite a bit of love for him.

When they pulled up to the tower, Jennifer had to strain her neck to see the top. They made their way to the elevator to take them up to the revolving restaurant. After being ushered to a table, John ordered a pitcher of beer. The waitress named Maggie gave them their menus before heading to get their drinks. When she returned, she poured into each glass and said, "Can I take your order?" John ordered for both the lobster dinner with baked potatoes and salad. Maggie asked about salad dressing, and they both ordered ranch. She thanked them and left. They sipped their beer while watching the restaurant circle around. They enjoyed their meal and, after paying, headed back to the hotel.

Going back to their room, she said she was going to change. John stripped down to his underwear and climbed into bed, and Jennifer came back wearing a blue nightgown. They spent several hours together before falling asleep.

The next morning when they awoke, Jennifer leaned over to give him a kiss. "I would like to relax by a pool today if you don't mind."

John said, "There is a water park not far from here, or would you rather go to the pool here in the hotel?"

Jennifer said, "It's too crowded at the hotel pool, so probably the waterpark. And if you don't mind, can we go shopping for swimsuits?"

John got out of bed and said, "We better get ready for breakfast if you want to do all that." They both got dressed and headed downstairs to the café for breakfast. They went to the breakfast bar. After they were seated, John got two fried eggs and hash browns. Jennifer loved bacon and loaded her plate with it with a small portion of scrambled eggs. The waitress came over and filled their coffee cups, leaving cream and sugar. After John paid, they left the hotel heading to the car.

They headed up Fairview to Niagara Plaza. They went to many shops and finally decided on a red bikini and blue swimsuit for John. They stopped in one store and bought two big beach towels with the Niagara Falls logo on them. They stopped for lunch at the Burger Bistro and had the le burger bacon and two ales before heading to the waterpark. Jennifer just did the lazy river, not wanting to do the tubes. After a couple of hours, they began to get tired and decided to leave. They went back to the hotel for a nap. After laying down, they didn't wake up until after seven.

"I guess we should just go to dinner here at the hotel," Jennifer said.

John said, "I heard Morton's Grille is good." They got ready and took the elevator down to the restaurant.

When the waitress seated them, they ordered beer when she handed them the menu. They sat looking out at the falls till the waitress returned with their beer. She asked if they were ready to order. John ordered for both. He ordered a steak with his medium rare and for her medium well done. He added a side order of baked potato and salad with ranch for both. They had a quiet dinner together. After he finished,eating John asked for the check. He paid with his credit card and put a tip for the waitress. They left the restaurant and headed back upstairs. When they got to the room, they turned on the TV and sat on the couch cozying up. They didn't watch much TV and were being affectionate and soon turned the TV off. They spent quite a while on the bed before deciding to go to sleep.

On the third day, they checked out and headed home. It took them till seven that night to make it back to Petersburg. They stayed in the same hotel for the night before heading back to Atlanta.

***

When Jennifer was finished with her story, Ruby said, "Wow! That was a great honeymoon. When you moved out, I was really depressed not having you to talk to. To tell you the truth, I started going to church with Susie just to see you. It was never the same talking on the phone. I remember the night you got back. You let me help move you to his apartment. I remember after we unpacked, we went out to dinner, and we had a great time. I know it was only McDonald's, but being there with you two made it great. I was sorry when John took me home even knowing I had to get up for school the next day.

"I got up the next day and got ready for school, and Susie came over and had breakfast together. I told my mom before she left to tell you hi."

Jennifer said, "She did when she got to work. I really appreciated what June did. I didn't have much to do the first day back. John was swamped with work, and I had to leave without him. He didn't get home till late, and I had to warm up his supper. By the next day, everything was caught up, and we had a lovely evening together after getting back."

Ruby said, "I'm glad I'm here with you even if Susie and my mother are over there not acting like I exist."

Jennifer said, "It is like a barrier between us, and we can see them but not talk to them." Ruby said, "I wish I knew what was happening. I'm a little scared."

Jennifer said, "I know what you mean, but we three are here together with Jim and Helen."

Jim said, "I know what you mean. I can't talk to my children and can't get near them."

Helen held Jim's hand to comfort him.

CHAPTER 16

SARAH WRIGHT

Sarah was remembering the wedding of John and Jennifer Conner while sitting next to June. She said, "I see them sitting over there and wonder why they aren't coming over here."

June said, "I'm not sure why they're on a different bus. I tried to go over and talk with them, but something prevented me."

Sarah said, "I see Ruby is over there with them while Susie is here with us. I know it's strange, and I already asked Susie, but she didn't know either."

June got up to try to go over to them and stopped when Jeff walked through the doors. June returned to Sarah, shaking all over. He looked over at them and tried to walk over but couldn't and went up to the ticket booth.

The ticket master said, "You are on a different bus. Please take your ticket and go sit down."

Jeff glared at the ticket master and said something under his breath. He went and sat down on a chair close to the wall behind John and Jennifer. Sarah felt a chill and couldn't understand why he made her feel fear. She could understand why June felt fear and only felt better when she saw he couldn't get to her.

Sarah started to remember her childhood and how afraid of her father she had become. She thought June was taking it better than she would because if she saw her father, she would have screamed. Her mind drifted back to the farm in north Georgia where she grew up. She could remember how beautiful her mother was with her blond hair and blue eyes. Her father was a rugged man about six-foot and was built with plenty of muscles. He worked hard on their farm and planted corn. They had acres and acres of corn stalks. Her mother Amy told her never to go in there without somebody because she could get lost. Her father had brown hair and blue eyes, and she was glad she took after her mother. Sarah had to come home after school and help out on the farm. Her mother always helped her do homework and would always go out in the field with her.

When she was twelve years old, tragedy struck. She was out in the field with her mother picking corn and putting it in a basket. Suddenly, her mother screamed and fell to the ground. Sarah rushed over to her but wasn't sure what to do. There wasn't anyone to help since her father had left early to go to town. She sat down on the ground cradling her mother's head in her lap and crying. It was several hours before her father returned. When he saw them, he rushed over.

She looked up at her father with tears in her eyes saying, "I think Mommy is dead." Greg picked up his wife and put her in their green pickup with Sarah trailing behind. He sped down the road to the hospital, but she was DOA. The doctor came out to them in the waiting room saying she had a heart attack, and there was nothing they could do. "You can call a funeral home to come pick her up."

Greg called Bernstein in Athens, and they came and got her and then followed them to the funeral home to make arrangements. The funeral director wanted to know if they had any insurance for Mrs. Wright.

"Yes, sir," he said.

The funeral director said, "Let's call them and see what we can do for you."

After calling the insurance company, they picked out a lovely coffin and did the paperwork to have her buried in Jackson Street Cemetery in Athens.

The funeral director said, "You have three days to find a preacher to hold the service."

Father said, "Thank you," and headed to the door. Sarah knew the next step would be hard since he had never taken one step into a church. Father found a nondenominational church called Living Hope, and the pastor said he could do the services. Father thanked him, and they returned home. Sarah went to her room, very upset about losing her mother. She refused to go to school till her mother was buried. Her father was quite upset too, and he didn't push the issue.

On the day of the funeral, she wore a black dress that her mother had bought for her and a pair of black high heels that her father bought, saying it would go good with the dress. When she walked in the room, her father could tell she was already becoming a young woman and resembled her mother.

Greg had on a dark suit and blue tie and said, "You look beautiful."

Sarah said, "Thanks, Daddy. Can we go now?"

Pastor Jones had the sermon at the funeral home since there were not many attendees. There was only one other family there, her mother's sister Amber. She and her husband, Ralph, and two children, Carol and Dan. They had never come to visit, and her mother was the only one who went to their house when her parents died. Sarah found out that they and her father never got along, and he refused to let them step foot in his house. Even at the funeral, they never spoke. Sarah greeted them and gave each other a hug. She asked her father why he treated them that way, but he wouldn't answer. After a small sermon, they followed the hearse to the grave site. Sarah broke down and started to weep after the pastor's words. Her aunt Amber came over to comfort her, but her father told her to get away from her. Sarah was glad to leave the grave since there was so much tension.

When Sarah got home, she went to her room and lay on her bed and cried and was still upset with the way those two acted, especially at her mother's funeral. Sarah knew her responsibility would increase taking over for mom, but at the same time, she lost interest in school and her grades began to show it. When her father saw her report card, he became quite angry.

Greg said, "I'm going to punish you," and grabbed her and pulled her over his lap. He spanked her and said, "Now you better pick up those grades."

Sarah cried and said, "I can't. I have too much work to do."

He said, "Are you talking back to me?" which made him very angry. He pulled her jeans down, including her panties, and spanked her tail red. "Now will you talk back to me?"

Sarah pulled up her jeans and ran to her room crying. She was never so embarrassed in her life. She never came out for supper and spent the rest of the night in her room.

The next day, she did all her chores before going to school. At school, she asked her teacher if there was something she could do to pick up her grades. The teacher gave her extra homework to complete. She soon brought her grades up so she wouldn't have that happen again. What she didn't know was that her father's affection for her was changing since she was looking more and more like her mother.

Sarah heard her father crying some nights and felt very sorry for him. She also felt depressed and didn't really feel like going to school let alone keeping up with the work. He was always yelling at her for not doing her chores. She kept up her grades so he wouldn't beat her anymore. She thought he was looking for an excuse to do so. On her way home from school, a boy in her class followed her. Sarah waited up on him to walk her home but was still afraid of her father. She tried to stop the boy, Jack, when they got close to the house, but her father saw him.

"Sarah, what are you doing with that boy?" he yelled.

"Nothing, Father. He was just walking me home."

"You better go away before I call the sheriff on you."

Jack got scared and ran, and Sarah knew she was in big trouble. Greg pulled her into the house and said, "Drop your pants." Sarah said she wouldn't, so he grabbed her up and tore her clothes. He put her over his lap and whipped her. She cried out that she had done nothing, and he had better stop. She got away from him and ran to her room, locking her door behind her. She stayed in her room crying hysterically. He knocked on the door several times and soon left her alone. She didn't come out the rest of the night being scared.

The next day, she went to school like nothing had ever happened. Jack asked her if she was alright, but she never answered him. When she came home from school, he acted like nothing happened and told her after supper to finish her chores around there.

Sarah ate her food that her father had fixed. She then cleared the table and washed the dishes in the kitchen sink. She left the house and went to the barn to collect feed for the chickens. She spread it out on the ground, and it was like a feeding frenzy. She knew that she had neglected these chickens and realized a reason for her dad's anger. Sarah then checked all the plants and made sure they were getting enough water before returning to the house.

Her father was sitting in the living room resting from a hard day. Sarah went in and told him what she had done. He said, "Good. Go do your homework and get ready for bed."

Sarah went in and took a shower and changed into her nightgown that her dad had bought her. She thought her gown was a little revealing but didn't put much thought into it. Sarah finished her homework when her father came into the room.

He said, "Are you done? You need to get some sleep for tomorrow."

She said she would, but he kept standing there staring at her. It made her feel nervous and asked him, "Is there anything else? If not, good night, Dad."

"In a moment," he said. "You look just like your mother." He came over and gave her a kiss and left. Sarah got into the bed, but her father had given her the creeps.

Sarah got up early the next morning and made a special trip out to feed the chickens and gather eggs for breakfast. She went into the kitchen and started the coffee and scrambled eggs for breakfast for her and her father. She realized that she was still in her nightgown and rushed upstairs to change. Her father was watching when she went by him.

She said, "There is eggs and coffee in the kitchen for you."

He said, "Why are you in a hurry?" She said had to get dressed for school. "You have got plenty of time. Why not come back with me and eat breakfast?"

She said, "I'll be right down after I get dressed."

He said nothing, and she hurried to her room. She could tell he was acting strange but didn't know why. After getting dressed, she went back to the kitchen, but he had already left. She warmed up her eggs and made her coffee with cream and sugar and sat there eating and looking at the clock. The bus would be there soon. She went upstairs to brush her teeth and hair and grabbed her books when she heard the honk of the horn. She rushed down the stairs and out in the yard to the bus. She felt her father's eyes on her while getting on the bus.

Sarah had a few girlfriends on the bus, and they talked about Ray, the cute guy in their class. The bus driver had to calm them down about their loud giggling. Sarah knew every girl wanted to get a kiss from Ray, but Joy had exclusive rights to be his girlfriend. So that's all they ever talked about, and no one wanted to hear her problem. She got off the bus heading for the school, and Jack came up to say hi. Jack had a crush on her but was still very shy and afraid to say anything, especially because of her father.

Sarah's day at school was uneventful and was soon back on the bus to go home. Her father was still out in the field, and she went in and changed to a pair of jeans and tennis shoes to go out and feed the animals. Pulling on her red T-shirt, she headed downstairs and out to the barn. She got the feed out for the chickens and scattered it all over the ground. All the chickens gathered to peck at their dinner. She put hay in the stall for their one cow. Going out to the field, her father called and said, "No need for you today. Go fix dinner."

Sarah returned to the house to make the pork chops he had left out for her. While frying the pork chops, she put on a pot of water for the potatoes. She was using a package since the potatoes in the garden weren't ready. Her father had put a bowl of green beans in the fridge. He must have brought them in earlier from the garden. She put them in a pot to boil before turning the meat over in the pan. Her father came in from the field and she said supper would be ready soon. He said he was going to wash up and would be right back. In time, he returned and she had set the table and put the potatoes and green beans in a bowl. Sarah then brought the frying pan over and put a pork chop on each plate. Replacing the pan on the stove, she poured out two glasses of ice tea.

Her father sat down and said, "You did a good job. Are you doing any better in school now?" Sarah said she passed her test today with a 100 percent. He began to eat and said, "That's good."

After dinner, she washed all the plates while her father sat in front of the TV. She went to her room and finished her homework. She laid down on her bed and read a romance novel she had from the school library. She had wished that she and Ray were the characters in the book. He was still the quarterback, but it was her, not Judy, he was in love with the book.

After her little fantasy, she decided to take a shower and get ready for bed. She went into the bathroom and put her clothes in a hamper and climbed in the shower. She was there a while letting the warm water roll off her skin before applying soap. She heard her father calling her. She got out of the shower and dried off, slipping into her nightgown. She walked out of the bathroom and her father stopped her in the hall. She saw he was looking at her strangely and realized she had nothing underneath. She tried to get past him to get her robe, but he wouldn't let her.

"Dad, what are you doing?"

He pushed her into her room and was on top of her before she could do a thing. He took advantage of her, and when he left, she felt wet and scared. Sarah got up from the bed and locked her door and started crying hysterically. When she knew he was back downstairs, she ran to the bathroom and locked the door. She stood in the shower stall with the water and blood running down her legs. She cried forever and couldn't understand why her father had hurt her. She went back to her room and locked the door, moving the dresser in front of the door.

The next morning, she got dressed and waited for the bus to honk before leaving her room. She sat on the bus in a daze knowing not what to do. When she got to the classroom, she didn't talk to anybody and acted like a vegetable.

The teacher called to her. "Ms. Sarah Wright, please come up to my desk." At first, she didn't hear her and slowly got up and walked up to the teacher's desk. The teacher could tell there was something wrong by the look in her eyes. "Sarah follow me out to the hall." She got up from her desk and took her by the arm and led her out of the classroom. Mrs. Rook said, "What is wrong with you? Do you need to go home?"

Suddenly, Sarah became scared and said with tears falling, "No. I don't want to go home. Please don't make me," crying.

Mrs. Rook said, "Did something happen at home?" Sarah became agitated trying to hide her feelings. Mrs. Rook said, "Let's go to the principal's office," and led her down the hall. Mrs. Rook sat her outside his office saying, "I'll be just a minute."

Mrs. Rook went into his office to talk to him. While she was waiting, the school resorts office came to the principal's office and entered. Sarah was becoming quite scared and felt like getting up and running but had nowhere to go.

Two police officers entered the building, and the one lady officer said, "I'm Officer Robins. Can I talk to you alone?" The principal gave them a room to be alone. "Now, Sarah, I know you are scared, and I just want to know what's bothering you."

Sarah popped up saying, "Nothing's wrong."

The officer said, "I can see that's not true. Let's go to your father and see if he can tell me what's bothering you."

Sarah really became nervous. "No. I don't want to go there."

"Why? Did he do something to you?"

Sarah began to cry, saying, "He hurt me. I don't want to go there."

Officer Robin said, "Wait here a minute. I need to tell my partner something." She returned in a minute and said, "We are taking you to the hospital. The doctor there wants to exam you if that is alright." They took Sarah in the patrol car to the nearest hospital and introduced her to Dr. Kelly. "She wants to exam you." The nurse took her into a room to get undressed and into a hospital gown. The doctor came in and examined her and went out to tell the officers about it. She told Sarah, "We will have to keep you here for a little while."

Dr. Kelly returned to the two officer and said, "She was raped." They left and went to her father's house. Knocking at his door, no one answered. Robin's partner, Officer Riley, saw him out in the field. He called Joan and said he was out there.

They walked out to the field and said, "You're Mr. Greg Wright?" He said yes. "Well, sir, you are under arrest for child abuse. You have the right to remain silent and to refuse to answer any questions. Anything you say may be used in a court of law. You have the right to consult an attorney before speaking to the police and have an attorney present during questions now or in the future."

They handcuffed him and took him to the squad car. "Do you have anyone to come and feed these farm animals?"

He said, "No. I'll have my attorney take care of it."

"You can call him when we get to the station."

At his trial, it was a clear case and pleading guilty got him a twenty-year sentence. Because there was no one to take care of the farm, everything went for auction and would be turned over to Sarah when she was twenty-one.

Sarah was resting in the hospital when an older lady came into her room. "Ms. Wright, I'm Mrs. Joy Lambert. I am your social worker. Do you have any relatives you can stay with?"

"My aunt Amber, but I don't know her last name." She said she would look for them. Tracing back her records, Mrs. Lambert found out that she had married Robert Zen in Savanna, South Carolina Mrs. Joy traveled to their home and told them what had happen.

Amber said, "I already have two children, and I'm divorced. Being a waitress, I have a hard time affording my two let alone another. I'm sorry. Even the little bit the state gives me I can't see that it'll be enough to take care of her, and I'm sure she is emotional wreck. I don't have enough time for that responsibility."

Mrs. Lambert walked back to her car feeling quite disappointed knowing how much the fourteen-year-old child had gone through to be rejected. She was not looking forward to returning to Sarah with the news.

The next day, Mrs. Lambert returned to the hospital. Walking into Sarah's room, she said, "I have some bad news for you. Your aunt Amber can't take you, so we have no choice but to make you a ward of the state. I'll be taking you to Macon to the Methodist Home. There are boys and girls there your own age."

Sarah began to cry feeling nobody wanted her, and she was scared.

Mrs. Lambert said, "Not to worry, I'm taking you myself." Sarah felt a little better but still asked about her father. "Well, there was a court hearing, and you didn't need to be there, and he will be gone a long time." She told Sarah to get dressed. "We will stop by your house for your clothes and anything else you would like to take."

When they got to the house, a sheriff was there with a key to let them in. Mrs. Lambert noticed that Sarah was a little afraid of the officer. She told the sheriff that she would go in with her, and he could wait there. Mrs. Lambert helped her to pack and asked her if she wanted any pictures. Sarah took a single picture of her mom but not her dad. Mrs. Lambert carried Sarah's blue suitcase out of the car and thanked the office. Sarah looked back as they drove away and was glad to get away from there.

It was a two-hour drive to Macon, and Mrs. Lambert tried to get her to talk but Sarah kept quiet. They stopped at the drive-through at McDonald's and got two quarter-pounder meals on the way. When they got to Pierce Street in Macon, they drove up to a big red-brick building. Sarah had never seen such a place; it looked like a mansion.

Going inside, it looked deserted with one desk in the middle of the room. Mrs. Lambert told, "Sit on that bench over there, and I'll be back to get you." Sarah went and sat down, and Mrs. Lambert went up to the desk.

The lady at the desk said, "Can I help you?"

"I'm Mrs. Lambert from Social Services, and I have an appointment with Mrs. Cartwright."

The lady picked up the phone and said, "This is Robin McGee at the front desk. There is a Mrs. Lambert to see the superintendent." Robin hung up the phone and said she would be right out. In a few minutes, a door open and a silver-haired lady came out.

Shaking hands with Mrs. Lambert, she said, "I'm Mrs. Nancy Cartwright." They walked over and she said, "Who is this young lady?"

"This is Sarah Wright, and she will be staying here."

Mrs. Cartwright shook her hand saying, "Welcome to our home. I'm sure you will fit right in."

Mrs. Lambert said, "Could I talk with you in private for a few minutes? Plus, I need you to sign the paperwork." Mrs. Cartwright led her to her office, leaving Sarah alone on the bench. Robin noticed how nervous she was and walked over to talk to her. Sarah saw she was a young woman in her twenties with black hair and brown eyes.

Robin said to her, "Don't be frightened. This place is alright. I grew up here and liked it so much I returned to work here."

Mrs. Lambert told Mrs. Cartwright about Sarah's problem and said she will need some counseling.

Mrs. Cartwright said, "We have excellent psychiatrists here."

"I hope you have a woman. I think she will have problems with a man."

"We have Ms. Regina Watts. She is new to us, but I'm sure she will do good with her. Well, let's go back, and I'll take charge of her."

Joy walked back to Sarah saying, "I must get back to work, and Mrs. Cartwright will show you around. I'll be back to check on you occasionally, so good luck." She gave Sarah a hug before walking out the door.

Mrs. Cartwright said, "Follow me," and headed to the double doors. Sarah saw there were classrooms on each side of the hall. Mrs. Cartwright said, "I suppose you are in the ninth grade." Sarah said she was. She led her to a classroom and introduced her to Mr. Thompson who would be her teacher. He put out his hand to welcome her, but she wouldn't shake it. Mrs. Cartwright said, "Come along," and said to Mr. Thompson, "I'll talk to you later."

Mrs. Cartwright went to a set of elevators and ushered her in, punching the number three. Turning to Sarah, she said, "The boys have the second floor and all the girls have the third." When the elevator opened, she led her to the room on the right. "This will be your bedroom. There are seven other girls around your age. We try to keep our girls in their age range."

Sarah noticed there were a lot of bedrooms on each side of the hall. Mrs. Cartwright led her to the end of the hall to where the cafeteria was.

She said, "Breakfast is served at seven and lunch at noon and dinner is at six, and if you are late, you will miss out. Now let's go to the other end of the hall." When they got there, she saw a large room with six computers and TV and radio and even a stereo with records.

Mrs. Cartwright said, "You will have to take turns doing your homework online. I'm sure your roommates will let you know the schedule, and you will meet them when class is done."

She led her back to a bedroom with eight beds and several dressers. She said, "That bed"—pointing to the last one on the left—"is yours and you have the bottom two drawers in that dresser over there to put your clothes. Well, I'll leave you now, and I'm sure the other girls will help you. You can put your clothes away and hang out in the entertainment room till they get back."

After she left, Sarah unpacked and looked around the room. The room was in white with brown dressers and gray slate for the floor. She walked out in the hall and saw a central bathroom. She went in and there was a line of toilet stalls and a shower room at the end with quite a few stalls and a supply closet with towels and washrags and even feminine supplies including dental and several kinds of soap. Sarah picked out a toothbrush and toothpaste and brushed her teeth since she hadn't since that morning. She also found a hairbrush, which she used. She took several things from the closet back to her room before heading to the entertainment room. Sarah played a few CDs before the rest got back from class.

The first girl Sarah met was an eight-year-old girl named Marcie. She was kind of cute for her age. She had brown curly hair and blue eyes. She came over saying, "You must be new," after she introduced herself. "I hope we can be friends," she said, "because I don't have too many friends here."

Sarah said, "Why not?"

"Well," she said, kind of shy, "everybody says I talk too much."

"Well, I don't mind," Sarah said, "and we can be great friends and you can help me to be informed about what's going on here."

Marcie said, "That would be great. I have been quite lonely here with no one to talk to." Just then, the other members of Marcie's class were coming in. Marcie said, "I'll see you later. Got to get to one those computers to do my homework." Sarah watched as Marcie got to the first computer and sat down. Others in her class frowned that she got there first. Sarah left the entertainment room and headed back to her bedroom to meet her roommates.

The first girl she met was a dark-haired girl with brown eyes. She was at least two years older than Sarah. She introduced herself as Judy. "I see you are replacing Ruth who has left at eighteen. Let me introduce you to the other girls."

The first two were blue-eyed blondes being fifteen. One was named Jane and the other Mary. Two were her age, a brown-haired girl named Betty and the other had brown hair, but her eyes were blue. She was Raven. Laura had red hair and green eyes, and Betsy's eyes were brown with coal-black hair.

Judy picked up her books and headed to the door saying, "We each take turns doing our homework. When I come back, it will be one of the other girls' turns. Since you are new, tomorrow you'll be last." They each took turns till six when they were called to dinner.

They stood in line for their tray of food. Sarah got her tray, which consisted of a piece of chicken and mashed potatoes and green beans. At the end of the line, they were handed a glass of ice tea. Mostly everyone sat with their age group except Marcie sat alone. Sarah took her tray and headed to Marcie's table and sat with her. Marcie was happy that someone was sitting with her. When they were finished, Marcie returned to her room, and Sarah walked back with her roommates.

Judy said, "Why didn't you sit with us?"

Sarah said, "She needed a friend," and nothing was said after that. Betsy was the last to return after doing her homework, which only left a half hour before lights-out. Sarah realized that she would have only a little time to do hers the next day.

Sarah woke up in the middle of the night screaming, waking up everybody in the room.

Judy told her, "Go back to sleep. You were having a nightmare." Sarah knew she was having that same dream of her father. Judy thought to herself that she would have to report it to Mrs. Cartwright.

In the morning, the lights came on in the room at six. Judy said, "Everybody, get dressed and make your beds. We must be at breakfast soon." The girls took their clothes and personal items to the shower room down the hall. They showered and brushed their hair and teeth. After getting dressed, they returned in time to make their beds. When they left their room, they formed a line to go to the cafeteria. This time their trays had two eggs, bacon, and toast and had their choice of coffee or milk. When they were finished, they collected their books and headed to the elevators to go to class.

Entering the classroom, Mr. Thompson said, "Sarah, your desk is that one there." She sat down where he pointed. He said, "If you look in your desk, you'll find everything you will need and take it with you when you leave. The only time you will be out of this room is at lunch and if you need to go to the bathroom."

They had math and history before lunch and science after. At two, class was over, and everybody got up to leave. Mr. Thompson spoke up and said, "Sarah, you are supposed to go to Ms. Watts's office, which is down the hall to the right."

The other girls headed left to the elevator while Sarah walked down the hall to the right. She didn't understand why she was going there. She knocked at the door and heard a voice telling her to come in. Sarah saw a young woman who had long black hair, which was straight on each side of her head.

"Hi, Sarah, you can call me Regina. Please sit down, and I would like to get to know you. I heard you had a nightmare last night. Would you like to talk about it? Sarah was quite nervous, not saying a word. "Do you like being here?" she asked. Sarah said it was alright, keeping to herself and only answering questions. Ms. Watts could see that Sarah wasn't ready to open up and said, "I'll see you next week at this time. Maybe you will talk to me then."

Sarah got up and left and headed back to class. Sarah was at the orphanage for the next four years and never talked about her experience. Her best friend was Marcie who was her mother till she left. Ms. Watts recommended Sarah be sent to the abuse center after leaving the orphanage. June was the only one who got Sarah to open up and led her to Christ.

While June was away, Sarah stayed in the parsonage and studied under Mrs. Marie. On Sundays, she would be an usher for the church. When June returned, she moved out of the parsonage. They were both happy to help in the church. Pastor Dodge had a good sermon, and Sarah sat down in the back row listening.

"How many of you here would rush into a building burning knowing your child is about to burn up?" Almost everybody raised their hand. "How many would do it for a stranger?" Not many hands went up. "That's what God is calling you to do to save people from a burning building. If you don't let people know about the Lord, they are going into the fire. Your loved ones need to be rescued, and I'm sure you hope someone will rescue you. God gave each one a mission to save someone. If we keep it to ourselves, you are condemning people. Someone came to your rescue, so you need to come to someone else's rescue. Everyone who didn't raise your hand needs to get down on your knees and pray. If you don't know the Lord, I would like to pray with you. I'm here to help you from that burning building because without Christ, you will be in that fire."

Quite a few people walked the aisle that day. Sarah and June passed the collection plates and gave them to John to count.

Suddenly, June shook Sarah out of her daydream saying they were getting ready to load their bus. Pastor Dodge got up to lead them to the bus. Everyone followed him while singing a church song. Sarah was glad to leave, especially with Jeff staring at them.

CHAPTER 17

JEFF BOYD

Jeff walked into the bus station. He looked straight at June and saw the fear in her eyes.

Jeff thought to himself, *I'll get her now, and none of those church people can stop me.* He headed across the room and ran into an invisible barrier. He was so surprised, and this made him angrier. Jeff went back to his seat behind Jennifer and John.

Jeff said, "It's all your fault, and you are lucky to have your man next to you." John got a little mad and told him to go sit down.

Jeff couldn't figure out why he couldn't get to June, and he was really fuming when everyone on that side of the room got up to leave. He yelled at her, "You better come back because wherever you go, I'll chase you down."

June didn't say a word as she walked out the door to the bus. The ticket master came over and handed him his ticket saying, "You're on the next bus." He turned to John and said, "You have a little while before your bus comes." Jennifer was glad that they wouldn't be on the bus with Jeff. Jeff calmed down and wondered why he was here. He began to think back to his beginning.

He remembered growing up in Atlanta with his parents. The house they lived in was quite shabby, and they never had money to fix it up. His father was a bus driver for the city and almost lost his job several times for drinking. He seemed to always come home grumpy and would take it out on them.

His father was a big man with brown hair and brown eyes. His mother was rather skinny with strawberry-blond hair and green eyes.

James would always go out for a drink before coming home. When he got drunk, he would start an argument with his wife, Gina. He usually used his fist on her, and Jeff would get knocked to the floor to protect her. Jeff's anger grew over time. He got tired of the beatings, and when he turned fourteen, his hatred for his father came to a boiling point. After getting beat and bloody, he waited till his father fell asleep and snuck in the bedroom and stabbed his father to death. When his mother saw what he had done, she was afraid for him. She told him to take off all his clothes and get in the shower. She took his clothes and hid them outside in their burn barrel. She came in and wiped the knife by putting on her own prints on the knife. When the police arrived, they took her in for murder. Jeff let her take the blame, and because of the physical abuse, they gave her twenty years. Jeff was sent to an orphanage. Before he left, he burned the clothes and never once visited her in prison.

Jeff was still angry and became such a bully in the orphanage that nobody liked him. He was too old to be adopted, so he spent the next four years there. When Jeff was seventeen, he saw this man hanging around out front of the orphanage and went out to talk to him. The guy dressed like a bum and asked Jeff if he wanted to get high. Jeff didn't know what he was talking about but lit up the weed that was gave to him. Jeff's head started spinning, and he enjoyed the feeling. One of the boys saw him and turned him in since Jeff was always picking on him. Jeff was punished, and the man was arrested. It didn't long before the man was back, and Jeff liked that feeling and snuck out for a smoke.

The man named Jim said, "You can have your own if you start selling for me, and I'll give you money too."

Jeff agreed and started selling for the guy. The boy that had squealed on him ended with a broken arm and never said a word again—too frightened. At first, he was only selling weed but soon began to sell heroin.

When he left the orphanage, he could afford his own apartment. One of his customers was a sweet girl of sixteen. Her name was Mary-Ann. She was quite lovely with her long brown hair and shining blue eyes. Soon she couldn't afford her habit, and Jeff started selling her out for sex. He kept all the money but kept her high all the time. He realized he could make a fortune selling girls for sex and soon had twelve in his stable. Jeff went on the internet to a dating site where he could lure more girls. One of the girls he was talking to be a girl named June. It took him a year to talk her into coming to Atlanta.

Jeff knew if he let June keep asking questions, he'd be in trouble. Jeff waited till she was asleep and drugged her. He figured he would turn her out with the rest of the girls. Jeff waited till she was hooked and told her what she had to do. Jeff left the apartment laughing to himself to see what she gets for asking. Jeff went to talk to his customers. He showed them the pictures that she had sent online to him. There were several nude poses, and he set her up with a few men at a hundred dollars apiece. When he returned home, she was gone with her suitcase full of clothes. Jeff was quite angry and started to bust things up in the apartment, especially things he had gave to her. He thought she went to her friend Jennifer, but when he got to the motel, he found that Jennifer had moved out. He went back home still boiling with anger.

I'll go to church tomorrow and get Jennifer to tell me where she is. He knew first he had to fix it with the guys he had lined up. He called each one offering other girls but had to return the money to two of them.

The next morning, he went to the church to find Jennifer. He went in and headed to her office. John saw him and followed. He went into her office without knocking, demanding her to tell him where she was. Jennifer was a little frightened but said she didn't know, and he needed to leave. Jeff grabbed her by her blouse and shook her saying, "Don't lie to me."

John rushed in and grabbed him, saying, "Let her go." Jeff took a swing at him and missed. John hit him, saying, "If you don't leave, I'll be calling the police."

When Jeff saw the pastor, he knew he had to get out of there. Jeff turned and left, saying, "I'll find out. You wait and see."

Jennifer at that time didn't know that June had left but was glad she did. The police came and were informed of what happened and told her to take out a restraining order. Pastor Dodge said he would get in touch with Jim Rhodes, and he would get it for you.

Jeff received the order, and he knew he couldn't go back to the church. Jeff had each of his girls watch the church after showing each one a picture. It took several months before Mary-Ann saw June entered the church. She went straight back to Jeff to tell him.

Jeff said, "I knew she would, sooner or later, show up," and gave Mary-Ann a free shot for a reward.

The following Monday, he sent Mary-Ann out to watch. The other girls reported nothing happening except Wednesday night services. That night while Mary-Ann was watching the church, she saw a woman walk up and opened the church. There were five others she let in, and they all seemed suspicious. Mary-Ann didn't hang around and went back to tell Jeff.

Jeff said, "Why didn't you wait and see what happens?"

Mary-Ann said, "I was excited to tell you about it, and I needed a fix."

Jeff told her, "Only if you have the money." Mary-Ann did, and he gave her the shot. "Next week I want you to find out about her, and if you get all the information, I may give you one for free."

Mary-Ann was there when she opened the door that Monday and waited till everyone left and followed the woman to the bus stop. When the lady got on the bus, Mary-Ann hurried to get on. She bumped into the woman on purpose, saying, "Excuse me."

The woman said, "It's alright. My name is Robin. What's yours?"

"My name is Mary-Ann, and I notice you coming out of that church. I didn't know it was open so late."

Robin said, "It's not. A friend of mine got me a key, so we could play poker there. I hope you don't tell anybody. It would get my friend in a lot of trouble."

Mary-Ann said, "Your secret is safe with me."

Robin said, "Thanks. If you want, you can come and play."

Mary-Ann said, "I might take you up on that."

"Well, I'll see you Monday. I get off here."

Mary-Ann watched her go into the apartment and noticed it was Garden Walk Apartments. She stayed on the bus till she got to Jeff's apartment and got off and headed upstairs. She knocked, and he let her in. She told him all she learned.

He said, "You earned your shot." After giving it to her, he said, "I want you back here Monday. You're going to join that poker game."

Mary-Ann said, "You know I don't have that kind of money."

Jeff said, "I'll be staking you, and I want you to find out the layout of that church and a way to get that key."

The following Monday, Mary-Ann got to Jeff's apartment. He let her in and said, "Here's two hundred dollars to play, and take this pencil and paper and make a map of the place." She took the money, and before she left, he said, "You do know how to play poker?"

Mary-Ann smiled and said, "I have played before, but not too good."

"I'm more interested in the layout, so don't worry about losing."

Mary-Ann got to the church at ten, and Robin had the door open letting everybody in. Mary-Ann called out for her to wait on her. Robin let her in and showed her to go in the left door, which lead to the cafeteria. Mary-Ann asked where the right-hand door led to.

"Oh! that's just the offices of the staff and pastor."

The group got busy moving the table to the center of the room and each brought a chair. Robin said, "We will go by our first names." They started introducing themselves. The first two guys were John and one guy was named Fred. The women, including herself, were Roberta, Mary-Ann, and Robin. Robin brought out the chips selling each person two hundred dollars' worth.

Mary Ann won a few hands of five-card stud before they changed the game to duces wild, and she started on a losing streak. She asked to sit out a hand while she went to the bathroom. The bathrooms were in the lobby, but she went straight across the hall to the door on the right. Going down the hall, she tried every door and found them locked. She came back out and tried the two doors in the front of the church. One looked like a nursery and the other was a Sunday school room. She seen on her watch that she had been gone a long time and rushed back to the cafeteria.

She said, "I thought I would never get off that toilet." Everybody laughed.

Mary-Ann played a few more hands before losing it all. She got up and said, "I need a drink of water," and went in the kitchen. She noticed a back door. Getting a drink, she walked back saying, "I guess I need to go."

Robin said, "Hold on a minute. I'll let you out after this hand." It wasn't long before Robin folded her hand and led Mary-Ann to the door.

Robin said, "Fred is having a lucky night. He's hard to beat."

Mary-Ann said, "I had fun. Maybe I'll be back next week."

Robin let her out saying, "I hope you do. Maybe I can get some of my money back," laughing and opening the door. Before leaving, she walked around back of the church to see where the back door was. It was in an alley with a dumpster. Mary-Ann went to the bus stop to wait on the bus. She sat down on the bench and drew a map thinking that Jeff would be pleased even if she couldn't get the key.

Returning to Jeff, she showed him the map. Jeff told her, "I need you to return next week to play again, but before you leave, I need you to unlock that back door."

Returning the following week after getting the money from Jeff, she returned to the church. Mary-Ann had a lucky streak and made almost six hundred dollars. She was so excited, almost forgetting to unlock the back door. She knew not to go back to Jeff's right away because he would take the money from her. She hurried and took the bus to her apartment. She got home and hid the money in the bottom of the closet where there was a loose board. Mary-Ann hurried back out the door to the bus and headed to Jeff's place. She went up and knocked on the door, and he let her in.

Jeff said, "Did you do what I said?"

She replied that she had left it unlocked, and no one saw her.

"I guess you lost the money," Jeff said. Being a little nervous, she said she did. Jeff looked at her and said, "Are you lying?"

She said, "No. I just need a shot."

Jeff said, "This will be the last one I won't need you anymore, and if I catch you lying, it won't be good for you." He injected her and said, "Leave. If you want more, bring me the money or I can set you up with someone."

Mary-Ann got out of there before he asked too many questions.

Jeff called his old friend Leroy, who was a locksmith. He came to the phone after several minutes.

"Who is this calling me up in the middle of the night?" Leroy said.

Jeff said, "I got a job for you. I want you to make some keys for me tonight. There's a church on Virginia Avenue called the United Methodist. Go around to the alley. The back door is unlocked, and I want a set of keys to every door in that place including the main door."

Leroy said, "It's going to cost you."

Jeff said, "If you do the job right, I will give you a thousand dollars."

"Wow! You must really want something. They got a lot of cash in there?" Leroy asked.

Jeff said, "Just get me the keys, and any cash in the place is yours."

Leroy said, "Don't worry. I'll be leaving in a minute, and I'll see you tomorrow for the money."

Jeff hung up and said, "It won't be long, June, before you pay."

Leroy pulled his black car behind the church making sure he didn't wake anybody in the parsonage. He found the back door unlocked as Jeff said it would be. He started with that door and made impression before heading inside. It took him several hours to make an impression of every door. He found the safe in John's office and finally got it open, finding very little money. He couldn't understand why Jeff wanted the keys; there weren't enough to make up for what he was giving. It was almost dawn before he was done and locked the back door. He left and got in his car heading to his shop.

By eight o'clock that morning, he had a key to every door in that church. Leroy said to himself, "This was an easy thousand." Leroy closed up his shop and went home to catch up on his sleep. He put on his answering service thinking he would answer them later. He got in bed at home and turned off his phone for a while. When he turned it back on, there were several messages from Jeff. He called him and said, "Don't worry. I got the keys. I'll be over tonight to collect, and I guarantee every key will work."

Leroy got dressed and went to his shop, answering all his calls before closing that night. He turned up at Jeff's around seven thirty with the keys. Jeff took the keys and handed him the money and asked him if he wanted a drink. Leroy drank a beer with him before leaving.

The next morning, Jeff went to the bank to get ten thousand dollars out of his account. He knew a guy who was in a biker gang who could get him the weapons that he wanted. Jeff drove to a bar off the interstate where this gang hung out. When he walked in, he looked around and saw his old buddy Brian drinking a beer alone at a table in the back. Jeff went up to the bar ordering two beers and walking over to the table where Brian was sitting.

Brian looked up as Jeff sat down saying, "Well, old buddy, I know you didn't come here just to sit and drink. What do you want?"

Jeff laughed and said, "You know me well. I'd like to buy some weapons from you."

"Depends on what you want and if the price is right," Brian said.

Jeff said in a quiet voice, "I want an automatic weapon with a dozen clips and a .45 automatic with three boxes of shells."

Brian said, "That's going to cost you."

Jeff said, "How about five thousand?"

Brian said, "I won't take less than seven in cash, and if I have to wait, it will be another thousand."

Jeff said, "Not to worry." He counted out seven thousand and handed it to Brian. He took the money and quickly put it away, not trusting too many of his friends.

Brian said, "Be here tomorrow night, and I'll hook you up. Park your car around back and come in the front. After a few beers, they shook hands and Jeff got up and left.

Jeff went home that night sitting and getting drunk. He thought to himself he pulled a fast one not having to put up the whole ten thousand. Getting rather tired, he staggered to bed and was soon fast asleep.

The next day after he got up, he made a pot of coffee. He sat there drinking and saying, "It won't be long before I get even with all of you."

After getting dressed, he drove to the nearest hardware store where he bought a length of chain and a sturdy padlock. He still felt hung over from last night and went back home.

"Well, I don't need to get there till tonight. Maybe I'll sleep for a few more hours." He crawled back into bed; the room still felt like it was spinning. He didn't wake up again until dark. Jeff got out of bed and looked at his clock and saw it was going on nine. He went in and took a shower to wake up. After getting dressed, he brushed his teeth and decided to shave. Soon he was ready and headed outside to his car.

Jeff arrived at the bar, drove around, and walked in the front like he was told. Jeff saw Brian with his two other friends sitting at a table, and he went over to join them. Brian hollered at the bartender to bring them four beers.

Brian said, "We got the stuff and will go out in a little bit and get it." For a few hours, they sat there drinking and smoking. Soon Brian told his buddies to meet him out back. They got up, finished their beers, and left. Brian said he would give them a few minutes before they go out back. They sat there drinking another beer before getting up and heading down the back hall. When they opened the back door, his friends were waiting. Jeff when over and opened his trunk. The one opened his trunk next to Jeff's car, and they transferred the weapons.

Jeff checked out the merchandise and was satisfied, closing the trunk.

Brian said, "We need to look like nothing is happening." Brian looked at his two buddies and told them to head back around front and go in and order some beers and sit at the bar till they come in. The two guys did just what they were told. Brian told Jeff to head back into the bathroom. When they got there, he told Jeff to wait a few minutes and headed back into the bar like you never left.

Jeff used the bathroom and washed his hands before heading back into the bar. He asked the bartender for two more beers and said to the guys, "You need one." They agreed and had the bartender to bring two more. Jeff said, "Why don't you guys join me at that table over there when you get your drinks?"

Jeff had just sat down when Brian strolled back in. He said, "I see you ordered us another round." Soon the other two came over and sat down. The four sat around talking and laughing. Jeff brought two more rounds before getting up to leave.

Jeff walked around back to his car feeling a little drunk and thinking he better be careful; he sure didn't want to be pulled over. He drove to the nearest Waffle House and ordered some coffee and some bacon and eggs. He sat and drank at least three cups of coffee and felt better after eating. He paid and headed back to the car and went home. When he got home, it was almost three a.m. He got ready for bed and slept half the day away. When he got up, it was almost two in the afternoon. He made a pot of coffee and sat and thought about his revenge.

Jeff knew a place that was quite deserted to take up some target practice. He took a shower and got dressed before heading out. He soon found the dirt road that headed into the forest and soon found a spot to set up. He took some old beer cans out of the car and set them on a fallen tree. Loading a clip in the automatic rifle, he fired, trying to keep it in a straight line. The gun kept trying to pull upwards, so it took him a while before keeping it straight. Next, he loaded the .45 and did better at knocking down the cans. It was starting to get dark, so he loaded up the trunk and headed home.

On the drive home, he thought, *I'll make sure no one will ever turn on me again.* He made it back to the apartment and watched some TV before going to bed.

Friday night came, and it was time to go around for collection. He made his tour around the city to the twelve girls he had working for him. Each handed over their cash for that week, and he gave each a gram to tie them over for a week. Mary-Ann was his last stop; he was going to get some from her. When he walked into her apartment, he found her passed out. He slapped her awake saying, "Where's my money?" He was a little angry thinking she blew his money on getting high.

Mary-Ann slowly awoke and said, "Your money is in the coffee cup in the cabinet." Jeff went into the kitchen and got the cup out of the cabinet. He counted it out and saw it was all there. Jeff came back in and shook her saying, "Where did you get that fix?"

Mary-Ann woke up and said, "John hooked me up." Jeff believed her since all his money was there. He had changed his mind of having her since she would be no good and will have very little response. He left feeling a little disgusted with her. He went to the local bar and decided to have a few beers. He was still feeling sexual and saw a woman sitting alone. He went up and asked if he could buy her a drink. They talked a while and soon she was drunk, and he took her to his apartment for the night.

In the morning, he had too much to do, so instead of recruiting her, he sent her home in a cab. Jeff made a pot of coffee and sat drinking while he went over the map deciding on a plan. He would park his car against the back door and chain the front. He thought this was a good plan and headed to McDonald's for breakfast. He ordered a big breakfast with pancakes eggs and bacon with a biscuit. He sat there in the restaurant eating and going over his plan making sure nothing would go wrong. He was too nervous to go home, so he strolled around the city looking in shop windows. He stopped for lunch at Burger King. He ordered a Whopper meal with a Coke. He sat there eating and saw several people come in from the church.

He laughed to himself, saying, *This may be their last meal.* When he was finished, he walked around some more. Jeff was starting to sweat and decided to go to the bar he saw ahead to cool off. He went in and sat at the bar and called to the bartender to bring him a beer. Jeff sat there for a few hours before getting up and going home. At the house, he put in the microwave a Hungry-Man TV dinner of fried chicken. Jeff went and turned on the TV to wait till it was done. When the microwave beeped, he went and collected his meal. He poured a glass of ice tea and sat down with his meal and ate in front of the TV. Jeff cleaned up his mess and sat in front of the TV before going to bed that night.

Jeff woke up Sunday morning feeling quite excited. As he made coffee, he thought to himself, *This is it, June. Today you pay with all the rest of your little friends.* He went and collected his bag and sat down and drank his coffee. He was too excited to eat. He made his way to his car and made sure no one was watching. He opened the trunk and filled his bag with the boxes of shells and the clips for the rifle. He noticed it was ten o'clock, and they would all be gathered in the church by now. He got in and drove to the church and parked his car against the back door.

He got out of the car and reopened the trunk and got out his two weapons plus the chain and the padlock. When he walked around the building, he could hear the service going on and no one was in the parking lot. Jeff smiled and went into the lobby. It was deserted, and the doors into the main church were closed. Jeff ran the chain through the two front doors and locked them with the padlock. Suddenly, the main doors to the service opened, and June and Sarah walked out with the offerings. June was shocked to see him standing there and turned around trying to run. He shot her down and the offering plates scattered everywhere. Sarah had just opened the door to warn people, but it was too late when bullets filled her back. Everyone panicked trying to get out of their pews when blood poured out of Sarah's mouth while she dropped to the floor.

Jeff followed her in with his automatic rifle spewing bullets. They were dropping in the aisles like flies. Pastor Dodge tried to get people in the rooms next to the stage. While a group of men tried to rush Jeff but died for their trouble. Some headed for the cafeteria knowing that there was a back door. Rita was in the kitchen and tried the back door, but it wouldn't budge. She and her daughter attempted to hide in the cabinets while others hid under the tables. Jeff waded through blood to the doors of the stage. He shot open the nursey door and filled the room with bullets; no one was left there alive. Jeff went to the other door, and when he got it open, the pastor was first to die.

Jeff returned to the cafeteria door smiling knowing no one could get out that way. Going in, he began shooting people under the tables. He could hear a banging at the front door knowing the police were trying to get in. While he was finishing up, John came out of his office and ran into the main church looking for Jennifer. He found her bleeding and picked her up and carried her back to the pastor's office and lay her on the desk and called 911 for an ambulance. He was hoping the killer wouldn't find them before the police got in. Jeff had made it to the kitchen and killed Rita and Ruby who were hiding. He knew the police would be in soon, and so he rushed to the door to the offices. He just started down the hall when he heard the front door break open. He checked all the offices, which were all empty, except the pastor's door was locked. Jeff sent bullets through the door, which went into Jennifer. When he got the door open, he shot at John, but the police were coming down the hall, so he turned to fire at them. Jeff suddenly felt weak as bullets entered his chest. He tried to hold the gun up, but it dropped into the hallway and soon he followed it as bullets kept flying. The police found John still alive and rushed him to the hospital. Many of the police vomited from the massive smell of blood. It took them quite a while to collect all the bodies out of the church.

EPILOGUE

Laura was watching the news when a special bulletin came on. The announcer came on saying that the United Methodist Church in Atlanta was attacked. The police broke in taking out the killer, but everyone was dead in the church except a John Conner who was rushed to the emergency room with several wounds. The police were there in time before the killer could make it to the Sunday school building. The children filed out to their parents. Everyone was crying and several children's parents were killed. The ones that were now without parents were taken in by other families.

Laura became frantic, calling her parents and telling them the news. She grabbed her car keys and purse and ran to the door and hoping she made it to him in time. It took her four hours to make it to Atlanta. She pulled up to the hospital and rushed inside. She was told that he was still in surgery and was shown to the waiting room. She called her mother and said he's being operated on. Mary said that they were on their way and should be there in an hour. Laura was very nervous and had a hard time calming down. She got a cup of coffee out of the vending machine and sat there drinking hoping to hear something. Her parents arrived, and she told them he was still in surgery. They sat and prayed for him and several of the nurses joined in. Two hours later, the doctor came out and was taken over by John's parents.

He said, "I'm sorry. I did all I could to save him, but he had lost too much blood."

All three broke down and cried. Mary said that they would decide for our son. The doctor left, and they walked out of the hospital with their heads hung low.

***

John came out of his daze at the bus station and watched Jeff and thirty others from the church line up to get on the bus.

Jennifer said, "We were not called. Our bus isn't here yet. I'm glad he is leaving. He gives me the creeps, and I'm glad he couldn't get to June. Pastor Dodge got on the bus earlier when you were asleep with June and Sarah. I called them goodbye, but I don't think they heard me. I was sad, but I didn't want to wake you up."

John said, "I'm sorry I fell asleep, but I wish you had. It seemed like I was having a nightmare. He said I died in the hospital and my parents were there."

Jennifer said that she had a similar dream, but it was in the church. Everyone on the other side of the room was gone, and her and just twenty members were left in the station. An announcement came on the intercom saying for them to line up at the door and get their tickets out. The bus conductor was at the door checking tickets and sending them onto the bus. After they were seated, she finally realized where they were headed. A few tried to get off the bus, but it was too late; the door wouldn't open. At least John was with her so she didn't panic and remembered suddenly that she was dead. If only she had paid more attention in church, she wouldn't be headed in this direction, but it was too late now.

www.ingramcontent.com/pod-product-compliance
Lightning Source LLC
Chambersburg PA
CBHW030131010826
48973CB00002B/509

9781964097541